HOUSE OF DRAGONS

Also by Jessica Cluess

HOUSE
OF
DRAGONS

JESSICA CLUESS

RANDOM HOUSE 🏠 NEW YORK

Text copyright © 2020 by Jessica Cluess
Jacket art copyright © 2020 by Sasha Vinogradova
Map art by Sveta Dorosheva

All rights reserved. Published in the United States by Random House Children's Books, a division of Penguin Random House LLC, New York.

Random House and the colophon are registered trademarks of Penguin Random House LLC.

Visit us on the Web! GetUnderlined.com

Educators and librarians, for a variety of teaching tools, visit us at RHTeachersLibrarians.com

Library of Congress Cataloging-in-Publication Data
Names: Cluess, Jessica, author.
Title: House of dragons / Jessica Cluess.
Description: First edition. | New York : Random House, [2020] | Summary: "When the emperor dies, the five royal houses of Etrusia attend the calling, where one of their own will be selected to compete for the throne"—Provided by publisher.
Identifiers: LCCN 2019018244 | ISBN 978-0-525-64815-4 (hardcover) | ISBN 978-0-525-64816-1 (lib. bdg.) | ISBN 978-0-593-30544-7 (int'l) | ISBN 978-0-525-64817-8 (ebook)
Subjects: | CYAC: Kings, queens, rulers, etc.—Fiction. | Contests—Fiction. | Dragons—Fiction. | Fantasy.
Classification: LCC PZ7.1.C596 Hou 2020 | DDC [Fic]—dc23

The text of this book is set in 12-point Dante MT.
Interior design by Michelle Gengaro.

Printed in the United States of America
10 9 8 7 6 5 4 3 2 1
First Edition

For Meredith,
the first and best
audience for my stories

STORMWAYS

ARCTICUS
SEA

HIBRIAN ISLES

HOUSE AURUN

ARDENNES

HOUSE VOLSCIA

AUREUS

CATALENIA
HOUSE ORETANI

BARCINE

CROTIAN SEA

ANTONINUS

KARTHAGO

HOUSE SABEL

Gods dream of empires, but devils build them.
—*the poet Valerius,*
prior to his exile in 735 AD (anno Draconis)

1

Emilia

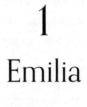

One day after the emperor had died and been eaten, the call went out to select his successor.

Emilia of the Aurun considered this on dragonback as she hovered one hundred feet above the rocky coastline. Frothing waves surged against the cliffs so violently she swore the spray speckled her cheek, even at this height. Salt-choked wind tautened her dragon's wings with a snap and tumbled her heavy red hair into her face. Maybe she really *should* wear it in a plait, as her mother suggested every other day. Chara's grumble reverberated in Emilia's bones. Shortening the reins, she petted the dragon's neck.

"It's all right. They won't pick me," she said, as if this were a conversation and not something she'd repeated in the locked room of her mind. *They won't pick me. They'd have to be idiots to pick me.*

Of course, Emilia privately believed that idiots had been running the Etrusian Empire for hundreds of years.

If her mother heard her say *that,* Emilia's hair would be the least of her concerns. After all, the House Aurun hadn't seated an emperor or empress in over three generations, and their family had the worst land holdings: the Hibrian Isles, two semi-large parent islands constellated by a smattering of smaller ones. Plunked down in the northwest corner of the empire, theirs was a frigid land of sea and wind, of winter and not-quite-so winter. The family needed an emperor in power to advance their fortunes.

They needed Alexander.

And there he was, a dot waving to her from the lip of the cliff. Emilia pressed Chara's sides with her knees, slackening the reins. The dragon snorted fizzling embers, tucked her wings, and tipped into a steep dive. Emilia lived for that plunge, that butterfly-flutter of her stomach. All the heavy pains of mind and body evaporated in midair.

She leaned back in the saddle as the cliff sped nearer, then pitched forward as Chara unfurled her wings and furrowed her three-clawed feet in the damp ground. The clean scent of upturned earth enveloped Emilia. Her brother came running while she rummaged through the saddlebag and removed a satchel, slipping it over her shoulder as she slid to the ground. She walked about to stand before Chara and stroke the dragon on her most favorite spot, at the juncture of jaw and neck. Chara nestled her snout at the center of Emilia's belly.

"Thanks, girl," she murmured, and stepped aside to let Chara flap her way up into the sky. There was still time for play before the calling.

Alexander appeared and wrapped an arm around Emilia. By the blue above, he was warm.

"You're a hearth f-fire. How?" Her teeth chattered as she spoke. Emilia clamped hands over her ears, twin curves of ice against her palms.

"Blood of the dragon. Obviously." He bumped her with his hip. "Pity you have none. You'd freeze on a summer's day in Karthago."

"You l-laugh now." Emilia pulled her purple cloak tight against her body. "Wait till I'm the one who's ch-chosen."

"Not to worry. I'll just pitch you over the cliff if that happens." Alex kissed the top of her head. Without teasing, he said, "They won't choose you."

It was some comfort. While technically any child of the five families *could* be called to the Emperor's Trial, only the Houses' eldest ever were. It was an unspoken tradition. They were all fortunate Alexander had been firstborn, not she.

His hair was deep Aurun gold, not her tangle of red. His complexion was fair as milk, as opposed to her deathly pallor. His laughter was easy, hers nonexistent. Unlike Emilia, he didn't have to be monitored carefully whenever they hosted the lesser Hibrian nobles at winter fetes or during the summer bonfires.

Unlike her, he didn't cradle death in his hands like a dozing serpent.

They walked the path toward the calling circle on the other side of the promontory, Emilia's heavy satchel a reassuring thud against her hip. She shivered as the icy wind knifed through her once more. She'd never liked Stormways, the family's oldest, draftiest, and most northern castle. Technically this was their territorial capital, though it was far from grand. A pity, then, that she hadn't left it in nearly five years, but that could not be helped. The far north was the most sparsely populated area. She could be inconspicuous here.

The Aurun banners, stark white emblazoned with a purple Aspis—the water serpent, their personal dragon—rippled in the gusts. Overhead, Chara and Alexander's dragon, Tarkus, dove and capered about each other. Both dragons had long, slender bodies with whipping tails, though Chara's scales were a creamy pearlescent while Tarkus was plum-colored. Aspises' heads were sleek, their scales silken, their noses doglike. Two horns corkscrewed on either side of their skulls. Unlike the other dragon breeds, an Aspis could spend time underwater and suffer no ill effects. Chara hunted whales in springtime and would float back home like a bloody wisp of cloud, blubber ragged between her teeth.

"Did you go flying to get a last look at the place before you become empress?" Alex teased. Emilia nudged him in the ribs.

"When I'm living in a golden palace at Dragonspire, I'll remember freezing my backside off with real fondness," she deadpanned. Suppressing a shudder, she added, "I, er, needed to clear my mind."

Alexander understood her. Normally, Emilia could be found with cooling cups of coffee and ink-stained fingers before the library fire, books and papers fanned out around her in a labyrinthine formation only she understood. But then the very fissures of her brain would spark, and she would have to leave before she hurt anyone.

Emilia stopped on the path. Ahead of them lay the evidence of what she'd done.

It *had* been a seagull. Amid the splatter of blood and the pasted smear of organs, gray and white feathers fluttered in the breeze. Back in her room, Emilia had felt the magic welling until she brimmed with it, like a cup. She'd hurried down the castle's winding steps, rushed out into the overcast day. She'd stalked toward the cliffs, been startled by a gull's circling cry. Her eyes had latched on to the bird . . . and the poor creature had uttered its last call.

There were two types of magic: the orderly arts and the chaotic ways. One type had built this great empire; the other had nearly destroyed the world. Order was creation, and chaos destruction. Emilia possessed no talent for order.

She was a natural at chaos, though.

If the other four families ever found out, death would be the kinder option. A chaotic couldn't be tolerated, not after the War of the Sixth House a millennium ago.

Alex hugged her tight. "It was an accident," he whispered.

Emilia knew how the castle servants gossiped. How they watched her. This was why she always kept her hair a heavy curtain and never plaited it; a curtain made it easier to hide. Her hands fisted until they ached.

"I know," she whispered back. They kept walking, the satchel banging at her side. "Here." She stopped once more, shrugged off the satchel, and looped it over her brother's arm. "It took some doing, but I had them bound."

Alex unbuttoned the pack and drew out several slim, cloth-backed volumes. Emilia immediately rearranged them in order, nervous to have her hard work inspected.

The Hunt. The Game. The Race. The Truth.

The four challenges that constituted every Emperor's Trial.

Each title stood out in embossed letters upon the covers. Emilia had also included a pair of parchment manuals labeled *Bestiary* and *Topography.*

"I had to do up the island maps by hand," Emilia said, happy to be boastful. Pride was such a rare visitor in her life. Alex nodded, flipping through one book after the other.

"You really think the Crotian Sea will be the first stop?" He looked up at her with one eyebrow raised. "I bet it'll be the Imperial Peninsula."

"We've factored in dragonflight's maximum speed, and compared the calling dates with the start of the first challenges. It requires a full twenty-four hours at least for everyone to assemble, even the Volscia and Sabel, and they're closest to the peninsula of all of us. That indicates a longer flight time. Or do you doubt my calculations?"

"Teasing. I'm teasing you." Alex shuffled through the books once more, put them away, and embraced her again. "Can't believe the day's here," he said softly.

Emilia closed her eyes and listened to the thud of Alex's heartbeat.

"We've prepared well, at least," she murmured.

"No one could've prepared me like you, Emi." He kissed the top of her head once again. "Remember what I promised you?"

Emilia recalled the shattering echo of screams. The stink of burning flesh. Blood everywhere. She remembered huddling in the corner of her bedroom, sobbing and raking her nails down her cheeks. Her brother holding her, swearing that he would make it right.

"Of course," she whispered.

"I'm going to keep that promise." He stepped away, held the satchel high. "With this. *Our* victory."

Emilia smiled, the corners of her lips twitching.

Since they'd learned that Alex would go off to the Emperor's Trial one day and never return, the siblings had studied every scrap of information on every Trial that had ever been held. Emilia made it her solemn mission to prepare her brother for every possible eventuality. Had she been a normal girl, she might have been permitted to present her findings at the Imperial University. She might have published.

Had she been a normal girl, she might have done a great many things.

The calling circle was over a thousand years old. A ring of moss-slick stones one hundred yards in diameter surrounded a large slab of granite in the very center, where the "chosen" dragon would stand. A few servants and liveried guard waited alongside the family, the bannermen holding House Aurun's flag aloft. As Emilia and Alex joined their parents, the sun pierced a cloud and illuminated the grass, sparking prisms of rainbow light in the dew. The family appeared to gleam in their stately purple velvet, the color of House Aurun. *We're a bunch of rare jewels,* Emilia thought to herself, smiling bitterly. *Pretty, and without purpose.*

"Emilia, what are you thinking?" Her mother sounded accusatory. She and Emilia's father often stared as if waiting for her to explode.

"Dangerous thoughts," Emilia muttered to the ground.

Lady Aurun huffed. Emilia's chest tightened to think of Tarkus settling on that granite slab, his tail swishing, summoning Alexander to fly away.

Emilia's parents tolerated her. They tolerated her lack of eye contact and tangled hair. They tolerated the perennial dark circles under her eyes, her headaches, her need to devour every obscure fact upon which she could lay hands, her halting conversation delivered in a voice roughened by lack of use. Her parents tolerated her chaotic soul, but Alex loved her.

Now, even if—even *when*—he won the Trial and became Alexander Sarkonus, Dragon Emperor of Etrusia, he would never be her brother again. They'd see each other twice a year, at the midwinter festival and during the annual congregation of the five families. No more private jokes. No more morning flights. No more companionship.

Loneliness was a starched gown in which Emilia could never grow comfortable.

Tears blurred her vision. Alex squeezed her hand.

"I won't forget you," he said.

She rested her head against his shoulder as the family's four dragons landed out of the sky to stand directly behind their riders, wings settling in anticipation of "the call." No one here had ever seen a calling before. Emperor Erasmus had died yesterday at age sixty-six, and had gained the throne at twenty. Emilia almost wished she could go along as a witness. There would be great research in it. Unfortunately, emperors were forbidden from speaking outright of what they experienced in the Trial. All the information Emilia and Alex gleaned had taken countless hours of cross-referencing different books, letters, even tax records.

As for the other competitors, there was no worry they'd share any secrets. The losers faced the Cut—and Emilia shuddered to think of that fate. *Please, don't let it happen to Alex.*

As the noon sun struck the stones and the family awaited the call, Emilia nestled inside her own head, a poisonous paradise. Her brain was the source of all her pain and delight. She hadn't seen anyone her own age in five years, apart from Alex. Once he was gone, she'd likely be alone forever. As the younger child, she'd been expected to marry and bear children to carry on the Aurun name, but how could she ever get close to a man without fear of splintering his bones or rupturing his kidneys? So she lived in dreams populated by phantom friends. Sometimes her imagination was a balm; sometimes it burned like acid, a reminder of what she could never have.

Through the haze of her thoughts, she heard someone shout her name.

"Emilia!" Alex gripped her shoulders, spun her to face forward. "Look."

Chara waited on the granite slab, her ruby eyes trained on Emilia. It was so jarringly wrong, like watching the sun rise in the evening, that Emilia didn't understand what had happened . . . until she did.

Chara had been called. Not Tarkus.

Not Alexander. Which meant . . .

"Chara, get down from there!" Emilia flung herself at the dragon, panic clawing up her spine. No. No, no, she couldn't be called. She was second-born. She was chaotic! She would lose. She would be *Cut*. "What do I do?" she yelled at her family. Yanking on Chara's bridle, Emilia looked the dragon in her shimmering red eyes. "Why are you doing this?"

Her dragon, the only creature in this world she loved as dearly as her brother, pressed her face against Emilia's body, over her hammering heart. Chara gave a deep sigh, her wings expanding. That reverberation that existed only between a dragon and its rider rippled through Emilia's blood and marrow. Emilia knew, as sure as if the dragon had spoken, that this was a natural thing. Some invisible force had called for Chara, and the answer could not be no.

"I have to go." Emilia could scarce hear her own voice through the blood pounding in her ears. Every hair on her body stood on end. She could feel the warmth filling her, like liquid. Power. Magic. Her fears. The chaos itched forward, screaming to be let out.

Her father's hand roughly pulled her backward by the hood of her cloak.

"No!" He was shouting at her mother. "They'll know we *lied*!"

Emilia tumbled to the ground, the magic within her spilling over. Anger squeezed the sides of her head, her jaw locked, and in the space between heartbeats she looked at one of the stones standing opposite her—she felt the thread of connection between herself and the stone. The fissures of her mind kindled, and magic surged.

The stone exploded in a shower of sharp fragments. The *boom* resonated through the air, echoing across the cliffs and out to the sea. Her mother screamed and recoiled. Oh no. *Blood*.

"I'm all right," her mother said, but her face was ashen. Her cheek had been cut. Destruction was Emilia's gift, and she couldn't hide it.

Now she'd be forced to compete with others. Monitored and scrutinized, how could she keep her magic at bay, let alone vie for an empire?

She couldn't. And if she didn't go right now, then the Cut . . .

Alex was by her side. He helped her stand and led her to Chara, giving a tight smile as he lifted her onto the dragon's saddle; only the tremor of his hands revealed his fear. "Long live the empress Emilia Sarkona," he said, and winked. He slipped the satchel of research back into her saddlebag.

Emilia settled on her seat, skirts rucked up around her waist—this was why a rider always wore breeches underneath her gown. Her feet slid into the stirrups, and she risked falling off her mount as she bent over and buried her face in Alex's shoulder one last time. He stroked her hair and stepped away. With a surge of wings, Chara rose, the circle and her parents and her brother diminishing in size until they looked no more than dolls.

Emilia felt numb as her dragon turned south and flew away from the Hibrian Isles, away from their rocky shores and green fields and sunless skies. Her shoulders ached with tension. Her head was bowed, her wind-whipped hair catching in her mouth. Where was she going? Only Chara knew now, answering a call inaudible to human ears.

How many years had she dreamed of breaking free from this place? How stupid she'd been. There were worse things than prison.

She'd seen them firsthand.

What am I going to do? Emilia thought. She pressed her knee against Chara—and felt the bulge in her saddlebag. The books. All those years of study and preparation in her hands.

Emilia's thoughts turned.

If they knew what she was, she'd be mutilated. Tortured. Killed.

But if she could somehow conceal herself . . .

What was she going to do? The whisper of an idea tickled her mind.

Why not try to win?

2

Lucian

W hen Lucian took a dagger to his braid, he was no longer of the Sabel family. Pride surged as he sliced. Burning the tail of black hair in a silver bowl, he felt free for the first time in four years. Since his first campaign.

"You'd understand," he said to the dead woman. Her picture hung in the center of the shrine, warmed by candlelight and framed in ribbons of incense. Karthago honored the dead as invisible protectors in the world beyond, their portraits set in ebony wood and surrounded by clouds of jasmine and white roses. One always prayed to a family guardian before undertaking a journey. Lucian's flight to join the Sacred Brothers would be his last. The great temple at Delphos was the seat of the orderly arts in the Etrusian Empire. It was where orderly magosi came to pray and practice, where acolytes from every walk of life studied in hopes of putting on the satin robes of the priesthood, and where the Sacred Brothers took vows of poverty and looked after the temple, its grounds, and the poor who came begging to the seat of order's power. Lucian would live a simple life now. He'd never return to Karthago or the campaigns.

He believed such a choice would have pleased the woman

in this shrine. She beamed down at him, the shape of her eyes and face so like his. Her hair, too, had been black—though his was now much shorter and bristled unevenly where he'd hacked it off. Still, where he was going he'd never look into a mirror again. Fine by him. He didn't relish seeing the face of a killer every morning.

"You'd understand, Mother," he repeated.

"No. She wouldn't," a cold voice behind him said. He turned to find his sister, Dido, studying him, one hand playing along the bejeweled hilt of a dagger at her side. She'd wanted to plunge it into his heart for years.

"Come for a final sparring match, Di? You should save your strength for the Trial." Lucian stood and walked side by side with his twin, their boots echoing along the marble corridors.

"I could beat you in under five minutes. Don't pretend to be some intense workout." She glared at him, her eyes the same copper color as his.

"Do you really want the last conversation we ever have to be full of insults?" he asked.

"Yes."

They both fell silent. Resentful brooding had always been more their style. Guards in livery embroidered with the blue Drake—House Sabel's personal dragon—stood at attention on either side of the hall, silver shields and spears at the ready. To the right, through the tall marble arches, Lucian looked down at the sparkling curve of the bay. The Sabel palace, the most splendid building in the entire capital of Antoninus, stood in plain sight of the great marketplace, the beating heart of Karthagon trade. Anything and everything you could want waited down there, and every price could be negotiated. Dates, spices, oils, bolts of crimson silk, blooms of white chrysanthemums, Masarian pottery, caged tigers, piles of oranges and barrels of wine: all for sale. Lucian recalled running through the labyrinth of stalls as a child with Dido chasing him, watching the colorful silk awnings balloon in the wind like a ship's sails. "The sun is a lemon," Dido had said with a giggle, squinting into the bright horizon. "Its juice stings my eyes." He'd taken off his cap to offer her shade, back when he and his twin had loved each other.

"Do you remember when we were little?" he asked.

Dido set her jaw.

"Yes." She sighed. "But I don't want to."

Lucian nodded. "That's one thing we have in common, at least."

The calling circle was at the heart of the palace, an open-air arena ringed by creamy blocks of sandstone. The first Sabel ruler of Karthago, Gaius, had carved water lilies into the stones. Legend said he'd done it to honor his queen, Ayzebel, the Flower of War. When the empire had expanded to Karthago's shores, Gaius arrived on the back of his fiery dragon, prepared for battle. Ayzebel, the dark-eyed ruler, sailed out to meet him with a thousand ships. In her lap, she carried her sword and a freshly plucked lily beaded with dew. She gave Gaius a choice: the sword or the lily. War or her.

The great conqueror looked at the warrior queen and was conquered in turn. Since then, the Sabel family had taken Karthagon customs and mates as their own. It was said that love ruled the Sabel men.

These were stories that victors made up to add a romantic sheen to their conquest. You could have as much fire and blood as you liked, so long as you followed it up with a wedding.

Lucian and Dido found their father in the ring, with their dragons perched and waiting for the call. When Lucian whistled, his dragon, Tyche, unfurled her wings and puffed out her chest. She was beautiful, the marbled black-and-blue color of all purebred Drakes. She shook out her triangular head with its tapering jaw. The electric-blue fringe along the ridges of her eyes expanded like ruffled feathers. Lucian couldn't go to her yet; first, there was his father.

"My children." Lord Hector Sabel embraced Lucian and Dido both. His kiss on Lucian's cheek was gentle, but Lucian felt it like a wound. It was hard to hate a man with such sad eyes. "I'm losing you."

Indeed. Dido to the Trial, and Lucian to the temple. He was lucky that his sister was firstborn. He shuddered to think if their positions had been reversed.

Hector frowned and glared when he took a good look at Lucian's shorn hair. Lucian couldn't help but wince in reply. Once Dido was empress—and she would be, unless the Volscia heir proved as dangerous as rumor suggested—she'd be sterilized per imperial requirements. No emperor or empress could have children who might attempt to claim succession. Lucian, meanwhile, would spend the rest of his life growing vegetables and spinning wool.

If that was the price he paid for ending the cursed Sabel line, so much the better. Soon, he'd find peace in rising before dawn, sweeping the temple floors, and feeding the hungry. Lucian imagined lines of ragged people flocking to him for help. He'd feed them, bind their wounds, comfort them in illness. It was too good a life for the likes of him, but he craved it.

Soon.

"My victory will be yours, Father. And the family's." Dido gave a stiff, military-grade bow. If the Sabels knew anything, it was war. She glared at Lucian; her irate expression was so like their father's. She and Hector really were similar. While both twins had the same eyes and brown skin, Dido had also gotten the pointed jaw, the braid of coppery hair—a true Sabel wore their hair long, a demonstration of their strength and power. She was a true Sabel, while Lucian took after his mother in all the ways that mattered.

"Ah yes. The family. *Nothing*'s more important than that." Lucian's gut roiled as he strode to stand before Tyche. She nudged his back with her nose, her breath hot on his neck. He stroked her snout, taking comfort from her presence. The sooner this was over, the better. Then he'd remove the royal-blue Sabel colors and don a homespun gray cassock.

He'd be free.

Dido stood to the right with her dragon, and his father to the left. They waited patiently as the sun hit its zenith in the sky, burning the shadows away. Sweat trickled down the back of Lucian's neck as he watched his sister's dragon, Hamilcar. The beast merely shuffled on its great stone perch and bobbed its head. *Come on. Move.* If Lucian didn't set out soon, he wouldn't make the temple by nightfall.

Behind him, Tyche gave a strange, trilling coo. She lifted off her perch with a leathery flap of wings. Lucian stared as her shadow flitted across the sandy ground, following her all the way to the center of the circle. As the blood drained from his face and as his legs grew heavy, he watched Tyche settle upon a slab of stone and fold her wings. She looked at him expectantly, her gold serpent's eyes attentive.

Come along, she seemed to say. *I'm waiting.*

She—and Lucian—had been called. Had any younger child of the Sabel house *ever* been called before? Maybe he should've spent more time studying the family history and less time hating it.

Maybe he should've jumped on Tyche's back directly after cutting his hair and taken off.

"*What?*" Dido's voice was an incredulous slap. She stormed toward him, hands fisted at her sides. "What in the black depths did you do, you *idiot?*"

Lucian's frozen shock melted.

"You think I want this? That I cut my hair for the fun of it?" He met her in the center of the arena, where she bared her teeth and thrust her face into his.

"You'll embarrass us more than you already have!"

Lucian pictured dragonfire melting fields of ice. Blood smoking on snow. His tears freezing on his cheeks as his sister scowled at him. Ashamed of tears spilled, not blood shed.

Lucian narrowed his eyes. "Our family's the embarrassment, sis."

With a grunt, she threw a punch and snapped his head to the left. Lucian took a knee, his jaw throbbing as he laughed. "*Good.* Real empress material." He glared at an incensed Dido. "Take your dragon and fly to the Trial. I don't want the honor."

"You can't refuse." Hector arrived, breathless. "The call, once heard, can't be resisted. If Tyche arrives at the Trial without you . . ."

Lucian's stomach soured. The Cut. Refusal of the call led to automatic disqualification. Maybe he *should* refuse to go—a monster such as he deserved oblivion.

But Lucian was too much of a wretched coward. He pounded his fist to the ground once, twice. "I was so close," he growled.

Dido swore colorfully as Lucian stood.

"Here." Hector unbuckled the sword at his hip. "The sword of Gaius Sabel. Let it bring you luck."

The longsword lay sheathed in a golden scabbard. Lucian pulled the blade free with a clean hiss of steel. Sunlight fired the rich rubies and cabochon emeralds inlaid in the hilt. It was a sword forged for empires and emperors.

And Lucian, whose bloody skill with the weapon surpassed even Dido's, was to be its new keeper.

Hector clasped Dido's shoulder. She looked murderous, but his father beamed. Lucian realized with horror that Hector now had what he'd truly wanted: a child to compete, and a child to govern Karthago and rear Sabel children. Thanks to this calling, the Sabel line would extend another fifteen hundred years. More children. More soldiers. More bloodshed.

How many had already died at the edge of Lucian's blade?

Lucian carried the sword to his dragon. Tyche extended her long neck in curiosity as he threw the weapon down at her taloned feet, kicking up a cloud of dust. Pointing at it, he said, "Tyche. Fire."

The dragon breathed a stream of white-hot flame, melting the sword on the instant.

Through the shimmering wall of heat, Lucian saw the distorted faces of his father and sister—Hector collapsed with a scream, Dido holding on to him. When Tyche finished, the sand where she'd breathed was fused into a sparkling circle of glass. The sword's blade ran in red, molten rivulets, its handle gone, the rubies and emeralds cracked and smoking. As Hector wailed, Lucian swung into Tyche's saddle.

From this day until his last, he swore he would never again take up a sword, never raise his hand to another living creature.

Dido stumbled around the sword's wreckage and over to him, hateful tears in her eyes.

"Bastard," she hissed. "You *bastard*."

Lucian closed his eyes.

"If only I were," he whispered as Tyche lifted off.

3

Vespir

Vespir had served faceless people since she was twelve years old. In the Ikrayina territories, commoners were forbidden from looking on the faces of the nobility. The lady Valeria Pentri, long-ago conqueror, had started that system. To look in the eyes of a highborn was to lose your own, as Vespir's grandmother had often grumbled.

It wasn't too hard not to look, though. Vespir always knelt whenever one of the family entered the aerie to get their dragon. She'd gotten to know the Pentri boots and slippers well. Lady Pentri favored jewel-tipped toes that were out of fashion, but which she felt properly conveyed her wealth. Lord Pentri kept his boots so immaculately shined that Vespir could see herself in them.

As personal dragon handler to the only child and heir of the House Pentri, Vespir was permitted to live in the palace at Khoryv, the noble House's seat. She had more honor than a servant could usually dream of. The food was much better, too. Most of the time, it was just her and the dragons, all the company she needed.

Most of the time.

Vespir swept the flagstones with a wicker broom, humming

to herself in the quiet. Usually, she had four snorting dragons to deal with. Old Lord Pentri's beast in particular was a hassle, always shitting sulfur and snapping when Vespir tried to clean. But the entire family and their dragons were at the calling circle now, waiting for Antonia to fly away. Vespir's stomach rippled at the thought.

"She'll be fine," Vespir said to her own dragon, the sole occupant of the aerie at the moment. Karina was perched behind a curtain, taking an afternoon nap. "She's going to win."

"Yes. She is." That voice. Vespir knew it as sure as she recognized the pair of green satin slippers, the mint-green silk gown, the swell of chest, and, finally, daringly, the perfect, smiling face of the girl to whom that voice belonged. Antonia of the Pentri stood in the aerie's doorway, the sunlight warm around her. Vespir was no poet—she never read poetry because, well, she couldn't read. But she imagined Antonia was the type of girl poets wrote about.

The sight of her stole Vespir's breath.

"Shouldn't you be at the calling, my lady?" Vespir prayed her nerves didn't show.

Antonia took a hesitant step nearer.

"I was thinking," she said, worrying an amethyst ring upon her finger. Her cheeks reddened. "There's a chance I'll never come back. The Trial is . . . dangerous."

Vespir's heart pounded.

"Yes," she murmured. Antonia drew even nearer, and Vespir tasted her pulse.

"If I'm going to die," Antonia said, "I want to die with no regrets."

She came in a whisper of silk, stood on her toes, and kissed Vespir. They had kissed before, a few days ago, a too-brief moment stolen down by the river, but not with this much feeling.

This much abandon. Antonia kissed Vespir as if she had nothing to lose.

Vespir wrapped an arm around the noble girl's waist and forced herself not to muss up Antonia's long black hair. If their daughter showed up looking rumpled, the Pentri might notice. Antonia gave a delicate sigh. She tasted like honeysuckle and peach blossom. "You taste like jam," Vespir had told Antonia breathlessly after their first kiss. Again, she was far from a poet.

Reluctantly, they broke apart. Vespir wondered what she should say. She wondered if she could still speak.

"I wanted to say"—Antonia's breathing shook—"I love you."

Vespir trembled, holding this girl in her arms. Seven words, all it took to give her the greatest happiness she'd ever known. Vespir could say nothing in reply. Nothing except—

"I love you. Too. I love you . . . so much." For years now Vespir had lain awake nights, mouthing those words to the empty darkness. She'd closed her eyes and wished and hoped that one day, if she were fortunate, she might hear those words returned. She couldn't believe it'd actually *happened*.

Vespir had never been particularly lucky before. Perhaps a lifetime's worth of luck had been held in reserve for this one perfect moment.

"I wanted you to know that I'm coming back for you." Antonia looked up at her, those dark eyes shimmering with hope. "If you feel the same—"

She couldn't finish that thought because Vespir's lips were on hers. Vespir kissed her again, twice more. Once more after that for good measure.

Finally, they broke apart. Antonia ran her fingers through Vespir's bob of black hair.

"Make sure you win," Vespir whispered, heart aching.

"If I know you're waiting, I will." Antonia sighed in contentment. "And you'd better be ready to come to Dragonspire when I do."

"So I'd be the empress's personal dragon handler *and* lover? That's so much work," Vespir groaned. Both girls laughed, giddy. That was one nice thing about the imperial throne: Antonia had told her that the emperor or empress could never have children, but lovers were fine.

"When I'm empress, you're going to have a much higher rank." Antonia sobered. "No one will ever make you look down again."

Vespir's heart fluttered even as a dark, unhappy voice whispered in her mind. *What about the other servants? Would they still have to keep their eyes down?* But Vespir pushed those thoughts aside. No, she trusted Antonia.

The girls started as the bells tolled midday. Antonia shivered in Vespir's arms. It was time. The calling waited.

The start of their life together was mere days away. Vespir was not losing Antonia; she was about to gain her.

"Go win." Vespir kissed the girl once more, savored the delicate feel and taste of her. Antonia's soft hand passed through Vespir's rough one, and she vanished out the door. Vespir picked up the wicker broom from where it'd fallen, then dropped it again; she couldn't stop shaking. Euphoria and misery clashed inside of her. Sighing, she glanced around the aerie, a much happier and, simultaneously, colder place than it had seemed a minute ago.

Usually, the aerie was the heart of Vespir's world, where she felt entirely safe. Since she'd been twelve, she'd spent most of her waking hours here, unless she was learning how to fly and to train dragons out in the Pentri arena. A domed, high-ceilinged building of gray stone, the aerie had housed generations of Pythos, the official Pentri dragon.

Vespir had spent much of her life learning to care for these beasts. She had broad horsehair brushes to smooth scales, tubs of beeswax to polish talons and horns, and rosehip ointments to rub into the thin membranes of wings during winter months when the air became dry. She knew how to ride a dragon without saddle or bridle, a custom all the Pentri observed. Antonia had scoffed at the other families' custom of forcing bridles onto six-week-old dragon hatchlings. Barbarians, she'd called them.

The decorative wall hangings had always cheered Vespir. They were beautiful, but more importantly they were a single reminder of what the eastern Ikrayina territory had been before Valeria Pentri's arrival hundreds of years ago. Images of dragons formed from stark geometric patterns of red and blue and yellow greeted Vespir wherever she turned. The hangings were edged in sharp lines of horns and talons to convey strength, and Vespir liked to imagine these woven tapestries hanging in homes out on the wide plains, back when her people had gone wherever they pleased with horses and hawks and bows.

For so many years, she'd been home here. Now the aerie was simply another reminder of Antonia. Of when Vespir had first glimpsed her at twelve while hiding in the rafters. Of how she'd placed her hands on Antonia's hips to adjust her riding position, cheeks flushing with the contact. Of years spent watching from afar, wishing. Of these last few perfect moments, these whispered promises.

But . . . what if Antonia did not come back?

Vespir suddenly hated this place. Wiping tears from her cheeks—she couldn't cry when there was work to do—Vespir hung up Antonia's extra tack and brushed out her dragon's stall. Daedalus wouldn't be coming back. Not for a long while, if ever.

Behind the curtain, Karina gave a cough and a yowling yawn. Vespir pushed the tarp aside and smiled. "Bet you wish you could see the calling," she said.

The greatest honor of being a dragon handler was receiving a dragon all your own. Of course, Vespir hadn't received a top-tier dragon egg; she wasn't nobility. But Karina, to her, was perfect. Sure, she was smaller than most dragons. The average length was twenty feet from snout to tail, while Karina barely passed nine. Her wings didn't curve, but appeared more batlike. She had no horns, a short face, and her scales were the brown of a riverbed, not green like a perfect Pythos. But her amber eyes were quick and intelligent. The dragon unfurled her wings on her perch, an iron bar set at the back of the stall. Straw littered the floor, and Karina's pet goat, Barnabas, stretched and bleated at his dragon friend. Dragons were like horses in their need for companionship. Karina leaned down and snuffled the tuft of white hair on top of Barnabas's head, then touched her snout to his. The goat's tail waggled.

"Boop." Vespir grinned. She always made a "boop" noise when they touched noses. It seemed right. Wiping a tear, she said, "I'll get your lunch, girl."

Vespir was tenderizing a fresh, bleeding leg of lamb with a wooden mallet when Karina began to cry. Dropping the mallet, Vespir yanked back the curtain. "What is it? Karina?"

The sounds were *terrible*. The dragon unfurled her wings, pitched her head back at the ceiling, and groaned like a dying cow. Barnabas bolted past Vespir, bleating in fear as he raced out the door. Vespir grabbed the soothing stick, a five-foot-long staff with peacock feathers clustered on one end. The color, movement, and sensation of the feathers often calmed a crying dragon. Teeth gritted, Vespir tried touching Karina, but the dragon flapped her wings and surged forward. Vespir barely had time to drop to the ground before Karina sailed past, skidding across the flagstones to hobble out the aerie's door. In horror, Vespir watched as her dragon took to the sky.

"Not today. Oh, why today?" she gasped, chasing after

Karina. Servants gaped as Vespir shot past them, waving her arms over her head. "Come back! You're going to get us killed!"

She wasn't exaggerating. If this interfered with the choosing, the Pentri would take both their heads. Vespir tailed her dragon through the peach orchards and across the back lawn of the Pentri palace. The day was bright, the sun hot, and Vespir sweated as she vaulted over a fence and down a sloping hill. Her boots sank in the mud from a fresh rain, splattering her trousers.

But when she saw where Karina was headed, Vespir nearly screamed. She would've if fear hadn't closed her throat.

Karina flew toward a circle of white standing stones, where much of the household guard, all in the green livery of the Pentri, clustered together. They surrounded Lord and Lady Pentri, Antonia, and their dragons. Karina was headed for the calling ceremony. Vespir was going to die.

"Stop," she whispered as Karina sailed past the family dragons. "Stop," she pleaded when Karina banked and lowered herself into the center of the circle. "Stop," she prayed when everyone—the Pentri, the guards, a horrified Antonia—turned to face her.

Vespir bolted through the ranks and halted before Karina. The dragon swished her tail and blinked her amber eyes. She appeared pleased.

"Why?" Vespir whispered. Her knees gave out. Vespir collapsed and prostrated herself before the Pentri family. Grass tickled her forehead. "Forgive me, my lord. I don't understand," Vespir cried as the faceless Lord Pentri's shiny black leather boots strode over to her.

Oof. A boot struck her in the hip. Stars of pain exploded behind her eyes as she tried to crawl away. "Forgive me," she wept.

Another blow, to her stomach. Vespir tasted acid in the back of her throat and curled into a ball.

"Thieving bitch!" Lord Pentri boomed. Vespir waited for

another blow, but it didn't come. The ringing in her ears nearly blocked out Antonia's voice as she screamed at her father. Vespir lay in pain, knowing none of the guard would help. If Lord Pentri asked, they'd kill her.

But they didn't touch her. Antonia did, lifting Vespir to her feet. Vespir kept her eyes locked on the ground . . . but Antonia raised her chin. Their dark eyes met.

Vespir heard the absence of everyone's breath.

"Don't," she choked out. But Antonia cradled her face and kissed her. Their tears mingled. Vespir's head throbbed. Her stomach trembled. She was going to be sick.

"How dare you." That was Lady Pentri's voice. Vespir didn't look at her. She stared only at Antonia, who stroked her cheek. Vespir's chin quivered.

"Promise me you'll try to win," Antonia whispered, tears streaming down her face. Vespir would have promised the world to this girl, wrapped it in ribbon to make a present. She would have told her any comforting lie under normal circumstances, but . . .

"I don't know how," she whispered back.

4

Ajax

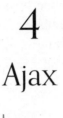

To Ajax, the word *family* tasted like blood, probably because his family always made him bleed. Like right now. Lysander's fist connected with Ajax's face.

Coppery warmth flooded his mouth as he fell backward to squint at his elder, and legitimate, brother. Lysander had it all: square jaw, shining blond hair, good height. He was also dumb as a block of below-average wood. Ajax might not have had the Tiber family name, but he had the brain.

Unless he got caught doing something dumb. Like right now.

"I told you to stop rigging two-bones-in-a-cup!" Lysander squared his already square jaw. Ah, two-bones. The finest dice game imaginable, allowing you to con so many mouth-breathing older brothers. Ajax had a ton of those.

"It's not my fault Demetrius never learns that I cheat." Ajax shrugged. "I'm the little brother, after all. I'm *supposed* to test him."

"Little bastard brother," Lysander corrected. Ajax stood and pulled his shoulders back. He came up to Lysander's chest. At five foot three, he still had all his growing ahead of him. Hopefully.

"Right. How could I forget for even one moment that you and Demetrius are the golden boys, while the rest of us"—he surveyed the arena of the calling circle, filled with twenty-seven of Lord Quintus Tiber's finest, ugliest bastards—"we're just lucky he squirted us out at all."

Lysander's lip curled. "Only a bastard talks like a commoner."

Ajax shrugged. "Only a commoner punches a bastard."

"Speaking of bastards." Ajax knew what Lysander was going for. His brother ripped the gold chain from Ajax's neck, the one with the Wyvern pendant dangling from it. The one Ajax had won almost fair off Demetrius. Ajax hunched his shoulders, pressure building behind his eyes as Lysander pocketed the pendant. "The official Tiber seal is for legitimate sons only."

"Demetrius is even dumber than you. Better shoulders, though." Ajax rasped his molars. His leg jiggled. "That should go to someone more deserving."

"Maybe. But that will never be you, Ajax." Lysander got in his face, smirking. "You're not even a first-rate bastard. That's why your mother couldn't be bothered to stay five minutes after she gave birth."

Ajax's vision blurred; a muscle ticked in his cheek. He had only a few what he called "berserk" strings, but his mother was one. He got to be angry at her forever for dumping him out in this freezing castle with its gray servants and punchy brothers, but no one else got to say anything about her. Ever.

Still, this was Lysander's big day. The choosing day, when his Wyvern would leave Vistlow, central city in the Wroclawian foothills, and take him to a glorious Trial that he'd hopefully lose. After all, Emperor Erasmus had been of the Tiber. Greedy to seat *two* emperors in a row, right?

So Ajax simply smiled. "If you've taught me anything,

Lysander, it's that you don't have to be an actual bastard to be a first-rate one." Lysander nodded, looking pleased. The insult had sailed right past his handsome, wooden head. "Good luck."

The older boy sniffed. "Right. Remember your place, brat." He left, and as he turned, Ajax palmed the dagger at his belt and sliced artfully through the material of Lysander's trousers. They split down the center, revealing Lysander of the Tiber's rosy ass cheeks. Some of the boys caught sight of it as Lysander strode down the steps and they hollered with laughter. Ajax, meanwhile, crawled onto the stone ledge beside his dragon.

"You just sat there while I got my lip split?" Ajax scowled at Dog, the stupidest dragon in the empire. "You're the worst."

"*Gawp,*" Dog replied helpfully, expanding his batlike wings.

One reason the five families tended to have few children was the scarcity of dragon eggs. Everyone of high noble blood needed a dragon—bastard and legitimate alike—and dragons laid rarely. The finest, largest eggs were kept for official family, the lesser eggs for dragon handlers and bastards. Ajax was the twenty-first bastard of twenty-seven and counting. As such, he'd gotten a pretty piss-poor egg.

The red Wyvern was House Tiber's dragon, but Dog looked like a brick-colored flying chameleon, with a curling tail that he liked to wrap around his perch . . . or Ajax's waist. Blue fringe traced his gullet, tiny horns decorated his head and nose, and his protruding eyes could swivel at any angle. Right now, Dog's right eye was trained on Ajax, while the left hunted a buzzing fly as it darted this way and that.

Eh. Ajax scratched the dragon's chest. Dog thumped his tail in enthusiasm.

"Just wait till next year. The army has no idea what they're getting." He grinned, thinking about all the opportunity war offered. There were battles to win, gold to gain. If Ajax couldn't make a name for himself in glory, he could at least get rich off being faster and hungrier than anyone else.

Far as he was concerned, the world was for the taking.

He looked out at the forum of the calling circle. The ring of marble stones waited below, while Lord Tiber's twenty-nine children and all their dragons sat on the tiered steps of the massive arena. The place was a zoo of noise, dragons snapping at one another, boys shoving and spitting and laughing too loud. Ajax wasn't sure if Tiber had never had a girl, or if he just didn't accept female bastards into his house. Whatever the answer, Ajax had grown up in a sea of boys, all jabbing elbows and funky odors. He scratched his own long dirty-blond hair, tied back in a tail that swung to the base of his neck.

Down front, Lysander and Demetrius waited.

The midday sun found its place in the sky. "Damn, how long is this going to take? We've got to get down to the docks. There's a card game I want in on, and the buy-in's going to be steep." Ajax said this to Dog like the dragon could reply. Actually, Dog appeared focused on the calling circle. Really focused. "I don't want you belching smoke all over the Corvus gang again, all right? You—hey! Where are you going, idiot?"

Dog soared down toward the circle. Oh, that stupid *dragon*. Ajax's cheeks flamed as he followed at a run, all the boys in the arena watching. Of course Dog would find a way to screw up the damn calling.

"Hey!" he called as Dog landed in the center of the circle. The dragon's eyes goggled as Ajax pushed after him, and he *hmph*ed when the boy yanked on his bridle. "Dog. No. Not our sitty-spot. This is Lysander's—"

Wait. A. Second.

Ajax looked at Lysander and Demetrius, both openmouthed with shock. He looked at Lord Tiber, sixty-four and bloated as a lazy toad. He looked at the crowd of bastard brothers, none of whom had ever paid attention to him.

But he had everyone's attention *now*. No other dragon came forward. Dog alone waited patiently on that rock to fly away, listening to a call no one else could hear.

Not *a* call. *The* call. Ajax, bastard of the Tiber, had been called to the Emperor's Trial. Forget the Cut or the competition. Finally, finally, everyone was looking at him with awe. With respect.

"You little *bastard!*" Lysander cried. To that, Ajax spat a stream of blood. It lay on the ground, pearled with spit. He grinned as the boys in the arena, all save Lysander and Demetrius, started up a chant.

"*A-jax!* A-*jax!* A-*jax!*" They rose to their feet pumping fists in the air, a sea of shaved heads and broken noses and crooked teeth. One of them turned, pulled down his pants, and waggled his backside. Beautiful. Ajax spread his arms, reveling in the shouts and knowing there wasn't a damn thing Lysander could do about it. For emphasis, Ajax made a rude gesture with his hands. Lysander screamed in fury, and the crowd cheered.

Ajax was going to represent the red Wyvern. He was of the Tiber now.

No. Forget Ajax of the Tiber. Ajax Sarkonus, Dragon Emperor of Etrusia, all at the tender age of fifteen.

The world was for the taking, and he would *take*.

5

Hyperia

Hyperia of the Volscia saw no difference between a suit of armor and a gown. Both were battle garb, one meant for war, the other for peacetime. A true leader understood that war and peace could be equally dangerous. In wartime, the people could rebel out of anger. In peace, the nobles could scheme out of boredom.

Her parents had made certain Hyperia knew her way around every bloody and beautiful battlefield. She thanked them for that.

For the calling, Hyperia had selected a gown worthy of an empress. She stood calm and tall and cool as the servants fluttered around her, adjusting and pinning. She wore gold, the Volscia color. The taffeta silk skirt was a cloud, the bodice of gold filigree lace so delicate, only the maid with the nimblest hands was allowed to touch. Pearls fastened the cuffs at her wrists, and pearls were woven into her golden hair.

Her personal maid traced a fingertip across both cheekbones, leaving gold dust like the trail of a falling star. Hyperia turned her face this way and that, her blue eyes examining every facet of her appearance. She knew she was beautiful. She didn't feel pride at it. Beauty was an accident, like birth. Only ability was earned.

Nineteen and the elder Volscia child, she'd been born to the Trial. But through years of sacrifice and pain, she'd truly earned her place.

"Good," she said at last. The servants exhaled in unison.

She added the final touch: a belt of weapons. Her sword rode on her left hip, her dagger on her right. She was ready.

The morning mist had burned away as she crossed the meadow to the calling circle. A cool wind teased the tendrils of her hair. Hyperia caught snatches of birdsong and smiled as laughter bubbled behind her. Normally, she'd take a dagger to anyone trying to sneak up. Anyone but her sister.

"Are you going to forget me?" Julia grabbed Hyperia's hand and ran forward, tugging her along. Hyperia didn't tend to smile—she didn't tend to do anything dishonest—but she smiled now.

"No. I'll never forget you," she said quietly.

Julia scoffed. "*You're* supposed to say yes, and then *I'm* supposed to cry like my heart will break." Julia had always been prone to flights of imagination. As a small child, she'd begged Hyperia to play make-believe and then acted out the parts of both the princess and the handsome prince herself. Hyperia had been relegated to the scenery. She couldn't understand such whimsy, but she could love it in her little sister. She touched Julia's braid of hair, all bound on the back of her head. Yesterday, that hair had tumbled around her shoulders.

"I suppose you had to grow up sometime," she said wistfully. In truth, fourteen was a bit late for such a thing. Hyperia had become a woman at twelve. But she didn't mind Julia staying a child longer. Her sister, shorter and chestnut-tressed, wrapped her arms around Hyperia's waist. Hyperia planted a kiss atop the girl's head.

"When you're empress, can you come and visit?" Julia asked.

"Sometimes." It wasn't a lie, though Hyperia didn't think

she'd ever crave a return to the Ardennes region. The Volscia land holdings were rich with sun-kissed vineyards and lavender fields, apple orchards and dense forests. They were the first dragon riders and the second-wealthiest family. Their primary family residence at Aureus was more opulent than any other in the known world, their commitment to art and music unparalleled. Julia adored all of that, the concerts and the masques. She could have sipped sparkling rose wine and eaten vanilla cakes smothered in fondant every morning.

Hyperia didn't like sweet things. The Volscia had begun as warriors and turned soft. The family hadn't seated an emperor in nine generations, longer than any other House. It was shameful.

Fortunately, Hyperia's parents had trained her to set things right. Now she was ready.

Though saying goodbye to her sister would prove difficult.

"Farewell to the nightingale," Hyperia murmured. Julia tightened her embrace.

"Hello to the lark." She grinned. It was a nursery song Hyperia used to sing when they were younger, one learned from an old governess. Hyperia had never seen the point of music. But Julia liked it, so it had value.

They came to the circle of obsidian stones, glossy under the high, hot sun. Hyperia's parents glittered in their golden finery. Julia ran to hug them; Hyperia did not. Her father came over and placed a heavy hand on her shoulder. She winced at his tight grip.

"Don't disappoint," Father said in a low voice.

"I never have." When he let go, she rotated her shoulder. Shadows flashed over the grass, and the family dragons lowered out of the sky. All dragons were magnificent, but the golden Hydra of the Volscia could not be matched.

Julia's dragon, Minerva, was splendid. But Aufidius, Hyperia's mount, was the finest dragon the world had seen since the empire first formed one thousand years ago. Aufidius's head was the rare, exquisite diamond shape. His wingspan stretched forty feet. Experts had measured the arch of his neck and declared it perfect. His scales, a deep gold, glowed radiant in the sunlight. His eyes, black as volcanic obsidian, shone with fierce intelligence. Most dragons were little more than beloved pets to their riders.

Aufidius was Hyperia's partner.

One day, he might well take her head off if she made a wrong move. That was exactly right. He was a dragon.

Dragons should be feared.

They were like emperors in that way.

Aufidius growled as Hyperia stood beside him and waited. Across from her, Julia waved. The minutes ticked by.

Hyperia did not panic as time passed. She'd never attended a calling before and trusted that it would all sort itself out.

She didn't fear when Minerva opened her wings and soared on an updraft. Julia craned her neck to watch, but Hyperia's attention remained fixed on the stones.

When Minerva landed on the center slab of obsidian, though, every muscle in Hyperia's body froze. The Hydra flared her wings and fixed Julia with an obvious stare. *Let's go,* it seemed to say.

By the blue above, *Julia.* Hyperia felt a spasm of horror. Her sister knew nothing of warcraft. She was second-born. She was too young. She would never be empress.

She would be Cut instead.

Hyperia strode to the center stone while Aufidius gnashed his teeth. Julia sobbed as Hyperia stepped in front of her.

"Please." Hyperia made her voice cool and reasonable. She

didn't know to whom she was speaking, but whatever *it* was, she believed it could hear her. "A mistake's been made. I am Hyperia of the Volscia, elder child of the House." Hyperia spoke formally, both because it was natural to her and because if she didn't she might give in to fear. An empress could not know fear or doubt. She must do what was necessary. "This is my right of challenge. *I* am the competitor for the dragon's throne. If you would call off this dragon and choose mine, I could come at once. Without delay." She paused. "If you would be so kind." She fumbled those words. An empress did not beg favors.

But she was not an empress yet, and for the first time in her life that position seemed in jeopardy.

Minerva lashed her tail and did not move. Hyperia's gown began to wilt under the hot sun. They were losing time. Soon, Julia would have to leave. Should her dragon arrive at the Trial without her . . . the Cut would be automatic.

"Don't let me go." Her sister's sobs wrenched Hyperia from her thoughts. She hugged Julia tight, letting the girl weep against her shoulder. "I can't do this!"

"It's all right," Hyperia soothed. She kissed Julia's forehead, squeezed her eyes shut. "My baby. It's all right." Cradling Julia's tearstained face, for one brief second Hyperia's fingers trembled. "Please forgive me," she whispered.

Hyperia drew her dagger and slid the blade neatly across her sister's throat.

Julia's eyes widened in shock. She spluttered and shoved at Hyperia as blood spurted from her neck, then she collapsed. Hyperia should have stood over her fallen opponent—because that's what Julia had become the minute she was called. But Hyperia knelt instead. She held Julia's hand tightly, leaned over so that her little sister could see the face of someone who loved her as she died.

"Farewell to the nightingale," Hyperia murmured as Julia twitched on the grass. The blood was warm on Hyperia's face and clothes. Her sister's grip slackened. "Hello to the lark."

When Julia of the Volscia died, Hyperia bit back tears, kissed her sister's forehead, and stood.

She heard a buzzing, like a fly. It took a moment to surface from her stupor and realize that the buzzing was actually her mother's wails. Lady Volscia had fallen to her knees. She reached for her daughters and screamed. And screamed. Lord Volscia held on to his wife, his face blanched.

Hyperia glared. "Stop that," she snapped. *I am your creation.*

The screams didn't stop. Hyperia stepped back and watched to see what Minerva would do.

The dragon hopped off the obsidian slab. She snuffled at the body of her mistress, prodding Julia with her snout. The Hydra keened, her song pure—beautiful and sad. Hyperia felt every mournful note echo through her bones.

Minerva opened her jaws wide and swallowed Julia's body in three goes. One: the girl's head and shoulders vanished. Two: only her stockinged legs were visible. Three: a trace of Julia's blood on the grass was all that remained. Hyperia nodded, feeling somewhat soothed. That was the end and the glory of all riders. To be recalled into the fiery belly of the dragon was to be immortal.

It was the greatest honor anyone could have. At least she'd given Julia that, not the ignominy of the Cut.

I love you, she thought.

Hyperia turned to the now-empty stone slab, blood bright against her golden front. She felt blood trickling down her cheek, reached to wipe it away, and stopped. Instead, she cleaned her dagger on her skirt and sheathed it. While her parents wailed, she narrowed her eyes, much as she did when sighting down an arrow toward a target.

"I am Hyperia of the Volscia, last remaining child of the House. The Emperor's Trial is mine by right. Go ahead." She held out her hands, palms up. She would wait as long as need be. She would wait forever.

"Call for me."

6

Emilia

Emilia hadn't imagined the world could contain this much blue. She'd woken an hour before, tied tight to Chara's saddle in traditional riding fashion. A well-fed and rested dragon could fly for a full day without stopping, and Chara had not responded to any of Emilia's tugs or pressed legs. The dragon had soared onward, listening to the invisible call. When Emilia fell asleep last night, they'd been somewhere over the eastern mainland of the empire. Now, with sun sparkling over the expanse of the sea, she could only stare in awe.

She'd grown up with the ocean a permanent background roar, but those waters had been dark and storming gray. Not like this, the shade of a summer sky, and so warm.

She'd been correct; that gave her a little flush of pleasure. The Trial's first location was the Crotian Sea. Emilia had studied the Crotian territory and knew that it was a land of eternal summer, of wild islands, of ceaseless blue.

"We almost there, girl?" Emilia's bladder felt near to bursting. In response, Chara glided down on the wind's current. Ahead, Emilia caught hazy sight of an island. "At last," she moaned.

Chara flared her wings, slowing and dropping. Eventually,

they landed on a wide, cleared patch of earth. Emilia's knees buckled as she slid to the ground, the insides of her thighs throbbing with pain. She'd never ridden that long before.

Shaking, she placed her palms on the ground and closed her eyes. She felt the thread of connection between her body and Chara, her hands and the earth beneath and the ocean behind.

As her heart beat faster, the warmth of magic began to fill her. Nothing had changed. Once again, Emilia was a blasted vessel for it. The flight here had shocked her so deeply that the chaos had held itself at bay, but it was resurging with a vengeance now. The magic—the prickling, boiling pain of it—demanded its liberty. She spun around and on her hands and knees looked down into the lapping waves. She focused upon a cluster of stones slick with algae, their tops shining when the water receded for one instant before sloshing back over again. Emilia saw the rippling dark of her shadow outlined by the sun's glare.

Her head throbbed; the blood pulsated at her temples. Biting her lip, Emilia focused on those rocks and freed her chaos.

The stones exploded, shards shooting every direction in the water. Enormous bubbles of air rose to the surface. The sea muffled the eruption, and instantly the tightness around Emilia's head eased up. The dull roar in her ears vanished. She was safe.

For now. Emilia had long compared these "outbursts" to a violent stomach illness. You could sense it coming, but you couldn't stop it. All she could do was try to find the best place to be sick. After, she felt empty. Breathing heavily, Emilia turned and stared at a pair of sandaled feet. The person before her wore a homespun brown tunic.

Oh no. No, no, did they see? Trying to remain calm, Emilia glanced upward. The person before her did not appear startled or frightened. Breathing out in relief, Emilia rose, dusting off her knees. The girl—yes, definitely a girl, not much older than she—gazed at Emilia with great calm.

"You're invited to wait," the girl said, gesturing toward a path that led up a small incline. "Their Graces will be with you in time."

"Oh." Of course, Their Graces, the high priests of the temple at Delphos. The administrators of order's magical power, the high priests spoke for the Great Dragon here on earth. They always administered the Emperor's Trial. Until a new leader was crowned, they were effectively the sole authority in Etrusia.

And Emilia would have to evade their notice. Nausea rocked her at the thought.

"Thank you." Emilia attempted a smile. *Try not to show too much teeth,* her mother had once warned her. Emilia's smile made people uncomfortable.

Chara snuffled behind her. Emilia went to remove her saddle—the poor dragon would have sores if she wasn't rubbed down soon. The hooded girl—the brown robe marked her as an acolyte of the temple, Emilia understood now—made a noise in her throat and took Chara's reins. The dragon let her.

"You're invited to wait," the girl repeated.

Emilia grabbed her satchel and walked. She threw glances at Chara over her shoulder, but the dragon appeared more than fine, puffing gladly as the girl loosened the saddle.

When Emilia got to the top of the path, she looked out at the temple beyond. Her eyes widened. She had anticipated beauty, but not . . . not like this.

Rows of marble columns led down a long, flowering courtyard and up to the building. Several steps ascended to the temple's single level, made of stone so white it was a glare in the sunshine. The doors gleamed brass, the triangular roof glimmered in accents of gold. A carved frieze displayed images of warriors on dragonback surging against a horde of snarling enemies. Near the start of the columns, mossy stone dragons had been set to guard the area. A rectangular pool lay in the center of the space, reflecting the azure blue of the sky. A fountain burbled at the far end, adjacent to the bronze statue of a man, his feet skating the pool's surface. The man raised an arm in triumph, while a dragon's wings extended from his back on either side. Emilia knew her history: this had been sculpted to commemorate Antoninus, the first emperor, who'd ridden the Great Dragon into battle against the Chaos House.

She shut her eyes; Chaos House. Her stomach churned to think of it.

This wasn't even the Great Temple at Delphos. This was another holy place, tucked away somewhere in the blue of the Crotian Sea. Emilia had never seen it on any map. Perhaps it had been built solely to gather those the Great Dragon selected. Emilia shivered with the realization that this Trial held mysteries that even she, with all her books and studies, had never discovered.

Within the courtyard, flowering shrubs and fruit trees bloomed in opulence. The pears and pomegranates practically quivered, ripe and ready to fall. Emilia's mouth watered. She wanted to pluck a pear and take a juicy bite—

Emilia felt the chaos surge again, her throat tightening with it. She was going to explode those pears, maybe the whole damn tree. Grunting, she sat down hard on the ground, digging her thumbs into her eyes. Magic boiled in her skull. Multicolored light splashed across her closed lids. The power bubbled in her blood, looking to burst.

Stop. I just released you. Stop, Emilia begged. She clenched her jaw and heaved a sigh as the chaos fizzled. The hum died down in her brain, and the knot of tension between her shoulders loosened. She'd stopped it in time. But why? She'd just given the magic its own way five minutes before; why should it suddenly appear again when she was thinking about *pears*? She had never experienced two bursts so close together. "Shit," Emilia whispered. Maybe if she was normal she could win this Trial with her books and her strategies, but this thing, this monster inside of her . . . If it showed itself at one wrong moment . . .

They're going to kill me.

Worse, they'd guess that Emilia's family had hidden her away to conceal her dark ability. Exploding rocks might be seen as relatively harmless, but Emilia had done worse. Far worse.

She'd exploded boys, as well. A boy, singular.

They're going to blame Mother and Father. She chewed her lip. *Alex.*

Her brother would lose his family lands and titles, if not his head. Emilia's temples throbbed dully. Why had she been called? *Why?*

They should have killed you when they first found out, she thought.

"Hello?" someone called to her right. Emilia shot to her feet and discovered the tall figure of a young man standing in a column's shadow. He stepped into the sunlight, which played on his shag of black hair. "Good. Someone else is finally here."

She didn't recognize the deep voice or the haphazardly cut hair. But those eyes were unmistakable: that liquid-copper color could only belong to one family. One person.

For the first time in five years, Emilia experienced the thrill of a pleasant surprise.

"Lucian?" she whispered, drawing nearer.

The Lucian she'd last seen five years ago had been half a head shorter than she, with round cheeks. He'd grown tall since then, and lean with muscle. Dark stubble boasted of his need for a razor. Emilia felt warm at the unexpected, entirely *admirable* sight of him. Different, yes, he was different, but also familiar. He was safe. At that moment, Emilia couldn't even wonder what he was doing here or where Dido was or anything sensible. What mattered was that *he* was *here,* someone who knew her from before her headaches began and her smile disappeared. Relieved, she trotted over to him . . . and stopped.

He looked at her like she was an alien creature. Horror lit his eyes as he raked his gaze over her body.

"Emilia?" he whispered. "What *happened* to you?"

7

Lucian

Lucian was seven when his mother died on campaign, slaugh-tered during an unexpected surge by the Wikingar clans against the empire's forces. Many highborn families had *tsk*ed among themselves and wondered why a noblewoman of that rank had gone into battle in the first place, but the Sabel prided themselves on being the only one of the five families that chose to fight on the front lines in the wars of expansion. Brave woman that she was, Lady Sabel had pressed forward until the end.

Her death had ripped Lucian's life out at the root. His father never forgave himself for being absent when his wife fell. The Sabel custom was to dress in deep gray for one week following the memorial, but Lucian's father had kept the family in mourn-ing for six months. He'd sequestered himself in his chambers, unable to even speak to his children. Lucian and Dido had been left with only their governess to watch over them. They'd run wild, frantic with grief.

Finally, Lucian's father had sent the twins to the Hibrian Isles, to stay with the Aurun family for the summer. Lucian remained in his room for three days after arriving, only want-ing to cry, refusing to play with the Aurun children. Then, one morning, a girl with wild red hair opened his door. Lucian was huddled in the center of his bed, knees pressed to his chest. He sniffled as he beheld this odd creature.

"H'lo!" She marched up to him. "It is very nice to meet you."

Lucian gave her his hand. She put her whole arm into shaking, nearly yanking him out of bed.

"Would you like to see the tide pools? My brother and your sister don't want to go."

That had been his introduction to Emilia of the Aurun, the girl he'd see every summer for the next six years. She'd taken him to study sea life at the tide pools, ankles grainy with sand, dress increasingly sodden, chortling with joy as she sketched every creature and wrote down every species' scientific name. (*"Strongylocentrotus purpuratus*! That's a purple urchin. I want to find a red one. What's your favorite color?") They'd swum together, boated together, crept out at night to tell frightening stories by the light of the full moon. Emilia had been unusual and lively. Her cheeks had been rosy, her eyes bright.

What had happened to that girl?

Now her tangled red hair hung heavy in her gaunt, pale face. Darkness ringed her eyes; her lips looked chapped from biting. She kept her arms huddled close by her sides and her shoulders hunched, as if trying to take up as little space as possible. "Are you unwell?" he said, before he could stop himself.

She lowered her chin. Her large gray eyes glared up at him. "That's a rude thing to say to somebody," she mumbled.

Lucian felt abashed and also strangely relieved. She was ready to scold him; clearly she hadn't utterly changed.

He laughed without thinking. "When did you ever know me to be polite?"

A small smile. "True."

She was right, though; he *had* been rude. "Sorry, Emi. It's just . . . I never thought I'd find you *here*." He went to put a hand on her shoulder, startled when she flinched and stepped away. Then he understood.

They were both here for a single reason: to win a throne or be Cut.

Only one could triumph. Being friendly wouldn't change that.

"Apology accepted." Her voice sounded hoarse. "While we're on the subject, what happened to *you*?" Her eyes scanned his hands, threaded with white scars. "My parents said you went on campaign with your father to the northern peninsula."

Images flashed in his mind: huts abloom with fire, roofs caving in; two charred bodies curled at his feet like a gruesome quotation mark.

"Yes," he said. "But I wasn't quite the perfect soldier he hoped I'd be."

"Really?" She seemed genuinely puzzled. "We heard you and Tyche cleared that barricade at the Vartl fjord. It was an impressive bit of strategy."

Yes. Tyche had fired when and where he'd told her, obedient as always. But Lucian had felt the dragon trembling beneath him. He had sat with her in the aerie during the night, trying to coax her to eat while she curled listlessly on the ground, her snout tucked beneath a wing.

Emilia continued. "Your father wrote to mine about how the emperor commended you for—"

He couldn't listen to this anymore. Not from her. Not from anyone, but especially not from her. She was one of the few fond memories of his childhood, and he didn't want to tarnish it by listening to her rattle on like a trained parrot about what a hero he was.

"Oh, I know how to kill," he muttered. "I just forgot to *smile* while killing."

"I'm sorry," Emilia said.

Shame flooded him. Why should *she* be sorry? She wasn't the murderer here.

Emilia cleared her throat. "Well, what are we going to do about this?"

He blinked. "This?"

She frowned. "Don't be obtuse." Unbidden, Lucian smiled. *Obtuse.* Most people would settle for a lesser, straightforward word like *dumb,* but Emilia had never settled for lesser. "If you're here, that means my calling wasn't an accident. A pattern is developing; likely younger children of all the Houses are being called this time. Now the question is, why?" Emilia placed one finger against her lips, the telltale sign that she was deep in thought. "Which leads me to the next question: Who or what *does* the calling? They say it's the Great Dragon Himself, but that seems like spiritualist nonsense. I suppose the priests can tell us. Have you seen them yet?"

"The priests are in the temple," he said. "But apparently they won't see us before tonight's reception."

He couldn't hold back the acid in his voice at the word *reception.* This island was beautiful, with the turquoise sea and the clear sky, the ripe fruit and the gilded temple. The reception would be luxurious, fit for the future ruler of an empire. An empire that didn't give a shit how much blood it had to spill to achieve its goals.

I should have just let them Cut me, Lucian thought grimly.

"My father heard you were headed to Delphos." Emilia seemed to sense the course of his thoughts. "You were going to take vows with the brotherhood?"

"Yes." He squared his jaw. "But not now."

"I'm sorry," she said quietly. He looked at her again. Whatever had happened to her these past five years—and something must have—it had clearly worn her down. After his first campaign at fourteen, he'd forgotten to write to her. No: he'd chosen not to. He'd hated her a bit for being innocent.

What if she'd needed his help, and he hadn't given it?

"I'm sorry, too, that you have to be here," he said. He wanted to reach for her, but stopped himself. "If it helps, I'm not going to fight. Coming here was weakness."

Emilia's eyes widened. "No, you have to at least try. I don't want you to be Cut." Her brow furrowed. "I don't want *any* of us to be Cut, but I suppose none of us has a choice." She slid fingers through her tangled wall of hair. "Now I wonder how poor Alex didn't go crazy."

Lucian extended a hand. She regarded him warily.

"I won't hurt you, Emilia. I can guarantee that." He gazed skyward. Where in the depths were the others, anyway?

"Well, there's at least one House that won't be surprised," Emilia said. "The Pentri. Antonia's their only child. She'll be here."

A dragon screamed overhead. They looked up to find a small brown creature hurtling to earth, a girl's shrieking voice merging with the beast's call. The screeching pair landed somewhere on the other side of the island. Emilia and Lucian frowned at each other.

"Whose dragon was *that*?" he asked.

8

Vespir

A mistake. Vespir mouthed the words while she slid off Karina's back. Her dragon panted as she laid her head on the earth. Vespir touched the poor creature's neck, the scales nearly burning her hand. An overworked dragon might suffer what handlers called a "flameout," the fiery acid in their stomachs rupturing and burning a hole from the inside. Karina was too small for such an enormous, nonstop flight. An hour ago, Vespir had been certain they'd plunge into the sea.

"Shh, it's okay, girl," she whispered. Karina closed her eyes and mewled.

A young man in a brown tunic and sandals appeared beside them, his shadow stretching over Vespir.

"You're invited to wait," he said. "Their Graces will—"

"Get her a bucket of water, not too cold. She needs to rest in the shade. Where's the aerie?" Vespir said all this while rubbing Karina's neck; thankfully, she felt it cooling beneath her hands. They were out of danger. Probably. Thank the blue above she never rode the dragon with a saddle. That might have tipped the scales into a rupture. "And food, too. Lamb'd be best." Vespir finally looked up. The young man blinked; clearly he hadn't expected her to be this talkative. Like Vespir, he had olive skin, high cheekbones, and narrow, dark eyes. Perhaps he was from the eastern Ikrayina as well. Perhaps he'd be sympathetic to her.

Then, reaching out his hand, he whistled low. Karina perked up, stood, and bobbed toward him. He touched her snout, letting her get his scent.

"You're invited to wait." He nodded at a small incline. "The temple's that way." All business. No sympathy. Karina bumped his arm with her nose, a classic, playful move.

I think I have to leave her with him.

This was all a mistake.

"Who do I talk to?" she asked. This time, the boy said nothing, merely led Karina away along a dirt path. Vespir cursed under her breath, climbed that slight hill the boy had pointed at, only to find herself before a damn *palace.* The white marble, the gold, the fountain—it all stopped her breath.

Antonia belonged here. This place was made for a girl like her. Vespir put a hand to her stomach, now painfully tender where Lord Pentri had kicked her. She must make it back to Antonia. The noble girl was Vespir's fixed destination, whatever the journey ahead.

"It's a mistake," Vespir whispered, and took off for the palace. She was bleary with exhaustion; having no rope to tie herself down, she'd had to stay awake all night to avoid falling off Karina's back. "I need to talk to someone."

"Hey!" A young man stepped into the path ahead of her, near a rectangular pool. He was dressed in royal blue. Vespir knew the other Houses' colors—this was one of the competitors. By the Dragon, he was *tall.* Built like a bull. Vespir locked her eyes to the ground as she fell to her knees. There was the sound of footsteps, and a girl appeared next to the boy. Vespir stared at the purple hem of her gown.

"It's one of the Pentri servants," the girl said, obviously

recognizing the green livery. She sounded bewildered. Good, she and Vespir had something in common. Vespir pressed her palms and forehead to the earth. "Where's Antonia?"

"Forgive me, my lady. I was called in her place." Vespir swallowed. Her throat was sore and dry. "But it's all a mistake."

"There've been many mistakes today," the boy grumbled. He stepped nearer. "It's all right. Let me help you up."

Vespir dared to glance at them. The girl's face—what Vespir could see behind a mass of hair—appeared blank with amazement. The boy narrowed his eyes. What was Vespir doing looking on the faces of nobility? She winced as she got to her feet and kept half bowed.

"If I could see someone . . . I need to speak to . . . This is wrong." Vespir groped for a full explanation, then muttered an apology and ran along the pool, sprinting for the bronze door. Her thighs screamed, but she blocked out the pain. Even when the world threatened to fuzz around the edges, she forced herself forward.

All she had to do was show up with dragon shit on her clothes and mud caked onto her cheap leather boots, and the priests or whoever would know this was wrong. They'd send her home.

You don't have a home anymore. Vespir nearly skidded to a halt. The Pentri would kill her if she ever showed her face again, and she hadn't seen her parents or her siblings in five years. For all she knew, they were dead.

Not right now. Inside the temple, the air was cool. The floors were creamy marble veined with gold, so polished that Vespir found an upside-down version of herself gazing back, like her soul had been trapped in a world beneath her feet. Her knees ached just thinking about the hours of work needed to achieve a shine like that.

Vespir ran the echoing length of the building until she came to a large pair of wooden doors. Two kids in brown robes—they all seemed to be kids here—waited on either side. Vespir moved to open the door, but they silently blocked her path.

"I need to talk to someone." Vespir's voice broke.

"Their Graces will see you in due time," the girl to the left said. She sounded cool and even a little bored.

"Who are Their Graces?" Vespir didn't give a damn that her voice was getting loud. These kids in their brown robes had to be servants just like her. No harm in shouting.

"The high priest and priestess." The girl curled her lip in disgust. "But surely you knew *that*?"

Vespir had heard that tone in noble voices a million times over. Astonishment at a peasant's ignorance; amusement at their earnestness; irritation, because how could *anyone* not know something so obvious?

But she would not let these . . . whoever they were . . . look at Vespir like she was trash. Something broke in her mind. Vespir lunged forward, shoving at the doors.

"Stop!" the girl cried, trying to push Vespir off. Vespir beat her fists against the wood, screaming to anyone who would listen.

"I need to talk to someone! Please! There's been a mistake!" she shouted.

And then, she could not move.

She could not even blink. No sound passed between her frozen lips. Her fists remained raised above her head; she could not lower them. She could still think and breathe, but otherwise she was trapped. A prisoner in her own body.

What's happening to me?

"Have you got her?" the brown-robed boy to Vespir's right asked. The girl huffed.

"I've never used stasis magic on a person before. I wonder if Their Graces will certify me." The two chuckled, and Vespir understood.

Even a peasant knew the three branches of the orderly magical arts: stasis, binding, and construction. A person was either born with the ability to become an orderly magos or not. No matter their station, any child who displayed the talent for order magic was taken as an acolyte and trained for the priesthood. There was no higher honor.

So. These two were training to become magosi. Magical priests of the Dragon Himself.

What was going to happen to Vespir now? Would she be kicked out of the Trial for her bad attitude? By the blue above, she could only hope.

Before her captors could do or say anything more, the wooden doors creaked open.

Vespir stood helpless as a man and a woman appeared before her, each wearing the satin orange robe of the priesthood.

"Release her," the woman said, her voice brassy with age.

Vespir's arms collapsed at her side. She stumbled over the door's threshold and into the room.

The walls were painted the deep orange of sunset. Golden pillars upheld the roof. The floor was colorfully tiled with a mosaic that displayed five different dragons whose combined flames formed a sun. Silken couches congregated around a low table of dark, gleaming wood.

Vespir collapsed to her knees and stared at the priests' embroidered slippers. She couldn't look up. Not due to stasis or anything. She'd just been trained too well.

"Now," the woman said. "Who exactly are you?"

"I'm nobody," Vespir said. She licked her lips. "I mean, I'm dragon handler to the Pentri family. But I'm nobody."

"Why are you here, Nobody?" The woman drew nearer. Vespir caught the scent of ambergris and rose; it must have been a lotion. "Where's the Pentri heir?"

Finally, someone understood how strange this was. Vespir trembled. "A mistake. My dragon was called instead of hers."

Silence. Then the man spoke for the first time, his voice high and harsh, "There are no mistakes."

Out of pure confusion, Vespir looked up. She glimpsed the faces of the priests for one brief moment. The woman had bright black eyes, a foxlike pointed nose, and shoulder-length hair of pure steel gray. The man's forehead was high, his eyes sunken, his jaw thin, his mouth bracketed by harsh lines.

They looked old and wary. *They're not gods,* Vespir thought.

Insanity. She bowed her head again. "Excuse me?"

"Petros means that we did not call you." The woman sniffed. "And the calling is never wrong."

Vespir swallowed. "My lady, maybe something went wrong just this once?"

"Your Grace," the priestess corrected. Her voice chilled.

Footsteps behind her. Vespir guessed the two competitors she'd seen outside had entered. The priestess's breath hitched.

"Oh. Now this is decidedly odd," she muttered, as if to herself. So the priests hadn't expected these two, either.

"We agree," the boy competitor said.

"Please, noble priestess." Vespir began to shake; the floor was colder than she'd expected. "Let me leave."

"No. I'm sorry." She sounded very far from sorry. "Petros is right. There are no mistakes."

"But you said this was odd." That was the other girl, the one in the purple dress.

"That was a personal opinion." The priestess clucked

her tongue. "The Great Dragon does choose in the most . . . mysterious ways."

"A creature that has been dead for one thousand years chooses the imperial candidates?" The girl sounded baffled.

"Dear child, logic is the enemy of faith," the priestess said. "As custodians of His sacred temple, we simply do as He demands."

Vespir wasn't the girl to debate logic or faith. She just wanted to get out of here.

"I'm going, if that's all right." She stood, her boots squealing on the floor.

"I wouldn't recommend it." The priestess *hmph*ed. "Not unless you want to be Cut."

Vespir blinked. "Cut?"

The boy and the girl made a noise of surprise and . . . pity?

"Oh." The priestess sighed. "Well, *this* is something I've never had to explain before." She stepped nearer to Vespir, who kept her eyes fixed on the satin hem of the woman's robe. "The Cut hearkens back to the dawn of the empire. The Trial was created in order to impartially select a new ruler from the five Houses. However, the losers could become . . . resentful. Therefore, the Cut was instituted to keep the unsuccessful competitors and their families docile."

Vespir swallowed, tasting bile at the back of her throat. "Let me guess. The losers are executed," she croaked.

"Perceptive." The woman sounded patronizing. "Yes, and in a manner of the victor's choosing." She gave a wry chuckle. "This is one excellent reason to get along with all fellow competitors; you never know who will decide whether to administer a painless poison or draw and quarter you to death."

Vespir didn't think it was that funny.

"But the Cut goes one step further," the priestess continued.

"How?" Vespir muttered.

"The losers' dragons are killed," Petros drawled. Vespir's head snapped up. Her mouth fell open. Spots danced in her vision.

Dragons. Killed. *Karina.*

"*What?*" The room tilted.

"The dragon is a rider's soul. Both body *and* soul must die, you see."

"You're going to kill my dragon?" Vespir swayed on her feet. The night ride, the lack of food, this madness . . . she couldn't stand much longer.

"Cut dragons are the most sacred to the blue above," Petros continued, as if reading lines from a dull book. "The Great Dragon considers them holy martyrs."

As a servant, Vespir had always known she might die on a nobleman's whim. She lived because they allowed it, same as all peasants. But Karina . . . a dragon . . . a beautiful, perfect creature . . . Vespir met the priest's eyes.

"You can't!" Her scream echoed.

"Thank you very much, we *can.*"

"But." What could she say to stop this? From the instant Karina had hatched and crawled to her, mewling and nudging against her knee, Vespir had understood how it felt to be complete. "But Karina's my heart," she whispered.

The priests regarded her with calm detachment.

Who grieved for the heart of a servant, after all?

❄

When she woke, it was dark. Vespir swallowed and sat up, sinking into the softest mattress she'd ever felt. She blinked at her surroundings. A golden lamp swayed from the ceiling, the light warping and flickering over Vespir's plush bed. The blanket was of fine green silk, the pillows tasseled with gold.

She vaguely recalled being brought here, feeling numb. The

instant Vespir's head had met the pillow, she'd been dead to the world. She coughed; her mouth felt tacky.

Vespir was in a rotunda, its columns upholding a round bronze roof. Her bedroom lay open on all sides to the night. White diaphanous curtains, the closest she had to walls, swelled in the breeze. The ocean surged nearby.

Someone had removed her boots, but she was still dressed in her handler clothes. The rough-spun green shirt itched against her neck. She shut her eyes, her head throbbing.

What do I do now?

"Hey." An unknown voice sounded to her left, startling her.

Vespir found someone small and blond watching her. His eyes glinted in the lamplight, and his smile was jagged. He drowned in a red coat that was far too big for him, its sleeves rolled several times.

"Guess I'm not the only bastard here after all," he said.

9
Ajax

———————➤

Ajax didn't get why everyone looked depressed. Maybe their lives back home had all been so wonderful that this was a step down, but for him it was the greatest opportunity ever. Granted, the clothes they'd laid out on his bed had been a little on the big side. The priestess, Camilla, explained that they'd tailored everything for the anticipated competitors. Whatever. Ajax hadn't been able to wear the pants, but the jacket worked fine for now. A little big, but fine. He'd long been denied the red cloaks of the Tiber family and was making up for that in a big way.

And here, another bastard. She couldn't be anything else.

But she glared at him. "I'm not a bastard. I'm a servant." She said it stiffly.

Ajax snorted. "Oh, excuse me. Didn't realize you were so fancy." He crossed his arms as she sat up. Damn, she looked taller than him, too. He'd been measuring himself against the others. "The reception's about to start. The fifth competitor should be arriving soon."

"This late?" The girl rubbed her neck.

"Yeah, apparently there was a holdup or something, the priestess said? Who knows." He waited. "Are you coming or not?"

"Are you always this polite?" Her cheeks flushed as she stared at the floor. "Sorry. My lord."

Oh, Ajax could get used to this. "You don't need to use my official title. Ajax is fine." He neglected to add that he didn't really have a title, but this made him look benevolent. A real man of the people.

"Vespir. I'll, er, join you," she mumbled, and sat back on her bed. He shrugged and strolled away, leaving the rotunda to flicker in the darkness like a lantern. In the distance, a line of torches flared, providing guidance for the last competitor's dragon. Ajax watched the sky, listened to the soothing hush of the waves.

So far, he'd sized up his competition. He could handle them all. The servant girl looked sick, so one strike against her already. The other girl, Emilia, seemed kind of weird. He couldn't quite explain it, apart from the hair thing and the fact that she wouldn't touch anybody, not even to shake hands. And Lucian, well, he was no trouble. Guys that big were often dumb.

That left this last, mystery competitor as all that might keep Ajax from the dragon throne.

He craned his neck as the flap of leathery wings sounded in the darkness. A massive shape surged down, thinning the torches' flames and snuffing some completely. A growl rumbled the earth as the dragon retracted its wings, its scales glittering in the remaining torchlight. Ajax trotted over to see a girl dismount. She walked away from her dragon, not even glancing back as the acolytes ran to take care of it. Her gown shone against the night.

Nice. A fancy girl. This might be fun.

"Hey." Ajax jogged up to her. She stopped and glanced down at him. Aw, damn. She was almost as tall as the big, dumb guy. He couldn't tell much about her other than that she sparkled, and he got the impression she was ready to leave if he didn't make himself interesting fast. "Ajax. Of the Tiber." He puffed out his chest. "Glad you finally made it."

"Mmm." She said it like she was barely humoring him and continued walking. Jerking on his collar, he strode after her. He didn't want to run, but her legs were *long*. "You're the Volscia heir, right?"

"Yes."

"The reception's this way," he said, trying to look like he was leading her and not the other way around. He slicked back his hair. "You, ah, want to change first?" She looked amazing, but also kind of worn. She had dirt on her cheek.

"We've wasted enough time already."

"Yeah. What happened? Your dragon sleep through the call?" He laughed.

She didn't.

In fact, she finally faced him head on, regarding him as she might an insect. Ajax blinked. She was the most beautiful woman he'd ever seen. She was stunning, golden from head to toe . . . and covered in dried blood. Blood had geysered onto her front in a dark stain. A splotch of it flaked rust brown on her cheek.

"You've got some blood on you," he said stupidly.

"Yes." Her eyes gleamed. "It's not mine." She walked away, leaving the delicate scent of lilacs in her wake. He trekked after her, a grin stretching over his face.

Oh yeah. *This* was his only real challenge.

10
Emilia

Emilia had tricks for keeping the destruction at bay. Slow, deep breaths focused her. The sensation of rubbing her thumb and forefinger together calmed her. Her shoulders were so tense that her muscles burned. Above all, she must avoid physical contact. Unfortunately, all of this looked odd when you had dinner with a group of people. Fortunately, shock and exhaustion had claimed everyone's attention. She'd have to do something truly wild to be noticed tonight.

She doubted she'd be that lucky for the rest of the Trial.

But she needed to contain her chaos tonight, of all nights. First impressions were important, and this was an opportunity to study her competition.

These four other faces at the table—some blank with fear, some stoic, some actually smiling—were all she cared about and took her appetite away. A pity, because the meal looked divine. A roasted peacock on a bed of fresh herbs occupied the center of the table. Oysters gleamed over ice, accompanied by glistening lemon wedges. Honey-drizzled sponge bread, creamy goat cheese, spiced yoghurt, curried fish soup, lamb medallions with coarse salt and rosemary, mounds of olives, and, of course, plump clusters of figs and grapes completed the spread.

For five years, she'd eaten roasted root vegetables, brown bread, and salted fish. Bland meals for a bland life. This much color and noise, so many smells, so much that was *new* . . .

It overpowered her.

The competitors sat on silk couches along the table, while Petros and Camilla occupied either end. After everyone settled, Camilla stood and raised a jeweled goblet filled with wine.

"Few high priests are fortunate enough to witness two successive Emperor's Trials." She gave a sharp smile. "Petros and I were not much older than you when we crowned Emperor Erasmus. We're both thrilled to lend guidance as you undertake the single most important tradition in Etrusia's long, glorious history."

Petros, meanwhile, looked on with the cheer of a cadaver.

The priestess is the true power. It didn't require a genius to see, but Emilia filed that away snug in her mental cabinet, where it would remain until she needed it. From her time spent studying the Trial, she knew that the high priest and priestess always oversaw matters. Why always a man and a woman? How were such elite priests selected for their positions? Emilia hungered for answers, but now was not the time.

"There are four great challenges in the Trial. Undoubtedly, you've all grown up hearing of them." Camilla smiled. "The Hunt. The Game. The Race. The Truth."

Emilia thought of her satchel back in her rotunda, its secrets awaiting her perusing eyes.

"I'll remind you that every single emperor who has ever been crowned has come in first in at least one challenge. Take them very seriously. But you should also remember that the Great Dragon judges smaller details as well. How you behave toward one another, and how you conduct yourself during the Trial, matters."

"Do people ever die during the Trial?" the blond boy, Ajax, asked while chewing.

"Oh, people die." Camilla said it easily. "It's common, but not typical. Thirty percent of the time?" She turned to Petros, who shrugged. "Forty? These *are* challenges fit for a dragon emperor. Accidents happen. Before I forget, I should remind you that killing one another, while not expressly forbidden, will result in a penalty. I'd recommend against it."

Vespir made a *hurk*ing noise and lowered her head to her knees.

"Now, we're going to leave you all to get better acquainted." Camilla gestured for Petros to rise. *Excellent.* Emilia had been afraid the older people would sit with them all night. "We know that the five families don't encourage much interaction between their children." True. Emilia and Lucian shared a quick glance. Their fathers' friendship was rare. Why be friendly with someone whose child might best your own in the great Trial one day? "But you should all support one another. The next emperor or empress is at this table, after all."

No one said anything. Apart from Vespir's labored breathing and the sound of the ocean, it was deadly quiet. Camilla walked toward the door. Petros dabbed at his mouth with a napkin, rose, and moved after her like a silken shadow.

The wooden doors slammed as they exited. Immediately, Hyperia stood and took Camilla's place at the head of the table.

Ajax cast a glance at the doors. "You'd think they'd be more interested in us."

"Odds are we're being watched right now," Emilia muttered. Everyone looked at her, and she wilted under their combined gaze. "The Trial has already begun."

Lucian grunted his agreement. The focus eased off her. Peering from behind her hair, Emilia surveyed the competition.

Lucian leaned one elbow against the couch. His thick black hair hung heavy in his eyes. She hadn't considered how different he appeared without his braid. He took his dagger, speared an apple with a juicy thrust, and began slicing off pieces to eat.

"Do you want a fork?" Emilia asked. He shook his head without looking at her.

"You don't get much use out of them on campaign." He shrugged. His tone was bitter, an indication something darker and angrier was being left unuttered.

Ajax regarded Lucian from the corner of his eye. "Impressive knife skills," the Tiber boy said. So fast she almost couldn't catch it, he snatched a dagger from his belt and sent it flying with a flick of his wrist. It landed in a leg of peacock, the handle quivering. A perfect throw. Ajax collected his dagger and the leg. Chewing, he waggled his eyebrows. "More impressive," he said with a grin.

Lucian gave a heavy sigh. "You and my sister would get along."

He wants Lucian to notice him. Emilia tucked all these little details away. It worried her, somewhere deep inside, that she looked at these other people as if they were test subjects to be studied. Shouldn't she . . . feel . . . more than she did?

This is no time for feeling. She narrowed her eyes. *They're all your enemies.*

The world is your enemy. Five years of brutal isolation had burned that lesson like a brand upon her soul.

"Hey, don't you want some meat?" Ajax studied Lucian's apple. "There might be one or two muscles you haven't developed."

"I don't eat meat," Lucian muttered.

"Because the Sacred Brothers don't?" Emilia wondered if

that sounded as casual as she wanted it to. She was so bad at making conversation.

Lucian frowned. "No. I can't stand the smell of cooked flesh."

"You know," Ajax said between bites, "you all look like someone pissed in your wine."

"There's a thirty to forty percent chance we could die during this contest, and an eighty-three percent chance of death at the end," Emilia said flatly. To her right, Vespir shifted on the sofa and held her stomach.

"I—I think the soup is bad," she muttered. Her eyes were glassy, and sweat beaded on her forehead. She'd never hold up under the pressure.

Lucian filled a glass with water and gave it to the girl. "Drink," he said, his tone softening.

"Thank you, my lord." Vespir took the cup but barely touched it to her lips.

She didn't really want it. She took it like receiving an order, Emilia realized. A weakness. Easily exploitable.

She shook her head. Emilia did not like those thoughts.

But if she wanted to survive . . .

Was it wrong to strive to live? Wrong to be just a little bit selfish?

Wasn't that behavior necessary in an empress?

"You don't have to call me 'my lord.' Really," Lucian said.

"Yes, my— Okay." Vespir drank.

Lucian tossed the apple's core onto a plate, licking juice from his thumb. "Well. What in the black depths are we all doing here?"

"I think the better question is, what are *you* all doing here?" Hyperia said. Swallowing, Emilia turned her eyes to the head of the table. The Volscia girl surveyed all of them, hands folded in her lap, the disturbing smear of blood as livid on her face as a claimed kiss.

Now, there was no ignoring her. She was the sun, and they, nervous planets in her orbit.

For a moment, even the chaos in Emilia's soul stilled. There was something so magnificently *orderly* about Hyperia of the Volscia.

"Actually, *we* were all the first choice." Lucian held the Volscia girl's gaze, his copper eyes gleaming with challenge. "I guess there's a reason Julia isn't sitting with us now." He gestured at Hyperia. "The truth's written all over your gown."

Hyperia didn't flinch. "Her calling was a mistake that I corrected."

White light pulsed behind Emilia's eyeballs. She squeezed her eyes shut and fisted her skirt. *Fearlessness. Utter certainty.*

What would it be like, to be so awful and calm?

"Like a real empress." Lucian clenched his jaw.

"As far as I'm concerned, the calling was the first challenge," Hyperia answered. "The Dragon wanted to know which of us would fight for their rightful place." She arched a perfect eyebrow. "I was the only one who passed."

"You're welcome to pass all the other challenges as well." Lucian leaned back against the couch. "I don't want anything to do with this."

"Come on." Ajax loaded up his plate with a second helping of peacock. "You've got to try to make it interesting for me."

"You?" Emilia said it at the same time as Hyperia and Lucian. Vespir continued to stare at the floor. Ajax ripped into the bird's leg, sneering.

"I'm a numbers guy, too. You." He pointed at Emilia. "You got one brother, right? So you had a fifty percent chance of getting called. Not that impressive. Same goes for you, Luce?" Ajax winked at Hyperia. "And you." To Vespir he said, "Wasn't Antonia the only Pentri kid? Man, some people really *can* screw up a sure thing. Whereas me?" He thumped his chest. "I had a one in twenty-nine chance of being called—that's only three percent—and look." He flourished his hands.

Hyperia made a noise of disgust. "I can't believe a bastard was admitted to the Trial."

"Could be worse." He blew a kiss. "I could be a murderer."

Hyperia sat rigid as a statue. Emilia chewed the inside of her cheek. This Tiber boy was either brave or an idiot. Probably the latter. Idiocy was definitely exploitable.

"You're not the only murderer here," Lucian said.

Emilia flinched. Unbidden, memories flooded her of Huigh, the cook's assistant, a handsome boy with dimples and russet hair. She'd stood on her toes to kiss him at thirteen, a daring moment stolen behind the aerie. The sweet touch of their lips and then the hot, salty rush of blood as it flooded her mouth, as it leaked from the corners of Huigh's eyes and dribbled from his nose when his lungs and heart exploded.

An accident, yes. But still murder.

She stared at Lucian, chaos crawling like ants under her skin. But he wasn't looking at her; he had eyes only for Hyperia.

"I've been on campaign," he continued. "You're not the only child killer."

Hyperia's lips thinned. Her already fair skin paled further.

"If you regret their deaths, then you regret your actions. In that case, you regret the empire's actions. The only thing worse than killing is killing without a sense of honor. You disrespect the dead."

"I'd rather my victims be alive. If that means I have no honor, so be it."

"This is our great hero of the northern expansion?" Hyperia

looked as if she smelled something foul. "There is no true nobility left, it seems."

Emilia had not imagined that creatures like Hyperia existed outside of epic poetry. A sea goddess determined to wreck the ships of a thousand men and string their hearts upon wire to wear about her neck or a flinty-eyed king who sent legions of soldiers to their deaths in the glory of conquest—those were Hyperia's true equals, not the people at this table.

Emilia loosened the guard on her chaos . . . and the table gave a faint tremor, just enough to rattle the plates. She held her breath as everyone started, paused, and then let it go. Earth tremors happened, after all. But she wouldn't be that lucky again.

"Next question." Ajax pointed at Vespir. "How did you get here?"

"Believe me, I've wondered that myself. My lord." The girl added the lord bit as an afterthought. A vein throbbed in the servant's neck. She looked like she was either going to be ill or start screaming.

"Maybe you're a secret bastard." Ajax twirled his dagger. "Maybe Lord Pentri holed up with your mother for a few—"

For the first time, Vespir looked up with confidence. "I. Am. Not. A Pentri," she said.

"You never know." Lucian shrugged, sounding sympathetic. "If you were secretly noble, that would explain how you got called."

"No. I'm not related to them." Vespir's voice cracked. Emilia bit her lip; this wasn't normal agitation. Something else lay under the surface here. Something too painful for Vespir to consider . . .

Oh. *Oh.*

"Let's talk about something else," she said quickly.

But Ajax was determined to be an absolute shit. "What's the problem? It's not like you've been—" Ajax clapped a hand over his mouth. "Oh, damn. Were you bedding one of them on the sly? Old man Pentri? Oh, that's gross." He shuddered, relishing the mayhem.

"I said stop it." Emilia crossed her toes to stave off exploding one of the goblets. Hyperia put her head in her hand and looked weary. Meanwhile, Vespir scowled.

"No, not *him*," the handler snapped. Emilia closed her eyes. Damn. Ajax's stupid theory was now practically confirmed. Vespir realized it as well. "I—I mean," she muttered.

"Well, if not him, then . . ." Ajax clapped and bounced in his seat. "The daughter! Who's got coin on the daughter? First off, who's got coin?"

Vespir rested her elbows on her knees and cradled her head in her hands. Emilia glared at Ajax, the best she could do with magic shouting inside her skull.

Even Lucian appeared to have had enough. "Leave her alone."

Ajax patted Lucian's cheek, an open invitation for the larger boy to strike.

He wants to see how far he can push Lucian, Emilia thought. She realized that Ajax's game might be similar to hers: assess your opponents and find their weakness.

Ajax's eyebrows shot up. "Damn. Your stubble's thick. Bet you can grow a beard in, what, five days? Probably started shaving when you were ten."

Lucian looked less than amused.

"Please stop fighting," Vespir muttered. She began to make more *hurk*ing noises.

"I cannot believe this." Hyperia spoke slowly, as if choosing her words with care. "I made the ultimate sacrifice to end up with the four of *you.*" Hyperia fixed each one of them with a glare. "Well, I thank the Great Dragon for my strength. If I weren't here, one of you would be crowned."

"Don't go decorating your throne room just yet." Ajax smirked. "We've still got a few days to enjoy each other's company."

"A bastard," Hyperia said. Her eyes flicked to Vespir. "A servant who ruts above her station." Her mouth thinned in an expression of distaste. Her gaze landed on Emilia. "A mouse of a girl."

Irrationally, Emilia felt hurt. For the sake of the blue above, it was *better* that Hyperia not notice her. Better that she write Emilia off. Pride, arrogance were Hyperia's faults, but . . .

Emilia craved approval in some lonely space within her.

Hyperia now focused on Lucian. She gave a beleaguered sigh.

"And the hero of the Vartl fjord, who turns out to be nothing more than a sniveling coward. The empire would crumble beneath any of you." She shut her eyes. "But I know this calling isn't your fault."

"Thank you for your benevolence," Emilia muttered. Hyperia's gaze fixed on her. An itch developed between Emilia's shoulder blades, but she'd had enough. "I just think that anyone who can kill her own sister might not be *my* first choice to rule." Emilia managed to raise her head. For a minute, the air between Hyperia and her was electric. The girl, golden and bloody, gave a slight nod. She seemed almost pleased.

"The Volscia have a story about our greatest general, Aufidius. The first dragon rider." She dipped her chin in a signal of respect at the name. "Fifteen hundred years ago, when magic and dragons were still young in the world, the forces of a forgotten civilization wanted to take the Volscia lands for their own.

Aufidius was a great warrior, but the enemy had a general who matched him in strength and ferocity. Caius Martius.

"Until Martius was cast out by his own people, by scheming politicians who hated his strength. So Martius offered himself to Aufidius, promising to help the Volscia destroy their enemy, the people Martius had once called his own. Aufidius agreed and came to love his new ally like a brother.

"But Martius betrayed Aufidius. When it came time to conquer his former people, his will was too weak to kill his old friends and family. He had too much chaos in him." At the word *chaos,* Emilia's heart plunged to her stomach. "And Aufidius," Hyperia said, "the greatest of our people, who never knew an instant's doubt or weakness, took a sword and carved out Martius's heart. Aufidius loved his friend, but he could not love weakness. He cleansed Martius of it, like purging a cancer." The girl's blue eyes glittered in the candlelight. "Aufidius summoned his dragon and burned the enemy to the ground. He showed no fear. He showed no mercy. That is why the Volscia have a right to be proud. *We* are the reason this great dragon empire stands today. And we have only one rule: when faced with weakness, cut out its heart."

She picked up Camilla's goblet, the first food or drink she'd touched that night. After a sip of wine, she smiled. "So if I am faced with weakness now, what do I do?"

Lucian regarded Hyperia with horror; Ajax's mouth hung open, displaying the chewed remains of a fig; and Vespir slumped off the couch, onto her knees, and threw up all over the tiled floor.

While Emilia wet a cloth to bathe the servant's wrists and forehead, she realized that this Volscia girl—this goddess, this future empress—despised chaos to the foundation of her soul.

Emilia had dreamed of many things in those lonely years

locked away in her family's tower. She had dreamed of friend-ship. Of love. And when the hope for those withered, she had prayed for something else.

An opponent.

And hadn't her wish been granted?

She looked up at Hyperia of the Volscia, the most beauti-ful and terrible creature imaginable. The girl who hated Emilia without even realizing it.

Emilia hid a smile.

11

Hyperia

Weakness is a cancer that must be purged. Hyperia knelt upon the cool tile of her chamber, her skin studded in gooseflesh as the night wind sighed over her. She'd washed her sister's blood from her face and removed her soiled gown. Clad in a nightdress of fine, pale gold cloth, her hair cascading to the middle of her back, she placed her hands over her breast and closed her eyes. She did not pray. There was no need, when the Great Dragon knew all. But she felt centered at night beneath the stars in the sky and found comfort in her own immovable soul.

Chaos is destruction; order stasis. Chaos is weakness; order strength. Chaos is experience; order purity. These thoughts repeated themselves on a comforting loop.

But the loop snapped when Julia's face emerged, as if floating up from the black depths of Hyperia's subconscious. Her beautiful, pale sister, a red slit open at her neck like a grim second mouth.

Stasis. Strength. Purity. Order.

The words dropped in her mind, like the tears streaming down her cheeks.

"Julia," Hyperia gasped, falling onto her hands and sobbing into the floor. Her breath washed back hot on her face.

She pressed her forehead to the tile, her nails trying to dig in, to find purchase on something. How could she sleep tonight? How could she sleep again? Yes, she had been the only right choice to come here, and, yes, she was needed, but the *price*. "My baby. I'm so sorry. I'm so sorry." She sat up, rocked back and forth as she wept into her hands. She wanted to run wild under the moon, tear every golden strand of hair from her head, plunge into the sea, and let the waves swallow her—

No.

"Weak." She braced and slapped herself hard across the face. The sting returned her to her senses. Her palm was wet from the tears. Unacceptable. Hyperia clenched her teeth before striking herself again. And again. And again. The pain ebbed, the chaos bled from her soul. Gasping, she got to her feet and smoothed back her hair. She was all right. This turmoil would pass quickly. It had to.

The curtains bulged in the wind as she turned to her bed, the blankets golden and lush, the pillows stuffed with goose down. The empire needed her, and she needed her rest for tomorrow.

But her fragile calm shattered when she found her sister sitting up against the cushions, her legs crossed at the ankle.

"Julia?" Hyperia blinked. The apparition remained, a perfect image of her sister with flowing chestnut hair, delicate folded hands, and a slit throat. Gore covered Julia's golden dress front, but her smile was the most disturbing decoration of all.

It was no dream. Trembling, Hyperia took her dagger from the table next to her and unsheathed it. Heart pounding, she stepped backward and felt the gauze curtain mold itself against her body. All the while, Julia smiled and watched her.

Why draw her dagger? What did she have to fear from a ghost?

Unless the dagger was for herself, because she didn't know

how long she could gaze into her dead sister's eyes until she ran absolutely mad—

"Hello? Are you all right?" a deep voice said behind her. Hyperia whirled around, thrusting the curtain aside to prick her dagger against Lucian's throat. He swallowed, allowing the dagger's sharp tip to almost—almost—pierce his flesh.

"I—" Hyperia glanced over her shoulder. Julia had vanished. She turned back to the Sabel boy with a cool air. "Why did you sneak up on me?"

"I was walking back to my room when I heard crying." He lifted an eyebrow. "I thought someone needed help."

She narrowed her eyes. "You ought to be more careful. Time away from war has made you sloppy." She pressed the dagger a millimeter farther to show her point. Unperturbed, Lucian held up his empty hands, displaying how utterly unarmed he was.

"I've sworn never to raise a blade against another living soul."

"What an idiotic vow."

She exhaled lightly and stepped back. He remained outside, dark against the night. Meanwhile, the lamp's fire warmed her back and, she knew, highlighted the brightness of her hair and clothes.

"I'm sorry you won't compete properly," she said.

He smiled. "That's a polite way to lie."

"I don't lie." Her temper pulsed. "You're the only competition that matters." The others were near her in age, but to Hyperia they might as well have been trundling around in a nursery for all the challenge they presented. "You're my equal, or near to it."

Lucian frowned. "I'm not sure that's a compliment for either of us."

Hyperia noted coolly—academically—that Lucian of the

Sabel was handsome. That his looks combined with his abilities, and even his deferential manners, would be attractive to people. Just not to her. It wasn't specifically him; Hyperia had not yet known desire. If she experienced it one day, that would be fine. But she wasn't going to force a sensation because the world deemed her age and, apparently, her beauty required it.

She did not want this young man, but she wanted to compete with him. She wanted a clean, honest victory.

Before she could speak again, he said, "Besides, you convinced me at dinner."

"What?" She finally lowered the dagger to her side.

"I wasn't going to throw myself into the Trial, until you started talking." His features were unreadable, but he seemed sincere. "I think the way you see this world is ugly. The empire is crying out for peace. I won't break my vows to achieve it, but I'll give everything I have otherwise."

His words warmed her. "Thank you. My victory will be honorable, at least."

"Don't think that." He let the curtain drop, so that he was little more than a talking shadow. "There's no honor for people like us."

He walked away, leaving her to sheathe her knife and get into bed. Julia wasn't beside her when she put out the lamp.

12

Lucian

———————◆———————

L ucian stood by the northern tip of the island and watched
  the flickering lights in the competitors' rooms. The sea
churned against the rocks as he finally wended his way toward
his own chamber. The competitors' rotundas had been placed
around the central temple like five points on a star.

He stopped outside of his room and turned his gaze to the
actual stars, picking out constellations like Draconis Major and
the Emperor's Bow. He fixed his gaze on his favorite star, the
brightest in the sky, chief ornament in the Celestial Diadem.
Then he knelt on the ground, placed his hands over his breast,
and bowed his head. The oath of the Sacred Brothers played in
his thoughts.

*I swear that I shall uphold my vows until the last breath of my
body.*

*I shall never take up arms against another, for every living crea-
ture that walks this earth and flies through the air is my brethren.*

Lucian pictured his father's horrified face as Tyche burned
that exalted sword . . .

*I shall forsake all worldly things, for temptation removes our
thoughts from good deeds and the suffering of our fellows.*

Lucian recalled an old man clutching a little boy, gazing up in terror at the dragon rider circling the gray skies over their village . . .

I shall cherish no one person over any other, for all people are equal in my heart.

Lucian's eyes snapped open at the surge of wings. Tyche descended out of the twilight and landed before him. Her tail skated along the ground, upsetting pebbles. Her nostrils flared, and in this darkness he could see the faint glow of embers. Holding up his hand, he let his dragon nose at his palm, and chuckled at the tickling heat.

"I can't cherish any one person," he said. "But the vows don't say anything about dragons."

Tyche tilted her head and made the light, chittering noise she always gave when playful. Sighing, Lucian sat back on his haunches and began to sing.

> *"They say that love should be boundless,*
> *As high and as deep as the sky.*
> *And yet no embrace can compete with the chase,*
> *Of a dragon for clouds passing by."*

It was a silly rhyme that he'd made up for Tyche when he was a boy, and he grinned as she fluttered her wings with the pleasure of it. The dragon tilted back her head and began to "sing" along. She made a series of lilting *ooo* noises, her tail swishing this way and that as she kept time. Lucian couldn't make it to the second verse before he had tears in his eyes from laughter.

Pleased with herself, Tyche thumped her tail and laid her chin upon Lucian's shoulder. He smoothed his hand down her neck, trailing his fingers along the silk of her scales. His girl made a purring noise in her chest, telling him she was happy. Happy just to be with him.

Lucian squeezed his eyes shut. He did not mind forfeiting his own life, but Tyche's . . .

My soul. The priests were right about that. She was all that he liked of himself.

"That's a pleasing tune," a girl behind him murmured. Lucian swiveled his head to find Emilia watching from a safe distance away. Her hair was still in her face, her shoulders still hunched. "Did you compose that yourself? I remember that you. Uh. Were fond of music." She spoke haltingly, as if trying to remember lines in a play.

"I did." He stood, dusted his knees. "Do you have any new theories on what we're all doing here?"

"I'm currently wavering somewhere between 'this is all a nightmare' and inarticulate screaming."

Lucian chuckled, and Emilia drew a few steps nearer.

"Well, let me know when you come up with a way to save us all. I'm counting on you."

"Oh? So I've got to shoulder this burden myself?" He could see she was smiling.

"I wouldn't trust anybody else. You were always the one with the plan."

"Yes, but . . . that was years ago." The smile disappeared. She ducked her head, and Lucian frowned.

"If you ever, well, want to talk—"

"About what?" she said abruptly. "We're trapped, and only one will survive. Isn't that correct? Being cordial and, well, chummy would only increase bitterness and, and enmity, wouldn't it?"

Well. Her feelings weren't wrong.

"I just don't want us to become . . . ." He searched for the best word. "Worse," he said at last. Emilia remained silent for a while.

"Some of us are as bad as we can be," she muttered.

Oh, she was right. She was righter than she knew. Lucian nodded grimly.

"I just want you to know that if you need help in any way," he began, and then nearly leapt out of his skin when something made a violent, banging noise behind him. A damn explosion. Lucian wheeled about, Tyche expanding her wings and squalling at the disturbance. He blinked as some pebbles scattered across the ground, but otherwise nothing was there. "Bizarre," he muttered, then turned back. "Emilia?"

But she'd gone. He heard the patter of footsteps as she raced away. Probably the noise had scared her. She was so high-strung. His heart sank to think of what might have happened these past five years to make her so.

I'll do something to help. I have to.

That was the path of a Sacred Brother, after all. Help those in need.

That thought gave some comfort as he left Tyche outside and entered his chamber with the blue bedspread and a blue gown lying on top of it. Bemused, he picked it up. It'd been measured perfectly for Dido. "Unfortunately, not my size," he muttered, balling it up and tossing it to the floor. He removed his cloak, sloshed water into a basin, and pulled off his shirt.

There was no mirror to let him stare at his scars. Good. Lucian washed quickly, scrubbing his face and dampening his hair. The scars, so pale against his brown skin, traced his arms like lines on a map.

Some drew raised eyebrows and gasps, like the white knob of scar tissue at the bend of his left arm. That particular scar had come from a Wikingar soldier with a broken broadsword. Lucian had cradled his arm, the injury raining crimson on the snow beneath. He'd been pleased to see his own blood spill for a change. Maybe he'd even hoped this would be the warrior to finish him.

He'd taken all his physical scars from practice and by an enemy's blade on the battlefield.

The invisible scars, those etched upon his soul, came from his father.

Every time he'd disobeyed or spoken back against a command, he'd been thrown into the brig, divided from Tyche, left to shiver through long winter nights. That discomfort had been nothing, nothing at all, to seeing the sadness in his father's eyes, the pain that came from Lucian's rebellion. His father, who could not seem to understand, no matter how fervently Lucian argued. That blind unhappiness had pierced Lucian to the core. A soldier needed to obey orders.

A son needed to love his father.

Lucian was a disappointment on both counts.

With a sigh, he turned to put out the light.

Two burned figures squatted at the foot of his bed and stared at him.

The eyes had disintegrated, their jelly boiled to sludge in the charred sockets, and yet he could feel their gaze. Lucian swore that he could still hear their fat sizzling.

The smaller one's face had become a mask of curling, crisped flesh.

Like roasted chicken, Lucian thought stupidly as bile rose in his throat.

The old man was skeletal and burned to a black cinder. His silent mouth opened and closed, the jawbones creaking, the hopeless gaping of a landed fish.

He had seen their faces in his dreams nearly every night. He'd stopped waking with a scream after the first year.

But this wasn't a dream. Lucian collapsed.

Finally, he thought.

Then sanity returned, and he ground the heels of his palms into his eyes. *No. No. No.* "You're not real," he whispered, his voice quavering. Hysterical laughter clawed his throat. When he looked again, the old man and the boy had vanished. The bed was empty.

Lucian's ghosts had abandoned him, but he knew they'd return.

They always did.

13
Emilia

———————+

Emilia woke to a bad headache, new clothes at the foot of her bed, and a dragon's snout poking through one of the curtained walls.

"Chara!" She thrust the blankets aside and went to her dragon, even as pain gnawed at the base of her skull. She placed a palm on Chara's nose and felt a gust of hot breath. The dragon had short, ticklish hairs at the top of her upper lip. Chara huffed in contentment, dipping her head so Emilia could stroke the long bridge of her snout. The tang of salt clung to her; she must have gone for a morning swim. Her pearly scales were soft. "Someone brushed you." Emilia smiled.

They're treating you well before they Cut you.

The dragon rumbled low in her long throat and pressed the side of her head against Emilia's leg. The warm, fizzing sensation of connection coursed through her . . . and she thought about never having that again. Dying, and her soul murdered as well. Drifting into oblivion.

Emilia looked away to gather her thoughts. Today the Trial would begin in earnest, and she had to be at her best. That stupid accident with Lucian last night could not be allowed to happen again. Thank the blue above it'd been dark, and the explosion minor. Just a couple of rocks. She had not expected him to sound so concerned. She had not anticipated that the way he spoke would ease a pressure that had long solidified in her sternum. But none of that mattered. She'd be stretched out on a table with nails pounded into her flesh if she did not learn to dominate this chaos in her soul.

The headache tightened as she studied the clothes on her bed: a plum-colored shirt, a jacket of sturdy fabric in the same color, and loose, tan trousers.

Beside the bed, someone had set a golden shield so polished that her reflection glared back at her. Emilia winced. She couldn't blame Lucian for his reaction yesterday. She looked hollowed out by a long, slow illness. With a sigh, she picked up the shield, and something behind it clattered to the floor. It was golden as well, a narrow tube about as long as her arm.

Emilia picked it up and flicked her wrist. Sharp protrusions shot out of the tube on either end. She studied the thing—the spear.

A spear and a shield for the Hunt.

The first challenge had begun.

"Nice to see you all properly dressed." Camilla regarded them coolly as she poured a cup of coffee from a gleaming copper pot. Emilia wondered how the clothes had been tailored so well for all of them. Probably the acolytes had worked their magic well into the night.

The competitors all sat awkwardly around the banquet table, mumbling thanks and eating. Emilia poured a cup of hot, syrupy coffee, her throbbing head practically shouting its gratitude. She took a sip and found it was sweetened with cardamom and cream. Her entire body softened with a shiver.

There were round loaves of freshly baked bread accompanied by oil and olive paste, sweet rolls dusted with cinnamon, fruit, and rice porridge stewed with raisins and dates. Emilia nursed her coffee. Ajax ate so quickly she wondered how he left room to breathe. Vespir sat cross-legged on the sofa, listlessly shoveling porridge into her mouth. Lucian, meanwhile, picked up his plate and sat down next to Emilia.

"How'd you sleep?" He offered her a cinnamon roll; he'd remembered they were her favorite. Emilia felt heat creep up the back of her neck.

"Uh. Well," she mumbled. Sitting next to him again relaxed her, let her mind wander . . . She could picture every capillary in his face bursting in one swell of crimson and his entire head exploding and bits of brain matter scattering over the cushions—

She stood at once and marched her coffee over to sit next to Ajax, who waggled his eyebrows. Sighing, Emilia stared into her cup. Lucian didn't try to sit next to her again.

Better he stay away.

At least her chaos had waned. Sleep and food did wonders for that.

Everyone took notice as Hyperia swept into the room, pouring herself coffee and taking a bowl of rice porridge. "The island's perimeter makes for a good morning run," she said conversationally, sitting apart from everyone else. No one said anything in reply.

"So. Can we get started?" Ajax asked.

"Your dragons are waiting." Petros snapped his fingers, and brown-robed acolytes entered to set leather satchels beside each of the competitors. "The coordinates are in here. Once you arrive at the island, the Hunt begins."

"What are we hunting?" Hyperia sounded pleased. Killing things had probably been a daily habit since she'd played dolls in the nursery.

"The island's residents have been under siege for some time."

"We're hunting the island's residents?" Ajax screwed up his face. "That's sad."

Petros's eyes fluttered shut. "No. A basilisk has been terrorizing them. You're hunting *that*. Whoever hunts it down, kills it, and brings back its head is the winner."

Emilia felt the coffee in her stomach sour. She'd studied every predator in the Crotian region and had consulted her notes as soon as she found the spear. They wouldn't be hunting a centaur—for that you need a bow and arrow—and no one would think to go after a siren without trawling hooks and nets, so that was out. Privately, she'd hoped for a giant boar or a lion, but no. A basilisk. She had to face a *basilisk*.

"Wow," Ajax breathed. Then, "What's a basilisk?"

"Didn't you read Pliny's *Natural History*?" Hyperia sneered at him.

"I can't read," Vespir muttered, so low only Emilia could hear. Then, even lower, "Forty percent chance."

Sensing Ajax was about to say something irritating, Emilia jumped in. "A basilisk is a land-based dragon." An abomination. A wingless dragon could never be a true one. "It walks on two legs and has a serpent's body with the head of a cockerel."

"A chicken dragon? Sounds fun." The idiot boy grinned.

Emilia's temper snapped. "If having acid for blood, sharp teeth, and a glance that can poison you to death is amusing, I *really* hope you enjoy yourself." She snatched a piece of bread from the table and forced herself to take a bite. Ajax stopped smiling. At last.

Lucian dusted his hands, swallowed the dregs of his coffee, and picked up the leather satchel at his feet. Emilia noticed that he had brought the shield, but not the spear.

"Let's go," he said as the other competitors grabbed their

weapons and headed for the front of the temple. Emilia hung behind with Vespir as Ajax and Hyperia jogged to be first on dragonback. The Tiber boy had to run to keep pace.

"Emilia." Lucian came up beside her. "Stay with me once we reach the island."

Thankfully, he didn't wait on a response. Lucian hurried ahead. She doubted he was trying to hurt her . . . but she could hurt *him*.

"Are you all right?" she asked Vespir as they walked side by side. The servant was making a little eye contact now. Progress.

"Sure. Basilisks are fun," Vespir replied, her voice distant as she checked the satchel's binding. It slipped open, revealing two extra loaves of bread and figs. Emilia frowned. The priests had already given them food for lunch; there was no need for more. Vespir noticed her notice. "It'll be a long day," she said. "I, er, get hungry."

"Of course." Emilia didn't say anything else. It wasn't her business.

Moments later she was seated in Chara's saddle, stealing a quick glance at the directions. She was ready. With a snort, the dragon flapped and soared upward. Emilia didn't look back at the others. She focused on the blue horizon, where the sea merged with the sky. She bladed a hand over her eyes and squinted into the bright day. She could practically hear her pale skin sizzle.

Basilisk. King of serpents. Alchemists claimed you could combine its blood with powdered human remains, red copper, and vinegar to make gold.

There'd be no alchemy today. Emilia's mind tarried over the facts in the files she'd brought, the books she'd slaved over. She'd no skill with a spear, and the sword at her hip would remain in its sheath if she could help it. To win this challenge, she would have to use her knowledge and her more . . . unique powers.

The pressure of chaos built at the base of her spine.

After twenty minutes of flight over sapphire waters, an island appeared. Emilia tugged on Chara's reins, peeling away from the other four as they rose on the wind to fly higher. Emilia could already see their problem: there was no landing space on the island. A thick forest covered nearly every square foot, and the rocky shore was too narrow. Most dragons didn't do well in water.

But Chara, as an Aspis, took to it naturally, and Emilia wanted to be separated from the group.

"Emilia!" The wind swallowed Lucian's voice. She felt a small stab of guilt but forced herself onward.

Emilia guided Chara around the island's perimeter until she noticed a tiny inlet of gentle water. She pulled back on the reins and squeezed the dragon's sides. They dipped toward the ocean, Emilia's hair whipping behind her. Chara huffed in delight when they splashed down in an arc of crystalline water. Emilia pulled her feet from the stirrups, trying not to get wet. While Chara dipped her snout into the sea and snorted, blowing a stream of bubbles, Emilia glanced at the shore ten feet away.

"Chara." She scratched the top of the dragon's head and pinched the knob of excess flesh at the base of her neck. Chara's wings expanded automatically on either side of her, the thin membrane rippling in the wind. Holding her breath, Emilia ran along the right wing, moving quickly so as not to apply too much pressure and bruise a joint or tear the membrane. She bounced effortlessly off the wingtip, landing ankle-deep in the sea. Onshore, she let the shallow waves play at her feet. Her dragon retracted her wings and trilled happily, flashing white and pearl as she frisked through the sea. "I'll be back. Stay here," Emilia called. Chara waggled her ears.

Emilia headed up the thin sliver of beach, scaled the rocky

slope, and walked into the tree line. The blazing sun extinguished neat as a candle. Splotches of yellow light carpeted the loamy earth wherever the sun managed to break through the branches. The ground sank beneath her boots as she hiked. Emilia sighed in relief. The viselike grip of her magic eased somewhat when she was on her own. Emilia had always preferred the privacy of her own thoughts. If she could have punctuated that quiet with occasional human contact, life would have been perfect.

And as dangerous as it was to be around the others, Emilia wished someone were with her at that moment. Every cry of a bird in the depths of the forest, every snap of a twig jolted her nearly out of her skin. Cringing, she kept her back against an old, mossy trunk.

Think.

She went over her plan. The others would undoubtedly make the mistake of trying to find the basilisk. All dragons had a tendency to protect their lairs; she doubted the beast would stray too far from home. It wouldn't dwell close to the sea. Emilia had spotted a dense patch of overgrown forest to the island's northwestern tip. The basilisk would likely dwell there. All she had to do was make her way around the perimeter. Then, once she'd located the lair, she would set off a small series of explosions to draw the creature to her. When it was within sight, she'd hide behind her shield so it could not poison her and use her powers to slice its head from its neck.

There were two potential drawbacks: she might simply obliterate the head, so that nothing remained to take back as a prize, and even if she *could* accomplish her goal, the priests might notice the head hadn't been severed with a blade.

She would draw her sword and trim the edges if necessary. Hopefully, she could get it done without anyone else seeing.

Though the plan was sound, fear ate at her. Fear of discovery, to be sure, but also of her competitors. Her competitor, singular. Hyperia.

Hyperia was hard and cold and *pure*.

Purity was the central virtue of the orderly arts, and the one Emilia most resented.

Snap. A twig broke underfoot . . . but Emilia hadn't moved.

Somebody was heading toward her from the center of the forest.

Damn. She didn't think the basilisk was the type of beast to tiptoe up behind people, but she also didn't want to take that chance. Wincing under the weight of both her satchel and the shield and spear, she trotted along a worn path and headed around the tip of the island. Sweat was already slick on her back and under her arms. Her headache's band tightened around her temples. Biting her lip, she glanced behind to see if anyone was tracking her.

"Ow!" she cried as her shin smacked against something hard. She pitched over the object and fell onto her stomach. Gasping, she rolled over to see what had tripped her, expecting a large root. Instead, she found a crude altar fashioned from gray stone. Flies buzzed around some shriveled plums and berries, and olive branches with browning leaves. Emilia smelled rotten fruit and crawled to her feet. An offering? Of course, the islanders were trying to appease the basilisk.

Something flashed on the path in front of her. Emilia gripped her blade's hilt on instinct. Much good it'd do; if she tried drawing, she'd likely drop it. "Who's there?" she called stupidly. Magic licked the hollow of her throat. The altar began to quiver with the nearness of her power. If she loosed it . . .

Someone stepped into a patch of dappled sunlight. Her eyes widened in horror.

"Lucian?"

"I told you to stay close to me!" He approached as Emilia cursed.

"Why would I? This isn't a team challenge." Emilia checked the altar. Thankfully, it had stopped vibrating, but she couldn't know when that would change. She had to get away from this fool.

"Because I want to help you." He shouldered his satchel as he drew nearer.

"You'll forgive me if I find the idea of one competitor helping another a little too altruistic," she snapped. She glanced at the empty sword scabbard on his belt. "Are you planning to wrestle the basilisk?"

"No. I told you, I swore—"

"Never to harm anything again, yes." She winced; the headache was starting to pulse behind her left eye. "I'm not sure how such a promise helps me. It seems like I'd be looking after you."

"There's no way I can win this challenge, but I'd rather you take it than someone like Hyperia."

Well, she couldn't blame him for that. If Hyperia won the Emperor's Trial, she'd probably boil them all alive. Emilia at least would be a merciful executioner.

"I don't think you were ever a great hunter. I can give you tips . . ." Lucian frowned at the altar. "What is this, exactly?"

"Hmm?" Emilia crouched to inspect the thing. In truth, she'd wanted a chance to study it, and since the basilisk wasn't currently breathing down their necks, this would probably be her best chance. She still needed to get rid of Lucian, but that could wait a moment. "If I recall correctly, the Crotian territories have mostly been brought under the empire's rule, but there are some islands that still retain the native culture. Look." Excitement loosened her headache as she traced her finger along a line of carvings. "The two eggs here—do you see? The Crotian people worshipped a sea goddess who gave birth to hero twins, a boy and a girl, by hatching them from eggs. The two eggs are supposed to designate the royal bloodline . . . or something sacred . . ."

"Emilia," Lucian whispered, but she was lost in thought. Whenever she had something new to toy with, Emilia left her body behind. It was the closest she got to freedom.

"These altars can't be for the basilisk, then." She frowned. "The symbol for evil in the Crotian region is the king of the sea, the goddess's brother. If they feared the basilisk, they'd carve a three-point crown, not the eggs. It's almost like—"

"Emilia!"

"What?"

She raised her head to find the tip of an arrow inches from her face. Emilia froze, glancing side to side. Seven or so people had crept out of the forest, wielding spears or bows. All were golden-haired and green-eyed, and none were smiling.

Lucian had his hands raised. Emilia felt chaos behind her eyes. If she loosed it now, she might get them out of here. But if Lucian saw . . .

She glared at him.

"I'm starting to resent your vow," she muttered.

14

Ajax

Ajax didn't care if people hated him. And even if he did care, what was he supposed to do? He tromped through the forest, wiping the sweat as it trickled down his face and stung his eyes. The shield and spear banged against his backside, and he'd started wearing the satchel around his neck. His arm got tired easily. This was a lot to carry. On top of that, it was so hot his balls were sticking to the inside of his thighs.

And he still only slightly cared if the others hated him.

Look. He was the youngest. He was the shortest. His dragon was the dumbest (but only he was allowed to say that). In a situation with this much against you, you had to show you couldn't be pushed around. Ajax wiped his face again, tracing the rough terrain of his acne. His hand registered his general lack of handsomeness. Lucian, of course, had probably been born with stubble and women swooning around him.

Lucian's the type everyone would bet on.

And Ajax would be palming their coin and running those bets. Maybe he didn't have the muscled-handsome-tall-brooding thing going for him, but he could get by.

Maybe there'd been a moment last night, when they all first sat down, where he'd imagined—just for a second—that he'd finally been let into the elite crowd. Even if they couldn't be friends for obvious reasons, they could at least acknowledge one another as equals.

They'd all looked at him like he was some piece of dirt, and maybe that'd stung worse than he'd wanted it to. So he gave them back what they expected. *Until I get what I want, and* then *they'll regret acting like a bunch of depressed, snobby—*

"*Gawp.*"

Ajax halted as a shadow passed above him, blocking out the few traces of sunlight and raining leaves and twigs down onto his head. Craning his neck, he swore.

"Dog! No! Go back." He waved his arms to the right. "Sit with others. Hey! Sit. With. Others."

"*Gawp.*" The branches quivered; the dragon was wagging his tail. Ajax gritted his teeth and trudged forward, wincing at the *shush* of the treetops as Dog crawled adoringly after. "My luck never changes," he muttered.

"Didn't you have a personal handler?" Hyperia asked.

Damn, she had appeared out of nowhere to stand right in front of him on the path. The crisp white of her shirt, accented with gold buttons down the front and embroidery along the edges of her sleeves, was a beacon in the dark forest. She'd woven her light-blond hair into a crown braid to keep it out of her eyes and looked cool as a drop of dew on the underside of a leaf. Had she even broken a sweat? Ajax slid the satchel off his neck and onto his shoulder.

Hyperia of the Volscia was asking *him* a question, even if she looked bored doing so.

"No," he replied, making sure to seem uninterested. "Too many bastards. We were searching the crannies of the rookery just to find enough eggs, you know? We couldn't have had a personal handler for everyone."

"Mmm." She turned to continue down the path. "Well, good hunting."

"You tell that to Lucian?"

Her slow turn and genuinely curious expression delighted him. Finding pressure points was the first step to making somebody do what you wanted. He drew nearer. The lines of Ajax's palms sweated, his pulse raced. He couldn't flirt with this girl— she was practically a goddess, how could you ever get close to *that*? He just wanted her to see him.

"When we landed, you two were first on the ground. We already know it'll come down to the pair of you." He started circling her. She didn't turn with him—she wasn't going to show her interest like that—but he knew she was listening. "But he's the one with the real hands-on experience, right? He's probably tracked soldiers before." Ajax really needed to brush up on the specifics of the empire's wars and territories. "If it's the two of you competing, fifty-fifty odds you come out on top. Maybe. I'd take that bet, myself." He halted in front of her, hands in his pockets. He didn't even feel the weight of the shield and spear now. "How'd you like to better those odds?"

She didn't move. The wind picked at a strand of her hair. "How?"

Got her.

"Join up with me. We won't go after his life, of course, but there are ways to trip a person." He let himself grin. His dealmaking face, he called it. "The other two don't stand a chance, and when you take the throne, you pardon me from the Cut and make me a viceroy of something. Second-in-command. You know." He wasn't actually going to be a viceroy, of course—he was going to be emperor. But if he were at her side, she wouldn't notice so easily when he put the knife to her. "What do you say?"

Her expression cleared. "A conspiracy," she said softly.

He winked.

She struck him with the back of her hand, sending him hurtling to the ground. His vision rattled. Damn, her knuckles had to be bleeding after that little display. Ajax had a rock-hard skull.

"So . . . no?" He spat a little blood mixed with saliva.

"You have no honor." She said it like she meant *you shouldn't exist*. Her long, beautiful neck corded with tension as he stood. Ajax spat again, and it just so happened to land at her feet. He picked up his satchel. Above them, Dog started gawping. *Easy, boy.*

"No. I don't." He smiled, even as his lip throbbed and fattened. "I guess that's a problem?"

She shook her head. "The Dragon selects who is fit to rule. If Lucian bests me, I'll gladly submit to the Cut. You would try to escape it?"

"Well, yeah. I don't want to *die,* you freak."

Hyperia's eyes tightened. "It makes sense. A dragon and a rider's soul merge as one the instant the egg hatches." She glanced upward, where Dog continued rustling and making a fuss. "Someone as unworthy as you could only ever have a fool for a mount."

"Careful." Ajax stilled. She was fingering that "berserk" string of his, and if she yanked on it . . .

She sneered. "You deserve each other. Both underbred and ugly to the bone."

Ajax bit the tip of his tongue. The girl before him went from goddess to demon without changing a hair on her head. "You don't want me for an enemy. I can make life unpleasant," he said, all kidding gone from his voice.

She gave a short, easy laugh. He stepped into her, and she swung at him again on reflex. This time, he took a knee and rolled. She made a startled noise as he leapt up behind her and flicked the back of her head.

When she shouted and spun with a kick, he ducked and

rolled again, this time coming up a good distance away. Damn, that girl could kick *high*. Hyperia seethed beautifully.

"If you manage to survive this first challenge, I'll . . ." She stopped in exasperation, because Dog was now being *very* loud. "Can't you send him away?"

"No." Sudden realization lumped cold in Ajax's stomach. "He's trying to send *us* away."

They both felt it at the same time, something watching them in the forest.

The basilisk, way thinner than Ajax had imagined it would be, slunk between tree trunks and bobbed toward them. Ajax halted, trying to process the sight of it. It stood fifteen feet tall, but maybe it'd be taller if it didn't hunch over so. Scales the green of old moss covered its body and legs. The reptilian feet had three toes each, and sharp black talons on the end of every digit clawed furrows into the earth. Emilia said it'd have a cockerel's head, which had sounded hilarious. But the head didn't look like it belonged to some fluffy white hen strutting around Lord Tiber's castle courtyard. It was the head of a bird that had been plucked, and plucked badly, with raw red flesh that drooped and sagged at the jaw. The open beak boasted rows of razor-sharp teeth.

The creature's right eye was gone, replaced by a swollen stripe of thick gray scar tissue. Ajax noted bumps studded all over the basilisk, realized that those bumps were the tips of arrows or spears that had been embedded there for so long flesh had grown thick and gnarled around it, incorporating the weapons into the thing's body.

A few ragged black feathers flared at the basilisk's throat like a threadbare collar. A line of drool dripped from its beak. Hyperia dropped to her knee at once, tore the shield from off her back, and hid behind it.

Really? The great warrior was going to hide behind a *shiny gold plate*?

"Use your spear!" Ajax choked.

"Use your shield!" she barked.

Ajax looked between Hyperia and the approaching beast, and made a choice.

He turned and bolted back down the path, the shield banging against his ass with every step.

Ajax prided himself on thinking fast, and he had come to a solid conclusion.

Killing the basilisk was a two-person job. He needed to find someone dumb enough to handle the dangerous parts for him.

And Hyperia? Well, of the two monsters, he hoped the basilisk won.

15

Hyperia

H yperia took a deep breath and let the beast bob toward her. If the basilisk caught sight of its own reflection and poisoned itself, her job would be easier. As the creature approached, Hyperia carefully slid the golden tube from its scabbard. With the expert flick of a wrist, the spear emerged. Step. Step. The monster loomed into view over the top of her shield. Teeth bared, Hyperia brought back her arm. All she had to do was wait for it to twist its head to the side . . .

Her objective was simple: blind the damn beast. Then the creature couldn't poison with its gaze any longer. True, its blood would still be acid and she'd have to take care while slicing off the head. But if she took its sight, the monster would be vulnerable, waiting for her to claim her prize.

Abominations did not deserve to live, anyway.

With a grunt, Hyperia prepared herself as the beast drew nearer. The scarred, blind right eye appeared first, so the creature was unable to see her as Hyperia rolled across the ground. By the time she popped up on its other side, the basilisk could not react.

Hyperia flung her weapon with a cry. The spear whistled through the air, its aim true.

The basilisk roared, ducked its head, and whipped its tail with a speed that she had not anticipated. Knocked off course, the spear buried itself in the trunk of a tree. Damn everything to the blackest depths. The spear quivered ten feet overhead. Hyperia was going to have to find a way to grab it. Not impossible, but . . .

The basilisk was certainly not going to help her.

Only the weak hesitate. Hyperia unsheathed her sword without pause and charged. Even now, down a weapon and with a monster looming overhead, she burned with excitement, not fear. Her muscles, tautened and trained, did exactly what was expected of them. When the basilisk lunged, serrated teeth prepared to slice her to pieces, Hyperia thrust her sword upward while quickly whipping the shield onto her back for protection. She felt the juicy entrance of her sword tip and heard the patter of the beast's blood on her shield. The basilisk howled, jerking roughly away and rampaging back down the path. Hyperia gasped, tossing the shield aside. The acid of the monster's blood melted down that golden surface. The shield had saved her, but at a price: the damn thing would be useless now.

She'd have to avoid the creature's eye at all cost.

"Damn. Damn," she muttered. If only she'd managed to get a clean swipe in, rather than an upthrust, she'd have taken the head in two seconds, claimed her rightful victory. Ah, but if she'd done so in that position, the blood would have got her for certain. It couldn't be helped; she'd done the best she could. But her best had not been victory. With a grunt, Hyperia wiped her blade on the ground to avoid the acid blood damaging the steel. Then she sheathed it, took a few steps back for a running start, and vaulted herself forward. Grabbing a low-hanging tree branch, she expertly swung herself up. Balancing, she jumped and caught her spear, wrenching it free from the trunk as she fell to the earth and rolled. Standing, Hyperia dusted her knees and gazed down the path after the basilisk. Drops of blood lay steaming on the earth, marking which way the beast had gone. Excellent.

Maybe she hadn't been able to take the head in one go, but she'd injured the creature. She would track it, and with or without the shield, she would kill it.

Hyperia made a fist. *Your sacrifice will be worthwhile, Julia.*

She hissed and strode down the forest path toward her destiny.

16

Vespir

Vespir sat on Karina's back and thought of home. All the competitors' dragons, save Chara, were nesting in the tree-tops, wings flared to fill with wind and keep them from becoming too heavy on the delicate branches. They bobbed on the leafy green sea like a deadly flock of ducks.

Vespir pictured Antonia, imagined she could smell the girl's favorite scent, honeysuckle and peach blossom. The mere thought calmed and focused Vespir. It allowed her to take the next step.

"We're getting out of here," Vespir whispered. She placed her forehead against the warm back of Karina's head and closed her eyes. The dragon chirped.

When they'd landed in the treetops, Hyperia and Lucian had moved as one efficient unit. Opening their satchels, they'd taken out the rope normally used for lashing a sleeping rider to their dragon, tied it to the saddle horn, and then slid down effortlessly into the forest beneath. Ajax had followed closely, sleek as a seal. Now Vespir was alone. No one would see her take off.

She breathed with Karina, focusing on the invisible thread that bound them as one. The Pentri rode their dragons without saddles, but they guided their beasts with pressed legs and gripped hands. Vespir did that, too, but she had another trick, something she called the Red.

When she closed her eyes and breathed with Karina, there would come a flash of red light in the darkness. The Red would form a brief image. It had taken some time and practice before Vespir realized the image created was whatever Karina herself saw.

The Red was the moment of locking in, of merging her mind with her dragon's.

And once that happened, all Vespir had to do was to think and Karina would obey. Pressed hands and knees were used as backup after that; the true test of a rider and dragon, Vespir believed, was that shared Red bond. No one else knew what she was talking about when she brought it up. Plotus, who'd trained her as handler until he'd retired last year, had thought she was crazy. Even Antonia hadn't understood.

Antonia . . .

Vespir saw that flash of red light and glimpsed the treetops and the other dragons. She was locked with Karina now and opened her eyes.

"Let's go," she whispered. Karina unfurled her wings wider, letting the wind carry them into the sky. They wheeled around and headed away from the island. Vespir looked behind as it grew small with distance and breathed properly for the first time that day. "They'll never find us."

So what if she lived without honor or had to go into hiding for the rest of her life? She and Karina would *have* lives. Antonia would go with them, if she could give up everything. If what they felt was strong enough.

At least Vespir was not a Pentri bastard. She breathed deeply, the tension unknotting between her shoulders. Despite Ajax's words at dinner, a moment's reflection had been enough to ease her worry. First of all, Vespir's parents had often spoken of the exciting first time they'd seen the Pentri family—two years *after* Vespir was born. And secondly, the Pentri line came from Antonia's mother, not her father. Since the girls were three months apart in age, it was impossible.

So Vespir tried to focus on the wide expanse of blue before her and wondered which island was nearest.

Besides, the Pentri hadn't specifically chosen her as their daughter's handler. It had been random chance. They'd stolen away all the children in the province to test the egg.

Vespir remembered the peach blossoms filling her pockets as she and her sister, Tavi, hurried home through the fields. It'd been late spring, two weeks before they would start making peach blossom jam, the most filling thing the family ate during winter. She remembered opening the door to their low-ceilinged hut to find a Pentri soldier in green livery waiting in the kitchen. He'd been so surprising, Tavi had dropped her apron, and blossoms had floated to the floor.

Vespir had been twelve, Tavi thirteen. The Pentri girl's dragon had hatched, the soldier said. The family needed a handler of a similar age to be trained immediately. Their mother, silver streaking her black hair, had wrapped her hands around a cup of tea, bowed her head in resignation, and let the girls go. No one had fought the soldier to keep his hands off the kids. Vespir hadn't cried, and neither had Tavi. They'd gone meekly, joining other children their age in an exodus out of the village. As she left, Vespir had noticed the fallen blossoms, carelessly squashed by the soldier's boots.

Maybe that was the worst part of all: how everyone just let it happen.

Vespir had been told it was a quick test with an egg.

She stood in a line with all the other peasant children. One after another, they were brought into a room. Five minutes later, each candidate was shuttled out. Vespir waited her turn, bouncing on the balls of her feet, and when she was let inside for the test, her only thought was of how hungry she was and how she hoped her mother was still making the jam.

She crouched on the floor opposite a large green egg with silver flecks in its shell. One minute passed. Then two. Vespir was about to ask the guard if she could leave early, when something happened. A crack appeared.

Stunned, Vespir squatted again and watched as, piece by piece, the egg came apart. A tiny brown creature with jewel-drop eyes and flappy little wings squeaked as it waddled over to Vespir. The length of Vespir's arm, the baby dragon nuzzled at her knee.

A love unlike anything she'd ever known stole over her. Giddy, Vespir picked up the dragon, still damp from its incubation, and pressed its head against her cheek. The dragon responded with a tiny, papery lick.

"It likes me!" Vespir giggled at the soldier, who nodded, opened the door, and shouted that a trainer had been selected. Prepare the convoy. They'd leave for the western territory that night.

And Vespir realized she wouldn't be going home. She started asking questions, and when they were ignored, she beat her fists against the guard's back, rushed out of the room shouting for Tavi. Her sister's face was waxen with horror. Howling, they were wrenched apart from each other. The last image Vespir had of her sister was Tavi's desperate face as the door between them slammed shut.

Five years had gone by. Even if she found her way back to the village, hundreds of miles across the grass plains, would her family still be there? Would Tavi be married by now? The future was so uncertain.

But it would *be* a future.

Until Karina dipped out of the sky.

The water drew frighteningly close. Vespir gritted her teeth as *pain* erupted behind her eyes, like a knife stabbing her brain. Karina's harsh breathing merged with her own. "What the depths?" she hissed.

Her eyes snapped open as she recalled what Camilla had said: you'll be Cut if you leave. Vespir assumed that meant they'd kill her if she tried to run, but what if it was something more? If the strange magic that had drawn Karina to the island could destroy her if she tried to flee the Trial . . .

"Turn around!" Vespir barked. Karina wailed as they dropped dangerously close to the sea, and screamed as her wingtip traced the edge of a wave—salt water was like acid to a dragon. Vespir bit her tongue as she clung tight with her knees, as she begged the Dragon above to save them.

They should have died then; Vespir knew it. But that Red bond flashed behind her eyes once more, and Vespir felt the sheer agony of effort as Karina turned herself around, as she managed to ride the currents of air above the waves and climb higher into the sky. The nearer they drew to the island, the stronger Karina grew. Vespir gasped in relief . . . until she realized that they were hurtling toward the dark middle of the forest, not the treetops. They were going too fast. She gritted her teeth and strained to imagine pulling up and reaching the treetops, but Karina mewled, wavering on the wind. She was too weak. Vespir bit down on her tongue, blood flooding her mouth as they plunged into the forest. The massive trunks loomed. Karina was small and quick, weaving around the trees. Her squalling was painful, her wings shuddering with strain. They turned left, right, went completely sideways to avoid smashing face-first into a trunk. Vespir plunged from horror to hope and back again as they rushed through the forest. When Karina banked, Vespir was catapulted into a thicket. The ground pummeled her body, bruised her hip. Rolling, she came to a stop and breathed, staring at sunlight filtered through the trees.

No escape. Vespir felt wrung out as a dirty rag and twice as used.

First they took her from her family and gave her a dragon; now they were going to kill her and her dragon both, and for what? Vespir had never felt more out of control of her own life . . . and she'd never had much control to begin with.

A rustle of leaves. Karina snuffled Vespir's hair, much as she had her pet goat. Karina tenderly touched snouts with her, and Vespir grinned through her tears.

"Boop," she muttered. The dragon blinked, pleased with herself. Vespir rubbed Karina's sleek head and stood. "Let's get you back up to the trees, girl." She looked skyward.

Vespir jolted at the sound of applause. She whipped around to find Ajax standing atop a fallen tree, haloed in the sunlight. He applauded with gusto, even threw in a couple of whooping noises.

"That," the boy said with a grin, "was *impressive.*" He leapt to the ground and strolled over. "My mistake for overlooking you. I thought you were just a servant."

Vespir frowned. "I *am* just a servant."

"That's a horrible word, isn't it? 'Just'? Cuts you into a small piece, makes you easy to swallow." Ajax waggled his fingers at Karina, who sniffed with interest. "Nice dragon." Back to Vespir. "No, you're not just a servant. You're a dragon *genius.*"

Well. Vespir had known for years she had a talent, even if common sense told her not to brag about it. Servants with too much pride weren't long for the whipping post, that's what Plotus had said.

"Thank you."

"That's why I think we can work together." The boy's grin grew lopsided. "Aren't you lucky?"

Vespir blinked. "Why would we work together when only one of us can win?"

Ajax shrugged. "Beats getting eaten by a basilisk, doesn't it?" Vespir didn't respond. "I promise not to be insulted by your lack of enthusiasm. Look, I'm an honest type. I'll tell you that you weren't my first . . . or second . . . choice to team up with. But. *But.*" He winked. "You *were* my third choice."

Vespir glanced at Karina. The dragon yawned, displaying rows of daggerlike teeth. *Me too, girl.*

"But if I'd known how you handle dragons, you'd have been first from the start. Here's my idea: You two fly through the forest. You find the basilisk, get it to chase you. With me so far?"

"Unfortunately, yes."

"See, we're having fun together. We can laugh about this. Anyway, you fly back here with the thing tailing you. Then." Ajax bounded up a small incline and pointed. "We're not too far from that patch of trees. See?" Vespir saw the trees, their low-hanging boughs concealing what waited not ten feet beyond: a sheer plummet into the ocean below. "You fly the basilisk there. Meanwhile, I'm waiting with a spear, hidden in the branches. I take out its left eye—it's only got one working eye, by the way, that's good for us—and it's blind. Can't hurt us anymore. Then you and me cut the head off, and it's a win."

"Are you saying that *you* want to *share* the basilisk?" Vespir regarded him with half-lidded incredulity.

"Friends share everything," Ajax said, hand over his heart.

"We're not friends."

"Allies share everything."

"We're not allies."

"Acquaintances—"

"Good luck with the basilisk." This scrawny little bastard was trying to lead her into a suicide mission. Despite her current misery, she'd rather live for Karina's sake, and in the hope she'd see Antonia again. As Vespir swung onto Karina's back, the boy waved his hands.

"All right. We'll have to battle it out for the head when it gets to that point. But wouldn't you rather go up against me than Hyperia?"

Vespir paused. Ajax certainly did present less of a challenge, though she didn't trust the runt. But she shook her head.

"I'd rather keep Karina safe." She petted the dragon's neck. "Ready, girl?"

As Karina's wings opened, Ajax said, "And if you don't win, your dragon's dead." For the first time, he sounded serious. Grim, even. "How's that keeping her safe?"

Vespir halted. Karina twisted around to gaze into Vespir's eyes. The dragon chirped, tongue flicking out in that adorable way of hers. Vespir stroked the top of Karina's silken head and sighed.

"Go over the plan again," she muttered.

She knew without looking that Ajax was grinning.

17

Lucian

Lucian had seen these faces before. Not the specific people, but their expressions. Up in the northern peninsula, he had killed many like these. They had looked afraid, perplexed, angry, wary: all correct responses to the soldiers' appearance. Lucian had watched grown men flee from him in terror. He would be damned if he gave these islanders reason to fear him, too.

"Emilia. Take out your sword and spear and toss them to the ground," he said calmly. The Aurun girl remained squatting before the altar, blinking at the arrow in front of her face. "Show them you mean no harm."

"Oh. Yes." Emilia fumbled at her belt, wincing as she drew her blade. Lucian listened to a bowstring tauten; his heart trammeled in his chest. It would be just if he met his end this way, but Emilia was innocent.

She tossed her weapons to the earth, then waited.

Slowly, the islanders relaxed their bows and spears. Birdsong struck up in the trees once more. Though the tension had eased, the men and women still watched them carefully.

"Lucian, let's try something. Follow my lead." Emilia dipped her head and spoke. *"Eyah shosh,"* she said, then widened her eyes at him. Lucian copied her, hoping he didn't stumble over the pronunciation.

The fear around them dissipated like smoke. The people smiled now and returned the greeting. Lucian exhaled deeply and gazed at Emilia. Color bloomed in her cheeks. She perked up, even laughed. It was a rough sound, but strangely musical as well.

"I was correct!" She appeared delighted with herself.

Lucian grinned. "How did you know that?"

"I've, er, studied the Crotian territories for years now. It's a formal greeting, but meant to convey goodwill." She bobbed her head in gratitude when one of the women offered her a water skin. Emilia drank. "The Crotians are an offshoot of the Hellini people. These islands contain the last of them." Lucian knew of the Hellini vaguely; they had been considered a great ancient civilization, before the rise of the empire. As a boy, he'd been instructed in some of their philosophies and poetry, but in truth he'd forgotten much of it.

"Can you ask them about the altars? About the basilisk?"

She shook her head, red hair swaying. "I know only a few words, and even then I'm not sure about pronunciation. Listen."

Two of the people began to speak to each other, the language unfamiliar and rich with rolling *r*'s and hushed *s*'s. Beautiful, but Lucian could not understand. On impulse, he opened his satchel and took out some bread. He offered it to the woman seated beside him. She accepted with hesitation, so Lucian tore a piece and popped it into his mouth to show it was harmless. The golden-haired girl beamed and began to divide the bread into shares. Within seconds, the group's mood had transformed into solid welcome.

This gathering had the atmosphere of a party now, but Lucian found that his mind trailed back to those charred figures seated on his bed . . .

The bread stuck in his throat. He glanced at the spear lying by a man's side.

The man noticed and gave it to Lucian to inspect. Turning it in his hands, he marveled at the craftsmanship. The carvings along the length were ornately beautiful flourishes of stars and ocean waves, a true masterpiece. Lucian whistled, handing it back.

"Impressive," he said. It was a relief, really, to see a people living with their own language, their own customs. Even if they had to survive under a blighted basilisk's eye . . .

"Oh, thank you!" Emilia cried. They'd given her a small leather flask. Lucian reached for it.

"Alcohol?"

"No, don't touch it." She lightly whacked his hand away. Well, if she wanted to keep it all to herself . . . "It's basilisk tears. You can smell." She unstoppered the flask and let him take a sniff. Lucian's eyes watered; it was like vinegar, and rotten eggs underneath.

"Um. Nice," he said, coughing.

"These are incredibly valuable." She plugged up the flask again and slipped it into her satchel. "They're the only known antidote against a basilisk's gaze. If the creature meets your eye, these will save your life."

"Thank you," Lucian said, gazing at the people seated around him. "Can we drink it now, as a precaution?"

"Definitely not. Basilisk tears are their own kind of poison. If you drink them without being envenomed first, they'll kill you."

"So I should be careful when hunting through your satchel for water, then."

Emilia laughed and then listened intently as one of the people began to speak to her. He was a boy, really, no more than ten or eleven years old. The child waved his arms about in excitement, repeating a word over and over as Emilia frowned and strained to understand. As she listened to the child, she absently twirled a bit of red hair around and around her little finger. A smile stole over Lucian; she seemed to know just about everything.

To think he'd come here to protect her.

"Oh, I got something." Her eyes brightened. The worn, weary look she'd sported yesterday had begun to vanish. Lucian drew nearer.

"What?"

"That word—*felash*. It's a bit ancient and formal, but I think it means 'guardian.'" She frowned. "That's . . . interesting."

"You say that like it's bad."

"I was thinking about the altar. If it had been meant to ward off the basilisk as evil, it would have borne the crown of the sea king, but the two eggs symbolize something sacred. Now this word, *guardian*. It could mean—" Emilia pressed a finger to her lips, her brow furrowing. "They're not feeding the basilisk to keep it away from them. They're honoring it as a sacred protector."

"Why would they do that?" Lucian felt a cold lump forming in his stomach.

"Well, think about it." She met his eyes. "Their practiced culture has become endangered. The empire often assimilates those territories it takes. If the basilisk keeps people away—"

"Then it keeps the empire out."

Lucian imagined this place with the basilisk gone. The island had no rich resources, but that might not be enough to stop expansion. Crotian territory fell under Pentri rule, and they had a reputation for being like a large fish, swallowing everything smaller in its path. Maybe the soldiers wouldn't come at once, but they would come. And when they came, they would not bring mercy.

Lucian bolted to his feet. The islanders regarded him warily, and Emilia blinked in surprise.

"What's wrong?"

"I have to stop this," he said. He ran away, unthinking as he broke through branches. Emilia's cries soon died behind him. He wasn't worried about her now. She'd be safe with the people.

But the people would not be safe so long as Hyperia stalked their lone guardian. Teeth gritted, Lucian raced through the forest and prayed to the blue above that he was not too late.

18

Ajax

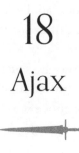

*C*ome on. Come on. Come on.

Ajax waited in the tree, crouched fifteen or so feet off the ground. His calves screamed from the pain of his position, and sweat studded his hairline and the band of his pants. Grunting, he shifted his weight to hold the spear against his left arm. He scratched his chin, then plucked at the rope tied about his waist. He tugged on it, and in the trees above him Dog gawped in reply.

"Stay there. Good boy," Ajax muttered. If all went well, Dog was going to get a jaw rub tonight, his favorite thing. As if anticipating it, the dragon began to puff in enthusiasm. Ajax wrinkled his nose at the acrid smell of smoke. "Stop blowing embers! You'll give us away."

"*Gawp.*" Dog sounded chastened. Good.

Ajax chewed the inside of his cheek as he scanned the dense forest, waiting for Vespir and that tiny dragon of hers to come careening around the bend with the basilisk in tow. Maybe Ajax had been stupid, and she'd run off laughing to herself about the good trick she'd played on the bastard. Oh sure, she'd be deferential and doe-eyed around the legitimate contenders, all *yes, my lord*-ing and *no, my lady*-ing. But Ajax? What'd a bastard piece of trash like him matter?

He felt that low, familiar hunger. His nose twitched, and his sweaty grip tightened on the spear.

Wouldn't they all gape to find him the victor? Wouldn't they all realize what a mistake it'd been to write him off?

Ajax would be the youngest emperor ever crowned in the Etrusian Empire's glorious history, and he would wear that gold circlet with pride. Lysander would kiss his boots if he asked. Soon. All he had to do was hold his arm steady and not piss himself with fear.

Ajax perked up as he heard the high call of a dragon echo off the trees. Then, soon after, the soft, dull *thud* of footsteps. Heavy, monster-size footsteps.

"Don't get scared," Ajax whispered to Dog, gritting his teeth against his own tremors. "You hear me? You get scared, I'll never forgive you."

Dog whined. Vespir didn't expect Ajax to be tied to his dragon. Once he stabbed the basilisk's eye out, he'd scurry up the rope and jump into Dog's saddle. One quick dive and a slice of his blade, and the head would be off before Vespir could turn around on dragonback. Nice girl, to help him like this. Too bad there could be only one winner.

Another squeal, this time nearer in the forest. The footsteps were growing louder now, and a deep, booming roar shivered the leaves and the branches around him. Ajax pressed a hand to the trunk and breathed. This was fine. Fine.

Karina and Vespir burst into view, the girl tucked against her dragon's back as they barrel-rolled through the trees. Brilliant. Partly it came down to the dragon being small, but Ajax had never seen handling like this. Vespir seemed more dragon than girl, insanely impressive when you realized she didn't saddle her mount. Ajax let out an involuntary whistle of appreciation. Genius. Sheer genius.

Ajax didn't have the talent, but he knew how to make use of it.

He'd calculated perfectly. The basilisk's bobbing head would come right up next to him. His stomach swirled as he hefted the spear to his shoulder. He would have half a second to blind the thing before its gaze met his. He could try closing his eyes when he thrust, but if he missed, he'd get eaten. Bad alternative.

Thud. Thud. The beast drew nearer, and Karina sailed right past his nose. Vespir's triumphant eyes met his for half a second. Yes, she'd done it. Couldn't be better.

The world around him seemed to hold its breath as the basilisk stepped into his space. The creature's eye would be level with his arm. Two steps more. Just one.

Ajax swallowed, clenched his jaw, steadied his nerves. A single thrust, and no one would call him bastard again.

He'd show his pig of a father what he'd squirted out.

Ajax brought back the spear as the venomous yellow disc of the monster's eye hove into view and—

"Stop!"

Someone screamed below, and Ajax froze. The basilisk came to a grinding halt. Ajax felt the spear tumble out of his grip.

Oh. Shit.

Before he could move, the basilisk's eye pierced him straight through. His vision began to melt; it felt like a swarm of bees was stinging his blood and bones. A buzzing scream reverberated in his ears. He opened his mouth, but no sound emerged. Ajax mercifully broke eye contact with the thing when it turned, interested more in whatever had shouted on the ground. He fumbled for the rope and tugged repeatedly, his grasp becoming clumsy. Hot tears streamed from his damaged eyes. He lost feeling in his right arm, which collapsed at his side.

Ajax screamed, the poison boiling through his system and slowing his tongue. He felt his brain start to burn.

Above him, sounding a hundred miles away, Dog made

horrible noises. Ajax wavered on his feet and fell backward off the branch, saved from the fall by the rope tied around his waist. Dog swooped up into the sky, Ajax's limp body bashing into branch after branch until finally he was pulled up into the world above, the sun screaming across his skull. Ajax's tongue swelled, filling his mouth.

He could only see flashes of images. The treetops beneath.

The sea and the sky.

Vespir, circling underneath on dragonback.

Vespir's concerned face.

The back of Dog's head, while hands tied him tight to the saddle horn.

No. No.

Unable to form words, Ajax howled as his dragon swung toward the horizon. Even dying, hatred swelled within him. Hatred for the basilisk, for the damn fool on the ground who'd screamed. Hatred for the servant girl with her dark, worried eyes and her damn helping hands. Ajax had been robbed of his victory, and now even his damn life.

He couldn't decide which was worse.

19

Hyperia

Hyperia had been patient as she stalked the monster through the brush, following the splatter of its poison blood. She'd been quiet as she tracked it to a glen in the center of the island, where it stopped to rub its jaw against a tree trunk, presumably to scratch away some of its crusted blood. She had not startled when a creature spun through the trees overhead and nabbed the basilisk's attention like an audacious fly before a frog.

Hyperia had been a bit surprised to discover that the servant girl—and her dragon—were luring the basilisk away. So. Vespir had more spine than Hyperia had given her credit for.

Excellent. Honor demanded a challenge.

Hyperia had raced after the monster and the dragon, tailing them across thickets and down slopes. She was used to running three or four miles at a time, and her muscles did not burn as she pursued them. Her breathing remained light.

When they neared the cliffs, Hyperia understood the girl's goal. Trick the monster into tumbling over the edge. She narrowed her eyes as she flicked her wrist, telescoping the spear to its full length. If she could find a good opening . . . Perhaps, if the monster plunged onto the shoals, she could summon Aufidius with a whistle and swoop down to claim her prize. There were three or four ways to go about this, and Hyperia saw them all clearly.

No need to worry. Victory was still within catching distance.

She came to a sudden halt as the monster slowed. Her lips pursed. Damn. If the monster smelled the trap, she would have to be cautious in her approach. Within the thick canopy of trees she couldn't call on Aufidius, and now that she had no shield she must be careful. Hyperia began to slink into the trees' shadows when—

"Stop!"

She whirled around, blinking at Lucian's idiocy as he barreled along the path to reach her. His fists pumped at his sides, and sweat gleamed on his face. He'd clearly run full out to reach her. Had he been racing all over the island?

What was he *doing*? The imbecile didn't even have a weapon; he'd left them behind because of his blasted principle or some other insipid reason.

"Don't kill it!" he shouted.

Hyperia heard some kind of strangled cry up in the trees and then the rustle of branches. Probably a bird taking flight.

"What would you have me do, then?" she snapped.

"Leave it and go." Lucian stopped, coughing and wiping sweat from his face.

"This is the worst attempt at sabotage I have ever seen," she snarled. "If you think I'm fool enough to simply stop the Hunt because you *asked nicely*—"

"I won't let you kill it!" He loomed nearer. His impressive size would be enough to intimidate the strongest men in her father's army, but Hyperia was worth ten of any common soldier.

"I thought you vowed never to raise a hand to another creature again. So. *How* will you stop me?"

He did not respond, but the flicker of a muscle in his jaw showed that he warred with himself. She gave a tight smile.

Lucian swore. "Look out!"

Hyperia felt the creature at her back before she heard its footstep or the slavering hiss as it bent down to tear her to shreds with its teeth. Sprinting away, she rolled and came up behind a trunk, watching carefully. The creature's blind side was turned to her. She could no longer see Lucian, but he was not her problem. Stupid boy. Don't kill the thing? How did he ever expect to win an Emperor's Trial if he wouldn't even complete the basic tasks?

Hyperia crept around, looking for an opening—the basilisk still had its backside to her. Her foot struck something. Glancing down, she found a second spear. Hmm? Whose was this, then? She looked up into the trees, but saw nothing. Vespir's, perhaps? Had the girl dropped it?

It wouldn't surprise me. She seems to know dragons, but little else.

Hyperia had an idea.

While the basilisk hunted for Lucian, Hyperia got out from behind the tree, readied, and threw the spear. It whistled cleanly through the air, landing exactly where she'd wanted: in the center of the monster's back. With a piercing roar, the basilisk turned, its tail whipping through the brush. Perhaps it had whacked Lucian. No. Hyperia would not be that lucky.

She stood on the path, catching the giant beast's attention, and then darted toward the cliff. She rolled back into the brush as the monster bellowed and followed at a fast clip. *Thud. Thud. Thud.* The ground trembled with its approach, and Hyperia prepared for her last throw. When the creature passed, she would blind it, send it hurtling over the edge, and then find a way to claim her prize with Aufidius. Battling in this dense patch of forest would never do. She couldn't get a clean swing.

As the basilisk ran forward, time seemed to slow.

Hyperia watched from the ground as it lunged into view, the yellow circle of its eye searching for someone to infect.

From back in the forest, Hyperia heard Lucian's frantic bellow. The moronic boy still wanted her to spare the demon's life.

She prepared to let her final spear fly—

The ground shook violently. Hyperia tumbled to her knees, the spear bouncing from her hand. The basilisk skidded to a halt, a hilarious sight for a creature its size. As it tried to turn back, the cliffside gave way beneath the brute's feet. With a deafening roar and a billowing cloud of white dust, the entire ten feet of rock and sand dissolved beneath the basilisk, and the monster plunged into the sea below.

20

Emilia

Emilia kept her fingers dug into the soft earth, shaking with gratitude that no one had seen her. Meeting those islanders had stilled the chaos in her soul, for a bit. She'd felt the power bulging inside of her as she ran, pregnant with magic. She'd followed Lucian as fast as possible, wheezing all the way. She'd never been athletic, and time spent locked in a castle had atrophied what muscle she had.

But then she saw Lucian fall and the basilisk lean down to devour him, and she blazed with fury.

Apart from Alex, Lucian had been the first person in years to make her smile. Emilia would not let some wingless dragon have him.

When the thing turned and darted for the cliff—sparing Lucian, thank the blue above—Emilia had given the power its own way. All she could think was destruction, explosion, chaos, death, death, *death* . . .

She had never destroyed an entire ledge of earth before. Her arms trembled, and her hands were cold. Emilia needed to eat something, but . . .

First, there was the basilisk. She crouched in the brush and watched as Hyperia emerged from the forest to stare down at the monster. Had it fallen into the ocean below? Was it beyond reach? Emilia gnawed her lip as Lucian sprang from the trees and got in Hyperia's face. He darted this way and that, his arms out, shielding the creature from her wrath. While the two shouted at each other, Emilia got a wild idea.

Why not . . . ?

She plucked the shield from her back. Taking the spear in hand, she crept through the forest, invisible to the arguing pair. All she needed to do was come up on the basilisk's side . . .

As Emilia moved forward, she heard the snap of twigs and the shuffle of feet all around. She paused in her journey, looked back, and let out a breath.

Oh no.

21

Lucian

I f Lucian had run twenty feet farther ahead, he would've been killed. He'd just emerged from the trees when the giant creature simply fell. The entire cliff had dissolved; he'd never seen anything like it. A wave of white dust rushed over him, stinging his eyes. Arm across his face, he coughed and inched forward.

Hyperia. Had she fallen as well?

"Hyperia?"

"I'm all right." The girl staggered out of the cloud of dust. Her face was streaked in white, her eyebrows powdered over. It lent her a look of blank surprise.

The basilisk. Had it died? Lucian breathed a sigh of relief. The beast screamed in fury and pain, but it was definitely not dead. It was trapped, probably broken on the rocks below, but its head emerged over the cliff's edge. Lucian put up his shield as caution and crept closer to Hyperia. She couldn't make a move now without going through him. He could at least block her.

"It's trapped," she croaked, coughing more dust from her lungs. But she began to smile as well. "Excellent." She seized her spear. "Out of my way, Sabel."

"You can't."

"You say that, but you haven't given a reason why," she growled.

"This creature guards the people on this island. It's not terrorizing them." He spoke quickly, his body instinctively falling into fighting stance.

"That doesn't matter. The challenge requires the monster's head," she snapped.

"So that's all it takes?" His temper flared. "They tell you to kill, and you do it without question?"

Lucian recalled Hyperia's blood-spattered gown at last night's dinner. The girl's eyes lowered for the briefest instant, but she was firm as stone. Firmer, even. Unlike the ground beneath their feet, she'd never crumble.

"Yes. That's all it takes," she said. "Don't be a fool, Lucian. Listen to it. That thing will never be able to crawl back up here."

He hated to admit she was right. The basilisk continued to scream, its roars deafeningly close, but it wouldn't last much longer. Its legs had to have been crushed in the fall; otherwise it would have already been trying to clamber up. The people would lose their guardian, one way or another.

"If you're not going to kill it," Hyperia said, "then stand aside. It would be nice to end this challenge before nightfall."

Hyperia turned when the voices began shouting. Lucian's stomach dropped as dozens of men, women, and children emerged from the trees.

One of them, the little boy with golden hair who'd given Emilia that vial of tears, threw himself into the dirt at Hyperia's feet. While the basilisk bellowed in pain, the boy spoke quickly in that tongue Lucian couldn't understand.

But he could read the terror in the boy's eyes all too well.

Please don't, the boy's eyes begged. *Don't kill it.*

Once again, Lucian had been sent to crush a group of people who had never hurt him.

How could he reason with Hyperia?

How could he suppress that hard voice that told him to

screw reasoning, to wrestle the spear from her and kill the damn thing himself? To win. The old way of thinking, black or white, win or lose. Nothing in between. The crown or the Cut.

Lucian shuddered.

The Volscia girl turned to speak, but her face paled in seeming horror.

"No!" she screamed, and charged past him. Lucian turned to find Emilia, crouched before the basilisk's remaining good eye with her shield held up. Trapped, the beast had caught sight of itself in the reflective surface and was screaming. It'd been poisoned.

Brilliant. But before Emilia could move to claim her prize, Hyperia was upon her. The Volscia girl leapt, striking her foot against Emilia's shield and propelling the other girl down. With a spinning twist, Hyperia flung her spear and lodged it perfectly in the center of the basilisk's remaining eye. Ensconced deep in the monster's socket, her spear jiggered back and forth like a baton conducting a mad tune. The now-blind monstrosity whipped its head about, screeching in agony.

Lucian's focus instantly shifted to Emilia, who lay on the ground. He ran for her as Hyperia yanked the spear out, vitreous fluid flying, then turned fast with a slice of her blade. Hissing drops of acid rained to the earth. The basilisk went silent and slipped apart at the neck. The head thumped on the earth, and the body disappeared into the sea below.

Lucian knelt by Emilia's side. Her face was pale with surprise, but she held up a hand.

"I'm all right. She stunned me, that's all," the girl whispered.

Together, they watched Hyperia pull a shimmering bag from her satchel. Using the tip of her spear, she nudged the head inside. Lucian watched, unwilling to move. The damage had been done, and she had the right of conquest.

Hyperia winced, and only then did he notice the bloody, teardrop-shaped boil on her left forearm. The acid had splashed her.

The little boy ran up to Hyperia, fists bunched at his sides while he howled in her face. She shoved the child back.

"As citizens of the empire, I have liberated you from this terror." She nodded. "You're welcome."

Her blue eyes narrowed as she cleaned and sheathed her blade. Hyperia hoisted the bag containing the basilisk's head to her shoulder, put her fingers to her mouth, and gave a shrill whistle. Within seconds, Aufidius appeared with a flap of his colossal wings and soared down to hover near the cliff's edge. Hyperia stepped onto his wing and ran to the saddle before rising into the sky. Lucian looked back at the people, a knotted congregation of grief.

I should have protected you, he thought bitterly.

"I almost had it," Emilia murmured. He placed an arm around her. She flinched but then relaxed into his grasp.

"Let's go back," he replied. Helping her to stand, the two walked into the forest to collect their dragons. As they went, they passed through the weeping crowd of islanders. Lucian watched them standing in a row, gazing into the sea to mourn their guardian.

Grim, he turned his eyes away. *Useless beast,* he thought with disdain. He did not mean the basilisk.

22

Ajax

Ajax was pretty sure he'd stopped breathing at some point. Waking in his bed felt like a miracle. Groaning, he sat up. His tongue felt thick, and he had a taste like rotted fish at the back of his throat. He fumbled with the blankets and staggered to the table in the center of his rotunda for a glass of water. Drinking, he squinted as Dog poked his nose through one of the dividing curtains, whining as Ajax shuffled over.

"You get me back here?" he croaked, rubbing the dragon's nose. Dog panted, letting his forked tongue loll from the side of his mouth. Ajax had spent weeks training him to do that. He'd wanted Dog to be more doglike. "You're a good boy."

"It wasn't just him." Vespir appeared in his room, shoving back a curtain. Ajax realized he wasn't wearing any trousers, only loose cotton undergarments. Ah well. He didn't think he was Vespir's type, anyway. The servant girl turned her face away while he lurched back into bed. It felt like a squadron of heavy-booted foot soldiers was stomp-dancing around his skull. "I tied you to the saddle."

"Yeah, I remember," he grunted, plumping his pillows before lying back. He decided he'd vomit later. Ajax thought she'd leave, but Vespir continued to stare at him. "So . . . you want a hug?"

"Aren't you at all curious why you're still alive?"

"Um. The priests did magic to make me better?"

"Lady Emilia brought an antidote back with her from the island. If she hadn't, you'd be dead now."

"Okay. Please tell *Lady* Emilia she's no longer my fourth choice for a partner," he muttered, and rolled over. Pain screamed against the left side of his body. It was the kind of pain that invited more pain over for a party and then upset the neighbors by playing loud music late into the night while drinking all your wine. "Mind telling me who won?" He winced. Talking was too intense right now.

"Lady Hyperia."

As if the day hadn't gone shitty enough. Groaning, he rolled onto his back and stared at the ceiling. A minute passed.

"You're still here for some reason."

"Lady Hyperia . . . Did you say something to her?" Vespir sounded hesitant. Though it was agony, Ajax propped himself onto his elbows.

"She finally admitted she craves me?" he drawled.

"She suggested we let you die. She said that anyone stupid enough to get poisoned by a basilisk's gaze is not fit to be emperor." Vespir frowned. "She also said you lacked honor."

Ajax bet he knew why this meek little dragon shit-scraper felt free to be this blunt with him. With the others, it was all Lord Lucian and Lady Hyperia, but with him? This common-born girl was legitimate. Even she had the privilege of looking down on him. Ajax let the anger fuel him.

"Palling around with *Lady* Hyperia? You're getting the hang of the highborn life pretty fast." He sneered. "I knew you had some Pentri blood in you. You and your *sister* must be close."

Vespir rolled her eyes, and Ajax felt cheap, which only soured him more. "Fine. Don't listen to me." She sounded exasperated now. "But Lady Hyperia . . ." She worried her lip. "Be careful."

"Oh, she's just jealous of me. She's only human." He sat up further, his skull practically melting as he did so. "Thanks for the assist, but I don't need a shitty attempt at friendship."

She looked at him with pity—he'd have preferred disgust. "Don't push her. I don't think anyone wants to see her angry."

With that, Vespir left him alone, and Dog retreated from the curtain, granting Ajax his privacy. He lay back in the bed, working his jaw. Fine. He hadn't won this challenge, but there were three more to come. The tasks couldn't all involve hunting mythical beasts he'd never heard of before. If he remembered correctly, next up was the Game. Well, he liked games. Besides, it wasn't his fault he knew so little about weird creatures. When they were six or so, all the Tiber bastards got piled into one dank room with one dim tutor and handed a haphazard education. Ajax could read and write—his spelling was terrible—and he knew some basic strokes of history. Beyond that, he'd sharpened his wits outside the castle's corridors.

He'd made a mistake. He could admit it. He'd gotten cocky. It wouldn't happen again.

He closed his eyes. When he opened them, he found a strange woman standing over his bed. Ajax bolted upright, swearing softly.

"Hey. Ah. Who're you?" he asked. She was a stranger, yet oddly familiar. The woman remained mute, her green eyes watery and bloodshot. A smattering of acne traced the corners of her mouth. Her dirty-blond hair lay lank against her face. Her nails were bitten to the nub, her fingers raw. She had a washerwoman's hands. And the way she regarded him, with those eyes that seemed so familiar—

Ajax's whole body went cold. He tried to speak, but she turned and vanished through the curtains. He struggled to accept what he'd just seen. It couldn't be real. There was no way *she* could be here. He'd thought the two of them looked similar, him and her, that was all. It was the poison making him delirious—

Someone screamed outside his room. A woman.

He fell out of bed and crawled through the curtains, bile choking him. On the path ahead, the one that led to the sea, there was . . . it was . . .

A pile of linens strewn on the ground.

Lord Tiber had surprised her while she was carrying them.

She screamed as he held her down.

No one came to help, despite how heavily trafficked the castle halls were at midday. People expected this.

Ajax had been just six years old when he'd heard another woman's screams and come running. When he'd shoved at Lord Tiber, the old cancerous toad, and told him to stop hurting the girl. Like it was a game that had gotten too rough.

He'd been dragged off by a servant, chastised with a branch. The girl kept screaming. Nine months later, Ajax had a new brother.

Now he stood, helpless, as a woman with his eyes and hair and crooked nose wailed—

"Stop it!" He pitched forward onto his knees, his temples throbbing. He heaved and spit bile onto the ground.

They were gone when he looked up. Vanished. It hadn't been real.

It's not real. It's the poison, he said to himself. This wasn't how emperors behaved. Emperors didn't act like bastards conceived with a horrific scream on a dirty floor.

No. Emperors were above all of that.

So if the others wanted to look down on him, pity him, they'd pay for it.

Stifling a sob, he stumbled back to his bed and yelled at Dog not to bother him.

23

Vespir

V espir stood silent outside the temple, waiting in a line with the others for the priests to appear. The summer air had cooled, and the columns' shadows stretched long and blue across the courtyard. The four, minus Ajax, were all dressed in outfits they'd found waiting for them upon their return. Vespir had breathed out in relief when she discovered a pair of trousers in forest-green velvet, along with a moss-colored doublet and cloak. At least the acolytes hadn't tried to fancy her up alongside the other two girls. Vespir had never enjoyed dresses. They got in the way of her work.

The sun settled on the horizon, casting them all in a reddish glow, when the doors boomed open and the priests descended the steps. Everyone straightened. Camilla walked ahead of Petros, carrying something golden in her hands.

"The first challenge is complete." The priestess's voice reminded Vespir of an antique bronze gong in the Pentri family's collection. "The Hunt tests the imperial merits of courage, strength, and physical skill. A true emperor must embody the warlike qualities of a dragon. Hyperia of the Volscia." The priestess extended her arms, proffering the golden gift. "This sword is yours, to use with pride."

Hyperia ascended the steps and collected her token. She strapped the gilded sword to her waist. There was no gloating as she surveyed the losers. Hyperia merely bowed to the priests and went right back to stand in line. Vespir watched with some tinge of admiration. Say what you would about Hyperia, but she behaved with dignity.

She was also a murderer, but you couldn't have everything.

Hyperia stared ahead, lost in her own thoughts. Emilia stood on her toes to whisper something in Lucian's ear. Vespir looked at her boots, trying not to let resentment get its teeth in her. Those two had clearly formed some kind of alliance. Hyperia needed no one but herself. Despite how stupid it was, Vespir had hoped she and Ajax might be on the path to, well, *something*. They were the lowborn, after all.

But here she was, trapped with nobles who either didn't notice her or hated her on principle, with challenges she could never win and Karina's life in her incompetent hands. Vespir winced. Idiot. *Idiot!* Why was she still bowing to these people, who took all that politeness as their due? Why did she care about the "right" way to do things anymore?

The world had turned its back on right and on her.

"Now," Petros said, his voice far less sonorous than Camilla's. "As for the other four, listed in descending order: Emilia of the Aurun in second place; Lucian of the Sabel in third; Ajax—"

"What?" Lucian and Hyperia both said it at the same time. Vespir's head whipped up.

"As we told you already," Petros said, sounding massively irritated, "every action matters in this Trial. How you conduct yourself is important."

"Were you . . . watching us?" Emilia's voice hitched.

"We do not choose. The Dragon does." So was the Dragon Himself watching them? Even to Vespir, that seemed impossible.

Petros gave an exasperated sigh. "We didn't have to explain in such excruciating detail during the last Trial."

Last time, all the right people were called, Vespir thought. Her heart pounded as she realized that the priests had named Ajax fourth. If so, that meant she was . . .

"And Vespir of the Pentri takes fifth place," Petros concluded, voicing her fears. Vespir swallowed.

"Why is she fifth?" Hyperia sounded confused. "She didn't get herself poisoned, like that Tiber fool."

"Because she tried to run," Camilla replied, her tone icy. "Isn't that so, Vespir?"

They saw. I don't know how, but they saw. Vespir shut her eyes, fighting a wave of nausea. She couldn't do a damn thing right.

With a sniff, the priestess extended her arm, the orange satin of her robe blazing in the sunset. "There is one other thing. The victor takes a trophy, while the loser—in this case, Vespir of the Pentri—must submit to a penalty." The woman gave a bloodless smile. "Of the high priests' devising."

Of course a penalty. Vespir looked up at the priests, and this time she let herself meet their eyes. It was as unnatural as breathing underwater, but she fought the impulse to hide.

Taking a deep breath, she said, "I'm not a Pentri. I served them, but I'm not one *of* them."

Camilla did not flinch. "Fine. Then Vespir, *servant* of the Pentri, prepare yourself for punishment."

That had always been the way. Vespir played by their rules and was dragged around by the nose because of it. The one time she disobeyed, justice fell hard on her. Meanwhile, people like Hyperia could murder their own sisters and catch a reward.

"I've never heard of something like this," Emilia declared.

"You cannot learn everything from books," Camilla replied, and walked down the steps. She halted before Vespir—the older woman was a few inches shorter, and Vespir took some small pleasure in making the priestess look up at her. "Now. You tried to run out of cowardice, the most shameless characteristic. To atone, you will face fear headlong."

"How?" Vespir muttered, trying not to curse at the woman. Even a servant could only be pushed so far.

"Hyperia. Take your new sword and fight Vespir in armed combat. The first blood drawn is the winner." Camilla stepped aside, just like that.

Vespir considered sprinting away, like a rabbit when it's caught a fox's eye. Hyperia had killed her own sister and worn the girl's blood to dinner. There could be no shred of mercy in such a person.

"What?" Hyperia sounded incredulous. Then, "That's not sporting." She turned to Vespir. "Have you ever held a sword?"

It took a minute to find her tongue. "I've used slings to keep rats away from our house."

"It's dishonorable," Hyperia said to the priests. She sounded horrified.

"No." Camilla stood beside Petros on the top step, wearing a wry smile. "Disobedience is dishonorable. Well, Hyperia?"

Of course, there was no arguing with that. Vespir heard muffled arguments from the other two, particularly Lucian, but she simply went through the motions. If she dropped her sword right away, maybe Hyperia would only graze her with the blade. Her legs trembled, her arms were leaden at her side as an acolyte appeared and offered a sword. It was heavier than Vespir had thought, and the grip slipped out of her hand. The blade clattered against the ground. Everyone watched with evident sympathy as Vespir fumbled for it. She stuck her legs at hip width apart and held up her sword. The blade wavered, tipping back and nearly slicing her nose. She trembled, which didn't help. Hyperia snorted in disgust.

"Pitiful," she murmured. Her evident sorrow for Vespir—

and dismay on her own behalf—nearly sent the servant girl over the edge. Blinking back tears, she looked at the priests. Emilia and Lucian were deep in discussion about something. Probably congratulating themselves on escaping this.

"Ready?" Petros called. Vespir planted herself, and gazed past the edge of her blade at Hyperia. Fine. In a few days, she'd be dead and gone. None of this mattered, anyway.

But Karina . . .

As the priest lifted his hand to signal the start, Lucian stepped between the two girls. Vespir almost dropped her sword.

"What are you doing?" Camilla asked.

"I have an offer." Lucian looked Vespir in the eyes. "Let me fight Hyperia instead."

24

Lucian

It had been Emilia's idea, and it was brilliant.

Hopefully, this would work.

"The rules say that the priests punish the competitor in last place. Is there anything to stop me from volunteering to trade positions?" Lucian asked. To their silence, he added, "I didn't even bring weapons to the island, and I actively tried to stop Hyperia from killing the monster. Isn't *that* dishonorable?"

"True," Hyperia muttered.

"We do not choose. The Dragon does," Petros said. Apparently, he was going to stick to the few lines he'd spent his life memorizing.

"But is there any rule outlined that says such a thing *can't* happen?" Lucian looked at Emilia, who nodded in encouragement. "If how we choose to conduct ourselves matters, isn't this also a choice? Doesn't it count?"

I'm hoping it's without precedent, Emilia had whispered. *If this has already been tried, it may not work.*

"You do realize that you're offering to be counted *fifth* in this challenge?" Petros said slowly. "You wouldn't merely take Vespir's penalty. You would assume her score and her ranking as well."

Emilia winced. She'd warned him, but hearing the priest say it felt more final.

Lucian had been prepared for this. He'd decided to play this game in order to bring peace to the empire, or at the very least keep Hyperia from ruling everything. He couldn't do that if he deliberately lowered his own score.

But Vespir . . . People like her suffered enough under the high lords' whims. It wouldn't work to play the game like they wanted—to be cutthroat and devious in order to gain the throne—and only after he'd won become good. Life didn't work that way.

Lucian was going to win *his* way, even if it meant losing tonight.

"I understand." He looked up at them. "All right?"

Camilla and Petros conferred very briefly. She nodded, he shrugged.

"Take up your sword, Lord Lucian," Camilla said.

"So . . . I'm in third now?" Vespir croaked. She picked up the sword and offered it to Lucian, but he shook his head.

"I'm not going to fight back." Never again. He would win his way. All of it, his way.

Hyperia snorted. "Oh, spare us your *nobility*."

Vespir took her place beside Emilia. The Aurun girl, peeking out from behind that tangle of red hair, gave a small smile of encouragement. That one smile calmed him, focused his senses. Yes.

He would force these people to witness their own cruelty.

When I'm emperor, I will show them. I will.

Lucian faced Hyperia, hands relaxed at his sides. The girl quickly pulled back her golden hair into a rudimentary bun.

Prepared, she crouched into a fighting stance. For a time she stood there, merely looking at him. Sunset glimmered on her blade.

Then she came.

Her form was exquisite; a high, well-practiced cut. Her sword didn't just swing; it sang. The air hissed with steel.

Lucian watched the blade descend, closer and closer. At the last possible second—the perfect one—he leaned back. The blade missed him by inches.

Then he was moving, too. He rolled across the ground, and quick as that, he was behind Hyperia.

She whipped around, ready to strike again. She shifted her weight, her eyes scanning him for weaknesses.

"Nicely done," she said. "I thought you said you wouldn't fight."

"I'm not fighting. I'm just not letting you hit me."

To his surprise, she appeared pleased.

"Ah," she said, and attacked once more.

She was phenomenal; he had to admit it. She knew every technique Lucian himself had studied, from the Masarian two-handed lunge to the Karthagon plow stance. A warrior goddess in the flesh.

And she was relentless. It wasn't long before Lucian's muscles burned and sweat slicked his chest. He felt the blood thudding in his veins, and his breath came in short gasps. He leapt through the air, dropped to the ground, and sprang to his feet an instant later. Her blade whipped with such grace and speed it was nearly invisible, but he managed to keep away. She was fast, but he was faster.

Hyperia had been forged in fire, her skills honed under the most elite trainers Volscia gold could procure. She had been melted down, her essence beaten and shaped until she herself became a perfect, golden weapon.

But a weapon set on a silken pillow, housed under a glass case.

Lucian had been forged in the fire of battle and learned his lessons in blood.

As the fight continued, Hyperia roared. Her face flushed; sweat beaded on her brow. She lunged, only to snarl in anger when Lucian deflected once again.

"How dare you!" she shouted.

Good, he thought. Again and again she lunged, her strokes growing messier, erratic. He jumped. He rolled. He ducked. With every defiant move, he drove her on to anger. The girl bared her teeth, a wild light crackling in her gaze.

Lucian wondered if he'd pushed her too far. Something dark peered out at him from behind those blue eyes.

Hyperia screamed and ran forward. When Lucian turned to the left, she surprised him: her blade was waiting. She had managed to trick him—trick him with lightning speed.

Lucian grunted as the sword entered his stomach. His eyes widened in agony.

"Lucian!" Emilia screamed.

He felt the earth tremble beneath his feet, a bit like when the basilisk had fallen. *Another earthquake?* he thought stupidly. But no, the tremors stopped at once, and the sword left his body. Blood warmed and wetted his clothes.

Too much blood. And far too fast.

"Oh." He tasted copper on his lips. "That's what it's like."

When he fell, he scarcely felt his head strike the ground. He simply gazed up at the twilight sky, the stars beginning to show themselves.

Numb, he watched Petros crouch over him, felt the priest's hand on his stomach. Lucian closed his eyes . . .

And opened them. Huh. He'd been sure he'd never do that again.

"You're all right now," Petros muttered.

Lucian sat up, wincing a little. His stomach was sore, and he touched where the blade had gone in. Eyes widening, he poked around at the slit in his clothes, where the cloth was torn and blood was heavy on the fabric. But the skin underneath . . .

"There's no wound," Lucian muttered. Then he closed his eyes. "Of course. Binding." The orderly magic of uniting things, including flesh and innards.

"Hyperia. That was . . . more forceful than we were expecting," the priest drawled as he stood, brushing off his knees. He made a pained expression, rubbing at his hand as though it were tender. Camilla came over to inspect it and confer with Petros, looking mildly worried. Perhaps such an intricate mending required a great deal of energy. Meanwhile, Hyperia sheathed her sword and stormed over, gripping Lucian by his shirtfront.

Lucian allowed the Volscia girl to bring her face near to his. Her teeth were clenched, her eyes tight with rage.

"How dare you!" she snarled.

"Excuse me?" he began, but she threw him backward with a cry.

"How dare you not fight?" She breathed harshly, her nostrils flaring. "You're incredible. You *monster!*" She clenched her fists. "How dare you not use such a beautiful talent?"

Stunned, Lucian lay sprawled on the ground while Hyperia left them all, stalking down the path and into the near darkness.

"First blood has been drawn," Camilla said, stopping overhead to regard him. "Everyone should return to your rooms. We leave tomorrow for the next challenge, and it will be something of a flight."

The priests strolled away with that, leaving Lucian on the ground. After they'd gone, Emilia rushed to kneel beside him, inspecting where Hyperia had stabbed. Vespir followed at a slower pace.

"Petros is an ass." Emilia frowned.

"He saved my life."

"Yes, but he didn't mend your clothing." She *tsk*ed. "That slit's still there."

Something about the way she said it made Lucian laugh. He slumped back onto the ground, spread his arms to either side, and laughed so hard that the deep pain of his mended stomach announced itself. Groaning, he placed his hands on the sensitive spot. Vespir crouched.

"I think," she said slowly, "that you're out of your mind."

He arched a brow. "No 'my lord'?" Vespir flinched, but Lucian's smile calmed her. "Sorry. Kidding."

"Yeah." Vespir grinned, the first honest grin he'd seen from her. "You're not funny, either."

"I never said I was."

The girl scratched the back of her head, rumpling her short, black hair. "Thank you."

"How's your stomach?" Emilia had backed away from them. Apparently, she liked her distance.

"Sore, though that's better than bleeding."

"What you need is a tisane," she said. To their blank looks, she added, "An herbal infusion. Like tea."

"Sounds . . . appetizing." He raised his hand. Vespir regarded it warily, like it'd bite. "Help me up?"

She smiled again.

"Okay," she said, and clasped hands with him.

"So you served my aunt and uncle?" Lucian said, when it was just him and Vespir alone in his rotunda. Emilia had gone to find herbs for the tisane. That left the servant girl, now hanging out at the edge of the room and a heartbeat away from running. The warmth of their shared after-battle moment had started to dissipate. She always kept her eyes trained to the ground, though Lucian thought it might be more out of habit than fear at this point.

"The Pentri are your family, too?" She glanced up in surprise. "I thought the nobles kept separate."

"They do." Each of the five great Houses governed an assortment of lesser noble families in their own territories and generally chose spouses from among them. Preserving the "authenticity" of the bloodlines was key to the lords and ladies of Etrusia. "But Lady Pentri's sister was my mother." Lucian knelt on the tiled floor and pulled his shirt up over his head. As he wet a cloth and wiped away the dried blood at his gut, he continued. "My parents met during one of the congregations in Dragonspire. They fell so madly in love that my mother left her inheritance and ran away to Karthago."

The great love of my life, that's what his father had called his mother. Livia of the Pentri became Livia Sabel, and Lucian could not recall a moment in his early childhood when his parents were not together. They'd overseen trade agreements together, ridden together, laughed together over supper. Every look between them had been soft with love.

Love ruled the Sabel men.

Apparently, it missed a generation, he thought.

"So Anton—Lady Antonia's your cousin." Vespir sat beside him, seemingly excited with the idea. She studied him now as if searching for the Pentri girl. "Oh, I see it. Your eyes, there's something about the shape. And your jawline."

"You miss her?" he asked softly. Vespir sighed. "It's fine if you do."

"I . . . Yes." Vespir pulled her knees to her chest, wrapped her arms around them. "She's so damn perfect, anyone would."

Perfect. Lucian winced. He'd given up on the idea of perfection.

"How long have you two been—?"

"It only really started a few days ago. But I've loved her since I was twelve." Vespir answered instantly and without fear. Then her face reddened.

"I think that's good," he said.

"Oh." A small smile. "Great." She picked at the tassel on a cushion so that she didn't have to look him in the eye. "She's not like her parents at all. She doesn't care about servants having to look down. Antonia wanted to change the Ikrayina territories, make things easier between the nobility and the common people. Give the people more land for themselves. She said she would if she became Lady Pentri. Maybe it's better that she didn't get called after all." The girl looked to the ceiling, the softness of a smile tracing her lips. "Now she can change things."

Lucian wished he could worship anything or anybody the way this girl did.

"That's good," he said again. Vespir scratched her cheek, her gaze darting here and there.

"Can I ask you something?" She finally looked up. "How'd you get all these scars?"

Lucian started to answer, but a footstep silenced him. Emilia was watching the pair of them, the curtain pushed aside. Her hands were filled with yellow and purple flowers and bits of green. Her lips formed a perfect O of surprise, her eyes fixed squarely on Lucian. Or rather, on his bare upper body.

"Sorry," she squeaked.

Flushing, Lucian grabbed a fresh shirt and yanked it on. "Sorry, I was cleaning up."

"No, no. Your torso is very robust and . . . symmetrical. You should be proud," she said, and hurried to dump the herbs on his table. She began crushing a few yellow flowers and some curled leaves; were her hands shaking? Done, she dropped the

Her life was a blank, clean void.

That realization spiked agony through her soul.

The pain shredded her thoughts as she hurried to make the damn tisane and escape back into the night. Now she trotted down the path, skirts clutched to avoid stumbling. Soon, she came to the edge of the island where the waves sighed over the rocks below. She sat, dangling her feet. To her surprise and delight, the rocks glimmered light blue, clearly defined against the dark water.

Bioluminescent algae.

The thought dulled her awe at once. Every amazing thing in this world had a simple explanation, one that leached away wonder. Emilia could explain everything.

Her headache tightened, and she closed her eyes.

This pain had kept her prisoner for five years. It had denied her kisses and battles alike. If only she didn't have this darkness crawling around inside of her, growing in the fissures of her brain like a fungus. If only she could be normal.

It was all the Chaos House's fault.

Once, this empire had been a loose collection of separate, friendly kingdoms. Once, six Houses had governed those king-doms: the Aurun, the Sabel, the Pentri, the Tiber, the Volscia . . . and the Oretani.

Once, two schools of magic had existed in the world: order and chaos. The orderlies maintained their temple at Delphos with its sleek white marble pillars and cultivated gardens. The chaotics housed themselves in great halls of crystal on the edge of the wild sea, dwelling in Catalenia, the far western territory.

The territory ruled by Lord Cassius Oretani.

While orderlies studied how to put shattered glass back to-gether or how to freeze a butterfly on the wing, chaotics delved into the far reaches of destruction. How to bring fire from air. How to melt flesh and blood. How to destroy a mountain with a wink and a thought.

Lord Oretani had come to believe that chaos was superior to order, and that the world could benefit from its bloody teachings. He and his chaotic magosi had searched the dark heart of chaos and returned from their journey . . . different. More than human. Beautiful, ageless, brilliant, passionate. Cruel beyond measure.

The Chaos House, as Oretani called it, soon believed that all should join in chaos's glory.

Join, or die.

And so the war began, the war between chaos and order, evil and good. The war that saw the Great Dragon, the only dragon in history who could speak the tongue of man, join with the five houses to stop Oretani. As one, they beat back chaos, confining Oretani and his followers to Catalenia. There, the orderlies froze chaos forever, trapped the monsters in stasis like insects in amber.

After that, the study of chaos was forbidden. Chaotics were killed on sight. Any child cursed with chaos's touch was inherently bad.

Emilia had been born evil, and nothing she did would change that.

She breathed and watched the waves. Chaos itched beneath her skin once more.

Still, even though she'd been born bad, she wanted to *choose* good. If she became empress, she could walk back the vendetta against chaotics, try to find a way to heal them of their power, not kill them.

Yes. That at least would give her wasted life some meaning.

She choked on the chaos, felt it bubbling up in her stomach.

Emilia gripped a stone at her side and closed her eyes. Let it out . . . let it destroy the stone . . . Then the pain would stop . . . for a while.

As she waited, her thoughts touched again on Vespir and Lucian. On their discussions of love and pain. And Emilia, barren of those experiences, couldn't help but smile.

Pop.

The magic came out different this time. Less like a sickness she needed to void, and more like a sigh. Emilia realized that she still held the stone in her hand. It hadn't exploded. Lifting it, her mouth fell open.

The stone had transformed from rock into gleaming crystal. Moonlight was slick on the faceted surface.

Transformation. Not destruction.

But . . . how?

"Emilia?" Lucian jogged down the path toward her. She jumped to her feet, hastily dusting herself off. "Why did you run away?"

"I'm. I'm tired," she croaked. For some reason, she hid the stone behind her back.

"Okay." He paused, then drew a few steps nearer. "You did amazingly well today, with the basilisk and Vespir." Was he patronizing her? Emilia had had her fill of people regarding her as some broken toy. "I kind of wish we could team up together more often."

"Well. We can't."

Lucian paused. "I know this won't end happily for all of us. But . . ." He adopted that look she remembered, the open smile, the offered hand. A boy with nothing to hide. "We can at least be friends. Right?"

Emilia felt a tug at her mind, the magic already itching for another release like a greedy child. With a grunt, she turned and flung the rock-turned-crystal out to sea, where it landed with a splash.

"Wrong," she said. "I'm not your enemy, Lucian, but an alliance is impossible." Without another word, she trekked back up the path. He didn't follow. As Emilia neared her room, Chara waiting outside with her tail curled around her taloned feet, she brushed the tears away. It would be so wonderful to sit on cushions and share stories.

If she could do it without killing anyone . . .

You deserve to be alone. You were born to be alone.

And then, the nasty voice in her head began to morph. That cruel voice had always sounded like her own, reminding her how terrible she was. But the hateful words dropped away. The voice became more soothing. More male.

Emilia. The voice spoke her name, and nothing else. *Emilia.*

She whipped around on the path.

"What?" she gasped.

But no one was there. No one but the night.

26

Hyperia

Hyperia did not usually feel nervous, but she also hadn't expected to return home this soon. When the priests announced at breakfast that the Game was about to commence, she could have cheered. Until they explained where exactly the competitors would be going—the Ardennes region.

Home.

She rode Aufidius through the deepening twilight, her gold cloak flapping behind her. As soon as they passed into Volscia territory, soaring above the lush green of the mainland and leaving the ocean behind, her gut cramped.

Aufidius, as if sensing weakness, growled.

Now, with the Volscia central palace growing nearer, gleaming against the foothills like a diamond pinned to a velvet fold of gown, she steadied her breathing. She was going to enter through those doors without Julia to greet her.

We know who's to blame for her absence.

Hyperia's heart beat faster as Aufidius dropped down out of the sky, swooping low for a perfect landing across the rolling lawn. What would her mother say? Hyperia didn't have much affection for her parents—they had actively groomed that emotion out of her. But her mother had loved Julia. Everyone had.

Including me.

The dragons landed one by one on the summer lawn. White-masked figures wearing gold velvet livery stood with torches flickering in hand. Five abreast, the competitors strode together toward the palace's entrance. Hyperia wore a bare-shouldered gown with long, slitted sleeves fastened at her wrist and a billowing skirt of gold cloth trimmed in ivory satin. Pearl-studded gold netting held back her hair. Elaborate curls framed her face.

Ahead, every window and doorway shone with candlelight—Hyperia thought of a thousand gleaming eyes all fixed upon her. Music and laughter crescendoed as they drew nearer. Hyperia walked with a straight back, refusing to search out the places on these grounds where she and Julia had chased each other during games.

Lord Volscia awaited them at the entrance. Despite his jowls and thinning blond hair, she recognized the strong Volscian nose and the imperious brow in herself whenever she gazed into a mirror. Camilla and Petros flanked her lord father. Hyperia's mother was not with them.

Hyperia could understand why she might not be her mother's favorite guest.

"Welcome, competitors," Lord Volscia said. He did not look at Hyperia. "Tonight, my family is honored to administer the great Game, the second challenge in our illustrious Emperor's Trial. We welcome our new emperor, whoever they may be, and salute those four who shall give the ultimate sacrifice to preserve our ordered way of life." With that, he and the priests stood aside and let the competitors through. Vespir stared at her feet. Ajax grinned and waved at the rows of silent servants. Emilia gazed straight ahead, and Lucian brought up the rear. Hyperia stole a moment with her father, while he looked like he'd rather be elsewhere.

"Yes?" he said. Hyperia alternated between wanting to weep

with him and wanting to unsheathe her dagger and pierce his heart. Yes, she had done what she had done, but he had contributed more than simply planting the seed of her inside her mother. He'd nurtured her, tended her, cultivated her like a trellised vine pointed toward a single destination: the dragon throne.

"I won the first challenge." She tried to keep the desperation out of her voice. *See what I've done. Be proud. It's all going according to plan, though we started badly.*

"Mmm. I know." He turned away. "It would be nice for all this to have a point."

That ringing madness began in her ears. "Everything I have ever done has been for you. Including *that*."

"You took away my chance at having an heir," he replied, as detached as if adding up numbers in a ledger. "We might have had another opportunity for the throne in a generation or so. Now my legacy is destroyed. The Volscia holdings will pass to my brother."

Hyperia stilled. If he should hate her, he should hate her because she had removed a beautiful, vibrant, and excellent daughter from his life. Not for this.

"Then I'm sorry for you," she growled. He merely nodded and led the way through the velvet halls of his palace. Hyperia watched as the others were taken aback by the sensory onslaught of a Volscia party.

Their principal family residence, located in the verdant heart of the Ardennes region, had been designed to overstimulate the senses with art. White marble statues of famous riders and swooping dragons occupied recessed alcoves, and frescoes of rich green countryside stretched into the distance in every direction. The red velvet and gold brocade wall hangings whispered at a touch. Soaring arches, polished banisters, chandeliers dripping with diamonds—every detail was designed to exceed the boundaries of opulence. But as beautiful as the carpets, hangings, statues, and paintings were, the sheer size of the palace and its winding halls had often made Hyperia think of some giant beast's intestines. The jagged white molding along the tops of the walls resembled teeth. She sometimes felt she'd grown up in a place poised to devour her.

The competitors passed down a hall of the eastern wing, stopping before the doorway of the "winter" ballroom, as the family called it, crowding together to gaze at its wonders. Mirrors on every wall replicated the swirl of dancers, and crystal chandeliers lent a frosty illumination to the proceedings. Everything within was silver and shimmer. At least two hundred people had congregated there in outfits of platinum and white gold, and the sound of mirth reverberated inside that great glass enclosure. Hyperia realized that every person here, save herself, the other competitors, and her father were masked. Musicians occupied a platform at the far end of the room, and music set the party's pulse.

"Wow," Vespir whispered.

"Not yet, competitors. If you please." Lord Volscia herded them all along, stopping before two large doors. The footmen allowed them through at his signal.

Hyperia knew they were going into the eastern parlor, with its large, floor-to-ceiling latticed windows that looked out onto the rose garden.

Sometimes, she and Julia had crept down here in the early morning to nestle under a blanket and watch the first blush of dawn touch the sleeping rosebuds. It was a moment of peace, before the hell of Hyperia's day would start—

Sentiment is weakness. Pay attention.

She blocked the pain and turned her eyes to the room around them . . . and discovered that this rosy parlor was filled with people.

Not just any people.

"Mother? Father?" Emilia broke the stunned silence first, walking to the Aurun in their purple velvet. The lord and lady greeted their daughter with cool nods; her elder brother (the one Hyperia *should* have been battling) was a bit warmer, enveloping his sister in a hug.

Beside the Aurun, the Sabel family, Lord Sabel and Dido, awaited their scowling competitor. Lucian trudged over, clearly staying out of hugging range. Not that his family seemed inclined to embrace him.

Lord Tiber, the pustulant cretin, and his two wheedling legitimate sons awaited Ajax. The boy strutted over, though none of them had anything to say to the other. Hyperia wouldn't be surprised if Lord Tiber had never spoken with Ajax privately before tonight. He might have even forgotten he'd spawned the boy in the first place.

And . . . Vespir. The servant girl's breath hitched as she found the Pentri family—yes, their daughter, Antonia, included—standing by the window and pointedly avoiding her gaze. Lord Volscia had to *harrumph* and practically force the servant forward. When everyone was surrounded by their respective families, Camilla and Petros appeared from a corner of the room as if by magic. Hyperia's father took his place by her right. She felt the cold absence of her mother to the left.

"Where is she?" Hyperia whispered. Her father didn't reply.

"The Game." Camilla rubbed her palms together, a vulpine grin stretched on her face. "A true emperor must have strength and courage, as evidenced in the Hunt. But the Game." She clucked her tongue. "The art of persuasion. Of anticipating what your opponent may want. Of strategy. Of cunning. Of intuition." She beamed at each one of the five in turn, rotating on her heel. "Politics is one, long imperial Game, and only the most adaptable players will come out on top. Tonight, in this most *splendid* palace, you are invited to a party. There's music, food, dancing, elegant attire, the most beautiful and fascinating people . . . and one goal." Her black eyes glittered. "Petros. Would you do the honors?"

The sullen priest walked to each competitor in turn and handed over a small velvet pouch with a drawstring. Hyperia felt the round outline of something through the covering. At Camilla's nod, everyone untied their pouches and reached inside.

Emilia pulled hers out first: a token the size of a coin. Holding it up to the light, she revealed the purple Aspis, her family's color and dragon, designed upon the silver medallion in pure amethyst. A treasure. Lucian revealed a coin with his family's crest in sapphire, and Ajax took out a ruby pendant. Hyperia reached within, and found . . . two.

Two coins.

Brow furrowed, she emptied the pouch into her hand. The golden Volscia crest and . . . the emerald Pentri.

"I don't understand." She looked at the Pentri family. Lord and Lady Pentri regarded her with tight smiles. Antonia stared at the floor, while Vespir turned her empty bag inside out.

Why had they given Hyperia Vespir's . . .

"Oh." Hyperia felt understanding hot on her spine.

"All of you—well, almost all of you—have begun with your family's token. The goal," Camilla said, ambling around the circle and looking them all in the eye, "will be to collect at least three. Three family tokens. Three families backing you for the throne. The first competitor to capture three wins the Game."

Hyperia understood. Two families would need to abandon their own competitor—their own child. They would have to believe that falling in line behind the next emperor mattered more than blood.

The Pentri hated Vespir, and Hyperia would bet that they had heard of her victory in the Hunt. Lord Volscia gave a discreet cough. So, he'd advocated her position.

She needed only one more family to win this Game. The promise of glory made her fingertips tingle.

Vespir appeared to deflate. Lucian scowled. Emilia pressed the tip of one finger to her lips and gazed at the ceiling. And Ajax, impossible to read, ran the pendant along his fingers as he might a common coin in a gambling den. Camilla went to the five and collected the tokens before gesturing to a table. A black velvet box waited there. Opening it, Camilla showed that every one of their names had been written upon a separate plaque and spaced equally apart. Beneath these plaques, the priests placed the family tokens. Hyperia watched as Petros placed both the Volscia and Pentri crests beneath her name.

Vespir deflated further.

"These will wait until the end of the Game." Camilla closed the lid. "The victor may keep their pendants. Each is worth at least fifty pieces of gold, so they're quite precious. I would recommend thinking *very* carefully about who to approach and how," she said as she and Petros departed for the ballroom.

Hyperia turned to her father as the others shuffled out. "Thank you." She did not hug him or smile. She simply gave what was due.

"The next-best candidate will be the Tiber. They and Pentri often have their affairs bound together." Her father sniffed. "You might take the dragon throne after all."

"Was there ever a doubt in your mind?" She looked over his shoulder. "I'm amazed Mother decided not to come for this."

"Hmm. I may as well tell you now." His voice was flat. "Your mother is dead."

Hyperia felt the words slam against her chest. Hyperia's

mother had never nursed her daughters, hadn't attended Hyperia when she was little and cried in the night. Hyperia had always thought of her as a stranger with whom she shared blood. But even so, Hyperia hadn't expected . . . *this*. Her breath stopped.

"What? How?" she whispered.

His reply was calm: "She hanged herself after Julia."

Hyperia clutched the edge of a table.

"Why didn't you write to me?"

He shrugged. "No one knew where you were. It hardly seemed necessary." Then, "I suppose I should thank you. I can remarry now to a younger bride and provide myself with new heirs. Perhaps this was all for the best." He nodded at the doorway. "I've arranged to meet Tiber in fifteen minutes. Shall we?"

The sounds of the party, the lilting cadence of violins and clink of glasses, washed over Hyperia like a wave on the shore. She barely noticed the other competitors as she took her father's arm. Somewhere, in the distant back of her mind, someone was screaming.

27

Emilia

———◆———

Emilia worked to keep her breathing steady. Her high-collared purple satin dress was tight, hugging the span of her hips and the width of her chest. By her feet, a ruffled train curled like an obedient dog. She'd completely forgotten what it was like to attend a party.

It was *loud*.

While she pressed herself against a wall and let people glide past, she comforted herself with the knowledge that she'd been right.

Emilia had long believed that the Game had something to do with trading favors. If one paid attention to the rise and fall of the five families after every emperor's ascension, a pattern emerged. This world and the people in it were all built on patterns.

With enough information, one could rule an empire.

Emilia had spent hours collecting every scrap of information on every one of the Houses that she could. Learning their weaknesses, their strengths, their hopes and dreams and dirty pleasures. She knew that the Pentri relied upon the Tiber for help in stabilizing the great grasslands. Her own family, the Aurun, had a strong navy and ruled the seas but were poor.

The Volscia hated the Sabel for being the first House to produce an emperor.

Over these past few days she had also taken the pulse of her fellow competitors. She knew what to do.

First: she'd guessed the Pentri would abandon Vespir in favor of Hyperia. Undoubtedly, they wanted an alliance with the Volscia, and their rich land holdings, not to mention Hyperia's triumph in the Hunt. Lord Volscia—Hyperia had a middling head for politics at best—would go to the Tiber next. It was the safest match, since Pentri and Tiber had a longstanding alliance.

She'd have to push a little on that.

Emilia sidled up to Lysander of the Tiber as he and his father and brother made their way from the parlor. Ajax had already disappeared. Clever boy. He knew there was nothing for him with these wretches.

"Yeah?" Lysander barely glanced at her. Emilia smirked. She may have been isolated for five years, but she could read the signals of people's bodies with startling accuracy. Men did not turn to her the way they did to Hyperia. Ah well. Sometimes the girl neglected in the corner could do the greatest damage.

"You all must be glad the Game is at the Volscia estate."

"Uh. Sure. Great wine, I guess," he grunted, scratching his ear. Classic hallmark of the Tiber: lazy, ignorant, pedestrian. Emilia's stomach curdled to be around them.

"The women of the Ardennes region are the most beautiful in the empire. Don't you find?" she continued. They passed by the open ballroom door as she said this and stopped to gaze at the finery—and the choice beauties—on display within. Emilia's tongue curled as Lysander's gaze slackened. He practically licked his chapped lips.

"Mmm. Yeah. True." Lysander left her then, but the seed had been planted.

Satisfied, Emilia sought out the others. She knew she had

her House's backing. She'd have liked to try for the Sabel, but Lord Sabel was devoted to his children. Besides, she couldn't bring herself to steal Lucian's family. With the clear, mechanical ticking of her mind, she knew that Volscia would never budge from his daughter. His pride, if nothing else, wouldn't allow it.

So Emilia needed Tiber and Pentri. She'd taken her first shot at the former. Now, to soften the latter.

She found Vespir pressed against the wall as well. The servant girl wore a distant look, her chin tilted upward. She appeared to have resigned herself to losing already. Emilia couldn't help feeling a wrinkle of sympathy.

"I hate this sort of thing," she muttered.

"I used to like parties." Vespir sighed. "I'd hang out in the aerie the whole night with the other nobles' dragons. Afterward I'd go down to the kitchens for a dice game, and there'd be all this cake and wine left over."

"Games *and* cake? That sounds perfect." Emilia cleared her throat. "You know what I think you should do?"

"What?" Vespir frowned.

"Servants love to gossip, yes? I'll wager someone who works here can give you all of the most scandalous stories on the Volscia." She waited to see if Vespir would connect the dots, but the other girl said nothing. "Maybe you can get Lord and Lady Pentri on your side if they think Hyperia's . . . well—"

"Deadly?" Vespir gave a muted laugh and plucked at her sleeves. She wasn't wearing a dress like Hyperia and Emilia. She'd been outfitted in a suit of green silk, a forest-green velvet cape slung fashionably across one shoulder, and looked as refined as a true nobleman. "If it's such a good idea, why not go talk to the servants yourself?" Vespir looked askance.

Huh. Emilia hadn't expected her to be so untrusting. She rather liked a challenge.

In this regard, at least, Emilia and Hyperia were alike.

Emilia shrugged. "They'll respond better to you. Besides." She tried smiling naturally. She'd been practicing. "I don't want Hyperia to win."

Vespir huffed. "Yeah. I think a rabid mongoose would be a better choice."

Emilia laughed and clapped a hand to her mouth. She wasn't used to hearing laughter, much less her own. It'd take some adjustment.

"Good luck," Emilia said. Somehow, she found that she meant it.

"Thanks." Vespir nudged her elbow. "Good luck to you, too." The girl walked away. Emilia watched the retreating figure, trying to read the signs. Would Vespir listen to her? Or would she take more persuading?

As Vespir passed a servant in gold livery, she halted, did a heel turn, and followed close after the girl.

Emilia pressed the back of her head to the wall and smiled as the party spun around her. She'd toppled the first two dominoes. For now, all she could do was watch the rest fall.

28
Hyperia

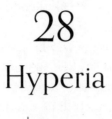

Hyperia sat as an empress should, with her back straight and a room of supplicant men fanned out around her. Lord Tiber, looking particularly mangy with his unkempt gray hair and bloodshot eyes, leered at her from his chair. His sons, Lysander and Demetrius, flanked him, looking vacant. Perhaps, rat though he was, Ajax *had* been the superior choice.

She didn't know where the little bastard had got to and didn't care.

Her father sat beside Tiber, giving the appearance of doing as little as possible.

"I'll cut to the point." Hyperia smoothed her skirts. "Withdraw your support from Ajax and give it to me."

Tiber puckered his lips. They were uncomfortably moist. "That's not especially convincing," he said. His two sons snickered.

"I triumphed in the first challenge, and I've started the second with two Houses backing me. Join now, and you'll have a friend on the dragon throne."

"You know, the last emperor was my older brother." Tiber grinned; his teeth were edged in gray. "Didn't give me any extra money or land or power, but I *did* get a new she-goat at every midwinter festival." Tiber sniffed, blew his nose in a handkerchief. He licked his lips with a swollen-looking tongue. "So, how are you going to sweeten my pot?"

Hyperia did not like the way he stared, nor the way his two idiot sons continued to snicker. But her father's eyes flashed a warning. Pursing her lips, she thought.

"More imperial troops will be sent to the northeast territories, to aid you in the fight for expansion. Once you take those lands, you'll be warden and their resources will be yours—"

"Nope." Tiber grinned. "Same old routine. My people fight those Wikingar dogs morning to night, long winter to long winter, but the fight never stops. More troops won't solve it. We don't have the Aurun ships or the Sabel trade or the Volscia fields or the Pentri population. We got mountains and snow and tired-looking women." Tiber's tongue peeked out from between his teeth. "My son was just telling me how *sweet* the Ardennes girls look. I'm inclined to agree. But you." He oozed to the edge of his chair. "You are by far the sweetest thing I've seen in some time. Huh, boys?" He waggled his eyebrows at his sons. "Nice, fresh little peach."

Hyperia's entire world seemed to drop away. She felt . . . exposed . . . lessened beneath this awful man's gaze. Drawing herself up, noticing her father's frantic eye movements all but ordering her to *remain calm,* Hyperia struggled with words.

"What. Are you. Suggesting?" she said through her teeth.

"Well." Tiber patted his knee, summoning her to perch. "I give a little, you give a little."

Lord Volscia became interested in the carpet's weave.

It would have been wise to, if not give in to his horrible idea, at least gently rebuff it. But all of Hyperia's blood revolted at this unwashed creature with his lewd, disgusting . . .

She shot to her feet in golden fury.

"A dragon does not give itself to a pig!"

Tiber's lip curled, baring his gray teeth. She wanted to cut him from ear to ear in a wide, bloody grin. Lord Volscia, meanwhile, cleared his throat and leaned closer to Tiber. He had seen this cancerous toad *proposition* her, and his inclination was to . . . to soothe him. Hyperia felt as if every inch of her were rotting away.

"So I'm a pig, am I?" the old man grunted.

"Perhaps the women of the Ardennes region might tempt you in my daughter's place?" her father said, all but falling to his knees with pleading. "How many would serve, do you think?"

"Father." Hyperia felt the blood leave her face. The women of her region, paid like a sack of potatoes to this . . .

"Mmm. They *are* the prettiest."

"I told you, Father," Lysander said, eyeing Hyperia as though she were hysterical. "They're quite . . . luscious."

Like fruit to be savored with one awful bite.

"All right, missy." *Missy.* His watery eyes tracked her form. "You're a sweet, tight little piece I'm sorry to be missing out on, but if you're willing to part with, say, twenty-five noble little ladies—you can throw some peasants in there, I'm not particular—I think we can come to an arrangement right here." The wet curl of his lips . . . the bleary shine of his eyes . . . the bobbing, excitable little monsters crouched behind him, probably waiting their turn at his leftovers . . .

Hyperia smiled. The men relaxed. At last, she was behaving like a good girl.

"My lord Tiber." She took his veiny, rough hand in hers and patted it. Then, she dug her fingernails into his palm. The man lurched forward, but couldn't extricate himself from her grip. She'd spent her childhood grappling, handling spears and the hilts of swords, climbing rung over rung to reach far-off pinnacles. Her hands were strong. This man had weakened himself on honor's dregs. "When I become empress, I will have my imperial guard sent to Wroclawia. When they arrive at your palace they will strip you naked, bind your hands, and force you to parade through the streets."

"Hey!" Lysander shouted. She gave one searing look, and he fell silent. So did Demetrius. Her father fumbled with apologies while she continued.

"I will have you walk until you finally reach Dragonspire. It's a distance of—what?—a thousand miles? More?" Her finger-nails drew blood. "I'll have them take the side roads."

"You—"

She grabbed his jaw and squeezed. His lips puckered, his veiny eyes bulged. He would never have anticipated this, be-cause he was a fool. He did not know that a girl's anger was her greatest weapon when handled with authority. Hyperia con-tinued.

"Once you have knelt before me and apologized, you will walk bloody-footed and naked into the Ardennes region, where I will line up every single woman and girl, from courtier to peas-ant. I'll have them walk through mud and rain and pig shit, so that all of the hems of their garments are sodden with filth, all so that you can get onto your worthless knees and kiss the hem of every. Single. One." She brought her nose to Tiber's; in his eyes, she saw the panic of a sow at slaughter. "And with every kiss, you will beg their forgiveness for entertaining the thought that a disease such as yourself could be worthy of touching them upon the shoulder, let alone . . ." She did not voice the un-savory thought. Sneering, she shoved Tiber backward. His chair nearly tipped over, and his sons scrambled to right him. Her father was on his feet now, but she paid him no mind. "So take that filthy slug between your legs and your ill-gotten spawn, and if you approach me again, by the blue above I will gut you." Her fists tightened by her side. "Do you understand, my *lord?*"

"Y-you . . . you can't," Demetrius choked.

Hyperia drew her sword in one seamless movement. The young men cowered behind their father's seat.

"I will have your balls on my mantel if you speak again," she said. Sheathing her weapon, Hyperia turned and strode out the door without a backward glance. Her blood thundered as she headed toward the bright cacophony of the ball.

She would find some other way. All she needed was Aurun or Sabel, and if she explained her right to victory—

"What have you done?" Her father grabbed her from behind, his eyes frenzied. "One word. We'd have taken the second challenge with *one word,* Hyperia."

"That man is trash whose mere presence degrades the dragon throne."

"If he goes, he can take Pentri with him, you fool!"

Fool. Hyperia flinched as memories flooded her, slaps, curses, cuffings, beatings with a silk cord so that her flesh should not be marred, because an empress must be pretty as well as strong—

"Do not speak so to me," she growled. She shook his hand from her shoulder.

"Tiber has the Pentri in his grasp. You must return and beg his forgiveness."

"I will never beg that bastard for anything." She narrowed her eyes. "When I am empress—"

"You won't be empress without me, you imbecile!" Spittle flew from his lips. Hyperia grew still as her father wiped a hand down his face. "Now more than ever, I regret your sister's death. He might have taken her for one quick spin and saved us all this trouble—"

Bam. Hyperia threw her father against the wall, her forearm pinning his neck. She pushed, choking him. His eyes widened as she stuck a knee between his legs, mashing his balls as well. Trembling, she bared her teeth in his face.

Julia. Julia, my beauty, my baby, my innocent.

At least I saved you from him.

"When I am on the dragon throne," she said, her voice as smooth as smoke, "I will have your head."

She left him choking in the hall. Hyperia did not listen to the sounds of the party. She took the main staircase to the second floor, and padded down to her sister's old chamber. Her mind dull, her hands shaking, she regained herself while standing in the center of Julia's bedroom, the gold-quilted bed immaculately made, the papers spilled across Julia's desk as colorful and untidy as she had been. Hyperia choked on a smile as she leafed through her sister's sketches and water paints. Pictures of Gus, Julia's tabby cat, of a sunrise on the vineyards, of Minerva while she slept . . .

Of Hyperia. The drawing was incomplete, the lines articulating her features blurred and half-erased. Julia might have been painting it as a remembrance, for when Hyperia became empress . . .

She stifled a sob and knelt on the floor, breathing fire from her lungs. Vision doubling, she recalled being eleven and perched at the edge of a gilded dining-room chair. Sitting before her father, her shoulders could never slope. A bone-china plate bearing the Volscia seal held a slice of yellow cake topped with cream. Hyperia had rarely been allowed sweets. Her father told her to eat. An order.

The cake tasted of lemon and butter . . . and of something dank with mold. When she tried to spit it out, he slapped her, blood mingling with pastry. She ate the entire thing, and then vomited in the lap of her pale yellow gown. Whimpering, she begged to leave the table. No. She must adapt herself to different poisons. An empress lived under constant threat. Even when she voided blood, her father wouldn't let her leave. Her shoulders must never slope.

Hyperia had sat down to the same dessert over and over, stuffed with different fungi and poison. She'd done so until her body was immune to all strains of death, and she hated sweet things.

Hyperia neatened the paintings on Julia's desk and tore up her own unfinished image.

29

Vespir

———————

Vespir knelt before the Pentri, eyes fixed on their silken shoes. Antonia hovered nearby, still wearing that scent of honeysuckle and peach blossom. Vespir closed her eyes. To be this near Antonia again was worth . . .

Everything. Including this awful meeting.

"Say what you've come to say," Lord Pentri barked. Honestly, even getting this audience with him had seemed impossible. A thought nagged at Vespir: maybe they'd agreed in order to have one last opportunity to kick in her teeth.

They couldn't have chosen a more perfect room. The curtains were of forest-green velvet, the moldings along the ceiling crafted to resemble bursts of wildflowers, while the carpet depicted a brilliant silk sky studded with clouds. The world upside-down: Vespir's life encapsulated.

"My lord, I've heard whispers from the Volscia servants." Vespir's voice shook. Yes, that girl carrying the tray of glasses had been more than happy to assist a competitor, particularly one raised up from the peasantry. In fact, the servant had snuck Vespir downstairs, where maids and footmen and kitchen girls offered her a thimble of cherry brandy, snuck from the cook when her back was turned. That brought memories of her former life flooding back. For the first time in days, Vespir had felt her spine relax. This was *her* type of party and people.

And the servants had been only too willing to discuss the secrets of their masters.

Vespir had expected something bad. She had not been prepared for what she heard.

"My lord, you know what a pit worm is?" Vespir did not dare look up. Lord Pentri snorted.

"A dragon that hatches with no rider present," he grumbled. At least he was humoring her.

Vespir had heard tales of such unfortunate dragons. They were wild, insane, raised in the bowels of the underground to avoid mishaps. Chained, baited, they grew increasingly mad until they were used as training for a proper dragon. Pit worms were thrown into an arena against a ridered mount as tests for dracomachia. Dragon battle.

The pit worms never came out alive, one small mercy in an otherwise brutal life.

"My lord and lady, Hyperia of the Volscia is . . . is a golden Hydra who was raised like a pit worm." Vespir worried her lip. "I've heard stories of what her parents did to her. They made her stand outside in the snow for an entire night because she disagreed with them at supper. They had her kill her own dog with a bow and arrow when she was ten years old because they thought it would teach her to take even the most difficult shots." Vespir's eyes stung with tears. She hadn't expected ever to feel sympathy for someone like Hyperia of the Volscia.

"We know that the Volscia have an investment in their daughter," Lady Pentri said.

Vespir clenched her jaw. "You know that she killed her own sister to be called to the Trial, then?"

"Some sacrifices are necessary in order to rule. Truly, I'm only sorry such a measure didn't occur to *others*."

Antonia moved a bit closer, and Vespir longed to diminish the distance between them.

"It's more than that. Hyperia has whipped servants for the smallest mistakes. She put one nine-year-old chambermaid through a window for spilling lamp oil on her sister's favorite gown." Vespir had met the girl, now twelve. The scars were still written on her cheeks and wrists.

"Perhaps it's a good method for dealing with wayward servants," Lady Pentri said, voice dripping acid. Vespir's eye twitched.

"She threatened Lord Tiber's life," Vespir muttered. Finally, that shut the Pentri up. Vespir had been below stairs when a servant burst in breathless with the news. She'd been eavesdropping on Hyperia's audience with the Tiber family, and had watched as Hyperia threw her own father to the wall and threatened him. She'd described the "madness" in the girl's expression. Vespir prayed to the blue above that she never find herself on the receiving end of such a vengeful glance.

This time, no snide comments followed Vespir's tale.

"How can we be sure it's not a lie?" Lord Pentri grunted.

"My lord, you may ask Lord Tiber. I'm sure he'll have something to say." Vespir clasped her hands before her breast. "I never wanted to be called to the Emperor's Trial, and I don't want the throne. All I've ever wanted since Karina's egg hatched was to be your servant." A lie, but close enough to the truth. "Please. Help me. If—if you do and I somehow manage to take the throne, I'll—" She swallowed, trying to unstick her words. "I'll give up the throne to Ant—to Lady Antonia. I swear it." She bowed her head to the carpet. "I've served you for many years, haven't I? I could still serve you now."

Her heart trammeled wildly as Lord Pentri walked to her. She saw the toes of his shoes.

"What is your family name, girl?" he asked.

"Um. Lutum, sir." Vespir Lutum. *Lutum* was the Latium, the imperial tongue, for *dirt,* assigned randomly to her family long ago when the empire came to the grasslands. Vespir had always envied the Caelums next door—the Skys.

"Vespir Dirt." Lord Pentri nudged her forehead with the toe of his shoe. Vespir's eyes watered. "A family of the dragon does not make deals with *dirt,*" he spat.

Vespir flinched, waiting for the kick that did not come. His words hurt worse.

"You took an egg from our rookery. You were gifted a place in the sky for all eternity, a nothing such as yourself, and in return you stole from us."

"Not on purpose!" she cried.

"You stole our daughter. Filth like you placed your grubby hands on her. Peasant trash." He placed his foot on the back of her head and pressed. Vespir made a frightened noise.

"Father, stop it!" Antonia cried. He pressed harder.

"You took her place in the Trial. Death is too good for such thieving scum." He removed his foot and bent low to her ear. "I only regret wasting a dragon upon a maggot like you. You, make deals with *me*? Be given *my* family crest? Never." He spat in her hair. Bile flooded the back of Vespir's throat.

"Get away from her!" Antonia was crying now. Tears flooded Vespir's eyes as well. She thought of Tavi's weeping face as the door closed between them forever.

"What about what you took from *me*?" she snarled. Lord Pentri gripped her hair and lifted her head. Vespir caught a flash of the lord's black eyes and furrowed brows before he slapped her across the face.

"Stop it!" Antonia pulled her father away, and Lord Pentri rounded on her while Vespir's vision shook.

"You could have had any noblewoman in our territory, and you chose filth like this? You're an embarrassment," he hissed.

Vespir struggled to her feet, ready to fight him for those awful words. Instead, Antonia shoved her father. Lady Pentri gasped in outrage.

"You're the embarrassment, not me!" Antonia howled. Vespir was numb with shock as the Pentri girl ushered her parents from the room. The family's heated argument grew muffled, and the door shut. Vespir wiped the spit from her hair and centered herself as Antonia came back to her in tears, on a cloud of perfume. And then . . . and then . . .

"I'm so sorry." Antonia looked up at her, a tear tracking down her cheek. The candlelight turned the tear into a gleaming ribbon.

"So am I," Vespir croaked. She did not look down. She did not wait for Antonia to make the first move.

This moment, them alone together, was the only thing in this world that Vespir wanted any longer.

She stepped close and cupped the girl's face. She wiped Antonia's tears away with her thumb. Then they were kissing, Antonia's lips soft as silk.

She clutched at Vespir's shoulders, gasped when Vespir's tongue stroked against hers. Vespir was all fire now, all light with this girl in her arms. She trailed kisses along Antonia's neck. Antonia gave soft, breathy utterances as Vespir pressed kisses to her pulse and then returned to her luscious mouth. Their kiss deepened, the world falling away around them.

Contentment settled in Vespir's chest. This was her one wish. Let the Pentri see how much their daughter loved being kissed like this.

She'd begun this embrace hot with fury, kissing Antonia as

much out of spite as desire. But the more they kissed, the more that pain evaporated. The more they kissed, the more Vespir felt as she had at twelve when hiding in the aerie rafters, still weepy after being forced from home. She'd spied on Antonia playing with her dragon hatchling, giggling when the little creature butted its head against her velvet-clad knee. Vespir had forgotten home in that moment; she'd watched a beam of sunlight halo Antonia's dark hair. Bracelets of amethyst and white jade circled the girl's slender wrists, clacking merrily as she waved her hands. Vespir's body felt full just looking at her.

Tasting her own pulse, Vespir experienced a revelation. The Pentri heir was not a goddess, but a girl.

And a few brief days ago, when they'd been exercising their dragons down by the river, Antonia had lain beside Vespir on the clay banks with the tall reeds sheltering them, and kissed her. If such a divine girl could love a nothing like her, Vespir thought, then maybe she was worthwhile.

"Vespir. Vespir." Antonia peppered kisses on her lips, but then pulled away. She put a hand to Vespir's cheek. Tears welled in her eyes once more. "I'm . . . I'm sorry."

"It's not your fault." Vespir stroked Antonia's hair, fingered the amethyst pendants dangling from her ears. "We don't need to worry anymore. They can't do anything to us now." She froze with a sudden thought. "Unless they've been hurting you?"

Antonia smiled, wiped her eyes, and shook her head.

"No. If anything, *I've* been terrorizing *them*. My parents tried to discipline me, but they just can't manage it. They never could. I'm their only baby, after all." Yes, Lady Pentri had delivered five stillborn children after Antonia. Every year, Antonia's birthday was the cause of massive celebration throughout the Ikrayina.

Well, Vespir thought that much celebration was only fair. It was Antonia, after all.

"So you've been yelling at them?" Vespir grinned in return.

"If they so much as mutter your name, I start a lecture. Father eventually had to go flying to get away from me. I trailed him all the way to the aerie."

"I wouldn't want you as my enemy." Vespir stroked Antonia's hair.

"No. I make a much better friend, it's true."

"Oh? Just a friend?" Vespir mock-pouted, then leaned in for another kiss. When it was only the two of them, Antonia and her, Vespir forgot to be afraid. Every tiny thing became a secret shared, another link in the golden chain that bound them together.

But Antonia turned her face from the kiss, so that Vespir's lips only brushed her cheek. The girl stepped away.

"I'll keep praying for you. I'll never give up hope." Antonia settled her shoulders. She sounded earnest, but . . . distant.

What?

"Well, that's nice of you," Vespir muttered, slow with surprise. When she advanced, Antonia retreated. A tremor passed through her body. Antonia was . . . pulling away. Antonia, the sole bright, unwavering spot Vespir had been moving toward since the calling, flickered. The nearer that light came to going out, the more Vespir craved it. "Come here." Vespir held out her arms. Antonia did not come.

"I can't," she whispered. "Every second I'm with you they'll get madder. They could try turning more Houses against you."

What a joke. Every other House looked down upon Vespir because of her birth. They were as turned away as it was possible to get. Vespir swallowed, thought back to Antonia's words in the Pentri aerie on the day of the calling. They'd filled Vespir with such fire. Vespir held up her head, repeated those words now.

"If I know you're waiting for me, I'll take the throne." She said it with determination. "I'm coming back for you."

"Oh. Of course." Antonia tried smiling.

All of Vespir's courage collapsed.

"You . . . you believe I will, don't you?"

"Yes. Yes, I do." She was trying so, so hard to lie well.

She was failing.

Stunned, Vespir understood. This had to look hopeless, didn't it? She'd lost the first challenge and was undoubtedly going to lose this one as well. Maybe she had a chance at the Race, but her dragon was the smallest. Size mattered. The fourth challenge, the Truth? What in the depths was that supposed to be? Vespir had no family connections, no book learning, no battle strategy. She had love—love for her dragon, for Antonia . . .

Love had nothing to do with victory.

Antonia would likely never see her again after tonight. She was . . .

She was trying to lessen the pain.

"All right." Vespir fought to remain still. The world tilted around her as she said, "You should go. My lady."

Antonia's chin trembled at Vespir's cool tone, and she buried her face in her hands. No, Vespir couldn't watch her cry. She'd do any wild thing if Antonia would only smile. When Vespir took her wrists, Antonia raised her tear-swollen face one last time. They looked in each other's eyes, the same way they had when they were thirteen and Antonia had decided that they should. *Just in private, of course,* she'd said. *So we can be friends.* To Vespir, it'd been like receiving a priceless gift.

"I love you," Antonia whispered. She raced out the door, leaving Vespir alone.

Alone again.

Vespir had been forced to trade her family for a dragon. Now she'd be forced to trade love and her dragon both for . . . nothing.

She was the empress of losers.

Vespir fell to her knees and sobbed.

No one came to check on her.

30

Lucian

Lucian felt the music in his fingertips as he stood against the ballroom's far wall, ignoring the flurry of dancers in favor of the musicians. As a boy, when swordplay was finished, he would be instructed by his music tutor in the finer points of lute-playing and the dove-pipe. Lucian had spent joyful autumn evenings beside the desert garden noodling with his own compositions.

The memory was all that could make him homesick now.

"What are you thinking?" Emilia appeared beside him. She had a habit of popping up and vanishing. She'd fetched two flutes of sparkling wine from a server and handed one to him. Lucian stared disapprovingly into the glass. The Sacred Brothers didn't ban alcohol, but it was frowned upon.

"I'm thinking . . ." He sighed as he gazed down at her pale, upturned face. *You're impossible to keep up with,* he wanted to say. First, she emphatically told him they couldn't be friendly and ran away, and now she showed up to have a drink and a chat.

Ah well. No need to chase her off.

"I'm thinking . . . that Ajax seems to be having a bad night."

The Tiber boy stormed along the edges of the ballroom, a dab of crimson amid the silver sea. His scowl was evident from fifty feet away. Wherever he went, looks traveled in his wake, along with smirks. Lucian imagined that Ajax had been shut out of the Houses thus far.

Undoubtedly, they'd dismissed him for his birth, his height, his age.

They love to run our lives based upon the things we can't control.

"Poor boy." Emilia frowned. "Even I've overlooked him. I made no notes."

"Notes?"

"Er. Cheers." She clinked glasses.

"I'm not sure I should drink this," he said. Not to be rude, but . . .

"Please. To being . . . friends." She smiled up at him, her shoulders hunching with shyness.

Lucian raised an eyebrow. "Friends? You had a pretty different attitude last night."

"It's been a difficult few days. I'm not always cognizant of my true feelings." How could he argue with that? Emilia gave a small smile. "I'm merely glad we don't hate each other."

All the warmth of their years together washed back over him.

"I could never hate you, Emilia," Lucian said, and drank. The wine was crisp, a trace of apples and elderflowers amid the spark of alcohol. It warmed his gut instantly. Emilia watched him over the rim of her own drink as Lucian looked back to the ballroom floor. Some of these people he recalled from his family's trade dealings. There were Lord Marcellus and his lady, who owned many of the vineyards along the southern Ardennes coast; Beckert, the northern merchant making a name for himself in timber, was dancing with his husband; even the Honorable Favonia, an eccentric old woman with marble quarries to spare, was seated by the edge of the ballroom and deep into a cup of wine, fluttering a fan resplendent with massive ostrich feathers and chortling at a joke nobody had made.

The sight of them enjoying themselves, not a thought given to what was outside these golden walls, made Lucian sick.

"It's crowded in here," he muttered. "Want to step outside?"

"All right," Emilia said after a moment's hesitation. Draining their glasses, they shuffled through the crowd of dancers and made for a pair of latticed windows by the side of the room. They emerged onto a balcony open to the night air, sweet with jasmine. The sky was a tapestry of stars. Lucian exhaled in relief and tugged at his collar. He hadn't realized how damn warm it had gotten in there. Side by side, Emilia and he stared onto the moon-silvered lawn.

Lucian glanced at the girl. She was rubbing her arms with the night's chill, but she appeared distant.

"Cold?" he asked.

"Mmm."

He unclasped his blue velvet cape and slung it around her shoulders. Emilia started, but wrapped the thing close.

"You're warm. Thank you." She huddled, an island unto herself.

"Emilia?" He had to ask. "Did something happen to you?" She didn't respond in any way, only kept her gaze on the rolling lawn. "I should've written."

"You couldn't have helped," she said softly.

So. Something *had* happened.

"What was it?"

"I got a little sick," she muttered, and shrugged.

"If there's anything you want to tell me, you can."

Finally, she looked at him, her white fingers playing at the edge of his cloak.

"You've always been good, Lucian." She spoke with such

simplicity—as if his goodness were as indisputable a fact as gravity. Lucian wanted to correct her. *You're wrong. Goodness doesn't exist. Only power, and guilt.*

But he didn't want to argue. Instead, they glanced at the sky, much as they had as children. He remembered summer nights sprawled out on the Aurun castle lawn, naming constellations and speculating about which stars were the dragons of old and their heroic riders.

That was the end and glory of a rider: to die, be eaten by your dragon, and then fly up to the firmament to live in eternal glory.

Glory. Heroes. Lucian's mouth quirked, and he laughed.

"What?" Emilia sounded baffled.

"Remember this?" Clearing his throat, he spoke in a deep voice. *"Upon the waves the boat did sail, a storm's embrace uproarious / Did soon allow Lord Lucian to demonstrate valor glorious."* Chuckling, he looked at her.

Recognition lit her eyes. Her mouth twitched. "'The Ballad of Lord Lucian and the Adventure of the *Petunia*.' How could I forget?"

When they were ten, Lucian, Dido, and Emilia had all gone boating by themselves without telling her parents, stealing a schooner called the *Petunia*. At sea, a sudden squall had nearly capsized the boat, and only Lucian's clear head had allowed them to make it back to the harbor. Though they'd all been soundly punished, Emilia's parents begrudgingly allowed her to present her epic fifteen-page poem (with illustrations) detailing Lucian's heroism at dinner. Emilia had taken certain liberties—Lucian hadn't fought a sea serpent, and the Great Dragon Himself hadn't come down out of the sky to bless the children with His wisdom—but it had captured the spirit of the experience.

"Oh, it's the greatest thing I've ever read." Lucian grinned.

He was so happy right now; the stars above appeared to smile back upon him. "That epic poem on the sack of Troia doesn't give nearly as much loving detail."

"Or bizarre rhymes." Emilia giggled, rubbing her forehead. "Did I really try to pair *unctuous* with *punches*?"

Lucian tilted his head back and laughed. He loved laughing! What a perfect night.

"When I was on campaign, I'd pull out the copy you gave me and read it." Even memories of warfare could not hurt him now. "Your writing made me feel . . ." He searched for the right word. "Heroic."

"I'm sorry." Emilia touched his arm. He felt the touch like lightning. "Sorry that you didn't have anything better to read."

"Something I didn't realize until this Trial started." Lucian rubbed his face; spots were whirling in his vision now. He staggered, but Emilia supported him. "I *want* to feel heroic again."

Emilia put a hand to his chest to help steady him. Lucian kept his arm hooked around her shoulders. It felt good to hug her again. Good to be friends. She was softer than he'd remembered, wonderfully so. Her hair smelled like rose petals.

"Thanks, Emi." He slurred her old childhood nickname. "Sorry to, ah, lean on you."

"No. I'm the one who's sorry." She sighed.

She had nothing to be sorry for, because she was so good and sweet and kind and smart and . . . and . . .

The bushes rustled, and Ajax popped up between them. He crawled onto the balcony, while Lucian threw himself backward with a curse.

"Where did you come from?" Lucian snapped.

"Uh, the hedge. Obviously." Ajax scowled, brushed fallen leaves from his jacket, and traipsed around the balcony, arms out in a balancing act. When the boy came to a trellis overgrown with ivy, he shook it, made sure it'd hold, and started climbing the damn thing.

"Where are you going?" Lucian demanded, unsteady on his feet. Ajax glanced over his shoulder.

"Uh, upstairs. Obviously." He scoffed. "Ease up on the wine, pal. How many have you had?"

"Just *one!*" Lucian shouted as the kid hopped onto the balcony above them and went on his merry way.

"Why can't he use the stairs?" Emilia asked quietly.

"There are so many mysteries in this world." On impulse, Lucian grabbed her and hugged her to him. "You can keep th'cloak," he murmured, bending to whisper in her ear. Her hair tickled his cheek. "Stay warm. I'm, um, so glad we're friends."

"Me too." Emilia sighed. Lucian grinned.

"Imma go talk to my father now." Lucian's tongue was clumsy, his balance off-kilter as he released Emilia. Ajax had a point. How could he be *this* tipsy after only one glass of wine? Perhaps he hadn't eaten enough. "Wait here. By hedge. This will be our secret hedge."

"Lucian." Emilia clutched his arm to steady him. "I'm . . . I'm really sorry."

Sorry he was making a colossal ass of himself? Ah well. To get through this night, he'd be as ass as possible. *As ass as.* He tried not to laugh as he strode back into the ballroom and through the sea of dancers, tripping over boots while he bungled to the exit. Grumbles littered behind him as he crashed into the hall, feeling rather wonderful. Screw all of them.

"What are you *doing?*" Lord Sabel wore an expression of horror on his oddly out-of-focus face. "Did everyone see you like this?"

Lucian blinked. He didn't remember getting to his family's sitting chamber. Every one of the five families had been given a parlor of their own, a private place to deal with the competitors. Lucian rubbed a fist into his eye. Why did his father appear so blurry?

"I had *one* drink." He put all his effort into not slurring his words and accidentally missed the chair when he sat down. Sprawled on the floor with an *oof*, Lucian scowled at his father and sister, who wore matched looks of disapproval.

"Good. On top of being a coward, you're a lightweight," Dido grumbled. She was wearing a cerulean gown in the Karthagon style, one shoulder bare, a slit in the skirt up to her knee. Her broad shoulders pulled back as she glared at him. Lucian glimpsed that jeweled dagger hilt at her side.

"Coward? *You're* the one who's afraid to pull a knife, Dido," he growled, though he took her hand to help him up. Sneering, she got in his face.

"Believe me, if it weren't for Father, I'd have followed Hyperia's lead! She at least knows how to get what she wants."

"Seems about right." He bared his teeth. "We all know you don't have any qualms about killing children."

Fury lit her copper eyes as Lucian wavered on his feet, and he wondered how exactly he'd gotten to this room and why, no matter what, he and Dido always seemed ready to do battle.

"Stop it, both of you!" their father boomed. The twins didn't listen.

"This is what I hate about you most," Dido snarled. "You act like you're the only one who ever felt pain in your life! My grief for Mother could never match *yours*. I had to keep twice as calm on the battlefield because *you* were always falling to pieces." Dido sneered. "I wish I could be weak like you."

"I'm sorry you see repentance as weak, Di." He stepped toward her . . . and tripped. His father put Lucian's arm around his shoulders.

"Why are you here, son?" The worst part was how tired his father sounded. Tired, yet gentle.

That hurt worse than any blade.

"Suppose I felt good and wanted to spend time in the warm embrace of my family." He shook his father off. "Foolish idea."

"What have you done to build relations with the other Houses? What is your strategy?" His father now sounded strained.

Strategies. Alliances. Give something, get something, sell a piece of yourself to move ahead. Destroy whatever you needed to—whomever you must—to win that prize. That was all that he should focus upon, wasn't it? The win. The kill.

It made Lucian wish he were drunker.

"Nothing," Lucian muttered. Dido swore and sat down hard on a couch. She was done with him. Hector rubbed his forehead.

"The first thing we'll do is reach out to the Aurun. Castor was always so fond of you when you were a boy—"

"That's Emilia's family!" Lucian loomed over his father. He was not afraid to use his height in order to make a point. "We won't steal her parents out from under her. Father, I thought you liked Emilia."

"I care for Emilia tremendously." His father placed a hand in the crook of Lucian's elbow. It was tender, that touch. "But our options are limited. We'll never budge the Volscia, and the Pentri hate us on principle because of your mother." At the mere mention of his wife, Hector's voice faltered. "You have such potential, Lucian. You could win this on your war record alone—"

Lucian sat down hard on the couch. His father knelt beside him.

"I committed atrocities. *We* did." He glared at his father's kindly face. "I won't take pride in that."

Hector sighed. "I will never abandon hope of you, Lucian."

Hope. Even when his father had locked him in a cell, admonished him before the whole camp, that hope had remained. Lucian had been forced to listen to his father's muffled cries afterward in his tent. Hector couldn't bear to punish his children, but he would never shirk duty. Not even for their sake.

"And I will never forgive you," Lucian grunted. He felt raw.

"How dare you?" Dido snapped, but Lucian's father held up his hand. He smiled.

"That doesn't matter, because I love you, my son." His father bowed his head, the copper-gold braid of Sabel hair slipping over his shoulder. "No matter how much you hurt me, my love will never change."

Lucian remembered standing in the snow, the world on fire around him. Back then, Hector's eyes had also been sad and loving. Lucian gripped his father's shoulder and whispered in his ear, "You're the best man I've ever known, Father." He gritted his teeth. "That's why it hurts that you're the worst, as well."

31

Emilia

Emilia tried to banish thought of Lucian as the guards announced her into Tiber's presence, but he nagged at her heart. Spiking his wine had been such a simple thing. Some of that viterian root from the island had proved useful after all. Logic dictated that, after Hyperia, Lucian would be the most attractive to the Houses as a potential emperor. He was strong, a leader, a seasoned warrior; of course they'd want him over a mumbling bookworm with tangled hair. She'd needed to embarrass him enough to lessen his appeal.

He . . . he truly did want to do good, didn't he?

The rosewood and citrus scent of his cape around her; the warmth of his body; the way his breath had tickled her cheek when he whispered in her ear . . .

You will never have that. Focus.

"Oh, the Aurun girl. What do you want?" Tiber grumbled, bored with her already. She stood in his appointed parlor and watched the old man pour more wine from a nearly empty carafe. "Get lost looking for your parents?"

"I've come with a proposition, my lord."

"Eh. Not sure you're the type we like proposing," Lysander grumbled. He and his idiot brother had congregated near the window. Emilia ignored them.

"What do you want?" Lord Tiber asked.

"No. What do *you* want?" Emilia pulled up a chair and sat before him, hands folded daintily in her lap. The urge to rub her fingers or fidget with her sleeves was overwhelming. "Your territory lacks resources, there are constant skirmishes on your borders, and you are the second-poorest House in the empire. Behind my family's, of course." Emilia waited as Lord Tiber scratched his scuzzy chin. "What if I could change your circumstances?"

Tiber snorted, and so did his sons. "No offense, girly, but how would *you* know what it takes to rule my land better than me?"

"It's not your land I'm interested in." Emilia pressed forward. "It's your rocks." She got an appropriately silent response. "Wroclawia is a region that boasts many different types of geographic features, yes? Wide plains, valleys. The Empire's Trident, in particular, has three mountain ranges all radiating from the same point of—"

"I'm losing patience, girly."

"You're sitting on a fortune, and you don't know it." Emilia stood, forcing her hands not to pluck at her skirts. Now she had their attention. "I've studied the reports on the material that makes up a large basin in your western territory. A certain type of shale. Fine-grained sedimentary rocks that, when mined and correctly processed and heated, become oil." At the word *oil,* Tiber's eyes widened. When he struggled to pretend nonchalance, she knew she had him. "That's right. You're sitting on oil enough to light the entire empire for generations to come. That kind of economic power could make the Sabels' trade look trifling in comparison." Her heart thundered as she leaned forward. "Back me as empress. I'll divert resources away from our wars of expansion and help you turn your territory into the greatest profit source this empire has ever known." She felt giddy now, ready to dance through the halls. Watching a man's face slacken as he realized she was right was power beyond anything sexual or magical.

"Tell me." Tiber's eyes took on a hard light. "Suppose I backed Hyperia and then mined as I please when she's on the throne?"

Emilia had anticipated this. "Have you forgotten the second edict of the Treaty of Interdependence?" The imperial constitution, written by the Empress Ismene I, guaranteed rights and privileges to the five Houses. "'The head of a House shall rule the vassals upon his or her land with supremacy. However, the empire's land itself shall forever belong to one individual: the celestial being who occupies the dragon throne.'" Emilia smiled as Tiber frowned. "Therefore, the basin itself belongs to the emperor. Tell me, do you think *Hyperia* will divert resources away from expansion, help you mine for shale, and then permit you to keep most of the profit instead of filling the imperial coffers?" She *tsk*ed.

"You've made your point," Tiber grumbled. He watched her with a narrow expression, a finger to his lips. "All right," he said.

"And?"

"I don't think so." He jutted his chin. "For all I know, this is a story you made up. I admire that—don't get me wrong—but I can't trust you. Even if you *are* right, there might not be as much oil as you say there is, and I could end up wrecking my chance at a Volscia alliance."

"Hyperia is insane," Emilia said gently. Tiber snorted.

"She's . . . high-strung." He licked his lips. "Cute quality in a girl." Emilia wanted to wipe the slime of his very presence off her skin. "Her daddy'll get her under control, and then we'll do business. I'm waiting until she enhances the deal. Sorry, sweets."

Tiber winked at her; Emilia wanted to vomit. "You wasted your time."

In a perfect world, she'd explode this pustule and leave bits smattered upon the walls, gobbets of him dangling from the chandelier.

"Hyperia's 'daddy' tried reasoning with her after they left your presence. She threw him against the wall and told him she'd have his head when she took the dragon throne." Tiber looked to his two sons, neither of whom seemed to know what to say. "She is out of anyone's control now, my lord," Emilia continued. "A person capable of killing her own sister in cold blood is capable of following any action, no matter how extreme, to its conclusion. I am much more reasonable." Emilia stood her ground and let her gaze meet the lord's. Her chaos, which had thankfully slept soundly this evening, began to stir. She imagined herself holding it down by its neck, telling it no. Establishing herself as dominant, not the other way around.

Because she *was* dominant now. Lord Tiber evaluated her. His sons, who had previously mocked her, now listened.

She was doing this.

She *could* do this.

Her future—and the future of all the other wretched, chaotic children—rested on these next few minutes.

"How do we know it's true?" Lysander asked.

"The story is getting around to all the nobles at the party. You may ask anyone you like," she replied. *Servants spread gossip like rats spread disease*—that's what her mother had once said. Emilia didn't love the comparison, but she had to acknowledge the point. "The Pentri know. It's lessened their interest in the Volscia. You both are allied in so many other ways. Why not here?"

"You can speak for them on that?" Tiber scratched his chin.

"Why not have them come in, and we can all speak together?"

"What do you say?" It was a mere twenty minutes later, and Emilia had managed to put both the Tiber and the Pentri into this one room. All of them were huddled close, speaking with the urgency of children sharing a secret. Victory breathed hot against the back of her neck, so hot that she couldn't even think about what Hyperia might do when she found Emilia had stolen her win out from under her. Then again, Hyperia wanted all the competitors to fight their hardest.

In a twisted way, it was the thing Emilia admired about her.

Emilia had re-explained her plan for the Tiber to the Pentri. As their lands touched and they frequently traded favors, what was good for one would be good for the other. Lady Pentri and Lord Tiber glanced across the room and nodded.

"All right." Tiber rubbed his chin. "You have us, girly. For the moment."

"That's all I need." Emilia got to her feet, trying not to explode. She'd done it. A few days ago, she'd barely known how to speak to another person, and now she'd *negotiated a deal*. "Come with me. We'll need to switch your votes over."

Before the crests could be assigned to the victor, they had to be registered with the priests. The respective parties had to sign beneath Emilia's name, and then—only then—would she win. She led the Tiber and Pentri down the hall, her heart jackrabbiting in her chest.

After this victory, she'd have a real shot at the dragon throne. Emilia hadn't allowed herself to hope for this. When she'd first got into the Trial, survival had seemed such a hazy prospect. But now . . . she *could* be empress.

And as empress, she could make changes. Lasting changes. First, she could reexamine the policies on chaotics, and . . . and . . .

One step at a time.

She found Camilla in the priests' parlor, the scorebook in her hands.

"I'd like to record the Tiber and the Pentri for myself," Emilia said, trying not to be offended when Camilla's steel-gray eyebrows lifted in surprise.

"Very well." The priestess opened her leather book with a flourish, produced a pen, and told the nobles where to sign. They wrote their names, and Emilia had to fight to keep the exhilaration from exploding everything around her. She'd done it.

She'd won.

She'd never won anything before in her life.

"So," she said breathlessly.

Camilla nodded. "So."

"So . . . how do we announce?" Emilia looked to the nobles and back to the priest.

"Announce what?" Camilla seemed genuinely puzzled.

"My victory."

"My dear girl, you need *three* Houses backing you to secure a victory. We explained the rules."

"Yes." Emilia blinked. "I have the Tiber and the Pentri."

"Two Houses." Camilla gave Emilia the book. "You need three."

But . . . but that would mean . . .

House Aurun had been scratched out from underneath her name.

"Who?" she whispered, throat dry. Scanning the page, she saw their name once more.

Under Lucian's.

32

Lucian

"Why are you doing this?" Lucian cried. Thank the blue above, his head had begun to clear of drink and he could have this conversation properly. The Aurun stood in his father's assigned parlor. At least their son, Alexander, whose eyes were red and raw, looked as angry as Lucian. One of the Aurun had sense, though sadly not the ones who mattered.

Lord Sabel stood at Lucian's back. Dido had removed herself from the discussion and was draped across a chaise, looking bored at the whole thing.

"What's there to question? We believe you should be our next emperor," Lady Aurun said coolly. She looked like a copy of Emilia that had been gradually erased, he thought, pale to the point of bloodless, her eyebrows plucked to nonexistence, her red hair faded with gray.

"You should support your *daughter!*" Lucian boomed. The Aurun didn't even blink.

"I agree," Alexander snapped.

"Father. Convince them." But Hector merely stood silent, an apology in his eyes. For Lucian or the Aurun, he did not know. Why? The family had always treated Lucian kindly, but this sudden pull of support from Emilia made no sense. Unless . . .

Unless someone had made a deal.

"Father. You didn't," Lucian growled.

Hector did not flinch. "I must do what's best for our family, Lucian."

"Honestly, it's not all down to Hector," Lord Aurun said. Lucian suddenly loathed the sound of the man's voice. "We think very highly of you, Lucian, and we think you can win. Emilia could never take the throne. She lacks the . . . constitution."

"Because you never believed in her!" Lucian felt himself coming apart. He rounded on the Aurun, who gazed up at him with guarded expressions. As a child they'd been kind to him, but he'd always despised the way they'd treated Emilia. Rolling their eyes at her passionate interests, mocking her posture and how unconsciously loud she spoke, asking her over and over why she couldn't be more like Dido. Emilia had seemed to let most of it roll off her, but he'd noticed during their childhood how she hunched in on herself. The words had eaten away at her, like constant rain upon a rock.

You always knew it couldn't be you and Emilia both on the throne.

But he didn't want it like this.

"I was going to become a temple brother before I got called to this Trial!" Lucian cried. "This whole empire is a bloated, fly-studded carcass! What good can I possibly do you?" Tears stung his eyes and throat. "Change your vote back!"

"No," Lord Aurun said.

Before Lucian could respond, the parlor doors opened.

Emilia looked at him, betrayal shimmering in her eyes.

33

Emilia

Emilia did not like being the center of attention. The Pentri and the Tiber stood smugly alongside Camilla in a corner, watching her with withering contempt. Camilla waited to see if she would or would not record a win. Lucian, Alexander, and Dido, meanwhile, clustered together beside the far window.

Her parents had her scrunched beside a bookcase.

"I negotiated the Tiber and the Pentri for myself!" Emilia's parents had never been openly affectionate with her, especially since her powers had manifested, but she'd never imagined they'd look at her with disgust. The pride at her own cunning fell away, and she transformed back into the person who'd grown up under their eyes: awkward, unappealing, an oddity who had no business being noble, or indeed much of anything. "If I take the throne, I'll give you whatever you want."

If you'd love me, I'll do whatever you want.

"You might win this Game, Emilia, but we all know you will never take the throne." Her father's words landed heavy as a slap. "In exchange for our support of Lucian, Hector has agreed to give us trade ports on the far eastern fringe of his territory. You in power is more dangerous than not."

Trade ports. That's all that was required to buy her parents' affection away from her.

"You don't know what I can do," she growled.

"Thank you very much, but we do." Her mother spoke low. "And none of it is good."

Emilia's stomach chilled. None of it was good. None of *her* was good. "I'm getting better at controlling it," she breathed.

"Keep your voice down." Her father sneered. "That's the other thing. In case you erupt in some disaster, we need to distance ourselves from you. Think of Alexander, if you can think of anybody beside yourself. Do you want him put to death on your account?"

Emilia could not help the misery that itched all over her skin. Unthinking, she began to rub her fingers together. Her mother slapped her hand.

"Have some dignity," she said. With them looking at her like this—less than nothing, worse than bad—she wanted to crawl under the carpet to where no one here would stare at her again. "Just don't look at me" had been the refrain of her childhood. At least, locked up in that tower, she'd been given the satisfaction that she wasn't hurting anyone. Sometimes she'd imagine all the happy things people were doing without her and took some relief that her presence wasn't making everything worse.

She repressed a sob.

"If we don't have a win," Lord Tiber drawled on the other side of the room, "I'm thinking of switching my vote. Lord Lucian. Now, that's the kind of profile you can imagine on an imperial coin. Don't you agree, high priestess?"

"It's not my place to give an opinion," Camilla said.

Emilia had not won anything. She couldn't even keep her own family. This was the one outcome she hadn't planned for. Emilia had never thought, not for one second, that her parents would back anyone else.

Her fatal flaw had been the belief that, beneath everything, her parents loved her.

Her father and mother turned away from her, signaling their position quite clearly to everyone in the room.

They were done.

Emilia trembled as pain began to slice into the backs of her eyes. Kill them. She could kill them for this. The rage merged with the chaos in her blood and burned hot. Her vision blurred with tears as she imagined her parents as trees in winter. Beneath their bark slept veins and capillaries, the slumbering buds that needed only the correct season to bloom. Emilia pictured her parents blossoming in crimson.

You're a monster.

Gasping, Emilia looked away from her parents and shut out the deadly images. She bit her lip and clenched her fists. They were right to turn on her. They were right to hate her. What normal person could ever love a monstrosity like her?

Emilia realized with horror that she was beginning to cry.

"Castor. Imogen." Lord Sabel said her parents' names with horror, and pity. Pity for Emilia.

A buzzing started in her brain, and it felt like sharp pins were being inserted underneath her fingernails as the whole room regarded her with expressions alternating between disgust and sadness. Tiber and the Pentri were already muttering between themselves and eyeing Lucian. Alexander had yanked their parents aside and was speaking urgently, his face bright red.

Lucian watched Emilia with the tenderest sorrow she'd ever seen.

If you knew what I am, you wouldn't care.

Bad. Evil. Monster. Vile. Freak. Wrong. Wrong. *Wrong.*

The buzzing turned into a hum, which grew into a grinding, awful sound in the center of her mind, like the clash of metal. Emilia tilted her head back and shut her eyes as she gave herself over to pain. Her body burned with hate.

The pulse of chaos moved through her.

No. Not here. Please, not here.

But as Emilia's eyes snapped open, she felt the power shoot out of her, rippling through the room, the hall outside, the entire building.

And that's when the screaming began.

34

Ajax

—————◆—————

"My lady, you look stunning this evening." Ajax brought a woman's hand to his lips, smelling the expensive lavender oil on her skin. She peered down at him through her mask, and even beneath the painted grin, her frown was evident. Ajax kissed each individual finger, sliding a ring off as he did so, one that sported a square-cut emerald the size of his eye with a ripple of blue in the center. Only the best jewels for nobles under Volscian rule.

The woman gasped.

"How dare you!" she cried.

Ajax was jerked about by some fancy guy in a silver suit, one positively dripping with clusters of diamond and pearl. The guy's weak chin quivered with feeling. Oh dear.

"What in the depths are you doing to my wife?" he snapped.

"Sorry. My mistake," Ajax said. The guy dragged him forward by his lapel.

"If you were not one of the competitors here this evening . . ." The fellow let the dangling end of that sentence imply something *truly* frightening. By the blue above, how would Ajax *ever* feel safe again?

"A thousand apologies, my lord. I didn't realize that the lady had such a big, strong defender." Ajax patted the man on his breast; no hard feelings. The guy snorted through his nose in the manner of the affronted rich.

"This is what happens when common blood gets into the Trial," the man huffed. Taking his lady by the arm (she was now swooning to have been rescued), the pair bustled off into the crowd. Ajax, meanwhile, gazed down at the treasure in his hand: a brooch of platinum and white gold, studded in pink diamonds with a fat, glistening ruby at the center. *Much* more valuable than the ring. The emerald had been bait to land a bigger prize.

"Prick," he whispered with a smile, before opening the pouch at his side and dropping the thing in. He surveyed his little magpie collection: a diamond bracelet; two emerald earrings (got off a lady who was five cups of wine into the night and singing drunken songs on the veranda); a gold ring bearing a family crest; a pair of crystal saltshakers he'd swiped from the buffet table; and now this brooch.

Oh. And the grand prize, of course.

He smiled bitterly at the little gleaming jewels as he tightened the strings of his pouch and went in search of another cup of that good, crisp wine. Ajax shouldered his way through a sea of sneers and whispers. Look at him. So short. So ugly. So illegitimate. So wrong for the throne.

He ground his teeth as he snatched a goblet from a passing server and leaned against the far wall. The room whirled on without him, letting him know how little they cared. Couldn't get an audience with *any* of the families.

Even his own father hadn't received him. The exact words Lysander had relayed, delivered with a simpering smile: "What for?"

All the other Houses had decided he had nothing to offer.

Ajax had spent much of his life taking whatever he could,

because nothing had been given. Well. Hopefully these rich pricks missed their little bits and baubles at the end of the night. He drank, but the wine soured in his mouth.

They'll be sorry, those mouth-breathing, weak-chinned idiots.

Ajax thought of that woman again, the one with the green eyes he'd seen outside his room. Maybe one day she'd see her own eyes staring back at her from the dragon throne, and she'd know the shit and the shame she'd gone through had all been for *something*.

Ajax let the sounds of the party pass through him like water through a sieve.

I'll make you sorry, you rich pricks. I'll make you beg on your knees for—

Ajax stumbled, catching himself on the edge of the buffet table as the ground shook beneath his feet. Glass shattered in every direction as the mirrors and latticed windows exploded. Men and women on the dance floor collapsed with cries.

"What the depths?" Ajax froze as a colossal *crack* sounded throughout the room. He looked up as a hideous fracture tore open the ceiling, radiating outward in a growing spiderweb of damage. A sound like thunder pealing throughout the ballroom. Plaster rained onto people's heads, and . . .

Everyone screamed as two chandeliers unrooted with a groan and crashed below. Crystal shards skittered across the floor as the fissure in the ceiling grew wider, like an ugly, looming smile. More plaster fell, the snap of timber started—

"Out of the way!" Petros boomed. The priest appeared as if from thin air, striding into the center of the ballroom. In his orange silk robe, he looked like flame sparking in a sea of ice. Hands up, he concentrated . . . and the crack in the ceiling began to knit itself as though it'd never been broken in the first place. It was slow going, and Ajax noticed that the old man had to pause and wipe his face repeatedly. The crack grew wider, then smaller, then wider again. The orderly magos was fighting a damned rough battle, it seemed. "Everyone, stay where you are!"

But panicked people don't listen well. They all rushed for the doors in a stampede of silk. Ajax was pulled along with them, though he kept craning his neck to check out the damage as it was repaired. He whistled.

Chaos.

Ajax knew that's what it was, a surge of the most evil power imaginable. He felt it in the fine hairs on his arms and the back of his neck. Better leave that disaster to the priests to fix. And yet, as he ran for his life alongside the screaming nobles, he couldn't help but admire it.

When Hyperia tore into the ballroom, Ajax made sure to lower his head so she couldn't see him. Though he'd have liked a dance with her, and maybe a chance to nab her pearl earrings, this was *not* the time.

Damn. Maybe it was the wrong way to think, but if only he could get the power of chaos on *his* side. No one would turn him away then.

35

Hyperia

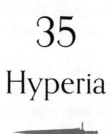

Hyperia entered the ballroom with one word singing in her ears: chaotic.

A chaotic had infected her ancestral home. Evil, disorder, destruction, death. It was a curse, and only she could stand bulwark against it.

Once she'd heard that the priests were healing the crack in the ceiling, she stormed downstairs and began ordering the guards. They followed her instructions with precision, golden pawns in a game of warfare. The one game she relished playing.

"The damage came from that side of the ballroom?" She glared at the musicians standing aghast on the stage, and the flood of people attempting to escape. "Stop them. Line them up by the wall—everyone who was here when it happened. If anyone left, drag them back." If anyone attempted to escape, well, Hyperia would act immediately.

The suspects' wails did not reach her. She waited as they were organized into rows, and a few at a time brought to stand against the far wall. With Petros at her side, she surveyed the shivering lot.

"Are you sure this is wise, my lady?" Petros grunted. The priest's eyes narrowed. "A chaotic's attack is horrifying, but Camilla and I can handle it. This is your challenge."

"This is my home," she replied. She dragged a man forward, knocking his dragon's mask off. He whimpered; the sound of his weakness sickened her. "Can you tell if he's the one?" she asked Petros. Hyperia recognized this man, some lesser noble from her family's southern territory. A floppy, drunk aristocrat, same as all the rest.

"M-my lady Hyperia, I swear I know nothing of—"

"Quiet." She unsheathed her sword and held the tip under the man's chin so that he knew not to trifle with her. "I don't want extra reason to suspect you."

"Suspect me?" The man's face reddened. "My family has served yours for generations, my lady!"

She did not even recall his name. Hyperia had never had her sister's knack for people. If only Julia were here now . . .

If only things had gone as they were supposed to from the start.

"This is not the way," Petros muttered, stealing close so that only she could hear him. His soft words sounded almost like a scold. "We have laws in place for suspicions such as these."

Ah. Yes. He was testing her.

He wanted to see that she would not yield.

"Your Grace, simply tell me what I want to know as we walk down the— Don't move!" Hyperia's blade came up to the man's throat as he lurched off the wall. He halted, face paling as he stared down his nose at her blade.

And then something exploded on the other side of the room.

Hyperia reacted.

A clean cut across the throat with a flick of her wrist, and then a splash of blood as the lord collapsed face-first into a pile of glass debris. Red seeped out from beneath him. *Like wine,* Hyperia thought.

She looked up to where the explosion had happened,

finding that, in place of chaos, one of the musicians had tripped and fallen over the shards of the chandelier, dragging the whole thing down in a cataclysm of broken crystal.

Oh. Hyperia gaped at the dying man at her feet. Only the slightest pressure, and this was the result.

Damn. Counting Julia, this made two people she had killed in the same week. *This is becoming a bad habit.*

The lord's wife screamed, a long, awful sound that stretched from one end of the room to the other. Hysteria bloomed as Petros tried herding everyone into proper formation. It was too late. The place erupted into full discord. Hyperia realized, watching the woman clutch at her dead, drained husband, that she had broken with all etiquette.

He might have been the chaotic, but he certainly had been a guest. She'd killed a nobleman with the same efficacy with which she might dispatch a troublesome servant.

Turning around in a daze, Hyperia found hundreds of nobles all looking at her with bone-deep horror. She'd broken the rules. She'd treated one of their kind with total disregard for rank.

Hyperia could feel the reins coming out of her hands, as surely as if losing control of Aufidius in a morning flight.

For the first time, she wondered if she wasn't losing the reins on her mind, as well.

36

Emilia

Alexander sat against the wall with Emilia, his arm around her as they witnessed the room's cacophony. Emilia's body was as sore as if she'd completed a ten-mile run. She'd never loosed that much power before. After the explosion in the ballroom, they'd all been told to wait in this parlor and not to leave for any reason until the danger was under control. Camilla had left, but soon returned. After all, one priest needed to be on hand to record a potential victory. Everyone else was standing about or seated on the furniture. Emilia didn't want to be close to anyone except her brother.

"Mother and Father are impossible," Alex muttered. Emilia nestled against him. He still smelled of home, sea salt and bonfires. Or maybe that was her own fancy.

"From a logical standpoint, it makes sense," she said lifelessly.

"Family shouldn't have to *make sense*, Emi," he hissed. He enveloped her in a hug, let his chin sit atop her head. Neither of them brought up the explosion in the ballroom. They both knew.

By some miracle, Emilia's power had projected several rooms away. She'd never done *that* before. Of course, she'd never hurt like this before, either. She felt flayed before the world.

Do something. You have *to win.*

"Wait. My lord." Emilia got up and hurried to the men, pulse fluttering in her throat. "What if I could offer you something more?"

"What else could *you* possibly offer?" Pentri snorted. "A frozen island in the northern sea?"

"Trade ports." She ignored her parents' horrified gasps. "My family has established new trade ports as a gift from the Sabel. Those ports border your own territory, I think, in the east." She felt all the gears in her mind clicking into place. "If I take the throne, they'll be yours."

Lord Sabel grunted, and for a moment, she was afraid he would change his mind. But he merely nodded at her in resignation. He and her father had been friends for so long . . . but Lord Sabel was teaching a lesson tonight.

"Sabel ports?" The Pentri husband and wife needed only a moment to confer. "Then we stay." Apparently, the anguish of family dishonor could be wiped away for a price.

"In that case," Camilla said, with a flourish of the pen, "Lady Emilia has won the Game!" She applauded, though everyone else in the room appeared stunned. "And to think, Lady Hyperia started off with victory practically assured. Isn't that the epitome of politics?"

Emilia turned to look at Lucian, and her stomach dropped. He was staring at his father with the most open, lost expression.

"Father," he whispered. "Why?"

"For you, Lucian." Lord Sabel blinked back tears, his voice trembling with emotion. "I would like your love again."

"My love?" The boy shook his head and pulled his father against him. Lucian hugged Lord Sabel forcefully. "Thank you. *Thank you.*"

Lord Sabel choked as he hugged Lucian back. Dido, the

most stoic girl, who'd met every challenge and obstacle in their childhood with nary a twitch of her lips, was now weeping into her hands. From joy, Emilia would guess.

She looked past the Sabel and their happiness to her own family. Her parents shriveled under the loss of their ports, but Alex . . .

He looked as if she'd slapped his face.

Oh. Oh *no.*

She'd stolen those ports from him as well.

Lord Tiber put a hand on her shoulder.

"Good job, girly," he whispered. She heard him lick his lips. "Here's to being in business."

This, Emilia realized, was politics at its finest.

37

Vespir

Vespir wasn't surprised when the bells chimed to signal the end of the Game. She'd sat cross-kneed on the floor after Antonia had left, waiting for Hyperia to be declared the winner. She just hadn't expected it to take this long.

She supposed the chaotic attack in the ballroom had set things back. At least she hadn't been there. This was one mess they couldn't blame on her, no matter how they tried.

Wiping her eyes, she sidled along the hallways until the guards herded her into the large, rosy parlor where they'd begun the competition. When she entered, something immediately caught her eye.

Hyperia looked as if someone had struck her in the stomach, hunched over, hands on her gut. Lord Volscia, beside his daughter, looked sickly, too.

What had happened?

Emilia and Lucian huddled with their backs to the walls. Only Ajax, arms crossed and legs confidently spread, appeared satisfied. No. No, it couldn't have been . . . *him*.

"Shall we?" Camilla said. Petros had only just entered the room, looking a bit pale. Whatever happened in the ballroom, it'd thrown their grand ceremonies off. Neither priest looked like they wanted to be showy now. "The winner," Camilla announced, "is Lady Emilia, with three Houses."

No one looked surprised, or at least, not that surprised. Vespir was too numb to be shocked by anything.

"Bring forward the box," Camilla said, gesturing to the table. One of the Volscia guards in his gold livery brought it. The priestess opened the latch, lifted the lid . . . and gasped. "What the—" she whispered. For the first time since Vespir had met her, she appeared dumbfounded. "Who has taken the pendants?"

The box was empty.

Everyone shared baffled looks. Vespir was half-afraid they'd start blaming her. After all, she was a commoner, and those jewels were expensive. Finally, Ajax snorted and shook his head, whipping his plait of yellow hair back and forth.

"You." Camilla narrowed her black eyes. She appeared *this* close to losing her temper.

"If I couldn't get a meeting with any of you fine lords and ladies, I figured I ought to take a souvenir of the experience." The Tiber boy bared his sharp little teeth in a grin. Vespir's chin wobbled as she tried to hold back shocked laughter.

"Where are they?" Camilla snapped. Instantly, the room's collective gaze went to the pouch at Ajax's side. The priestess ripped it away and poured out a glittering handful of fine jewels. The pendants, however, were nowhere to be found.

"You think I'd keep them in a *sack*?" Ajax winked. "Use your imagination, *Your Grace*."

Vespir struggled to control her breathing. Her shoulders began to shake.

"Where are they?" Camilla snarled. "Return them, or there'll be consequences."

"I thought you were saving the killing-me part for later."

"How did you even get in here?"

"Come on. Let me maintain my aura of mystery."

"High priestess, I swear the door was locked and the guard posted," one of the soldiers stammered.

"Doors." Ajax *tsk*ed. "I'm *way* beyond doors these days."

That did it. Vespir collapsed to her knees and burst out laughing. The room stared as she pointed with a shaking hand at every one of them in turn.

"Look at your faces," she gasped amid giggles. All these poncy lords and ladies, priests and soldiers, undone by some little . . . "And you." Vespir grinned at Ajax. "You're . . . so . . . *stupid*," she said, barely able to get the words out. She wrapped her arms around her stomach and rocked with laughter.

"Um, let's finish this," Petros muttered to Camilla. He had a point. The longer this went on, the more humiliating it'd be.

"Fine," the priestess said, taking a book from Petros's hands. She spoke at a clipped pace now, as if running against the clock. "Emilia of the Aurun, take the collected wisdom of our most recent emperor, Erasmus. Let it guide you on the path to great statesmanship." The priestess all but shoved the book into Emilia's hands, while the girl blustered her thanks. With that, Camilla turned glinting eyes to the rest of the room. "As for the other rankings. Lucian of the Sabel shares second place with Hyperia of the Volscia, with one House each. Vespir, *servant* of the Pentri, and Ajax of the Tiber tie for last." Camilla practically bared her teeth. "Normally, the penalty would apply to both of you, but due to Ajax's *unorthodox* manner of playing, he descends to last place on principle. Therefore, the punishment is entirely his."

Well, that was one good thing to happen to Vespir. And the boy didn't seem all that perturbed by his loss.

"What'll it be? Is Hyperia going to punch me in the face?" Ajax worked his jaw. "I might enjoy that."

Vespir heard the Volscia girl scoff.

"Pride in an emperor is commendable; arrogance is the opposite." Camilla glanced at Petros, who appeared to understand her implicitly. The old man nodded, the bags under his eyes growing more pronounced with his smirk.

"Arrogance is often a marker of the lowborn," Petros continued. He eyed Ajax from head to toe. "You will strip yourself and your dragon of the Tiber family colors and partake in the next challenge as you began this Trial: a humble, illegitimate boy."

The grin withered on Ajax's face. He touched the collar of his crimson cloak as if it were a talisman. Emilia and Lucian appeared sympathetic, while Hyperia seemed to relish this.

"Can I . . . go change?" the boy muttered.

"Here, *Lord* Ajax. If you please," Petros hissed.

Vespir watched the boy fumble at his cloak's clasp, let it slip from his shoulders to pile to the floor. He took off his jacket, his lips pursed in a hard, white line. Ajax threw the jacket after his cloak and stood there in his white shirtsleeves and black trousers. Without the fancy attire, he was a scarecrow of a boy.

"Give me my bag," he growled, snatching at the sack and kneeling to shove his treasures inside.

"Of course," Camilla purred. "A little thief deserves his loot."

Ajax froze, fist tightening around diamonds.

Throw it in their faces, Vespir thought. But he tied up his pouch and got to his feet. The two Tiber boys snickered, but Ajax would not look at them. He kept his fists at his sides, and gradually everyone's glance slid past him. Forgotten, as usual.

Only Vespir saw the one, brief moment that his chin quivered.

Camilla clapped her hands. "With that, the Game concludes, and the Race begins. To dragonback, everyone. Your next and final stop is the capital."

As Vespir climbed onto Karina's back, she prayed for another glimpse of Antonia. The girl wasn't standing next to her parents, who looked smug about how the evening had played out. They sneered openly at her. Vespir, blind with rage, barely restrained herself from going over there and kneeing Lord Pentri in his highborn balls.

Karina chirped, bending her long neck to glance over her wing at Vespir. The dragon nudged at her shoulder, and Vespir touched her forehead to the dragon's snout. Karina gave a coarse lick with her forked tongue.

Just like when you were born, girl.

Vespir's eyes burned to imagine those priests cutting her beautiful baby's throat, her dragon screaming for Vespir as her life bled away. But Vespir would be dead herself by then.

No one will ever know about me or Karina. It'll be like I never existed.

The ultimate sacrifice, and none of these fine people cared.

Next to her, Ajax climbed onto his dragon. The boy's face was wan, his eyes puffed. Astride his dragon, who gawped with abandon as he spread his batlike wings, Ajax spared her a sour glance.

"What?" he asked.

"They don't get it," Vespir replied, nodding at the nobles in their finery, jewels winking in the torchlight. "They'll never understand what it's like to be us." She petted Karina's neck. "I should've been last. When they snubbed me, I gave up. At least you fought back."

Ajax sniffed.

"Yeah. Thanks." He looked to the sky. Vespir rolled her eyes; she didn't know why she bothered reaching out to this kid. "Vespir. Catch."

She jumped in surprise as something arced through the air. Vespir grabbed it, thinking it was a coin. When she opened her hand, she found the Pentri crest. The silver disc was cool against her skin, the green Pythos dragon insignia set in emerald. Ajax cocked his head, a smile returned to his lips.

"Where'd you hide this?" she asked.

"I've got ways." With that and a dry chuckle, he took off into the sky, Dog snuffling in contentment as he swooped after the others. They were growing distant, outlines against the moon. Gritting her teeth, Vespir rose with Karina to go after them, not bothering to look back at the Volscia palace. There was nothing for her on earth anymore. No home. No family. No Antonia.

All she had was Karina, who purred as they cut through a wisp of starlit cloud.

Karina, her only reason to live.

To fight.

All she needed was one single victory to have a shot at the throne.

The Race was on.

38

Vespir

———◆———

N o one had slept. As the sun rose over the ocean, Vespir
found everyone seated perfectly straight in their saddles
without the aid of sleeping ropes. They had left the mainland
sometime past midnight and flown toward the Imperial Peninsula, with moonlight sparkling on the waves far below. At least
it hadn't been cloudy.

Vespir and Karina kept a careful distance behind Dog, riding
the larger dragon's air current. Ajax turned in his saddle, cupped
his hands, and yelled, "Hey! How long till we get to Dragonspire?"

The golden capital, the greatest wonder of the civilized
world. Or so Vespir had heard it described.

"No idea!" she shouted back. He yelled something that the
wind ate. "What?"

"I said, *How do you piss while riding?*"

Vespir blinked. "If it hits me, I'll kill you!"

"I'll hold it! Thanks!"

Beside her, Emilia and Chara rose up on a gust of wind. The
ripple effect made Karina waver back and forth, but the dragon
soon steadied herself.

"We should reach the peninsula in a couple of hours," the

Aurun girl called. She'd kept to the back of the racing formation, occasionally dropping away far below, almost to touch the
waves. Odd, but then again, she rode an Aspis. Emilia certainly
had a good breed for this race.

Aspises: good with water and could sustain themselves for
longer flights. Weakness: the length of their bodies, and the natural serpentine movements of their tails, could make hairpin
aerial turns difficult.

Vespir had been checking on everyone's dragon throughout the night, guessing how they'd try to pull ahead during the
final descent into Dragonspire. So far, they all congregated together on the long flight. In fact, their dragons instinctively co-
operated, adopting a constantly shifting V flight pattern rather
like geese in migration. There was no sense in racing right now.
Putting on an aggressive burst of speed would only result in
tiring out their dragons. At best, they wouldn't be able to pull
ahead when the finish line was in sight. At worst, the poor creatures would spiral into the sea out of exhaustion or suffer a
flameout.

Vespir went over her plan again.

Lucian managed Tyche with one hand on the reins. Drakes
were more nimble than any other breed, and their triangular snouts and dart-shaped torsos let them cut through the
air with ease. Weakness: also the most delicate dragon. They
tired quickly.

Ajax had both his hands over his head, Dog's reins flapping
free in the wind. The dragon gawped with glee as they swayed
side to side, Ajax's pressed knees the only guidance.

"Will you hold on to the reins?" Lucian twisted around in
his seat, and shot the other boy a look of withering contempt.
"You're going to disrupt the formation."

"You're all a bunch of toothless old women. Look at this!"

Ajax crowed, gesturing to the expanse of ocean, the rising sun streaking the sky gold and pink. He stood in his stirrups, pumped his fists. "We are *gods!*"

Vespir caught Emilia's eye. The Aurun girl shook her head, then clasped her hands over her throat. The signal was clear: *kill me.* Vespir laughed. Emilia hastily looked away, but Vespir caught a pleased grin.

"Stop. Wrecking. The formation!" Lucian shouted, swearing as Dog tried getting alongside Tyche in midair. The finicky Drake swooped away, chittering and lashing her tail. When a dragon lashed its tail in a flying group, the message was clear: *don't touch me.*

"Hey. Stop, you moron!" Ajax finally took the reins and brought up Dog's head. He rapped his knuckles on the dragon's skull. "Be a good boy."

"Gawp," Dog replied mournfully.

Wyverns: the hardiest breed of all, capable of the longest distances and the heaviest battles. Weaknesses . . .

Well. Dog was . . .

Weaknesses: Dog.

A shadow swept over Vespir and Emilia, and a growl reverberated through the air. Instinctively, Vespir ducked her head as Aufidius passed. Hyperia had been bringing up the rear for a while, to rest her dragon. Wise. Now she was shifting into the lead, presumably to get away from the shouting and Dog's weaving and bobbing.

Hydra: the supreme dragon breed. The keenest natural intelligence. The longest claws. The hottest flame. The Great Dragon Himself had been Hydra.

Weaknesses?

Aufidius was a god among beasts.

Weaknesses: none.

Well. Except maybe temper. As Dog ballooned his wings and soared upward to join Aufidius, Vespir craned her neck to watch the poor, dumb dragon nuzzle at the Hydra's snout. Snout nuzzling was an invitation to play, and now not even Ajax's yanking on the reins could get the Wyvern to stop.

Vespir heaved a sigh. Ajax was one of many, many brothers. Dog had probably come from a crowded aerie, with all sorts of siblings to play with.

It wouldn't occur to the dragon that anyone wouldn't want to be his friend.

Aufidius lashed out and snapped in Dog's face. The Wyvern escaped having his nose ripped off by dropping swiftly, nearly collapsing onto Emilia and Chara. After a near-midair collision, the dragons wobbled back into formation. Aufidius pulled ahead, letting out a roar so massive Vespir's vision trembled with its power.

"Keep your dragon under control." Hyperia did not need to turn around for her voice to carry.

The other four kept away from her and the Hydra's lashing tail.

Aufidius was the most furious creature Vespir had ever seen. She began to shiver.

"Listen." She called to the others when they were half a league behind Hyperia. "That dragon hasn't been properly trained. I'll bet they kept him muzzled for close to a year."

"What do you mean?" Emilia asked. Her red hair whipped about behind her like a stream of fire.

"When they're still hatchlings, dragons need to be weaned off biting. Sometimes, handlers put muzzles on them to make the point. You have to do it before they get too big, or you can't control them." Amazing, that these dragon riders did not know how their own creatures had been trained and reared.

"But you have to switch between using the muzzle and connecting with the dragon. You feed them by hand, play with them, and make them trust you. Then they don't want to bite. But it seems the Volscia handlers just kept Aufidius muzzled. They made him angry so that he couldn't connect with anyone."

"So they didn't know what they were doing?" Lucian sounded baffled.

"No." Vespir watched Aufidius's retreating form, feeling sick to her stomach. "They knew *exactly*. They wanted to keep him wild, so that only Hyperia could control him. The more feral a dragon is, the stronger it becomes. They tortured him from the time he hatched."

Monsters. Aufidius was a beauty, and they'd ruined him.

After that, they flew in silence for an hour or two, and Vespir closed her eyes to "lock in" with Karina once more. That flash of the Red, and then it was as if her breathing itself had synced with her dragon's.

When they reached the peninsula, everyone would spread apart on instinct. They'd be coming to the capital soon, and the dragons would want to be ready. Vespir had written off Chara and Dog. They didn't have the proper handling to make full use of their strengths. Tyche would pull ahead to begin with, then tire. What Vespir wanted was to fly underneath Tyche and Aufidius, to wait for their final descent. Because to brake the speed and redirect themselves, they'd have to pull up and bank, flap their wings, and then . . .

Then they'd provide a gust of wind that would propel Karina forward. The smallest, lightest, and sleekest dragon, if Karina could keep hurtling ahead of the others, she could win. They'd lose all control in the descent—they'd be no better than an arrow released from the shaft, so they'd need careful aim. But it was their only chance to beat the larger dragons.

All Vespir had to do now was remain calm and wait.

As the sun rose higher into the sky, the thin green line of the peninsula came into view. Everyone's shoulders hunched forward on instinct, and every dragon's tail began to lash in anticipation.

Except Dog, who had been cowed by Aufidius's harsh reaction and desperately yearned to make a friend.

"Stop. Stop!" Ajax yelped as his dragon shook its head free of his rider's lead and urged toward the Hydra's tail. Vespir inhaled deeply and tugged on Karina's own bridle. Ugh, she *hated* that those priests had forced a saddle and halter onto her baby, one with green silk tassels at the snout and green embroidery upon the leather.

But the harness was the least of her problems right now. She, Lucian, and Emilia all cried out in horror as Dog flapped harder, trying to overtake Aufidius. Whimpering, the dragon tried to bounce his snout against the Hydra's.

Friend? Friend? The poor creature's need couldn't have been more obvious.

"You fool. Get away!" Hyperia shouted as Aufidius lashed out once more. This time, smoke curled from his nostrils. Vespir's heart beat faster.

No. No, no, not here. If that dragon breathes fire . . .

They were too ill matched for dracomachia.

Dog would be killed in the battle.

"Ajax!" Vespir stood in the stirrups and tried to get alongside the boy. He fiendishly yanked at his reins, but Dog would not be turned. "Guide him down!"

"I can't!" The Tiber boy's voice tightened with fear. "He won't listen!"

"I'll try to pull away," Hyperia snarled, doing her best to guide her own dragon's head to the right. She was no fool; she

225

knew the dangers of dracomachia this high up. "By the blue above, keep that idiot creature off my tail!"

Vespir looked over her shoulder to find that Emilia had pulled well away. She was a full fifty yards or so behind now.

Smart girl. She'd already won a challenge. Better to place last here than get in a fight.

Dog gave a long, yowling cry as Aufidius swooped farther away.

Lucian and Tyche flew up beside Vespir. The Sabel boy cursed as Dog and Ajax sped for Aufidius.

"Damn it," Lucian muttered. "What do we do now?"

Vespir's throat was dry.

"Nothing," she whispered. "It's too late."

39

Ajax

Ajax screamed, sat hard in his stirrups, and pulled up Dog's head.

"Don't make him angry, you idiot!" He dug his heels into the dragon's side, and Dog yelped. Ajax didn't want to ever hurt this fool but better Dog get kicked in the ribs than die. "Back away. Go down!"

Aufidius wheeled about, and Ajax could feel himself trapped in the creature's obsidian gaze. Oh, *shit*. The golden dragon opened its jaws—and roared. The full-blooded roar of a bull Hydra was said to have the power of five adult lions. Now practically deaf, Ajax urged Dog to circle away from the massive beast. Vespir wheeled overhead, safely out of the way as smoke spiraled from Aufidius's nostrils and heat rippled from his mouth. Despite Hyperia's shouts, it was too late.

Time slowed as Ajax tried to scream. All he could manage was to whisper Dog's name.

Aufidius flared his wings, stopped midair, and spewed fire.

Ajax huddled himself behind Dog's body, trying to pull his knees in as close to his chest as possible. Dog puffed out his chest, taking the brunt of the flames as they licked harmlessly off his scales. Ajax's eyes watered, and he choked on the sulfuric stink. The attack seemed to stretch on for hours, though it couldn't have been longer than a few seconds. His legs trembled to hang on as he looked down into the seemingly endless fall to the ocean below. One slip was all it would take to hurtle him into a blue oblivion. When the flames died, Ajax began to shudder violently.

"Go. We have to go," he wheezed. But Dog was no longer listening.

Ajax could feel the fury vibrating through his dragon. Aufidius had nearly hurt Ajax, and that couldn't be allowed. Not for a loyal creature like Dog.

There were no friendly gawps now. Dog roared in reply, only half as loud as Aufidius but impressive nonetheless. Ajax's entire head shook with the deafening sound, and he clutched the saddle horn to let his dragon take him for a ride. From around Dog's shoulder, past the flaring wings, Ajax got brief flashes of their competition. Aufidius flapped to remain in midair, then struck out with his legs. The talons that tipped his toes extended, obsidian and fiendishly curved. Oh no.

"Pull back!" Ajax shouted as Dog yelped; one of the Hydra's talons had sliced him across the haunch. This was bad. Even as Ajax yelled and pulled at the reins, yanking so hard he nearly slid out of his stirrups, Dog breathed fire in response. Ajax watched as the flames licked harmlessly across Aufidius's broad chest. Ajax saw Hyperia duck, same way he had, plastering herself to the dragon's back in order to avoid being hit. The two dragons circled, kicking out at each other with claws, breathing fire when they missed. Ajax kept tugging, and his efforts finally paid off. Dog managed to put enough distance between himself and Aufidius to avoid being struck by the flames. Aufidius unleashed another fiery attack, which didn't touch them. Ajax coughed; the smoke was still terrible, of course. His face was slick with sweat, and his forehead scalding to the touch. Much more of that and his flesh would've started to blister.

"Ajax!" He heard Hyperia's voice. "Try taking him lower. Signal defeat!"

Right. Right, the code of dragon honor, or whatever it was that these beasts naturally did during battle. The dragon who went down on the wind would be spared; he'd never be alpha, but at least he wouldn't die. For most dragons, pride wouldn't allow that kind of surrender. Better to be dead than lesser.

But Dog wasn't like most dragons. To him, being loved mattered more. Damn moron.

Eh, but Ajax could be alpha enough for the both of them.

"Come on," he snarled, digging his heels so deep into Dog's sides that Ajax knew it had to hurt. He'd apologize later with a jaw rub and half a rabbit. Later, when they weren't dead.

Mercifully, Dog listened. Whimpering, the dragon bobbed lower on the wind, signaling his defeat. Ajax peered up at the hovering Hydra, its tail lashing like a golden whip through the air. *Just leave us alone.* If Dog accepted defeat, then Aufidius might listen to Hyperia and fly away.

Instead, the Hydra roared once again and lunged. The monster flew down toward them like an arrow aimed with deadly accuracy, its jaws open, flame kindling in its mouth. Ajax couldn't think; he couldn't try to guide Dog away or anything at all smart. He could only sit there in wonder and horror as his death came hurtling at him out of the sky.

At least his death would be huge and gold and awe-inspiring.

Move, you idiot! Move!

But Ajax couldn't . . . he couldn't . . .

Boom.

Tyche sped up out of nowhere, her passage knocking Ajax and Dog aside in a sheer gust of wind. The Drake was a black-and-cobalt blur against the sky. As Ajax watched and Dog keened, she struck Aufidius's neck with her snout, knocking the charging beast off his course. The Hydra snarled at the Drake as she pushed off with her legs to fly before him in challenge. Lucian sat forward in his saddle.

Right. How fitting. Ajax's dragon was the runt again. Dog had previously been the runt of the Tiber family aerie, so Ajax was familiar with the position.

Most dragons—Tyche included—would step in to protect the runt. Even though Dog was larger than Tyche, or Karina for that matter, the pod of dragons had adopted him as their smallest, weakest member. And unlike humans, who saw smallness and weakness as an opening for brutality, the dragons would defend their runt.

Shit. Now Lucian and Tyche were going to get into it with Aufidius, and if the Hydra was still keen on blood, they were going to end up with a ton of it and—

Out of nowhere, Aufidius banked on the air and turned himself around. With a gigantic roar, the dragon started winging hard to the peninsula. Ajax gave a shriek of relief, his heart a painful hammer in his chest. Shaking—he might've wet himself, though he hoped to the depths he hadn't—Ajax flew over to Tyche and Lucian.

"Thanks," Ajax gasped, his voice trembling. "Wh-why'd he do that?"

"They're trying to win the race." Lucian sounded amazed, pointing toward the thin line of land in the distance.

"Against *who*? You're here. Emilia's here. Vespir's—"

Ajax halted, scanned the sky. No, the servant girl was definitely not here. She must've taken off during his battle with Aufidius. Smart girl. She had the smallest dragon, after all, and there wouldn't be many opportunities to distance herself from the rest of them.

But the way Aufidius was wound up right now . . .

Oh. Oh no.

"He's gonna kill her," Ajax rasped.

40

Hyperia

———————

At least Aufidius had turned away from Ajax and that damned nuisance of a beast. Hyperia did not want to spill blood. She would be penalized and she could not accept that, not now. Not after all she'd accomplished. Instead, she leaned into the wind, narrowing her eyes as she gazed over Aufidius's golden shoulder. The little dot of Vespir and Karina grew in size as they came into sight of the mainland.

"You didn't have to attack the boy like that," she whispered, almost certain Aufidius couldn't hear her through the rush of the wind. "I ordered you to move on. There is no honor in attacking a defeated creature."

Beneath her, Aufidius growled. He shook her to her bones, and she clung to his saddle, half-certain he'd chuck her into the ocean if she disrespected him again.

What a monster. How proud she was to ride such a beast.

If that servant had any common sense, she'd let the Hydra pass without incident. Hyperia had a grudging respect for Vespir's attempt at taking the lead. She'd been clever enough to understand that she could accomplish nothing at the dracomachia. She'd tried to win this Race, Hyperia would give her that. The servant girl had tried her best.

But Vespir's best would never be Hyperia's.

As Aufidius came up on Karina's tail, Hyperia felt his sides growing hotter beneath her legs. Her pulse stalled. No. No, he didn't need to fire upon them.

"Aufidius. Stop!" she cried.

But of course, her dragon would not be ruled.

Hyperia cried out as Vespir glanced over her shoulder at the coming onslaught. Vespir's eyes widened, the wind ruffling her black hair. The servant shouted something at her own mount, and Karina dove out of the way as Aufidius unleashed a fireball. It did not strike the girl, and Hyperia closed her eyes in relief as they surpassed Vespir, taking the lead.

Hyperia would win now, and Vespir would take second place. That was admirable, after all. Not a win, not worthy of a crown, but enough that Vespir would meet her death with pride.

A noble death was all that people like Vespir could hope for, and, Hyperia thought as Aufidius winged his way toward Dragonspire and victory, it was something that she would happily grant the servant girl when the time came.

41

Vespir

Vespir coughed, eyes stinging as Aufidius passed them with ease. Karina hovered on the wind as Vespir struggled to catch her breath. Behind her, the other three were dots on the horizon. She would not be last in this challenge, but . . .

Karina would die if she did not win this Race.

How? How do we win?

Her heart sank as the voice of Plotus, the old Pentri handler who'd trained her, replied, *You can't. Your dragon can't overtake that Hydra. She's not built for it.*

Vespir's hands trembled. Her original plan might have worked if it weren't for poor, sweet, stupid Dog. Now Vespir couldn't nestle between Tyche and Aufidius in the hope of sling-shotting ahead. The only way to benefit from the Hydra's great surge of wings would be if . . .

Her head whipped up. This would require the most idiotic move possible.

Karina chirped, as if to ask what Vespir was thinking.

That chirp was all she needed. *My dragon is going to live.*

"Steady, girl." Vespir unfastened Karina's harness and bridle with cool hands, and let the damned bit of leather fall to the earth.

Getting the saddle off would be a greater challenge; to ac-commodate a dragon's wings, the saddle buckled along the belly in an X formation. Vespir had to scoot back, knees balanced on Karina's hindquarters, while she reached down and fumbled for the clasp. Vespir's thighs began to shiver with strain, but finally she felt the saddle give. When it slid off and away, Vespir settled onto her dragon's back with a sigh.

This would require balance. Karina wasn't Vespir's pet to ride. She was her partner. The better half of her heart. Vespir closed her eyes once more, and the Red was instantaneous. They were one person. One soul.

"Okay, girl." Vespir pressed herself fully against Karina, slid-ing her arms around the dragon's neck, slipping her heels down to hook under the dragon's hindquarters. "Let's go."

They stayed well behind Aufidius for much of the next few miles. When the river they'd been tracking began to widen and the horizon shone with gold, it was time to move. Ahead of them, in the distance, Vespir caught sight of a great black ban-ner that spanned the length of several city streets. Enormous golden pillars upheld that banner, marking the finish line.

Dragonspire was near.

Vespir would appreciate the grandeur of the capital once she had survived these next few minutes. Burying her head against Karina's shoulder, she pictured what she wanted to happen.

The dragon instantly obeyed.

Karina put on a burst of speed, just enough to get out ahead of the Hydra. The wind screamed in Vespir's ears, and tears bled from her eyes. She had never gone this fast before, and adren-aline spiked through her. They were doing well, but Karina couldn't keep up that pace forever. They didn't have to, though. They just had to match . . .

"Now," Vespir whispered.

Karina pulled up and slowed a bit to settle just below the Hydra. They were riding parallel with Aufidius, Vespir's back mere feet beneath the dragon's talons. She pressed her face against Karina's neck, smelled the baking-bread scent that was peculiar to her own dragon. Aufidius grumbled above them, but as long as they weren't touching, hopefully he wouldn't care.

One minute crawled past. She heard Aufidius snarl: he sensed the intruders beneath him.

Vespir stifled a scream when Aufidius's talons—each nearly as long as a table—swiped the air a hairbreadth from Karina's wings. If caught, those talons would slice through them like butter. Just a few more seconds before the descent would begin. Only a few, but it needed to happen now. Now. Now. *Now.*

Why wasn't the Hydra banking? Karina was starting to tire. Much longer, and the dragon would spiral out of control. They wouldn't make it to Dragonspire. They'd crash in the fields.

Please. Please.

Aufidius pedaled his taloned feet once again, and once again he just, just missed them. Vespir knew in her gut that the third time, the Hydra would not miss.

Please.

And then . . .

Aufidius pitched back, ready for his descent. He banked, and his wings provided a surge of wind.

Vespir clung to Karina as they shot ahead.

Be like an arrow, girl.

No one needed to ask directions to the finish line. All they could do was fall, and hope.

Hyperia gave a bewildered cry as Karina and Vespir shot ahead. Karina folded her wings against her body and hurtled toward the earth, the capital rapidly spreading out beneath them. Vespir cracked her eyes and watched the buildings come into view: the golden towers, the marble arches, the aqueducts

cordoning off the edges of the city. Terra-cotta rooftops and pi-
azzas with elaborate fountains. The crowds' cheers grew louder
as she spiraled to the finish line.

Vespir could no longer see; she could only hold on.

Behind her, Aufidius roared. Vespir could hear the creature's
wings flapping hard to catch up. Closer. Closer. She smelled
acrid smoke. If that beast tried to roast her now, Karina would
not have the power to move out of the way.

The great black silk banner grew nearer. Vespir squeezed
herself against Karina, the crowds screamed, the air around her
split with roars and—

Vespir raised her head as Karina zoomed past the banner
and into the city.

First.

Her dragon spread her wings and slowed. She soared over
the crowds' heads as the others flew in behind. Vespir put a hand
over her racing heart and whooped. She could not hear her own
voice in the cacophony. Children leaned out of windows and off
balconies to fling handfuls of pink and white flower petals into
the air. Bands played a triumphant march below as the competitors sped along the main boulevard, soaring toward the heart of
the city. Women waved handkerchiefs and tossed bound stalks
of dragongrass, which grew on the fabled banks of the imperial river. Vespir pumped her fist, and the crowds roared their
approval. She was air, now, air and light. People threw gold and
silver coins to sparkle in the air, and Vespir caught one. Shop
windows gleamed like fire in the afternoon sun; as they rose,
Vespir saw the fabled rooftop gardens, lush with date palms and
tamarisk.

Before them the palace of Dragonspire loomed, a one-
hundred-foot-tall mountain of gold-and-white marble. The tall-
est building ever constructed.

Vespir and Karina rose overhead to make for an elegant landing, and from this height she noted that the building looked teardrop-shaped, with a sharp, narrow tip that slowly widened and rounded out. At the teardrop's point waited guards clad in the imperial black livery, all of them standing in two straight lines to allow the competitors' dragons to touch down between them.

The tip of the teardrop was the landing strip; the round base held the gardens and pools. The middle consisted of a tiered building, brilliant with gold. At the top tier, someone had built a fifty-foot spire—hence the name Dragonspire. Legend had it the Great Dragon had ordered it built as a beacon to riders everywhere.

Vespir landed, legs trembling as she slid from Karina's back. She cupped the dragon's face in her hands and nuzzled her velvet snout.

"Boop." Vespir giggled as Karina merrily chirped. "Thank you, girl." Turning, Vespir wobbled down the landing. The priests waited—how they'd arrived before the competitors, Vespir was not certain. Camilla and Petros wore even more magnificent robes now, tangerine silk with gold embroidery at the sleeves and collar, jeweled medallions with the imperial seal around their necks.

Vespir grinned, her cheeks rough and wind-chapped.

The guards stepped aside as Aufidius landed a moment later, and Hyperia dismounted. The Volscia girl stalked toward Vespir, her heeled shoes a brisk slap on the pavement. Oh no.

Vespir considered how to dodge the blow.

Hyperia extended her hand.

"That was the most brilliant bit of flying I have ever seen," the Volscia girl declared.

Soft with shock, Vespir shook hands.

"Th-thanks."

Lucian landed next, then Ajax, with Emilia last by a hair. Everybody approached Vespir in awe. Ajax didn't even seem pissed about losing. The four crowded her, and every one of them whispered congratulations. Every one of them smiled.

Vespir finally turned to the priests. She trembled with happiness, the ruler of the skies.

For the first time, she felt like a damn empress.

"Well?" she asked, beaming.

Camilla smiled in return.

"The Race is forfeit," she said silkily. "There will be no victor."

42

Lucian

Surely Lucian hadn't heard right.

"Excuse me?" He stepped up beside Vespir. Camilla and Petros exchanged glances, and then Camilla placed her hands together as if in prayer. She gave the most insultingly brief shrug.

"There was a skirmish on the edges of the peninsula—a dracomachia. Unfortunately, such behavior falls outside of the acceptable range of competitor combat. As a result, the Race is off. There will be no victory and no penalty." With that, the priestess gestured to the landing strip, the black-liveried guard waiting in a perfect line. "Welcome to Dragonspire. Rest well, for tomorrow is the final challenge. You will be taken to your quarters—"

"*No.*" Lucian felt as he used to when presented with an enemy's surprise charge. Tamping that emotion down, he took a deep breath. He would not let himself be that person, but this . . . was *wrong.* "The rules never said anything about dracomachia. Vespir and Karina weren't even involved."

"It's simply impossible to ascertain who would truly have won under these circumstances," Petros replied. His whining tone was like a needle inserted directly into Lucian's ear.

"Meaning what?" Vespir raised her head. Her voice was rough. "Karina and I couldn't have won normally?"

"It's impossible to know," the priest said.

Lucian glanced at the others. Emilia hung back, looking paler than usual; perhaps the long flight had done her in. She was rubbing circles at her temples. Hyperia appeared absolutely livid, and Ajax bristled.

"Didn't you see?" he barked, pointing at Vespir. "She got that tiny-ass dragon to go faster than a bull Hydra! Who *does* that?"

"Our rules are sacrosanct," Camilla said.

"Your rules are dragon shit," Lucian seethed. Beside him, Vespir seemed to lose the will to fight. She gazed at her feet and muttered something he could not catch.

Hyperia shifted through their small knot of a group, her passage as smooth and golden as she. The Volscia girl looked the priests in the eye.

"Vespir won this challenge with as much honor and ingenuity as I have ever seen." Lucian imagined her voice as an ice-encrusted diamond. "Give her the victory."

"My lady." Camilla sighed. "Your every word is redolent with command, but you are not an empress yet. There is much difference between a truly accomplished dragon rider and a handler's tricks. I assure you, this is far less impressive than you may think."

Vespir flinched as if she'd been slapped. Lucian's temper frayed to the breaking point.

"You were never going to give it to her. Were you?" he snarled. "From the moment she arrived at the island, you'd already decided her fate!" The old him wanted nothing so much as to grab Petros by his shirtfront and shake some damn sense into him.

Vespir's hand on his arm stilled him. Instantly, Lucian turned his head and quelled that hideous voice. How could he bring peace to the empire when he couldn't be peaceful at the slightest provocation?

"Thank you," Vespir said to the priests. "I always knew this Trial wasn't fair. At least now you're being open about it."

Camilla smirked.

"Rest, and we'll dine at eight. Do enjoy the palace grounds. Come this time tomorrow, four of you will no longer be able to." With that, and a swirl of her robes, she glided toward the entranceway with Petros at her side.

The five were left surrounded by the armed guards, whose presence suddenly felt less than welcoming.

Lucian shook his head. "The Dragon saw what you really did."

"The Dragon doesn't care about people like me," Vespir grunted. One by one, the competitors' dragons were led off by an organized flurry of handlers, taken to the aerie at the very tip of the platform. The imperial guard would escort each of the competitors to their rooms. Hyperia turned back to Vespir, pursing her extraordinary mouth.

"I'm so sorry," she said, before striding away.

"The five of us should have a drink or something after dinner," Ajax suggested as they entered the palace.

The ceiling soared twenty feet overhead, tiled in gold. Jewels winked in decorative swirls upon the walls, creating mosaics of the five Houses' dragons. Wyverns studded with rubies and Drakes dense with sapphires glistened as they passed. Golden statues of long-dead emperors and empresses saluted them from recessed alcoves. The marble floor echoed with their footsteps.

Ajax spun, taking it all in. "Just the competitors. If this is the last night of my life, I don't want to spend it with those priest clowns."

"My thoughts exactly," Emilia groaned, peeling off from the rest when one of the soldiers asked her to follow. She waved goodbye but seemed distracted. Lucian frowned as he followed her with his eyes.

"See you later," Vespir muttered, and soon she and Ajax had left Lucian with the captain of the guard.

The fellow wore plated ebony armor with the silver imperial seal on the chest: five dragon heads radiating outward, like a five-pointed star. His helm had two great, stylized horns of obsidian curling around it.

"Which way to my room?" Lucian asked, then gasped as the guard removed his helmet.

The captain grinned, a familiar smile in a wonderfully familiar face.

"Rufus?" Lucian cried.

"Hey, one captain to another now." Rufus clasped forearms with Lucian. "Though, last I heard, you were giving all that up to weed gardens for the Sacred Brothers."

"Something like that." Lucian grinned.

Rufus was a Karthagon boy from the deep desert territories, conscripted into the army when he was barely twelve years old. The two had met in the snowy terrain of the northern expansion. Soon after Lucian's first battle on dragonback, he'd left the luxury of his family tents and the officers' mess to rough it with the foot soldiers. That's where he'd met Rufus, when the boy had been awed by Tyche and Lucian had encouraged him to pet her. Where they'd trained together, pushed each other to better things, made fun of each other for their bumbling attempts to talk to girls.

Rufus had started off scrawny, Ajax's height. Now, he was nearly six feet, broad-shouldered. His smooth, dark skin had lost its adolescent roughness. The snapping light in his eyes, though, was still him entirely.

"When did you get *this* job?" Lucian slapped his friend on the shoulder. "I thought you were transferring to a division on the Masarian frontlines, closer to home." It had been over two years since they'd parted. Lucian had been sorry to lose a friendly face.

"Your father put in a good word for me at the top. I transferred to the corps here, and then right after the emperor started getting sick . . ." He lowered his voice. "The old captain of the guard just offered his resignation and left overnight. Next thing I knew, I was promoted."

"At least one of us fulfilled his potential," Lucian said, trying to smile. Rufus lost his own grin.

"I don't know how in the depths you got into this Trial, but may the bright stars guide you to the throne," he said.

In Karthago, they had worshipped the stars long before the dragon riders arrived. Karthagons believed that the stars were their ancestors, every one reborn as a god in the sky. Gaius Sabel, due to his wife Ayzebel's influence, had allowed the people to keep their religious customs so long as they did not flaunt them. Generous, most people called it. Basic decency was Lucian's opinion.

A ruler should accept all his people, not a special class of them.

But after the Race, Lucian felt like the Trial was simply dragging all five of them along, up to the edge of a cliff and then over it. Justice didn't exist here. Only power.

Rufus had once told him "there is power in the stars, and in the hearts they govern." An old saying from an older Karthago. Lucian had smiled bitterly at the idea that there could be anything graceful or loving in power.

This was not something to tell Rufus. There'd been so many

things Lucian had never told him, for the sake of the other boy's happiness.

So Lucian clapped his brother-in-arms on the shoulder.

"Pray for me," he said, "and the stars will do the rest."

Dinner had been a silent affair, everyone scraping their plates and eyeing the priests at either end of the long table. The dining hall was a long, echoing chamber with wooden walls and the shields of each of the five families on proud display. The table, twenty feet of polished mahogany, had been set with crystal and linen, decanters of gold, the plateware pewter with heavy cutlery of the princeliest silver. The roast boar and flamingo tongues had been exquisite, but no one had eaten very much. Lucian had had to make do with bread and figs. When the meal was done, the five trooped out in formation to find a parlor far away from the sour-faced priests.

They found one, a room with tall windows facing the east. The river was a bend of silver in the moonlight, and the whole of Dragonspire was lit with twinkling lights. Fireworks erupted in the distance, blossoming red and green in the sky. The people were celebrating their new soon-to-be emperor.

Emilia sat on a low silken couch. Lucian placed himself next to her. Vespir perched cross-legged on a chaise opposite, and Hyperia took her customary golden place at the head. Ajax whistled at a servant; a whole line of them in imperial black waited at the corners of the room, perched liked trained ravens.

"Wine," Ajax said. Then, "A *lot*."

So they all drank together.

Wine from the imperial vineyards was very good and *strong*. It had only taken a single cup to soften everyone's hard edges. Two or three cups to relax them.

Now, after four cups, Lucian felt almost happy.

Hyperia slowly put a hand through her magnificent hair. She had to move slowly so she didn't wobble; whenever she spoke, she spoke very clearly, as if proving that she was in no way drunk. The trouble was she'd say things like, "If I die, and you die, and we all die, then no one else will die. Correct?" and look around for confirmation.

"We should get some food," Emilia groaned. She rested her head against Lucian's shoulder. Her hair smelled nice.

"Y'know, I was jus' thinking the same thing, about everyone dying." Vespir smacked her lips, turned to Hyperia. "If we all get Cut, would that mean no one's emperor?" She chuckled. "That'd be funny."

"No, it'd be civil war." Emilia tried pouring some more wine and sloshed it. "That happened in the pre-empire days, you know? They used to have civil wars *all* the time. You could, er, schedule them, they were so regular." She gave a tiny belch. Lucian privately thought it was adorable, but he didn't say anything.

"I want a civil war!" Ajax climbed to his feet. "Can you imagine everyone on dragons just, I don't know, dragon-ing?" He sat next to Vespir with a triumphant smile. "I would win."

Vespir snorted into her cup. "No. No. You'd go down first." She wiped her mouth, giggling as she roughly elbowed Ajax. "Didn't you learn anything from this afternoon? Your dragon is *so dumb*," she hissed, then clapped a hand over her mouth, her eyes bulging. Incensed, Ajax looked like he was trying to puff himself up. *Like a puff adder,* Lucian thought. *Or a puff fish. Something small that puffs.*

"Dog is not dumb! He's . . . crafty."

Everybody looked at him askance.

"I'm sorry. I love dragons!" Vespir waved her hands,

apologetic. "I'm a friend to all dragons. Dragons are my people. I like dragons better than anyone else." She placed her hands over her chest, looking sincere. Then she snorted. "But your dragon is *so, so dumb*."

"Well, your dragon's *small!*" Ajax thrust his face into Vespir's. She grinned and knocked her forehead against his.

"Boop." That cracked her up, but no one else got it. Wiping her mouth, she said, "Your dragon is so sweet, but so dumb." She paused. "Your dragon's so dumb . . ."

Oh, Lucian couldn't resist.

"How dumb is he?"

Vespir's eyes lit up. "Your dragon's so dumb that he tries to migrate south for the winter with the geese."

Vespir kicked the table at her own joke. Even Hyperia chuckled, but it could be that she enjoyed Ajax's humiliation more than anything.

"Your dragon is so dumb," Vespir whispered, "that he thinks the dragon throne is a place where he gets to take a shit."

Vespir fell onto her side and curled her knees to her chest, laughing with unbridled joy. Ajax looked like a grimy, closed fist.

"Your dragon's so dumb," Emilia said, lifting her head with a grin, "that he mistakes the Platonic dracomachian hypothesis for Calliphon's theorem of draconic hierarchy." Hyperia and Ajax gazed blankly at her. "Well, *I* thought it was funny," she grumbled, and slumped back against Lucian.

"I think," Hyperia said in low, dulcet tones, sitting regally with one hand against her cheek and her eyes closed, "that I may have to vomit soon."

"We need more of this." Lucian shoved the pitcher at a servant girl. "And something to eat. Bread, grapes, rice, uh, bread? Yes. Thank you."

"We're missing a good opportunity for a symposium here, you know." Emilia poked Lucian's side.

"First." Ajax held up one finger. "What's a supposition?"

"Symposium. Back in the empire's infancy, it was a party where everyone would drink wine and debate philosophy and science and the meaning of the universe." Her eyes sparkled at the thought.

"That sounds awful," both Hyperia and Ajax said. If they noticed their brief moment of unity, they didn't show it.

"No. It was wonderful if you were *intelligent*." Emilia wrinkled her nose. "For a few hundred years, discourse was treated with reverance. But in the past century or so, debate and philosophy have been deemed essentially useless. Right around the time the conquering spirit infected every aspect of Etrusian life. What's the point in expanding the base of human knowledge when you can just expand lines on a map?" She went for a drink and found her cup empty. Emilia waved it in the air while she looked for the servant. "What's in this stuff?"

"Wine," Lucian whispered. She elbowed him.

"Careful. That sounded almost treasonous." Hyperia's soft, chilled voice indicated that her brief moment of not being herself had ended. Damn.

"Well, soon I'll be dead, so it's fine if I get a little angry," Emilia muttered.

"You don't know that," Lucian said, more roughly than he'd meant to. She blinked at him in surprise. Clearing his throat, he said, "You could win. You won the Game, after all." Despite the full understanding that only one of them could triumph in this Trial, and despite wanting that throne for his own reasons, the idea of Emilia dying . . . and on his order, if he were victorious . . . filled him with despair.

"If only the Truth was a debate. I know I'd win that." Emilia sighed and Ajax snorted, chugging a new cup of wine.

"I know how to talk to people. Trust me, the priests would be amazed by what came out of my mouth," he said.

"Trust me, they already are," Emilia replied. Lucian laughed before he could stop himself.

"Watch me. Listen to how brilliant this is." Ajax hopped onto the sofa, wobbling a bit to keep his balance. Beside him, Vespir craned her neck to watch.

"Should we look away?" Emilia muttered as Ajax made big, sweeping bows.

"Would you even want to if you could?" Lucian replied.

"This is a supposition," Ajax cried. Emilia sighed. "A, er, talk about why I'm going to be emperor, or why I really should be. So . . ." He paused, screwing up his face as he organized his argument. "I should be emperor because I am all about expanding. You know? Expand the empire. Expand the boundaries. Why?" He ticked the reasons off on his fingers. "More expansion means more land. More land means more people. More people means more taxes. More taxes means more money. More money means I get richer. More richer, I mean, I get richer means I'm in a good mood. More good mood means we're all in a good mood."

He paused, letting that brilliance sink in.

Everyone did their best to be polite.

"Also," Ajax said, with the air of someone who knows he's got a crushing point. "I'm going to get girls. *Girls.*" He threw his head back and crowed to the ceiling. "*Giiiiirrrrlllllssss.*"

"That is hardly a fitting argument," Hyperia began, but then Vespir leapt up beside the boy.

"*Girls are amazing!*" Vespir shouted, grabbing Ajax's shoulders. "But don't be creepy, though."

Ajax shook his head emphatically. "No, no, I will not be creepy about it. If I walk up to a girl and say, 'Hello, Miss Girl, would you like to come back to my golden palace?' and she says, 'No,' that is *totally* fine. But there's, I think, a sixty percent chance she will say yes, because I am an *emperor,* and I have a *golden palace.*"

"*Yeah, golden palace!*" Vespir shouted. She looked positively delighted by the idea. "My turn!" she cried as Ajax bowed to no applause.

Ajax threw his arms around her and hugged her tight. "Yer my bes' fren. Boop," he said, releasing her from the hug and collapsing into his seat.

"That's not how it works, but good try." She wobbled in place, was silent a moment to compose her thoughts, and began.

"I don't know how to write my name," she said. Good start. Lucian noticed—and saw Hyperia notice—that the servants appeared to be intently listening to Vespir. "I come from a small village, the kind of place you pass through to get to somewhere that's actually worth visiting." She wavered, but found her balance. "When you talk about 'expanding,' you know what I think of?" She wasn't asking Ajax so much as the whole table of them. "I think of hundreds of soldiers camping all over my village, hogging our two wells so they can water their horses. I think of soldiers loading up on our chickens and grains and potatoes because they're hungry. Because apparently *we* never get hungry," she grumped, rubbing a hand across her face.

"*Yeah, hungry,*" Ajax called through his cupped hands. It seemed like he was trying to support her more than he understood what was going on.

"So after they take our water and our food, the soldiers plant a flag in the ground and say we're part of the empire and then move on. But they leave behind some guy who sits at a desk and tells us that now we have to start paying more money and more chickens and grain for . . . I don't know what.

"And the guy behind the desk never gets his hands dirty, but he starts telling us how to run our land and when to hand over our children for the army or to work in their palaces or their fields. And no one cares when they take us, because why would they? We belong to them from the day we're born." Vespir stopped wavering; in fact, she stood frighteningly still. "They tell us how to run our lives, and then have us die for them, and then write letters saying how sorry they are that we're dead. Only we can't even read how sorry they are, because no one thinks it's a good idea for us to read."

Vespir's voice grew louder as the room got quieter.

"My older brother Casca. He got pulled into the army when I was eleven. I came home one day to find a wooden box on our kitchen table and my mom crying. She had a letter with the Pentri seal on it. We knew one of my brothers and sisters was dead in the wars. They burn the body, put the ashes in a little box, and send them back to the family." Vespir's eyes shone with unspent tears. "Mom couldn't read the letter to find out who'd died, so I had to run it down to the local imperial outpost to get some guy behind a desk to read it." She sniffed, rubbed her nose. "He told me Casca was a deserter, so they'd killed him on sight. And all I could think, when my mom and dad wept and prayed at the little family altar that night with the clay figures of the Pentri family and asked for forgiveness for raising a coward . . . all I could think was, of course Casca ran. He wasn't a soldier. He told jokes. He overslept and ate too much rice porridge. His trousers never fit because he grew so fast. And they squashed his whole long, skinny body into a little box on our kitchen table.

"Y'know, before the Etrusian Empire came east, my people were horse people. Not dragon people." Vespir blinked away her tears. "When Valeria Pentri came through to conquer us, we put up such a good fight that she married one of our nobles. Kinda like they did in Karthago, the Pentri started looking like us. But it's still mostly Etrusian, right? So my family name, the words I speak, the clothes I wear . . . it all comes from Etrusia. Sometimes, I wonder what my name would've been in some other language. I don't know.

"So, what are we left with?" Vespir asked, snapping out of her self-reverie. "Not enough. They ask more of us when we have less, and why? Because someone put a flag in our village or something."

She mumbled this last bit to the floor. Ajax roared with applause, and quiet glances darted back and forth between the servants. Lucian saw all of them twitch or nod slightly. Ajax hugged Vespir when she sat beside him. "Mine was better, but yours was really good, too," he said.

Lucian poured the girl another cup of wine, trying not to let his hands tremble. What she'd said was simple truth.

"You didn't explain the key part, though." Hyperia curled her lip, revealing small white teeth. "Why should you be empress?"

"I mean. Why *should* I?" Vespir grumbled.

Emilia, meanwhile, twirled a strand of hair around and around her finger, adopting that far-off look that Lucian had once known so well.

"Lucian?" Hyperia glanced his way. "Do you have anything to add to this symposium?"

This would've been a good time to say no, to drink and toast to whoever would win and keep his thoughts buried deep. But after Vespir's speech, and all the wine, Lucian felt his tongue loosen. And even though part of him shouted to stay silent, he found himself speaking the words.

"When I was a boy," he said slowly, "I *worshipped* my father."

Finally, Lucian told the full story of his first battle when he was fourteen years old. He told how he had been raised to wield arms, how he had vowed at age seven to one day avenge his mother and murder the northern barbarians who'd taken her away. Lucian had trained with a sword and a spear, imagining with every hack and thrust that some Wikingar monster died beneath the blade. When Tyche hatched, he had worked to be an aerial menace worthy of the Sabel name.

He remembered how, when he and Dido turned fourteen, their father declared that they were ready to do their duty for empire and family. Hector, who always put duty and honor before everything else, who took exceptional care to teach his twins to be proud and noble as well as fierce and strong. How Lucian had loved him.

The first time he and Tyche had flown into battle against the northern hordes, Lucian's new armor had fit snugly, his fur-lined cloak flapping behind him in the frigid northern air. He and Tyche had landed alongside his father in a dense forest, the Drakes nimbly alighting with ease. And Hector had explained the plan.

Ahead of them, through the gnarled winter trees, there was no battlefield, no barbarian horde. Lucian could see only huts and the smoke from cooking fires. He heard children's laughter.

"But, Father," he'd said, "this is a village." Lucian recalled feeling like the whole day was a drawing that wasn't turning out the way he'd imagined.

His father told him that in real life, victories came from everyone doing their part. Wikingar soldiers were headed east to meet the imperial troops in battle. Lucian's job, he said, was to make certain that any survivors would return to find their homes gone. No families. No shelter. They'd be cut off at the legs. So the ground troops charged the village, and Lucian took to the air on Tyche.

Lucian recalled setting fire to those thatched roofs, the burning sap and resin smelling sickly sweet, like toffee.

War looked so different from fifty feet in the air. The villagers mostly comprised the old, the sick, and those too young to wield a weapon. Lucian and Tyche mowed them down wherever possible, easily dodging the few arrows that were shot their way. Lucian felt sick as he moved along the village, destroying every home and building he could.

And then, beneath him, as Tyche reared up and prepared another fireball, he saw the old man and the child.

The man's beard was long, his eyes sunken. He pointed at Lucian in horror. The order to fire stuck in Lucian's throat as the old man clutched the little boy against his chest. His grandson? Probably. The child, no more than eight or nine, looked up at Lucian and the dragon and screamed in fear.

"Tyche. Fire," Lucian whispered, and his dragon spewed a stream of pure flame.

Later, when Lucian had his father's hand on his shoulder and was taking a victorious stroll through the ransacked village, they came across two bodies.

One was a man, the other a little boy. They were both charred beyond all recognition, but Lucian knew them. The man's arm was tucked around the boy, his body curled about him in protection. Their fat still sizzled, like something roasting slow over a fire.

Lucian realized, in that moment, that he was not and never would be any kind of hero. While the soldiers cheered and their few prisoners wept, Lord Sabel kissed Lucian's cheek and said, "You are my worthy son."

Lucian stopped his tale then and drank more wine.

Emilia sat fully upright now, her gray eyes soft with horror. Across from him, Vespir leaned over and put her head in her hands.

"What did you do then?" Emilia whispered.

"I yelled that I hated him." He wiped his lips. "That I hated this whole rotten empire." Lucian closed his eyes. "He slapped my face. He'd never struck me before. That was the first time he put me in the brig. It wasn't the last."

"You fought to expand the borders of something you hate?" Hyperia shook her head, her eyes hard. "There's nothing worse than a hypocrite."

"You don't know." Lucian leaned closer to Hyperia, every hair on his arms and the nape of his neck standing on end. Fury sharpened his focus. "You lived your whole life in golden palaces, like Ajax was rambling about. People like you don't understand what it is to have no choice."

"We all have a choice, every day," Hyperia said.

"No. A few of us have a choice. You. Eh, even me," he growled, because he knew she was right. He could have flown away on Tyche at any time, even if it meant paying the price. He had slaughtered and burned for the sake of his family's pride and in the interest of saving his own skin. "But people like Vespir don't. Even Ajax." He glanced at the two of them. "You can't talk about choice when they have none."

"I know what it's like to make a terrible choice." Hyperia stared out the window.

"Your sister wasn't a choice. She was a victim." He expected her to attack him over that, but Hyperia didn't respond. "So that's why I want the throne. I can't accept a world that didn't have room in it for that old man and boy."

Silence.

Finally, Hyperia spoke. "Antipone wrote the only law of empire we'll ever need." She held up a hand, palm forward, pinkie and ring finger bent. She'd adopted the classical stance of the philosopher. Lucian could tell by Emilia's raised eyebrow that even she was impressed. Hyperia was well educated. Lacking in imagination, yes, but not in education. "'I thank the forces of order that give me a tongue to speak the truth and a mind to comprehend it,'" she said, quoting the first rule by heart. She continued. "'Our empire is the only true and orderly and good thing in this world. How else would those civilizations condemned to chaos and primitive life be raised up with medicine, law, agriculture, and the arts? An empire provides honorable work for its soldiers. Their labor, steeped in blood for the future's glory, is a sacrifice that lets all prosper.'"

The wine fired Lucian's gut.

"'An emperor receives the fruits of war and gives greater meaning to the world as he conquers it. He prospers.

"'The nobles take bounty from the emperor's outstretched hand, allowing them to breed soldiers and scientists and philosophers, who in turn bring meaning and hope to the people. They prosper.

"'The people are safe and fed, and find meaning as they work for the stability of the empire. They prosper.

"'Those who live in chaos struggle and die. The empire restores order. Free from chaos, all nations give their people and riches to the empire, a tributary feeding into a greater river. They prosper. Thus, only an empire generally, and this one specifically, is moral and right.'"

Finished, Hyperia leaned back in satisfaction. Emilia cleared her throat.

"Dragon shit," she said cheerily, sweeping her hair back from her face.

Lucian gave a shocked laugh.

Hyperia's eyes narrowed. "Excuse me?"

"Antipone wrote that in the second century AD, long before the war machine was ascendant. Also, the second rule discusses temperance, how important it is not to simply conquer for the sake of conquering. Antipone specifically said that an orderly empire could only remain healthy by creating spells of peace as well as war, like the rotation of crops. Funny how no one ever remembers the second rule when they quote her." Emilia frowned. "Besides, didn't you hear Vespir and Lucian? Hungry people grow hungrier. Poor people grow poorer. Innocent people are burned alive. How does tearing families apart stabilize anything?"

"Temporary suffering is needed to make the future greater," Hyperia answered automatically. Lucian imagined the Volscia girl's mind as a system of cards; get a question, pull up the proper response without even considering what you'd been asked. He watched Emilia, feeling a surge of excitement. *Yes. Get her.*

"You know, I read a lot," she said conversationally. "I love statistics."

Hyperia groaned, but Emilia continued.

"The Imperial University did a recent study on the conquered Wikingar clans." Her words stung Lucian's heart. "When we first began our conquest, they had a twelve percent infant-mortality rate. Years later, it was discovered that the twelve percent hadn't changed. But one number *did* fluctuate, greatly. Care to guess?" She leaned nearer to Hyperia. "The death rate for people aged sixteen to twenty-five nearly tripled, because our empire keeps shoving them onto the front lines of even more wars. So with the same number of dead babies and fewer new families, how exactly do the Wikingars prosper? We're the only ones who get anything from it."

Hyperia did not respond for a moment.

"You cannot compare a dragon to a cow," she said at last. "They serve different needs."

Lucian felt as if he'd been struck. Emilia took a hissed breath, but her words remained calm.

"If a dragon eats too many cattle, the situation worsens for cows and dragons alike."

"What would *you* do, then?" Hyperia's voice dripped acid. Emilia didn't flinch.

She rested her cheek in her hand. A sigh ruffled the curtain of her hair, which had fallen back over her face. "I'm simply saying that this current system doesn't work. Maybe it would be all right, conquering these people, if we really did make them prosperous and happy, but we don't. We promise order, but we're making the world more chaotic."

"The empire is the furthest thing from chaos imaginable," Hyperia spat.

"All I know is that for anything to get better, something must change."

"Be careful." Hyperia's voice chilled the room by several degrees. "Be sure you don't start speaking like the chaos lord, Oretani, or his fanatics." The girl stood and wobbled only slightly. "I'm going to bed. I'll see you all for the final challenge in the morning." Hyperia swept from the room, the servants bowing her out the door. Ajax rose as well and set his cup down with infinite care.

"Guess our happy-family moment's done," he grumbled. Vespir followed him, and Lucian stretched. It had to be past midnight by now. If this was to be his last sleep, he felt it would be a sound one. Hopefully.

He still feared seeing those two charred bodies at the foot of his bed, but after speaking of them, the pain had lessened.

As he and Emilia walked into the dark halls, he said, "I like the way you think."

She gave a weak smile. "I have no idea what's coming tomorrow. I've spent years searching for every scrap of information on this Trial I could find, and there's nothing on the Truth." She gazed up at Lucian with cautious eyes. "I have to ask. Have you . . . seen anything odd?"

His heart picked up pace.

"Visions, you mean?" he whispered.

She nodded, biting her lip. "What do you see?"

"The burned bodies of the old man and the boy. The ones I told you about." He frowned, but exhaled in relief. "You see things as well?"

"Yes. I wonder if that doesn't have something to do with whatever we face tomorrow." She spoke low as they walked, checking over her shoulder in case they were being followed. Lucian didn't blame her. It felt like secret eyes studded this entire gilded palace. "I haven't questioned Ajax or Hyperia, but Vespir told me she's seen her family. That's all she'll say."

"And you?" Lucian stopped them. "What have you seen?"

Emilia was still for so long he thought she wouldn't answer.

"When I was fourteen, I saw a girl executed for being a chaotic." She began to rub her fingers together very fast. He'd noticed her doing that off and on. "Sometimes . . . I see her again."

"That's awful." Even though his flesh crawled at the word *chaotic*, Lucian felt a surge of sympathy. He'd heard stories—the nails, the blood—but he'd never seen the specifics. Monstrous as those abilities were, Lucian had always thought the practice of putting people to death was vicious. Apparently, Emilia felt the same.

"If I see that tomorrow, I don't know what I'll do," she muttered. Lucian took her hands in his, stilling her rubbing.

"You'll face it. You've always been brave," he said.

She shook her head, hair tumbling into her face again. "You're wrong."

"If it can't be me, I hope it's you," he whispered. "You're smart and you're good and you're brave."

He'd meant it to be kind, but Emilia pulled away.

"I'm smart, at least."

She fled then, her slippers a soft patter as she sped down the hall and made a sharp right. Lucian ran a hand through his hair. Where had *that* come from?

As he headed for his bedchamber, Lucian's foot struck something that skittered across the floor and glinted in moonlight. He knelt and discovered small shards of crystal, picked them up.

Odd. They were shaped like teardrops.

43

Hyperia

Hyperia cleaned her blades with dry cloth. She laid out her best gown, a silken affair with exposed shoulders and gold sequins stitched in five-pointed stars down the bodice. She polished her calfskin slippers until they gleamed with candlelight. A cloak of pure gold cloth with exquisite beading in the shape of flames completed her outfit for tomorrow. On the bedside table, her pearls and diamonds stood in rows like soldiers awaiting a command.

"Good," she breathed at last, spotless and ready for her destiny.

She didn't need to turn around to know that Julia waited at the foot of the bed. She'd be smiling ghoulishly, serenely, like always.

"There was a reason for what I did," Hyperia said, laying her jeweled dagger in her lap. "Don't worry." Hyperia checked for Julia's reflection in the mirror of her blade. "You're going to be so proud that I killed you."

44

Hyperia

The next morning, the final test waited outside of the palace, deep within the labyrinthine gardens. Hyperia, Emilia, Vespir, Lucian, and Ajax stood before the entrance to a void.

Whatever they had expected, this had not been it.

The gate nestled between two sharp cypress trees, with bushes of wild roses crowded on either side. While the blooms were lovely, Hyperia noted the dense snarl of thorns and resolved to be careful. The void, or whatever it was, lay framed by gray stone doorjambs, a lintel on top. If one were passing casually, one would never notice it.

Through that doorway waited darkness of the most impermeable, inky sort. No noise came from it, not the drip of some faraway water, not the wind. In fact, she got the impression the void actually swallowed sound. Hyperia imagined that, should she set foot inside, she would merely . . . cease to be.

Is this truly the magic of order? She nearly pinched herself for thinking such a thing. This world held many mysteries, not all of which could be understood by a person like her. That was why they had priests.

"We just . . . go inside?" Emilia asked. It was only the competitors and the priests. The imperial guard was nowhere to be seen.

"Yes. The final challenge awaits," Camilla said.

"We can't tell you what's within, because we hardly know ourselves," Petros explained. "When Emperor Erasmus returned, he merely said he'd seen the Truth." The priest nodded. "I'll give you this piece of advice. Most of the emperors or empresses who have been selected passed this challenge."

"Passed? Not won?" Emilia asked.

"So far, you've competed against one another. In this challenge, it is said that you will compete against yourself. There is no ranking. You either pass, or you don't."

The Truth, it seemed, was more important than anything prior. Hyperia felt her shoulders relax. She had never avoided facing unpleasant truths head on.

"How do we know if we pass?" Lucian asked. He took a deep breath, his gaze unwaveringly straight.

"You'll know," Petros replied. Hyperia pursed her lips. Not terribly helpful.

"Go." Camilla waved the competitors forward. "One at a time, but you can all be inside at once." Hyperia watched Emilia enter first—even the relatively thin girl had to turn sideways and squeeze. Then Ajax, then Vespir. Ever the gentleman, Lucian gestured for Hyperia to go, but she shook her head.

"I'm happy to be last," she said. Hopefully, she didn't sound frightened. Shrugging, he squeezed his muscular frame inside. Hyperia crouched and turned herself. She feared nothing, but she hated tight spaces. Those were the opposite of what a dragon needed.

But she inched into the dark bowels of that doorway. The five shuffled forward. The air here was still, almost . . . blank. Hyperia peeked back and discovered that the doorway's light had grown watery, even though they hadn't gone that far in.

"Where are we?" she asked. Her voice didn't seem to carry,

as though there was some presence close on every side, trapping her and her words. Her flesh beaded at the thought. "Hello?" Hyperia whispered. The others did not respond. They'd vanished.

The world around her was darkness and silence. Hyperia rocked on her heels and gripped the dagger's hilt at her side. She would wait for something to come for her, and then if need be she'd kill it. She always felt better with a plan.

Something breathed in the dark.

Hyperia turned, and her hand fell from the hilt.

"It can't be," she whispered.

45

Ajax

A jax stood in a room filled with gold. From nothing to every-thing, dark to bright in two damn blinks. He kicked at a pile of coins, which fell in a shimmer. On his knees, he picked up a handful and found them imprinted with his own face. Ajax Sarkonus. He slipped them through his fingers, waterfalling them back to earth.

Sapphires, emeralds, daggers encrusted with diamonds, golden chairs in the shape of dragons with velvet cushions red as blood . . . all the wealth he'd ever wanted sprawled before him. Ajax felt ravenous, ready to gorge himself on every plea-sure he'd ever craved. He wanted to roll through the piles of treasure but had to restrain himself. No, he must be an emperor about this.

Ahead loomed a large, four-poster canopied bed with red velvet coverings and silk drapes.

In the bed . . .

Ajax froze at the screams.

She screamed and battled him, their forms shuffling in that bed, defiling it . . .

Defiling it with *him*. Ajax recognized the red velvet of his father's bedchamber.

Something stuck out in the midst of the treasure: a sword with a dragon's head as its hilt, the mouth open, a gleaming ruby for an eye. Ajax wrested the sword out of the mountain of coins. The blade shone in the candlelight, the hilt warmed his hands. He could imagine pulling back those hangings, bringing the sword point down through the old man's back. Stab and end it, end it, end it, make it all *stop* . . .

Ajax froze as he listened to those wails and grunts. The shame of it, the dirty shame . . . he couldn't look at where he'd come from.

What he was.

Evil. Hateful. A smudge on the sheets.

"Stop," he gasped, dropping the sword into the coins and falling to his knees, fingers weaving behind his head as he rocked back and forth.

"Stop," he moaned, but he could not move to stop it.

And then—

46

Lucian

L ucian discovered the old man and the little boy unburned
and alive. He'd anticipated coming across their smoked
corpses and choked in relief.

"Hey!" he yelled, but they did not notice him. Instead, they
looked to the sky, the old man sheltering the child in his arms.

Lucian's stomach seized to find his dragon, his Tyche, flaring her wings midair in perfect battle stance. She stretched out
her blue-and-black neck and gave an unearthly shriek, her war
cry. Her tail lashed, her wings beat heavily. Lucian felt his hair
move in the wind she created. His tongue lay swollen in his
mouth.

"Tyche! Girl, stop! Stop!" Lucian waved his arms, desperate
for his dragon's attention, but she kept her focus on the huddled
man and boy. Her jaw dropped, heat rippled from her mouth.
The first sparks of fire began. She was preparing to burn. To kill.

No. Not again. Lucian ran for his dragon, and his foot struck
something heavy. Looking down, he found a golden sword, hilt
in the shape of a dragon's head. A red ruby eye gleamed up at
him. *Take me,* it seemed to say. Lucian reached . . .

But he had sworn never to pick up a blade again, and why
should he take up arms against his own dragon?

Lucian shielded the man and boy with his body. Tyche glowered down at him, smoke streaming from her nostrils. She smelled of autumn bonfires, a scent he'd always loved.

"Stop, girl! It's me!" Lucian cried.

When Tyche opened her mouth and the flame billowed toward him, Lucian fell against the man and boy in his panic. As their bodies roasted together, as the agony of dragonfire obliterated his senses, his last thought was that he had saved none of them.

And then—

47

Vespir

Vespir was not permitted to raise her eyes. Here, on her hands and knees alongside her family, she was in her natural state. She glanced to the side and noted that Casca was among them. He smiled at her, that gap-toothed grin from their childhood. Vespir allowed a small shake of her head. No fooling around. The fact that he was dead didn't trouble her; they had bigger worries.

The Pentri regarded them, and she had to remain silent.

How . . . how had she gotten here, though? Vespir blinked, something tickling the back of her mind. Her mother nudged her—apparently Vespir wasn't being obedient enough. She bowed her head again.

"You." Lord Pentri's boots stopped before her face, and Vespir touched her forehead to the ground. "You *nothing*," the lord said, kicking her. Vespir grunted as a sharp pain lanced through her body. She crumpled in on herself, preparing to succumb to a shower of blows. What else could she do? There was relief in this submission.

But more blows did not come. Peeking up through her hair, Vespir watched as Lord Pentri pulled Casca to his feet. Dusted him off. Horror froze her blood as the lord selected more of her brothers and sisters to stand. Vespir crawled back to her knees, shivering while her mother wept and pled with her not to do anything. *Keep small. Don't let them see you.*

It's the best we can get.

But Vespir could not look away as the lord kicked her brother's knees out from under him, as he slumped to the ground. As Lord Pentri bent her brother's neck, unsheathed his sword.

He was a deserter.

And who was she to say no? What was she? Lutum. Dirt. She was nothing.

Nothing at all.

But . . .

As the lord lifted his sword above her brother's neck— despite knowing that there was no bringing Casca back—Vespir lurched to her feet. While her parents gasped, she threw herself forward. It was pointless, she had no weapon, and her mother shrieked when Vespir knocked Casca aside and raised her empty hands—

Clang. Steel met steel.

Vespir found that she'd parried the lord's blow with a sword of her own. The blade shuddered in her hands and nearly slipped from her grip. But she managed to hold it.

Lord Pentri stepped away, the rage melting from his face. He was rendered doll-like as Vespir rose, hefting the sword. Knowledge flowed into her muscles. Suddenly this weapon felt so . . . so right. Easy. A dragon's face snarled up at her from the hilt, a ruby glinting in its eye.

Vespir pointed the sword at the nobleman's gut. Lord Pentri fell to his knees as she approached him. So easy to slice his throat, watch him bleed out.

But he was Antonia's father.

Should she drop her sword and beg forgiveness? Or gut the man?

A choice. Vespir had to make a choice.

She made it.

And then—

48

Hyperia

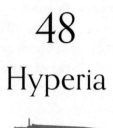

*J*ulia. Hyperia had found Julia in this darkness.

Not the one with the slit throat and the vacant smile. This was the real Julia, with soft, chestnut hair and softer hazel eyes. Her little sister gathered breath for a shriek of relief. Her shoulders lifted.

Hyperia prided herself on never acting impulsively, but she launched herself onto her sister. Julia sobbed against her shoulder. The strawberry-and-vanilla scent of her, the lavender oil of her hair. Julia was a physical weight in her arms.

Hyperia hadn't killed her.

"My baby, you're here." Hyperia sobbed. Why stop her tears? They were alone in this darkness. Somehow, even though she could see Julia perfectly, there was no source of light in the cavern. Hyperia didn't care. She didn't care. Her mind spun, relief coursing through her veins. "I missed you. Really missed you."

"Can we go home now?" Julia wept.

"Of course. How long have they kept you here?" Hyperia stepped back to cradle Julia's face, wipe her tears away.

Something clattered to the floor, right alongside Hyperia. She crouched to inspect it and lifted it up.

A sword, with a golden pommel, the hilt fashioned to

resemble a dragon's head. The emperor's sword, passed from one serene imperial hand to the next.

"I won." Hyperia beamed, giddy. All the misery of her childhood, the pain of the past weeks, all worth it now. "I won!"

But nothing changed. There were no celebratory trumpets, no beating of drums. The two sisters remained in nothingness, and Hyperia did not understand.

Until Hyperia realized, with dreadful and creeping certainty, that she hadn't been set free after all.

Julia watched with haunted eyes. Her lip quivered. Did she remember?

Hyperia screwed up her face, trying to remind herself that this was fake. Her sister wasn't in front of her. This was a phantom. Not real.

Killing her would mean nothing, because Julia was already dead. Hyperia had been a frightened fool to think otherwise. She hefted the longsword over her shoulder, so easy in her grip. The next Volscia empress, hers for the taking.

She only had to do the thing she hated most.

"Please no," Julia wept, backing away with her hand outstretched in some flimsy attempt at protection. "Hyperia, no! Not again!"

Hyperia flinched, biting down on her tongue. *It's trying to trick you.*

This time, the crown would be hers, and her sister would already be dead.

"Please!" Julia's ghost sobbed.

"I'm sorry," Hyperia said. With a cry, she swung the sword and sliced through the phantom's neck. Julia vanished in an instant, and Hyperia was left alone in the dark, the sword dangling from her hand.

Was that it?

Hyperia traced a thumb across the ruby set in the dragon's eye. She waited in that darkness, waited for the fanfare of trumpets. She waited for a moment of serenity that did not come, and an indescribable feeling began to bloom in her chest like some poisonous flower.

The void, the Truth, whatever this place was . . .

She felt like it was *looking* at her.

Judging her.

What if . . . what if she'd chosen wrong? As the seconds crawled past and she lingered in nothingness, her pulse began to race as unwelcome thoughts bombarded her. If this was wrong—if she'd done the wrong thing now—then she must also have failed before.

When she . . .

"No!" Hyperia screamed into the blackness.

And then—

49

Emilia

———————✦

After Emilia exploded Huigh's heart and lungs, she became difficult to manage. By the time she was fourteen, she'd been locked away in a castle and under her parents' eye for nearly a year. Emilia had insisted that this treatment was barbaric. Why couldn't she leave the castle grounds? Why did she have to stay so far north, where the sun barely rose in the winter? Finally, her parents seemed to relent. They took her and Alexander to the nearest village. A chaotic had been discovered in their midst.

A girl, barely older than Emilia.

As the lord and his family watched, seated on a raised dais, comfortable on velvet cushions with cups of spiced wine in hand, the villagers had jeered while the girl was led to a platform. The girl had worn the helmet signifying a chaotic. The locals called it a "beetle helm," but to Emilia it resembled a crude bird's head. A black metal contraption affixed in two sections, the upper part of the helmet jutted out a bit, sort of like a beak. There were no eyeholes, no mouth hole, so whoever was locked inside the thing could not see or communicate in any way. Apparently, inside the helmet's lower section, which was strapped around the neck, a kind of clamp held a chaotic's tongue to prevent them from casting spells.

I've never needed to speak to do magic, Emilia had thought, but wisely said nothing.

They started by unshackling the girl's hands and removing the helmet. Beneath, the crowd discovered a scrap of a thing, pale, with wide blue eyes and a snub nose. Someone had cut all her hair away with a knife; her scalp bled in patches. The girl began to hyperventilate as the constable took a hot blade from a nearby brazier. Its tip glowed molten orange as they forced her head back.

"Please. Stop this." Emilia had tugged at her father's sleeve, and he'd given a withering stare.

"Watch and learn," he'd growled. Emilia's guts had felt full of twisting worms when the constable sliced out the girl's tongue with one deft movement.

Emilia recalled how the girl's mouth overflowed with dark, rich blood. *It looks like berry sauce,* she'd thought numbly. Then she'd started to shake.

Her chaos slept dormant in her soul. The horror on display overpowered every sense.

The girl had been laid out on a table, chained, and the wound of her mouth cauterized so she didn't drown in her own blood. They'd made a science of torture.

First, they drove iron nails through the girl's hands and feet, binding her to the table completely. Emilia flinched with every pound of the hammer. The girl was pinned like some sick imitation of a captive butterfly.

Then they'd taken boiling lead and blinded her with it. The muffled screams, the way her legs shot out like she'd been struck by lightning, remained in Emilia's mind more vividly than all the blood. She clung to Alex's hand. Her brother bore the half-moon imprints of Emilia's fingernails for hours afterward.

They then sliced open the girl's belly in front of the crowd, pulling out her liver, examining the jellied red-and-purple of it, unspooling her intestines like yards of pink sausages. That thought, of breakfast sausage, nearly made Emilia throw up.

"Contain yourself," her father had murmured when she started to breathe heavily and bent over to clasp her knees.

Emilia didn't know at what precise moment the girl died. She had clearly soiled herself before it happened or perhaps at the instant of release. The constable threw each of her organs in turn into a fire, and the smell of roasting offal and shit wafted through the air as the people cheered, and dancing began. Emilia caught sight of two people, a man and a woman, both prostrate on the ground with grief. The girl's parents.

"It's over now." Alex had kissed her head.

When they returned home, her parents asked if she wanted to prance around the Hibrian Isles doing as she liked. She went to her room and lay in bed for two days straight. Emilia couldn't close her own eyes without seeing the girl's. She smelled blood in every cup of tea her brother tried to get her to drink.

That had started her love of coffee, actually.

And when Emilia finally started crying, and cried for almost eight solid hours while trapped in a corner of her room, her power splintering her dresser and exploding the heads of her dolls, only Alex had been brave enough to come inside, knowing she wouldn't hurt him. He cuddled her on the floor and made a promise.

"When I take the throne, my first order will be to stop butchering chaotics. I swear to you." He kissed the side of her head. "Just hold on a little longer, Emi. I'll make it all right."

✳

Emilia had not seen this girl in four years and had thought never to see her again. Now Emilia stood by the executioner's table, hands limp at her sides as she looked upon the victim. They'd already nailed her hands and feet and boiled her eyes. They'd even vivisected her, her stomach sliced open and the raw red of her innards on display, though the feeble twitch of limbs showed that the girl was still somehow alive.

"I'm sorry," Emilia whispered, reaching out to touch the thin white arm.

Out of the silent darkness a mass of people emerged. Emilia's head snapped up. She looked at the cheering, jeering throngs on every side of her. They began to clap, to throw things, and to shout, "Death! Death!"

"She's a child. She's only a child!" Emilia screamed at them, turning every which way, but wherever she looked she faced rows of snarling, ravenous faces.

We were born with an evil affliction, Emilia had thought when she first beheld the girl. Evil. Yes, they'd been born evil, though not by choice. At the time, she hadn't thought this butchery was wrong. Horrible, yes, but not wrong.

But now . . .

Alex had told her he would make it all right when he took the throne, but Alex was not here. *She* was. Emilia felt the prickle of power along the ridge of her spine, and the flow of chaos deep in the lines of her palms. Her body was a vessel, filling with a naked and uncontrollable energy. Her hair seemed to spark at its ends, and she tasted something metallic on her tongue.

"You. You *good people,*" she snarled, looking at their cursed faces. The girl continued to mumble and sob, struggling to free herself. Emilia blinked.

Who had placed a sword beside the girl?

It was gold, the pommel shaped like a dragon's head.

Emilia brushed the damn thing aside. She had other, better weapons.

People always feared a girl of too much feeling.

She would show them they'd been right to fear her.

Gritting her teeth, Emilia held out her arms on either side, her palms up.

"Should I do this?" she whispered, more to herself than anyone else. But that voice that she had heard on the island right after the Hunt—that rumbling, masculine voice—echoed through her head . . . and spoke her name.

Emilia.

She felt the power sizzling under her fingernails, welling beneath her rib cage. Emilia opened her eyes and looked out at all these good, ignorant, self-righteous people, and she felt the hatred rise. The chaos mixed with that hatred—and she let go.

She unleashed the power, watched as the world around her ripped away.

The girl on the table vanished. The people in the stands vanished. The darkness itself vanished.

A screeching began, the squeal of twisted metal. Emilia clamped her hands to her head but could not force that sound out. In this churning gray void of nothing, images flashed in her mind.

A leather vial.

A golden throne.

Some symbol, lines and curves she could not understand.

Emperor Erasmus, hands placed over his breast, his eyes closed in death.

A great orange dragon's eye as it opened. As it beheld her.

And . . .

Dragonspire in flames.

The buildings reduced to rubble, smoked to a cinder. The smell of charred human flesh, as sickly sweet as roasting pork, heavy in the air. Bodies, dozens of them if not hundreds, scattered about as numerous and pitiable as a drowned colony of ants. In her gut, Emilia felt the tugging horror of inevitability as she beheld this dead world.

And in the rubble, she glimpsed five particular bodies. Hers and the other competitors', all blood-soaked, with lifeless eyes turned toward the blue above.

Emilia!

And then—

✸

Emilia stared at the clear blue sky. Her body shivered as she pushed herself up on her elbows. Around her there were coughs and moans as the others rolled about on the ground. Lucian. Vespir. Ajax. Hyperia. They were all here.

And the Truth . . .

Now it looked like any other stone archway in a garden. Through it, she could plainly see a stone bench and a bush of pink flowers. Emilia tilted her head back and found Petros and Camilla standing over her, blocking out the sun.

"What in the depths *happened*?" Camilla cried.

50

Vespir

Vespir sat beneath a pear tree, clenching and unclenching her jaw. How long until the priests would fix whatever had gone wrong with the test? How long until they would know who had won? If she had to wait much longer, she might go screaming mad. Ajax sat to the right of her. For nearly an hour, they'd been stewing together.

"Think they're gonna get it set up again soon?" Ajax muttered. His outstretched leg jiggled rapidly. Ahead of them, the two priests circled the stone doorway. Camilla would walk through it and Petros would follow, clearly arguing with each other. Camilla began flapping her arms out of sheer frustration, like a great gaudy bird.

"I don't know." That had been her constant refrain to Ajax's questions. Vespir regarded the other three competitors, clustered together out in the sun. Emilia sat by the edge of the pond, hair shielding her face as she trailed fingers through the water. Lucian stood beside her, hands on his hips, the pose of some heroic statue—he often unconsciously did that. Hyperia had seemed oddly disturbed since they all were thrown out of the gateway. At first, she'd sat away from the others, rubbing her arms as if cold. Now she seemed to have returned to herself and spoke to Lucian while casting glances at Vespir and Ajax. Her attention set Vespir's teeth on edge.

"Here." Ajax flung something up into the branches, and an instant later a pear with a knife's handle sticking out of it plopped beside Vespir's hand. It smelled divine.

"Thanks." Vespir took a bite, the flavor exploding in her mouth. She wiped her chin, passed the fruit to Ajax.

"Uh, I thought you were gonna cut a piece, but sure. I'll eat your spit," he said. Vespir chewed as she leaned her head against the trunk and closed her eyes. Why had the doorway broken? And . . . had she passed the test? Vespir tried to recall everything she'd seen.

"What did you see in there?" she asked.

"Isn't that supposed to be private?" •

"I don't see why we can't talk to each other about it. Besides, I thought you didn't care about rules."

"Yeah, but in a smolderingly appealing way, not a stupid way." Scuffing his shoe along the ground, he said, "I don't think I passed."

"Why do you say that?"

"A feeling. Am I not allowed to have feelings anymore?"

"Well, you don't need to take my head off," she said.

"Trust me, if I win no one's getting their head cut off. I'll be generous. For the execution, I got the idea of this amazing twelve-tiered cake that you guys had to keep eating until you died. At least you'd go out with a smile. And cake."

"Anything else?"

"It'd be chocolate."

"No." Vespir sighed. "During the test. Anything like . . . images?"

Silence. The wind rocked the leaves above them.

"A weird eye? A throne?" he asked softly. Vespir's breath hitched.

"The city?" she whispered. Ajax shifted.

"Dead." The word dropped heavy on the ground between them. Neither wanted to pick it up. "All of us, too. Dead." His voice cracked. Vespir's throat constricted. She'd been hoping that the competitors' dead bodies was a nightmare vision all her own.

"I wonder if the others . . ." Her words trailed away as the three strode toward them. Even after the Race and their talk last night, Vespir still felt the urge to lower her head when the "legitimates" were around.

The five of them knotted together, and Vespir noticed how Hyperia and Lucian instinctively blocked the view of the priests. They were in their own world now, united.

"We wondered if you saw anything odd during the test," Emilia said.

The whole experience had been odd, but Vespir knew what the girl meant. She didn't have a chance to open her mouth before Ajax leapt in.

"The flask. The throne. Uh, some weird symbol. The emperor. Some freaky eye. The city." He swallowed. "Us." He and Vespir got to their feet. "You too?"

"Perhaps it's part of the test?" Hyperia said. Her face was ashen. The Volscia girl had spent so much of this Trial separate from them that to have her in their little group was weirdly unsettling.

"Maybe." Emilia pressed a finger to her lips. "But it happened just before we were thrown outside. Judging by the priests' behavior, this can't be normal."

Vespir peered past Lucian to find Camilla with a hand on the stone lintel, speaking rapidly. Impossible to catch the words, but Petros's high, furious swear was easy to understand.

"I can't stop seeing the fire at the end." Hyperia shuddered. "It felt like I was there."

"You *were* there, remember?" Ajax muttered. "You were covered in blood. Though I guess you're more used to that than the rest of us."

Hyperia flared her nostrils but did not look at the boy.

"That's not what I meant." Hyperia sounded hollow. "I felt like it was about to happen, and I couldn't stop it."

Silence. Everyone agreed. Vespir shut her eyes and rode out a wave of nausea.

"So we all see a weird set of images, then the Truth breaks and we're shoved outside." Ajax stroked his chin. "Is it, like, a puzzle?"

"It couldn't be, or the priests would have anticipated it. They've conducted an Emperor's Trial before," Emilia whispered. Her voice naturally lowered when discussing the priests. "No, whatever transpired in there had to be unusual."

"Does anyone think they passed the challenge?" Hyperia looked to each of them in turn. Both Ajax and Lucian cast down their eyes.

Vespir had felt sick to see Lord Pentri kneeling, right before those bizarre images appeared. It'd been as unnatural as snowfall in summer. That couldn't be winning, could it?

"What happens if none of us passed?" Vespir murmured.

"Maybe that's why the Truth kicked us out?" Lucian guessed, turning to Emilia.

"It's possible," she said.

"The lack of an emperor would explain why Dragonspire was destroyed," Hyperia croaked. "And we all died."

"Looks like we might get an answer. Their Graces are gracing us with their gracious presences," Ajax muttered. The five spread apart, opening the group from a tight bud to a bloom. Camilla and Petros wore scowls that could mean nothing good.

"There's been a problem with the gateway of Truth," Camilla said gravely.

"Yeah, mine breaks all the time, too," Ajax said. Vespir elbowed him.

"Unfortunately, no final decision shall be rendered until it returns."

Hyperia made a noise like she'd been punched. Vespir imagined that the girl was halfway convinced she'd been right. There'd be no ruler, and chaos—and death—would follow. It made Vespir a little sick, too.

Emilia had questions, of course. "Does this gateway communicate with you? Does the Dragon? Are you certain that this test was able to take the measure of each of us? What even *is* it? Is it a naturally occurring phenomenon or the result of orderly magic? How do we know the gate will return? What are we doing to retrieve it?"

"Allow faith to guide you, my lady," Petros said, eyes narrowing. "You must trust in us."

Vespir glanced at Emilia. *I don't think Emilia trusts anybody.*

"Uh, while you're both here, we had some questions." Ajax jiggled his leg at an incredible speed; clearly he was nervous. "We all saw some things that—"

"No." Camilla's voice was like a slammed door. "It is forbidden for us to hear of what you saw."

"Yeah, but I think you really want to know about this. See—"

"If you attempt to speak of it again, you will be thrown into a cell. Do you understand?" Vespir shrank a bit. She'd never heard the priestess this angry before, and she had certainly seen her mad. Ajax jutted out his chin but said nothing else.

"What should we do while we wait?" Lucian asked, trying to maintain the peace.

"The five of you are confined to the imperial palace, but you may go anywhere you wish." Camilla settled her shoulders. "When a winner has been selected, you shall be informed."

"But how—" Emilia began.

Hyperia cut her off. "Thank you, Your Graces." As the priests walked back to the stone arch, Hyperia shot Emilia a withering look. "They'll think you're questioning their authority."

"Why can't I?" Emilia frowned.

"Would you like to spend your remaining hours in prison?"

Emilia didn't reply.

"I don't trust the priests, anyway," Vespir said. She sensed Hyperia was about to respond with something scathing. "Not after what they did to me in the Race."

"Well." Even Hyperia had nothing to say to that. She sighed and pressed a hand to her forehead. "Is the Truth really that we're going to die and the city fall?" The girl pinched the bridge of her nose. "My own death doesn't matter, but I can't stand by as the capital burns. I *can't*."

"It may not be hopeless." Emilia edged into the center of the circle. "What if the other images we saw were a way to counteract that fate?"

"What do you mean?" Vespir asked.

"What if the Truth, or whatever it was, wanted to communicate with us? Tell us what *could* happen if we don't do something. Maybe the answer is in those images."

"Okay, I'm lost," Ajax said.

"Shocking," Hyperia muttered.

"Think about it like pieces of a puzzle. Like what you said earlier, Ajax," Emilia continued. "Things have gone wrong from the beginning, haven't they? The wrong people were called to this Emperor's Trial. Then in the middle of the Truth challenge, the one that's supposedly the most important of all, we're shown a seemingly random set of images and a gruesome outcome. I don't think this can be a coincidence."

"Meaning what?" Lucian asked.

"Meaning I think the other images could be a way for . . . *something* to communicate with us. To warn us in order to keep that disaster from coming to pass."

"A warning?" Lucian furrowed his brow. "But from whom?"

"The Dragon Himself?" Hyperia inhaled sharply at the idea.

"Maybe," Emilia said, though she sounded doubtful. "I don't know, but I've an idea where to start. The first image: the leather vial." Emilia looked to every one of them in turn. "I'll show you." She started to walk away, but no one else followed.

After all, Vespir had no idea if any of this was true. She had no idea if Emilia was right. All she had was the lump in her stomach that told her she *would* die and the city would burn. Could she really do anything about it?

But what if she *could*?

"So you want us to freak out over a bunch of weird images, then spend our last few hours solving a puzzle that may not even exist?" Ajax crossed his arms, one hip cocked.

"You have other plans?" Lucian frowned.

"Uh, drink? Order too much food? Get a massage? Live like an emperor?"

"You disgust me," Hyperia sneered.

"Love and disgust are practically the same emotion, you know."

"I didn't realize love also induced vomiting."

"Frequently."

Vespir didn't want to watch this play out to its violent conclusion. She tried to look Emilia in the eye.

"I vote yes," she said. "I want to know why I'm here, if possible. I don't see how it can hurt, anyway." Like Hyperia, seeing her own bloodied corpse had shaken Vespir to the root.

"I'm in," Lucian said. "It's damn better than sitting around doing nothing."

Hyperia swallowed and looked aside. "Do you really think it's a way to stop that abomination from happening?"

"I can't be sure. But it might," Emilia said.

Hyperia nodded.

"Then I have a duty," she said simply.

"Since it's no fun being debauched alone, I'll join you," Ajax grumbled. "Now. This leather vial thing. You know what it is?"

"Come with me," Emilia said.

51

Emilia

Emilia had spent five years locked in a room of her parents' castle, with the sea and the wheeling gulls outside for company. Her parents had often traveled to their other estates, taking her brother with them. Emilia might spend half the year in utter solitude. The servants were instructed not to speak to her, to merely serve her table or clean her chamber and then hastily depart. Emilia spent most days with the rain outside and a single candle to light her reading, speaking the words in her books aloud to hear any kind of voice.

Now she had four other people crammed into her room. Given the circumstances, it probably shouldn't have made her as happy as it did.

Hyperia and Vespir sat on opposite sides of the bed, with its purple velvet hangings and purple blanket. Emilia hated the color purple. Her family's color, yes, but wouldn't it be nice to have something in her actual favorite color, sea gray, for once in her life?

Lucian guarded the door, as if to block an unexpected attack.

Ajax slouched against her dresser, both legs vibrating with energy.

"Okay." Ajax sniffed. "What's this big secret?"

"You of all people should care about this," Emilia muttered, sliding open her bedside drawer and palming the rough leather vial. "I received this during the Hunt. These are basilisk tears." She tossed the vial to Ajax, who caught it one-handed. "They saved your life."

Ajax had no smart remarks, though he made an unpleasant face as he uncorked the vial and took a whiff.

"Disgusting. What do these disgusting tears have to do with anything?"

"Lucian." Emilia turned to the boy at the door. "You were with me when we found the islanders."

"Yes." He winced at the memory. Of everyone gathered in this room, Emilia believed—no, she *knew*—that Lucian would be able to follow her line of thought.

"Do you recall the word that boy repeated? *Felash?*"

"It meant 'guardian.'" He nodded.

Emilia's mind had been spinning over this bit ever since she was thrust out of the Truth. She'd considered it by the garden's pond. She'd toyed with it when the priests had explained the delay. Now she felt increasingly certain.

"Well, that's the archaic form. I chose it for the translation because the main bulk of my Hellinical studies consisted of classical literature. The sack of Troia? The three principal goddesses were all guardians of different—"

"Could we get to the point, please?" Hyperia asked.

"Let her finish," Lucian said, pushing off the door. Then, to Emilia, "I remember the poem. The *Troiaka.*" He smiled at her. "Go on."

Lucian's smile made it a bit difficult to remember her point.

"The more modern translation could roughly mean a 'protector, a wise person.'" She paused. "Or a 'priest.'"

The others all regarded her with silence.

Ajax bolted upright. "Oh!" He then slumped back against the dresser. "I don't get it."

"You mean like the high priest and priestess?" Vespir at least was trying.

"It does seem a little far-fetched," Lucian said, his tone conciliatory. "Wouldn't the islanders have a holy person of their own?"

"But why would that vial appear in the vision?" Emilia had to be careful, because she was getting excited. When she became excited, the pressure of her power could build. She had unleashed it inside the doorway—in fact, she might've been the one who'd broken the damn thing—and she believed that outburst would keep her stable for a while. But that could change. "Suppose the priests visited that island before sending us. Perhaps our hunt for the basilisk masked some ulterior purpose?"

"I have an idea." Ajax raised his hand. "Maybe they decided to vacation on some island, and when they got there, they went 'Shit, there's a giant monster here, we should take care of that,' and lo, here we all are."

"That sort of makes sense," Vespir admitted.

"But the islanders only began talking about priests when they gave me this vial," Emilia said.

"Yeah. It's an antidote," Ajax grumbled.

"Only if you've looked the basilisk in its eye first. If someone drinks these tears *without* that, it's poisonous."

"How poisonous?" Hyperia asked. She appeared lost in thought.

"Deadly."

"It's still all a cluster of what-ifs, though." The Volscia girl stood, smoothed her golden skirt. "I don't see how any of this can be proven or what it's even supposed to prove. I can't see how it relates to Dragonspire." She was testy. Hyperia, after all, hated wasting time.

She sounded strained. They all did, Emilia realized. They were coming up on the end of this Trial, four of them about to die. Perhaps all five, if that hideous vision held any truth. No one wanted to spend their final hours chasing a dead-ended mystery. If Emilia could tell them the truth of what had happened in that void and what she had seen and what she had *felt* . . . If only she could tell them of the power she'd sensed, as well as the doom. She palmed the vial again and set it back in her drawer with a sigh.

"Well, it was my first idea," she muttered at last.

"It was better than any of us could have done," Lucian said. Emilia felt her cheeks flush. A foolish, chemical reaction.

"What's next?" Vespir asked.

"The imperial throne," Lucian said. "I've been in His Excellency's presence a few times. I know the throne room well."

"When he commended you for your bravery in the expansion?" Hyperia's honeyed voice was laced with bitterness. Emilia found she wanted to strike the damn Volscia girl.

Emilia prayed that no one else noticed the thin, spiderwebbing crack that suddenly formed in the wall by her bed.

"All right," she said. "To the throne room."

52

Lucian

Lucian wasn't sure that walking as a group was the subtlest way to go about things. He was not even sure why he felt the need to be secretive. A gut instinct, perhaps.

Shortening his stride to match Emilia's, he spoke low to everyone, "Act naturally."

"Right." Ajax nodded. "If anybody asks, we're going to drink and make out with each other."

Lucian gave the deepest sigh of his life.

"You're certain you remember the location?" Emilia asked. He understood her concern; it was two stories overhead, directly underneath the spire. The group followed a twisting stair to the second level, which was both smaller and more impenetrable than the main floors below. "A serpent's knot," Emilia called it, sounding impressed. The hallways coiled around and around the centerpiece—the throne room. There were multiple doorways that led to different "coils" of the snake, and someone who did not know the way could end up accidentally going in circles for hours.

"I remember," he said. Lucian and his father had been led through these hallways by the old captain of the guard soon after the Vartl fjord triumph. Lucian had entered an egg-shaped golden chamber and knelt before Emperor Erasmus.

Lucian did not remember much of his audience with the emperor, but he remembered veiny hands that trembled as they settled a gold medallion about his neck, and he recalled eyes in a withered face, with hollow cheeks and a well-trimmed beard. Lucian remembered, also, that there'd been a little dried egg yolk at the corner of the emperor's mouth. Lucian had wanted to wipe it away, feeling embarrassed for the feeble old man.

"When I saw the emperor," he said to Emilia, "I thought it seemed strange to have a human being on that throne. It was like placing a piece of rotting meat in a golden box."

"Well. One of us may soon be the rotting meat of choice," she said flatly, but he caught the quirk of her smile.

Lucian brought them to a halt outside a golden door ten feet tall, ornately embellished with curls of abstract flame. The imperial seal—those five dragon heads in a star's formation—hung directly in the center of the door. Before it, Rufus waited, wearing his horned black helm.

Upon seeing Lucian, the captain grinned.

"Sabel. Come to get a look at your future throne?" Rufus removed his helmet and held it against his side with one arm.

Hyperia stiffened. "How dare you be so informal, Captain," she growled.

Rufus's smile dimmed, and his gaze flicked to Lucian.

"Apologies, my lady. *Lord* Lucian and I are old comrades-in-arms." Rufus resettled his helm onto his head. "Unfortunately, my lord, much as I would like to permit you entrance, the throne room is off-limits until the Trial is complete."

Lucian glared at Hyperia, who refused to be cowed. *You made our job more difficult.*

"Rufus." Lucian clapped the captain on his shoulder or, at least, the armored plate covering that shoulder. "There's nothing to do until the priests get that final challenge fixed. It's a bonding experience."

Rufus snorted but didn't remove Lucian's hand.

"Bonding? How so?"

Ajax took the lead. "We're gonna drink and make out with each other."

Lucian froze. Both Emilia and Vespir made noises of disgust.

"I'd sooner die, you worm," Hyperia growled.

"With tongue."

"I will *kill* you."

Rufus burst out laughing. He bent over, slapped his knee.

"Oh. You highborns are so *bizarre*." He laughed harder, and Lucian joined in. Soon, all but Hyperia were chuckling.

"Only one of us can triumph. We all wanted a look before we meet our fate. Come on." Lucian held up his hand. "Just five minutes?"

"For you . . . Ah." Rufus tilted his head in Hyperia's direction. "I'd hate for anything to get back to Their Graces."

"We wouldn't dare say anything." If Lucian had to yank Hyperia aside and explain the concept of subterfuge, he would. Rufus nodded.

"All right. Five minutes." With that, the captain stepped aside, and Lucian led the way into the imperial throne room.

The chamber was round, the walls arcing toward a point overhead—an egg, as Lucian recalled. Pure gold leafed those walls, with no windows to break the gilded absolute. Only a few candelabra dotted the edges of the room, while a great golden chandelier hung overhead, providing warm illumination. A few censers of pure gold, shaped like dragon heads with incense puffing from their jaws, lent the air a hazy quality and the smell of sandalwood.

"It's like they expected us," Vespir said in a daze.

"The candles and incense are lit every day, and the door guarded whether the emperor is dead or alive," Lucian replied.

The floor was obsidian, a carpet of red velvet leading like a serpentine tongue to the raised platform at the room's center. On top of that dais sat a golden throne. Two golden dragon's wings formed the back. The red velvet cushion was cradled between great talons made of pure gold as well. The sides were scaled. The armrests had been designed to resemble a dragon's clawed feet.

They stood in an ancient chamber, a space more sacred than even the white-pillared temple at Delphos. Everyone held their breath.

"Huh." Ajax audibly swallowed. "Little much, isn't it?"

"Shut up," Hyperia hissed. She ascended the steps, though she did not sit on the throne. Her fingers hovered mere inches above the armrest. "It's the most beautiful thing I've ever seen."

Lucian saw, to his shock, that she had tears in her eyes.

"We have five minutes." He gestured to the throne. "We should use them."

The others had no problem touching. Ajax settled himself onto the cushion, wiggling his hips to get comfortable. When he leaned back, he grimaced.

"Not very cushy. Does the emperor have to sit here all day?"

"I believe it's only required for formal audiences." Emilia sniffed the air and rubbed her temples. "The incense would drive me insane."

"I don't see anything," Vespir said, crouched behind the throne. She rose slowly, studying every inch. "I don't even know what we're supposed to be looking for."

"I'm starting to think this is all crap." Ajax stepped off the platform and strode toward the door. "Maybe the Truth or whatever flashed a bunch of things that we had on our minds before it broke. It's the Truth, after all. Maybe it sensed we were all feeling anxious, so it made that freaky picture of the city. And of us."

Lucian had to admit that it was a plausible explanation,

and unusually sophisticated for Ajax. Sighing, he stood beside Emilia against the wall.

"But what about that strange symbol?" Emilia asked. "In that language."

"What language?" Hyperia frowned.

"You remember." Emilia traced her finger through the air in strange half-loops and swirls. Lucian remembered it as well:

"I've never seen it, either," he said. To Emilia, "Is it ancient?"

"It could be an archaic form of the pictograph language from pre-empire Ikrayina, out toward the Temmurian plains. It could even be runic. There are old stones on the Hibrian Isles that predate—"

"I know what it is," Vespir said.

"*You* know?" Emilia cleared her throat and tried to sound more polite. "I . . . I thought you couldn't read basic Latium."

Vespir's nostrils flared. "I know what a put-waste-here marker looks like. It's standard in every aerie stall. It lets the handlers know where to sweep all the dragon dung." She blinked. "Have none of you *ever* cleaned out your own dragon's stall before?"

The room filled with awkward silence. Lucian scratched the back of his neck; he'd never looked after Tyche's basic needs, not even during campaign.

Vespir appeared disgusted.

"So, now we need to clean out some shit? This is officially the worst treasure hunt ever," Ajax muttered. "I vote we go back to the parlor and drink wine until they fix the doorway. Who's with me?"

"I've no objection to the wine," Hyperia growled, "though I'd rather miss out on your company." But Lucian noticed the relief seeping into her voice. She believed that this was all some shared fear that they'd witnessed together in the doorway of Truth. And really, he found he hoped for the same thing. It would certainly be less frightening than a cryptic warning.

"So that's it?" Vespir looked around in bewilderment. "We're all into this until it involves your dragons?"

"No, until it involves their *shit*," Ajax clarified.

But Vespir would not be moved. "Well, I'm going to look in the aerie. If I have to deal with dragon shit, that's just another normal day for me."

The girl left without any shred of deference. Emilia put a finger to her lips.

"That was different," she murmured.

"Different, but not bad." Lucian hated to think of Vespir shoveling out the aerie stalls on her own, even if he was now halfway convinced there was nothing to find. "One last stop. If there's nothing there, we end this. Anyone with me?"

"I'll go," Emilia said at once.

"I suppose," Hyperia muttered. "I do hate to leave anything unfinished."

"And *then* the wine. Okay?" Ajax said.

53

Vespir

Never even cleaned up after their dragons. Vespir kept her rude opinions to herself—or at least muttered them under her breath—while she inspected Karina's stall.

Her dragon hopped down from her perch when Vespir entered and nudged at the back of the girl's neck while she shoveled the waste from one corner to another. Vespir coughed; this was never the most pleasant part of her job. Dragon aeries smelled like no other place on earth. Sulfuric, with that rotten-egg element that took a while to get used to. But then there was the fragrance of the rosehip ointment for their wings, and the warm campfire smell of their breath. The musk of the straw, the citrus of the polish used on their claws, the pine tree sap treatment of their tack.

The imperial aerie was located at the tip of the palace's landing area, a gigantic, egg-shaped dome with the very top snipped off, providing an unbarred look into the sky beyond. The dragons could fly in and out through that opening. For people, there was a wooden door on the southern wall. The whole circular chamber was built of cool gray stone, and every dragon's stall had plenty of room. There was enough space here to house ten dragons comfortably.

"And their riders are all too important to muck out a stall," she grumbled to Karina, who nipped at Vespir's hair. Even Antonia had learned, under Vespir's guidance.

Vespir used a rake and a wicker broom to clear the floor and saw the standard marker.

Nothing looked different or special about it.

"Sorry, girl," she breathed, sweeping the waste back in its proper place. She'd just dirtied the floor and made life harder for the imperial handlers, whoever and wherever they might be. Vespir frowned. Slackers. If she could take over this place, she'd have the aerie well run in no time. She edged out past Karina, pushed the tarp curtain aside, and took a deep breath of fresher air.

In addition to the five competitors' dragons, the priests' dragons also dwelled in the aerie. A Wyvern and an Aspis, Vespir had managed to get inside and examine their areas. Nothing. Wiping the back of her hand across her brow, Vespir laid the tools against the wall.

"Nothing?"

A giant gawp from one stall, and Ajax staggered out backward before falling onto his ass. Dog poked his head through the opening, his forked tongue hanging out the side of his mouth as he panted.

"I said *no*, Dog! No playtime!" Ajax stood, dusting himself off. "Damn dragon wants to snuggle."

"Why wouldn't you?" Vespir stretched out her hand, and Dog nudged at her palm. She petted him between his nostrils. "He's just a big, precious baby."

"I didn't see the mark under all his crap." Ajax crossed his arms as Lucian and Emilia emerged from their respective stalls.

"Nothing," Lucian said with a shrug.

"Nothing," Emilia echoed. She appeared rather sheepish. "Perhaps I was mistaken."

"Well, what about Hyperia?" Vespir shouldn't have taken this personally, but the sight of them giving up . . .

Why, because they had to stoop down to the level of a handler and clean out dragon shit? Because *now* it was too hard?

Or . . . was it because Vespir longed to discover a reason for being called? It would be nice if her life—and death—had some meaning.

"Vespir." Hyperia's voice came from behind her dragon's tarp. "I need your help."

Hyperia's admission of weakness stopped everyone cold. Vespir pulled back the curtain and found Hyperia with a pitchfork in her hands, the rake and wicker broom leaning to the side of Aufidius's stall. The golden Hydra snarled when he saw Vespir, and his tail, wrapped serpentlike around the dragon's taloned feet, began to unwind. The bull was ready to lash out. Vespir swallowed, her throat dry.

"What?" she whispered.

"He won't let me inspect his area. I need you to distract him."

"Maybe we should just say we checked them all," Ajax muttered.

"Okay." Vespir turned to the side, her head down, and gazed at Aufidius out of the corner of her eye. "Here, boy. It's all right." Slowly, Vespir raised her right arm to shoulder level, inviting the bull to take a sniff. Aufidius's obsidian eyes glinted as he unwound his tail and took one, then two shuffling steps forward. *Scrape, drag, scrape, drag* went his claws. His guttural growl weakened her knees as he stretched out his head to sniff Vespir's hand.

If he rejected her, he could bite her arm clean off.

"Please hurry," she muttered, watching Hyperia shuffle around to the back of her dragon. It was a miracle, really, that the Volscia girl was doing this just to search for *something* that might not even be there. A noble usually had the luxury of sending others to do the dirty work. Then again, if Hyperia had ever wanted anything, it was the truth.

Bitterness swirled in Vespir's gut, along with a keen admiration of the Volscia girl's bravery.

Aufidius bared his sharp white teeth and snapped. Vespir jumped but kept her arm outstretched. The heat against her knuckles, then, the velvet-paper bump of scales against her hand. Fingers trembling, she touched Aufidius lightly on his snout.

"I did it," she breathed.

Aufidius lunged forward, and it was a miracle that Vespir managed to fling herself away before he bit. The Hydra snarled, tail curling once again around his feet, the end of it flicking like a whip. Lucian grabbed Vespir, pulling her back, his arm around her waist. Emilia knelt by her side, face white with shock.

"I've never seen a dragon do that." Her voice wavered.

"He's feral." Vespir wanted to call Aufidius what he truly was: a pit worm; an unbridled, wild monster. It didn't matter that he and Hyperia shared a bond.

Well, maybe it did. Maybe it explained everything.

"There's something here!" The Volscia girl sounded numb. "I don't believe it."

"Seriously?" Ajax bounded ahead, skidding to a halt before Aufidius. "What?"

"It's a door in the floor. It's been painted over to look like stone, but . . . I think it's a plaster facade. There's a keyhole in the symbol. I think it's locked. No." A moment later. "It *is* locked."

"Is there any chance it's some kind of storage unit?" Emilia asked Vespir. The Aurun girl began to chew on her thumbnail. "Perhaps a place to dump the waste?"

"No. We keep tack and supplies in cupboards, and the waste chute's by the front door. A handler would never keep one in a single stall, or locked." Vespir's mind worked to find a logical explanation. Maybe it was an extra entrance for staff? But why? And why disguise it?

She got up and began to search the rest of the aerie, looking for some type of key on the tack hooks and in the cupboards. But there was no key.

"How do we get in?" Ajax muttered as Hyperia left the stall. "I don't feel like hanging out with Aufidius while we try a bunch of different ideas."

"Maybe the images are supposed to help us," Emilia said. She gazed up at the ceiling with a faraway look in her eyes. Her lips moved, shaping her thoughts noiselessly. "I'll go to the library and see if I can discern anything from Erasmus's old writings. He was fairly prolific." Vespir wasn't quite sure what old, dusty volumes of philosophy had to do with all this, but then again, she didn't think Emilia was the world's most practical person. "Hyperia should stay and see if there's any other way in, since she's the only one who can get past Aufidius. Lucian?"

"I can find Rufus again, see if he knows anything. He's worked at the palace for a while now."

"Good. Ajax, you should—"

"I'm headed back to the throne room," the blond boy said.

"You won't be able to get in." Lucian sounded annoyed.

"I'm way past doors at this point. Remember?"

"Fine," Emilia said. "Vespir, you should . . ." She paused, clearly trying to think of something. "Can you speak with the handlers? But don't ask outright about a key. For now, I think we should keep the door as secret as possible."

"If they've been in there, they probably know about it," Vespir offered, but Hyperia seemed less sure.

"The plaster looks exactly like the surrounding stone, and the keyhole was carved into the symbol itself. If I hadn't been looking for it, I wouldn't have noticed. Someone worked hard to disguise it." If Hyperia of the Volscia was prepared to turn conspirator, they must all be onto something.

"All right." Vespir sighed. "I'll go talk to the servants."

As they left the aerie on their separate missions, she considered how fitting their roles were: Ajax to intrigue, Emilia to books, Lucian to soldiers, Hyperia to her monster, and Vespir to servants.

It was all that could be expected of her.

54
Emilia

Emilia had not felt this comfortable since before the Trial began. She sat in the imperial library, at a long table with the soft glow of candlelight to guide her reading. The moss-green carpet was lush under her shoes. Two cream silk-upholstered chairs with wooden feet carved to look like dragon talons hunched before the fireplace. The smell of moth and vellum lay heavy in this library, the scent so comforting she would have worn it as perfume.

Emilia perused *Imperatoria,* Emperor Erasmus's musings on the worthiness of an empire, the book she'd received upon winning the Game. Emilia would have loved to just read the book cover to cover, but the others were counting on her to find . . . something. What, she did not know. She had gone on this mission based on a sensation in her gut. "Hunch," her brother would call it. The others were counting on her.

Lucian was counting on her.

At the thought of him, Emilia felt a tickle somewhere beneath her left rib cage and down the back of her neck. She quickly focused her energy on a flower; she'd gathered a hasty bouquet from the garden in case of an outburst. A twitch of her eyelid, and the flower crystallized. She picked it up. A petal, now sharpened, pricked her thumb, and she dropped it with a curse.

Things were changing, weren't they? These past few days, her headaches had begun to abate. Her panic had slowed. Maybe it was all the fresh air. Maybe it was sitting with Lucian and the others, drinking, sometimes laughing, now working together.

What if solitude had been the worst possible medicine? Perhaps isolation had sharpened her affliction.

There is so much we don't know. Emilia couldn't help the pang of regret. Once, there had been the crystal chaos towers in Catalenia, a library made of glass that had contained the studies of chaotics across history.

A library that had been smashed, and all its volumes burned, when the chaos nation was defeated. Emilia's existence was an amalgamation of questions, and anyone who could have answered was a thousand years gone. She frowned as she read. Was she wasting her time?

No. If they wanted to survive the priests, knowledge and power might be the only way out. And Emilia, more than any of the others, had knowledge and power to spare.

She could imagine Lucian regarding her with awe as the walls crumbled about them, and she forced the group's way past those simpering priests. He had sworn never to harm another soul. His rough hands were gentle now; the scars on his body would never let him forget. They'd both endured so much since they'd parted five years ago. And Lucian, tall and battle worn as he was, had kept the most important pieces of himself intact. Still trusting. Still brave. Still kind to her; the kindest person she'd ever known, besides her brother. She thought of Lucian watching her unleash her power, imagined his look of horror at her freakishness. Emilia was evil. Born evil. As she felt the creep of chaos, a march of ants along the fissures of her brain, another flower shriveled and died.

"How are you doing?" Hyperia asked.

Emilia screamed, slamming the book shut and jumping to her feet.

She only just managed to suppress her power, imagining it as a stack of china cups teetering in her hand. The Volscia girl appeared bewildered at the outburst.

"Er, you startled me. No luck with the door?"

She brushed the dead flower to the carpet as Hyperia took a seat.

"We need the key." Even in private, Hyperia sat on the edge of her chair, as if waiting for an order. She scanned Emilia's book with a distasteful expression. "I fail to see how Erasmus's teachings will help."

"We all saw the emperor in that vision." Emilia tucked a strand of hair behind her ear; Hyperia's appraisal made her shy. "When you get to know a person, you can start anticipating how they'll act. His books are the only real chance we have to understand him."

"It seems like our time would be better spent finding the key."

Emilia felt a small flame of anger. "Books can teach you how to make a key."

"But you only like philosophy, it seems. Thinking *about* thinking." Hyperia scoffed. "Waste of time."

"Thinking makes us human," Emilia said. "There's also history and theory; those are important for an empress. Who won and lost the great battles? And why? The fight against the Oretani, for example." She swallowed; chaos prickled her skin. She must be careful. "I've read histories that declare he and his chaotic followers had the eyes of wolves in human faces, and that to awaken the static chaos nation requires the sacrifice of a noble heart's blood."

"Stories. Lies." Hyperia's nostrils flared. "I hate lies."

We've all noticed.

"Just because something hasn't been proven doesn't mean it's a lie." Emilia fought against a smile. "Besides, there's power in stories. Did you ever hear of Emperor Tiberius the Fifth?"

"Of course."

"How did he die?"

"He passed away in his sleep, after a well-earned victory and a hearty meal." Hyperia sniffed. "Dull fact."

"Not according to Plautus's *Secret History of the Empire*. According to him, the emperor loved honey and banana puddings. He ate so many that he needed to use the bathroom, pulled up his robes, and . . ." Emilia fought not to laugh, her stomach cramping with effort. "They found him dead in the morning. He was so stopped up, he'd had a heart attack trying to relieve himself."

Hyperia looked as if she'd been slapped.

"That is obscene! He was an emperor, anointed by the Dragon Himself!"

"He was." Emilia couldn't stop the giggles now. "But he also really, really loved pudding."

To her surprise, Hyperia's own lips began to twitch.

"Not funny," she said fiercely. The sight of Hyperia struggling so valiantly not to laugh made Emilia laugh harder, and soon the sight of her howling broke Hyperia as well. Hyperia clapped her hands over her mouth, and Emilia leaned so far back she nearly knocked her chair over. Wiping her eyes, Hyperia groaned.

"That's not actually true, is it?"

"No one knows for sure. But you'll never think of Tiberius

the Fifth in quite the same way again, will you?" Emilia shrugged. "That's power."

"You're confusing." Hyperia sighed. "Of everyone here, I understand you the least."

"Likewise." Emilia could anticipate Hyperia, much like she could anticipate how a lioness would hunt its quarry. But what went through the animal's mind? Emilia would never be able to guess.

"But I certainly don't like you least." Hyperia adopted that unnerving stillness. "Would you say the same about me?"

Emilia was smart enough not to voice her opinion, but not quick enough to decide what to say in its place.

"I . . ."

"It's fine." Hyperia gave a brisk nod. "I admire your honesty." She seemed truly pleased.

Emilia opened Erasmus's book again. She found her place and was about to flip to the next page when something caught her eye. She frowned, leaned nearer.

"What?" Hyperia muttered.

"This note in the margin. This was the emperor's personal copy." The emperor had underscored a passage about the concept of "infinite cruelty." In the margin, he'd written: *Cont'd in vol. 24.*

Emilia checked the spine. This was the twenty-third pamphlet of Erasmus's writings. Why make that note? And why "infinite cruelty"? Strange words for an emperor to write.

Getting up, Emilia went to the shelves and searched. There was no twenty-fourth book. No matter how she looked, going up and down the ladder to read every spine available, the book did not appear. She hissed in frustration as Hyperia joined her.

"What does this mean?" Hyperia asked, clearly puzzled.

Emilia said the words she hated most. "I don't know."

55

Lucian

L ucian sat in the guards' mess, a room with wooden floors
and bare stone walls one flight of stairs beneath the emper-
or's domestic level. The palace of Dragonspire was something
else: five solid levels of kitchens, bedrooms, gardens and balconies, of servants' quarters and chambers fit for entertaining in
imperial style. The emperor's personal guard got to live directly
below him. They had their own chambers, their own kitchens,
and their own barrels of wine.

They'd been eager to show those off first.

"A toast!" Aidan, a recruit from the Hibrian Isles with a pale,
triangular face, clunked a goblet against Rufus's. "To the next
emperor of Etrusia, Cap'n Lucian!"

Cheers from the men and women all around the room.
They were soldiers gathered from every corner of the empire,
from the Ardennes to the farthest reach of the Ikrayina. In this
guards' mess, where they came from mattered far less than
where they were. These folk probably hadn't seen their families
in over a decade; this had become their true home, their real
family. Lucian had known this kind of bond on campaign. Here,
he saw scars much like his wrapped around biceps. After the
toast came a loud song about a fish named Cyrus and his many

naughty nautical adventures. Lucian rubbed his forehead, and Rufus snorted into his cup. Aidan, meanwhile, sat down on the table, pinched off a bit of bread, and held it up to his neck.

"Here, boy. Here, Mungo."

A white ferret popped its head out of the guy's collar, and nibbled the bread. While Aidan cooed at his pet, Lucian elbowed Rufus.

"I wondered why he smelled so . . . musky."

"The ferret's clean. Aidan's the one who needs a bath." Rufus drank and grabbed Lucian by the back of the neck. "I know it's not up to the guard to decide these things, but most in this room'd be happy if you won the throne. Think there's a chance?"

"Truthfully, not much." Lucian cocked an eyebrow. "You wouldn't want to follow me anyway, Rufus. I'm a reformed man."

"Ah, that's right. The kindly monk, yeah? Gardening?" Rufus screwed up his face and drank, wiped his mouth, slammed the cup to the table. "You always wanted to change things, Sabel, but you never went about it the right way."

"How's that?" Lucian smiled.

"You've always been ashamed of what you can do."

"Killing is not something to be proud of." Lucian's smile died.

Rufus ran a hand down his face. "What do you know about gardening? Hmm? 'Bout medicine? How can you feed and heal the sick when you're no good at it?"

"People learn new skills. I know I'm too old for it, wizened age of eighteen and all, but I could try."

"You're not just good with a sword, Sabel. You can make people like you. Eh? When you stop moping around, you can make people *follow* you." The boy tsked. "Not right now, of course, right now you look like you've got a sign around your neck that says 'Please punish me.'"

"You sound like you know my problem so well," Lucian muttered.

"I do. The emperor was sort of the same, at the end."

The rest of the noise around them seemed to dissipate. Lucian focused hard on Rufus.

"What do you mean?"

"Well." Rufus scratched his tight curls. "I served here 'bout two years, yeah? Always seemed like the emperor was mad about something or sad about something else. Not just the regular pain of running the place. The old captain, Leonidas, he told me that the high priest and priestess would only visit the emperor a few times a year at his palace, as tradition. But by the time I got here, they were coming several times a month. Sometimes they'd stay one end of the month to the next."

"Do you know why?" Something was cold against Lucian's skin. He'd felt it in battle before, that instinct that a man with an ax was right behind him.

"Sometimes we'd all hear 'em. The emperor, mostly, yelling at the priests. Then he shut himself away and started writing. He'd always been a bookish sort, the old man, but now he wouldn't come out. Started demanding that he prepare his own food. Remember a while when he'd only eat figs he'd picked himself from the garden. He started muttering to himself in the halls. Remember one night, there was a crash in his chambers. We ran in, and the priest, Petros, he was standing by the wall lookin' scared. The emperor had thrown over his entire writing table, bottles of ink smashed, papers scattered. Took a while to clean up."

"Why was he angry?"

"Who knows? Doctors said brain disease got him in the

end." Rufus drank again, but his eyes were sober. "One time, I helped him off his throne when he was too weak to make it up and down stairs by himself. Know what he said to me?"

"What?"

"'You're trapped, Rufus. Like the rest of us. We will be burned alive and set free by dragonfire.'" The captain shuddered. "That night I slept with a candle lit. The old man seemed so deadly serious." Rufus sighed heavily. "He took to his bed, and a few days later he was gone. Brain disease." Rufus raised a cup in salute and drank. "Pray I don't go out that way."

Lucian raised his cup as well. "You were there when he died?"

"Mmm. Went peaceful, at least. Had a nice parting line. He said, 'Please. No more tears.'"

Rufus toasted again and chuckled.

Lucian did not.

56

Vespir

"A future empress must be a bit plump." The head cook, Hestia, grinned as she ladled more lobster soup into Vespir's bowl. Curls of fragrant steam wafted upward. "Plumpness lets people know she's got plenty of money for the best foods and lots of time to eat."

"I really want this job now," Vespir said.

"Oh, the whole kitchen staff hopes you'll take the throne." Hestia's dark eyes gleamed with approval as she bustled to the stove and stirred a saucepan. "Emperor Erasmus wasn't fond of Ikrayinan cooking, and I'd love to have excuses to make cheese fritters again. Maybe a sweet yoghurt as well!"

Vespir sipped at her soup, the creamy broth and the bite of tarragon warming her stomach. She grinned as Hestia turned back to slide more mutton dumplings onto her plate. A mint dipping sauce waited in a little golden bowl. Hestia had insisted on bringing out only the best.

Vespir appreciated the fine china, but she cared more about the mutton.

"My mother used to make them the same." Vespir's eyes rolled in her head as she took a bite, her teeth breaking the crisp fried skin and sinking into the juicy meat. She groaned and wiped the sauce from her chin, barely remembering her manners.

"Nothing's more important than food." Hestia sighed as she cracked an egg into a sizzling skillet. "Whenever I'm lonely or homesick, I make a dish of lamb and noodle stew, just as my mother taught me. A pinch of rosemary and a dash of cinnamon, that's the secret. I always say you're never alone so long as you've got a family recipe."

"Mmm. Though even my family didn't make anything like this." Vespir surveyed the table. There were the dumplings, the soup, a glass of chocolate with salt and cinnamon crusted around the rim. Thin pancakes wrapped around raspberry jam waited at her elbow for dessert. Finding an eastern Ikrayinan cook in this kitchen, seeing Hestia's long black hair tied in the traditional side braid, had been the tonic that Vespir needed.

She nearly forgot why she'd come.

Within five minutes of questioning one of the servants, Vespir had been escorted into the imperial kitchens. The room had to be over fifty feet across, the ceilings ten feet high. Vents had been carved to allow smoke and steam an escape. The walls were painted cream, and at the center of the kitchen a large window boasted a view of the river. The place smelled and sounded like the Pentri kitchens.

Plucked fowls hung by their feet overhead, alongside bunches of dried herbs. The copper pots bubbled on the stovetop, while two brawny-armed boys grunted as they lifted a bit of roasted hippo from the oven. Kitchen girls with wrapped hair sang a chanting song as they plucked capons for the evening meal. Vespir ate at the long wooden table, with girls on either side of her chopping herbs and kneading dough. No one stood on ceremony with her here or acted as if she should be gone.

Vespir had asked everyone about the aerie, and every single

person had shrugged and said that no one went in there much. The lead dragon handler, a woman named Sylvia, had said the aerie was far grander than most, but still a simple aerie.

Vespir sipped the salted chocolate, enjoying the tug of sleep. After a good meal, she'd love nothing more than a steaming bath and a bed. She shouldn't be surprised that the servants hadn't known anything. What did servants know of emperors, besides the way they liked their eggs, or the changing span of their waistline?

Vespir untied the basilisk vial from her belt and set it on the table. She'd showed it to everyone, from the steward to the second and fifth footmen. No one had known a thing about it, which made Vespir feel far less clever than when she'd gone back to Emilia's room to retrieve the thing. Maybe she wanted to believe that she would find the connection that had escaped the likes of Hyperia and Emilia. The girls who'd spent their lives studying music and philosophy and epic poetry would then be astounded by Vespir's keen mind.

"Oh, is that your medicine?" Hestia asked while Vespir took another mouthful of soup. The cook grinned, revealing deep dimples in her steam-reddened face.

"Oh no. It's—"

"Erasmus used it." The cook sighed, adding some sliced carrots to a boiling pot before wiping her hands on her apron. "Maybe it would have saved him, poor man, if the disease hadn't been so far along."

Vespir paused.

"The emperor was taking this . . . medicine . . . when he was sick?"

"Yes. Some newfound treatment discovered on one of those sacred islands down south. Her Grace Camilla brought it to me, asked that a drop or two be put in his food with supper.

Supposed to be hard for his delicate stomach, so it needed to be introduced gradually. Their Graces took such care of the emperor in the end." Hestia mopped her face. "I'm sure if anyone could've saved him, would've been those two."

"You're sure that the medicine came in this vial?" Vespir tried to keep herself from shouting. "This exact type?" She dug her nails into the table as Hestia picked up the vial, uncorked it, and sniffed. The cook made a face.

"Ooh, I'd never forget. The smell, especially. Smells like sulfur, doesn't it? And vinegar. It was strong medicine. They tried, but in the end, he lasted only about a week more. Where did you get this, then?"

Vespir snatched the vial back.

"Thank you for the delicious meal." Vespir stoppered the flask and ran from the kitchen. Pity there was no time for sweet things.

57

Ajax

———————◆———————

When Ajax was emperor he would change many things, but he would not change this throne. Not for all of the riches of the Karthagon spice trade, not even for the chance to force Lysander and Demetrius to compose poetry about his brilliance and recite it naked in the streets. No, this throne room had been built for him, and him alone. He strode up the dais and settled himself upon the velvet cushion. Left leg crossed over his right knee, he gripped the armrests and surveyed the room. His narrowed eyes darted from golden wall to golden wall. The incense tickled his nose.

If I were an emperor, what secrets would I have?

Ajax could live like many emperors before him. He could drink and dance and leave all the spiritual things to the priests, and the war things to the military, and spend his days doing whatever best pleased him.

But Ajax wanted to be worthy of the commemorative golden statues of emperors and empresses past, for his memory to be as revered as that of Ismene I or Commodus IV. He wanted to be Ajax the Great, the Ajax against whom all others would compare themselves.

Sometimes, a vein in his temple throbbed to picture that

glory so clearly while remembering that he was not yet sixteen. In many ways, he was a kid wearing his father's clothes, cuffs drooping well over the tips of his fingers. But Ajax would grow. If he were allowed to live, he would grow.

If I were an emperor, where would I hide things?

Likely, Erasmus's everything had been monitored. His clothes checked, his wine tasted, his shits inspected. An emperor's body belonged to the people, not to himself. Holding on to the things he cherished would be like trying to keep a mound of gold coins in well-oiled hands.

When I am an emperor, Ajax thought, slipping his dagger from the hidden sheath by his ankle and tapping it against his teeth, *what will I want to keep close?*

He turned his weapon to the throne. Delicately, he traced the tip along the golden claws and wings. He tapped the flat of his blade against the throne's legs. He reached over and stuck his knife against each individual golden scale.

Tap.

Tap.

Tap.

Tap.

Tick.

Ajax paused; he'd hit something hollow. Sheathing his dagger, he got to his knees on the cushion and bent over, his braid flopping as he gazed upside down at the fifth scale on the first row. Ajax touched it, tapped it again. Then, he tried flipping it upward. The hinges squeaked.

Success.

A little hidden compartment in the dragon throne. Glad for the first time that his hands were small, Ajax reached inside. His index finger traced something metal. Drawing in a breath, Ajax pulled out a small iron key. He flipped the scale closed, concealing the hiding place, and held the key overhead in triumph.

He stood and gave a showy bow. He imagined his father and all the bitter families as they were forced to bend their knees. He imagined a woman with his eyes standing somewhere in the back, watching with muted approval.

Ajax palmed the key.

"All hail the emperor," he said.

58

Lucian

L ucian arrived at the aerie to find Hyperia gone, and he paced while waiting on everyone's return. Idly, his hand strayed to his side to grip a sword hilt that was no longer there. He sighed. Why did he reach for a weapon the way others clutched at a sentimental trinket?

Rufus's words had set his teeth on edge. Lucian's "gift" was warfare. Did talent decide a person's fate? Was it wrong to focus your life around something you weren't naturally good at? He tried turning his mind to more important matters. What had the priests been up to?

Footsteps. Two women. His ears had been well trained from long nights spent listening for an ambush. Emilia and Hyperia came through the door. Emilia carried a book, and her cheeks had high color.

"Did you find anything?" she asked breathlessly.

Hyperia moved to Aufidius's stall, looking less excited than the Aurun girl.

"Gossip, mostly." Everything Rufus had said about the priests had set Lucian's teeth on edge, but suspicions were not proof. He looked at the book. "You?"

"Something interesting." Her smile lit her eyes. It was the truest smile he'd seen from her since this nightmare began.

"Erasmus left a note implying he'd written at least twenty-four books, but we only found twenty-three in the library."

Normally, Lucian would suggest that the mysterious twenty-fourth volume must have been misplaced. But after the conversation with Rufus, everything about Erasmus seemed murkier than before.

Hyperia turned, skirts swirling as her hand gripped the dagger at her side. Lucian flinched. *Just like me.*

"Someone's coming," she said, but relaxed when Vespir raced into the aerie. The girl nearly crashed headlong into Emilia. Trembling, she held something over her head. The basilisk vial.

"They killed him." Vespir coughed. "They murdered him!"

Lucian froze, as did Emilia and Hyperia. The air in the room seemed to grow thinner. He felt an invisible snare closing around his foot.

"Who?" he asked. Vespir checked over her shoulder.

"The priests," she hissed. Hyperia snorted at that. "The cook recognized this vial. She thought it was my 'medicine.' Said that the priests had her put a drop of this into the emperor's supper every night. He died a week later." Hyperia's skeptical expression flattened. Emilia's hand went to her mouth. "Don't you believe me?"

"Yes." Lucian swallowed. All the separate elements merged seamlessly. "Rufus said the emperor's last words were 'Please. No more tears.'"

Hyperia made a noise like she'd been struck.

"So he knew what they were doing to him?" Emilia breathed.

"And could perhaps do nothing," Hyperia grunted. "The high priest and priestess are the second-most powerful unit in the empire, and Erasmus had been raving for a while near the end. No one would have believed him, and few could have done anything even if they did."

Lucian pressed his thumbs into his closed eyelids, trying to think. Rage and fear merged, and also a horrible giddiness. This empire was a festering boil, like he'd always said. It needed a good lancing to drain the disease.

What can we do?

More footsteps. Hyperia thrust her blade forward on instinct.

"Shit!" Ajax skidded to a halt, the tip of Hyperia's sword steady at his throat. He knocked it away and shut the door with a kick. "I'm gone for an hour and you all fall apart."

"Find anything?" Hyperia asked, sheathing her sword.

"Oh. No."

Lucian noticed the discreet palm Ajax laid against his trouser pocket.

"What is that?" Lucian strode nearer.

"What's what? Aaah!" Ajax yelled as Hyperia grabbed him by the collar and pinned him against the door. She reached into his pocket while he squirmed. "Wait. Wait. This is my number-two fantasy, but you need to be gentle."

She made a disgusted noise as she pulled out an iron key.

"Once a thief," Lucian growled.

"Twice a rich man. Isn't that how the saying goes?" Ajax bared his teeth. "Look, I enjoy our little bonding exercises, but this is still an Emperor's Trial."

"The emperor was murdered," Hyperia said.

"*What?*"

Hyperia took the key to Aufidius's stall. Lucian stepped toward Emilia, keeping his back slightly to her in case the dragon lunged. The Hydra blew a line of troubling smoke as his rider approached. Apparently he was not in the mood to obey anyone right now.

"I can try luring him out with candied pork." Vespir paced behind Hyperia. "I'm sure the cook will let us have some. We could also try coaxing the dragons into song. That often relaxes the alpha—"

"Aufidius." Hyperia's voice boomed. She extended her hand, long, slender fingers curling. "Come to me now."

The Hydra gnashed his teeth and growled; embers flared in the smoke. Vespir cursed, knocking back into Lucian. He gripped her arm, trying to get the girls and Ajax out of the aerie. If that damn monster blew flame in here, they'd be reduced to ash within seconds.

"*Now,*" Hyperia snarled. She bared her teeth in the same manner as her dragon. Lucian felt the twitch of something intangible between the pair of monsters. "*Now, Aufidius. You are mine.*"

"What's happening?" Emilia whispered.

"She's challenging him," Vespir muttered. "If he doesn't accept her as alpha, he'll charge."

The Hydra extended his perfect neck, jaws open. One step. Two. The monster shuffled out of the stall, tail dragging behind him. The golden wings opened, the span so enormous they were all nearly knocked to the floor, and then shut. Hyperia pressed her palm to the creature's snout. Aufidius closed his eyes and gave a rumbling growl that Lucian could feel in his breastbone.

"*Stay.*" She nodded to the others. "Come, and don't dawdle." She swept into the stall, knelt, and fit the key into the lock. With a click, Hyperia lifted the door.

"I want her to crush me," Ajax whispered.

Lucian led the others to the hole in the floor. It was dark, though Lucian could discern a few stone steps and smelled stagnant air. He made a face.

"I'll go down first," he said. Quickly, he went out and grabbed a few tallow sticks and flints, standard for nightly visitors to the aerie. They lit a torch each, and he stepped into the blackness below. A few steps later, Lucian was lost in the dark.

The light barely showed him the next step; the black was that oppressive, like a body standing in his way. He dimly heard the others as they followed, their flames lighting the close, mildewed underworld. The steps were uneven, sporting dips that had been pounded into the stone by generations of climbing feet. Cold seeped into the pores down here; Lucian guessed this tunnel led somewhere back into the bowels of the palace, but he couldn't guess where.

Bare sconces began to appear. Once, torches had lit this path. The walls nearly scraped Lucian's broad shoulders, and he winced as a spiderweb broke across his face. Slowly, the tunnel around them widened, and four more steps led to a rounded chamber. Lucian halted abruptly at the change of scene, and Vespir and Ajax barreled into him. He entered the room cautiously, holding his breath as if it might be filled with poisonous gas.

Pillars carved with constellations supported the room. Upon the ceiling, the faded painting of a great orange eye observed all below. Unlit candles waited all around the chamber. With Vespir's help, Lucian lit them. Gradually, the room glowed. Parts of the rounded walls were mirrored, morphing the reflection into an endless, wavering sea of light.

There were also bookshelves in this chamber, at least eight, and all of them stuffed to capacity. In the center stood a writing table and chair, with pots of ink, pens, and a stack of papers. Emilia went right for the desk, lifting a page off the top. She frowned.

"'I believe that this is the end,'" she read aloud, squinting. Lucian peered over her shoulder. "'This next volume must wait until another comes in my place to finish.'"

"Erasmus?" Lucian asked.

"I think so. The books." He went to the shelves with her, Emilia glancing quickly across the spines. "Here!" She pulled a thin leather pamphlet and raised it over her head. A flaking gold number had been stamped upon it. "Volume twenty-four!"

"What is it?" Lucian asked.

She read the title. *"On the Depravity of Wrongful War."*

"What?" Hyperia's voice was like a slap. "What kind of an Etrusian uses *that* for a title? No, the emperor didn't write that. This is clearly storage for seized heretical literature. It's not . . ." Her voice failed.

Emilia continued. "Here's the first page. 'I, Erasmus Sarkonus, once of the Tiber, never a good man, sit upon a mountain of corpses as I write these words: I declare wrongful war to be a chaotic action. All that which is wasteful, all that which is cruel, and all that which is unsociable is to be found on the unlawful battlefield.'" Emilia flipped the page, scanned more, flipped, and repeated. Lucian marveled at the way she slipped through the maze of words straight to their meaning. "He differentiates between defensive war—defending your home from invasion or marching to stop a threat, which safeguards the empire—and offensive war—plundering a territory solely for its resources, which creates strain on the empire, and all that the Etrusian army currently does."

Could this really be the man who had slipped a golden medal around Lucian's neck and declared him a hero? For defeating an enemy that had been lean and hungry-eyed, whose defenses could not hope to last against the inexhaustible Etrusians and their dragon lords? Lucian had felt so alone the day he received his medal, so numb to the applause, and all along Erasmus had been twice as lonely and twice as cold.

"He doesn't say that!" Hyperia roared, charging for the book. Lucian shoved himself before Emilia, stopping the Volscia girl's advance.

"Think," he murmured. "The emperor was poisoned by the priests. Why do you think they did that?"

"If this is true, maybe the emperor—" Hyperia bit her lip, as if to stop the words.

"Deserved it?" Lucian finished. "We all remember what the orderlies at Delphos consider the most sacred rule of the church. Care to repeat it, Hyperia?" She turned from him and leaned against the desk. "'The emperor is the living embodiment of the Dragon on earth, and all that is order flows from him. Therefore, his life is eternally sacred and inviolate.' But the priests couldn't stand what he was thinking. From what Rufus told me, the emperor argued with them all the time."

"There's more." Emilia had started snatching additional volumes from the shelves. She crouched behind Lucian, flipping through pages. "Two volumes later, in a book titled *The Northern Conflict,* Erasmus talks about wanting to halt the war against the Wikingar clans. He says the ongoing struggle is depleting the empire's resources and killing its soldiers for very little hope of reward. The Wikingars don't threaten us like the Wroclawians did when we conquered them, and they don't offer a rich prize like Karthago or the Ardennes. But he writes that 'their eyes are all around me, and there is no one to trust.' These books were part journal, part manifesto." She flipped through more and more, lost in her thoughts. Lucian stood guard over Emilia, but Hyperia's shoulders sank further with every word. Her shoulders had never sloped before.

"What's this mean?" Vespir asked.

"It means . . ." Lucian had never felt so tired. "The emperor was against everything the empire stood for, and the priests killed him because of it. Maybe he was planning to pull troops, and they panicked."

"Perhaps," Hyperia said, "this is why the calling was so off. If the priests violated the most sacred commandment, perhaps the Dragon chose differently in reaction."

"I still don't think the Great Dragon chooses anything," Emilia said, standing. "But, Hyperia, that's a decent theory." A strange glow lit her eyes. "The priests set the world out of balance. Into chaos. And ironically, before that they'd had too much order. We keep expanding the boundaries of our empire not because we need to, or to save us from a threat, but because that's just what we've always done. It's mindless. It's tradition without thought."

"Uh, getting back to the point. So we're all here because the priests are murderers?" Ajax frowned. "But *why*? Why us?"

No one had an answer to that.

"What do we do now?" Vespir murmured.

Lucian helped Emilia reshelve the books.

"We can't let Petros and Camilla get away with this," he growled. His eye twitched to think of Erasmus trying to end the bloodshed, and the priests blocking him at every turn. Monsters. Liars. Murderers.

Lucian had no right to judge anyone else for murder, of course.

"We do nothing," Emilia said quietly. Ajax snorted. "Not until one of us is crowned."

"Why wait?" Vespir asked.

"Until a new emperor is chosen, the priests are the sole authority in the empire. It's tradition." Emilia looked quite pale now. "If we tried to reveal what they've done, they might be able to silence us. The imperial guard is sworn to obey them until one of us wins."

Lucian understood.

"So, whoever wins takes control of the guard and arrests the priests—"

"Exactly. And . . ." Her eyes widened. "Pardons the others from the Cut."

"Excuse me?" Hyperia turned.

"If we were called because of a crime the priests committed, that means there was an error in the selection. So none of us should face the consequences of losing." She grabbed Lucian's arm. "Everyone swear right now."

"All this swearing in a circle and hugging bullshit is too much," Ajax grumbled.

But to Lucian's surprise, Hyperia agreed first.

"Fine." She stared at the eye painted above. He could not guess at her feelings.

"Yes," Vespir said, elbowing Ajax in the side.

"Fine," he grunted.

"I don't think I need to ask you," Emilia said to Lucian. The corners of her mouth curled lightly in a smile.

"No. You don't."

"Of course, the winner will be one of you three." Ajax headed for the stairs with his hands shoved in his pockets. "We already know it won't be me or Vespir."

"At least you'll be alive," Hyperia snapped, following. Lucian trailed the others, stopping quickly to blow out the candles, leaving the room in smoky darkness. As he walked behind Emilia, he wondered how he should feel. Ah, but there would be time to decide how to feel. If they all made it to the end of this damned Trial, there would be time for everything.

"Hey," Emilia whispered. She stopped on the stair, and he fumbled into her. She looked over her shoulder, and her breath tickled his temple. "Will you meet me tonight, after everyone goes to bed? I need to discuss something."

"Of course. What?"

"Not now. Tonight."

He wearily followed her back outside, another mystery ahead of him.

59

Emilia

Emilia had never known fear like this, not even when Chara first settled upon the calling circle and demolished her tidy life. As the city bells tolled midnight, she left her rooms and walked to the back gardens. She hurried along the gravel path, past the night-blooming jasmine and the gentle murmur of the fountain. Now she looked out onto the vast spread of flickering lights. They kept the public lamps lit from dusk to dawn, every boulevard and avenue illuminated for the emperor's pleasure. In Dragonspire, there was no such thing as going to bed at a reasonable hour. The city was the imperial playground, a feast of many different delights.

If she became empress, honesty would be the sweetest delight of all.

And if someone else won the throne . . .

Right now she could scarcely think that far ahead. She was numb enough with fear just anticipating the next few minutes.

Fear is the darker twin of love. The poetess Acantha's words flashed through her mind, startling Emilia. *No.* Her face felt hot. Ridiculous, fanciful musing.

No, she was afraid for a much saner reason.

The crunch of footsteps made her turn and force a smile

as Lucian arrived. She felt her pulse in the very tips of her fingers. Already the chaos clawed at her throat, begging for attention.

"What did you want to talk about?" Lucian yawned, pressed the back of his hand to his mouth. His sleeve slipped, and Emilia got another look at the muscled arm and the light pattern of scars against his dark skin.

"You may have noticed that I have been a little . . . odd . . . during this Trial." By the blue above, why couldn't she have a natural conversation? Why did she start discussions as if delivering a formal lecture?

Lucian laughed. Oh. She was funny, apparently. Emilia had to suppress a flare of happiness.

"You've always been odd. That's why I like you."

Don't say something awkward. Don't say something awkward.

"I . . . like that you like me." Emilia's skin felt too tight. For the sake of the Dragon Himself, she wasn't looking to seduce this boy.

"You like me, too. Yes?" He stepped nearer; Emilia tasted her own heart. "I only mean, you agree we're friends."

"Yes." She inhaled. "If you still want to be."

He frowned. "Of course I do."

"Say that again in a moment." She extended her left hand to a rosebush situated nearby and flexed her fingers. The chaos tickled her brain. Lucian gasped as the roses hardened, transforming from bud to crystal. The leaves frosted over, and soon the entire bush looked as if it had been blown painstakingly from glass. The thorns glittered with starlight.

Lucian crouched to inspect it, and as he did, Emilia pressed her palms together and prayed to the Dragon above, the one she didn't believe could hear her.

Don't let him run away.

"How did you do this?" Lucian whispered. Now. Too late to turn back.

"Chaos," she said.

He sprang to his feet. *"What?"*

"I'm a chaotic, Lucian." The words stumbled on their way out. *I'm evil,* she might as well have said. "It started when I was thirteen. The first boy I kissed, I . . . I exploded his heart and lungs." She had to tell the truth, no matter how unpleasant. "I didn't mean to," she added quickly. "But the power comes and goes. It's unstoppable. At first it was all destruction, the way chaos has always been, but then I discovered I could do *this.*" She gestured to the rosebush. "No one ever told me about transformation. When we first arrived at the Trial, I was so afraid I'd hurt somebody, but I'm starting to think that sustained interpersonal contact lessens the effects. I—" *You're sounding like a textbook again.* She hurried, afraid he'd try to cut in. "I crumbled the cliff and brought down the basilisk, and I broke the ceiling at Hyperia's palace. The ability seems to be linked to my feelings, but I'm controlling them better now. There's so much I want to learn." Her entire body began to quake, but she stood her ground. "After what we discovered, I wanted to tell you the truth. You alone. I hope that you won't hate me." The boy who had burned people alive was the boy who might understand what it meant to be monstrous. "And. And maybe, even if you're afraid of me, you could get to know me—the *real* me—again."

At that, her breath failed, and Emilia sat down hard on the edge of the wall. She gripped the stone and refused to look up.

He knelt before her, took her hands in his. She jolted from the contact.

Lucian tilted her chin. "I'm so sorry you were alone."

Then he pulled her close and wrapped his arms around her. He simply held her, warmed her. Emilia began to shake. Thank the blue above she'd already spent her chaos, because this would have turned the whole garden to glass. Emilia gave a deep sigh, feeling her body expand in his embrace. She wrapped her own arms around his neck and laid her cheek against the warm slope of his shoulder.

She had forgotten how nice it was to be held.

"This is why your parents wouldn't let you come to Karthago with Alexander." He swore. "They said you were engrossed in your studies. I was an idiot."

"It's not your fault."

"No. It's not *your* fault." He pulled away then, held on to her shoulders. Their faces were near enough that she felt the heat of his breath. She had not been this close to anyone since Huigh. The heavy awkwardness of her body lifted. "You are not evil, Emilia."

She had yearned for someone who was not Alex to say those words. She imagined settling back in his arms and simply resting.

"I had to keep it secret because—" she began.

"I know." He winced. "The priests. They're the ones who've done wrong. It's not your fault you were born with an evil affliction."

Emilia's smile withered.

"I'm not sure my 'affliction' is evil," she muttered.

"But . . . it's chaos." Lucian appeared puzzled. "Oretani tried to burn everything to the ground with it."

"I'm not Oretani," she snapped. The bubble began under her skin again, the hissing in her brain. Emilia stood. "Didn't we just learn how the priests have lied to us? Who knows what's true about chaos. Did you ever think I could do *this?*" She waved again at the glass roses.

"All right. All right." Lucian adopted that tone she despised: the concerned, patient tone used to silence tantrum-throwing children. "But you can't pretend that chaos hasn't been used to kill people! That's irrational."

Irrational. Emilia had poured her life into books specifically to avoid that label. Irrational. Chaotic. Feeling. Madness.

"I don't think *you* should lecture me about killing," she growled. Her chaos nestled against her, whispered in her ear. "Considering what you've done."

Lucian's face darkened. "All I mean is that I understand you," he snapped. "We're both murderers."

"No. You killed because someone told you to. Huigh was an accident!" she spat, and turned on her heel.

Emilia stormed through the palace and down the hallway to her chamber. Tears constricted her throat. Why, why, why had she believed Lucian would understand?

But hadn't he? He'd said she wasn't evil, her *affliction* was. That was all she'd claimed to want, but . . . She didn't desire mere tolerance; she craved acceptance. Now she knew that it would never, ever be hers. If Lucian could not give her that, no one else could. Emilia stifled a sob.

The others slept soundly within their own rooms. She passed Hyperia's chamber and Vespir's . . . and paused outside of an open door. Ajax's. Frowning, Emilia peered inside.

"Emilia," Lucian hissed, coming up behind her. "What are you doing?"

She forgot, for one moment, what had transpired in the garden.

"Ajax." The bed was pristine and unslept in. "Where is he?"

60
Ajax

Ajax stood outside of Dog's stall, a dagger in hand. Dog poked his nose through the tarpaulin curtain for nuzzles, which Ajax had no time for.

"Be a good boy, all right?" Ajax knelt before the dragon and shoved his head away.

"My *lord* Ajax," Camilla said as the high priests entered. Petros wrinkled his nose at the aerie's smell. Camilla held up a handkerchief to mask the odor. She'd addressed him in the most condescending tone possible, and Ajax's balls retracted a little. "Might we ask what prompted you to request our presence?"

"This." Palms sweating, he held up the basilisk vial. He'd swiped it from Vespir. It hadn't been hard. Neither priest spoke. "I know you murdered Emperor Erasmus. If the world found out, you'd suffer a death even worse than a chaotic's, wouldn't you?" He licked his lips. "But you don't have to if you do as I say."

"What, pray tell, must we do?" Camilla murmured. She didn't sound so bold now.

"Two things." He flipped his dagger in a shining arc, catching it by the handle. Just for show. "First, no matter who really wins, you crown me Emperor of Etrusia. And second, you pardon the other four from the Cut. Nobody dies." He had to do this; the others would never understand, but he *had* to. There was no other way he could win, and that woman with her sad green eyes must find him on the dragon throne one day. The whole Tiber household must bow to him. Emperor Ajax, Ajax the Great. He must. He *must*.

Besides, he would still pardon the others. That was awful grand of him, right?

This was an Emperor's Trial, after all.

"Those are your only demands?" Petros sounded wary.

"Do that, and I get rid of this vial. No one needs to know."

"What led you to this theory?" Camilla asked. Smart. No confirmation.

"I have my sources. If I'm wrong, you can just walk out of here, can't you? But you're probably wondering what other proof I might have. Let's say I do have it, and you won't know what it is until I'm crowned and safe. This is your one chance to avoid execution. Take it."

He pressed forward, a dragon. *The* dragon.

The priests exchanged unreadable glances.

"You're right," Camilla whispered. Her black eyes found him. "We did kill Erasmus."

So close, so close to that golden line of glory.

The vial tumbled from his hand, and so did his dagger, both clattering to the floor at his feet. His body was a block of stone; he could not blink. When he tried to speak, not even a whimper emerged.

Oh. Oh, *shit*. He'd forgot about the damn stasis magic.

"But if you think we'd ever set a bastard upon the imperial throne, you are as ignorant as you are ugly," Camilla finished. She grinned, showing her teeth. "What shall we do with him?"

"Hmm." Petros stroked his chin. He touched the priestess

on her shoulder with two fingers, gave a little shove. "It would not be the first time a competitor lost his nerve and took his own life."

"We had one of those last time, didn't we?" She chuckled. "Pentri?"

"No, Aurun. She poisoned herself. You recall finding the body?"

"The puffed face?" Camilla rolled her eyes back and stuck her tongue out the side of her mouth. Petros gave a high, whinnying laugh. It was, Ajax thought, like watching two old friends reminiscing. The fond camaraderie made him sick.

"Well, my dear. Does he go over the side, or do they find him in bed with his wrists slit?" Petros mused, pulling at his lip.

"Cutting him and getting him back into bed requires coordination, and we're not young anymore, Pet." Camilla tsked. "Send him over the edge. I'll write a note and leave it on his pillow, though I must make sure to misspell a few words. He doesn't strike me as the bookish sort."

Ajax's eyes stung from staying open. Move. He had to move! *Help me! I'm an idiot!*

"Whatever was the Dragon thinking when he sent us this runt?" Petros clucked his tongue and walked toward Ajax. "I'll lift him, if you get the feet."

Ajax wanted to scream, run, and throw himself into Vespir's room to hide under her bed. She was the first one he thought of for protection, more so even than Lucian or Hyperia.

I'm never going to get to tell her how sorry I am.

As Petros drew nearer, a shape lunged out of the stall to Ajax's left. Dog threw himself between the priest and the boy, and this time the dragon did not gawp.

He roared.

Petros and Camilla screamed as the dragon's cry trembled

the rafters. Dog expanded his wings, and his tail lashed to signal aggression, breaking a wooden stool against the wall. The dragon must've shaken their concentration, because Ajax could move again. He dashed the tears from his cheeks, swiped his dagger, and climbed aboard. Without a saddle, he felt the baking heat of Dog's body, the rumble of his fire-acid stomach.

"Fly, boy," he whispered. Dog lifted off the ground. Two flaps, and they were out of the aerie, the priests' astonished faces rapidly diminishing. Ajax looked to the stars above, tried to think. He had to run first and then find some avenue of getting back here and warning the others of his mistake. Mistake? No, his damned idiotic notion—

"No!"

Ajax gripped Dog's neck as the dragon stiffened and plummeted ten feet to the ground. Mercifully, they landed on the runway and didn't plunge to their deaths. Ajax dismounted and tugged at his dragon's face. No. No.

Dog was frozen; they'd locked him into stasis. He whimpered faintly, so apparently their hold on him was weaker than on Ajax. Just not weak enough. Ajax touched the dragon's face.

"Fight. You can get out of this," he whispered as the priests exited the door. Ajax crouched, dagger in hand. "Come on!"

"As if we'd engage in knife fights," Camilla scoffed. She gave a low whistle.

The night exploded with a uniform line of guards running in lockstep. In perfect formation, they surrounded him with their swords unsheathed. Numb, Ajax's dagger fell to his side.

"It's always best to be prepared." Camilla's smile was acidic. "Your note gave us some pause."

Ajax played what few bad cards he had left. Fear ruptured his mind.

"She poisoned Emperor Erasmus! They both did!" he

screeched, looking around at the soldiers. A circle of expression-less eyes watched him from beneath shadowed helms. "They used basilisk tears! Ask the cook! She thought it was medicine and put it into the emperor's stew!"

"Ah, *Hestia*." Camilla clucked her tongue. "Poor woman. Such terrible eyesight. Makes so many easy mistakes."

Ajax realized that he had now doomed the cook as well. He was stomping on innocent lives left and right. Frantic, he struggled to rebound. He had to be persuasive, smart, smarter than the damn priests.

"I, I mean, maybe she did. Maybe I made it up! To, uh . . ." He'd cratered everything around him, his words more destructive than a chaotic's touch.

"Arrest him," Petros said. Guards seized Ajax and pulled him away from Dog. The creature was still able to move his protruding eyes; they swiveled to track Ajax's every movement. More whimpers poured from the dragon's throat.

"I'm telling the truth!" Ajax wailed. "I . . . I have proof!"

"Proof is nothing to power." Petros gestured to one of the guards. "The dragon."

The guard obeyed without hesitation. Dog whined as the man stood before him, sword at the ready.

Ajax could not breathe. Dog. The colorful, bug-eyed, gaw-ping, idiot love of his stupid life whined as the man lifted his sword . . .

"Stop! Stop!" Ajax didn't care if he sobbed now. He would have crawled to the priests if they let him. "I made it all up! Just don't . . . don't do this! Not Dog! Please, not my dragon!"

The last word came out as a ragged shriek. Ajax would hear it echoing for the rest of his life.

"The eyes," Petros said simply.

Dog whimpered.

Ajax screamed as the soldier sliced through the dragon's protruding eyes with two clean strokes.

Wild with pain, Dog must have become too much for the priests to hold. He stampeded forward, bellowing in agony as his wings flared and receded. His head whipped side to side, drops of blood spattering onto the ground like a cruel rain. Dog began to wipe his poor head along the flagstones, as if all he needed was to get the blood out of his eyes to see again. He did not spew fire, and in his gut Ajax knew it was on his account. Dog would never do anything to hurt his rider. Not ever.

Ajax could not move. He was helpless.

No emperor, no Ajax Sarkonus. Just a fifteen-year-old boy.

"Dog." He wept. The dragon gave a low, mournful cry as he hopped forward. The guards stayed out of his way, and the priests laughed.

"Such a *noble* creature," Camilla drawled. "So, my *lord* Ajax? What have you to say now?"

Ajax could not see through his tears. He could not speak.

Someone broke through the crowd of soldiers. A protective wall of a boy stood in front of Ajax.

"What have you *done*?" Lucian shouted.

61
Lucian

When he'd found Ajax's undisturbed bed, he'd known the boy would be working trouble somewhere, but Lucian could never have imagined this.

And the *dragon*. This mutilation was heresy, like crude words carved into the walls of the sacred temple. He imagined Tyche like this, and the pain was fierce.

Dog continued to wipe his face and wail for help, lost in a dark world.

Camilla tilted her head back and filled the air with remorseless laughter.

For the first time since burning Gaius Sabel's sword, Lucian regretted his vow to live without violence.

"What did you do?" he bellowed. When one of the soldiers reached to restrain him, Lucian leapt away. Soldiers blocked him on every side.

"Give him a sword," Camilla prompted. Petros made a discouraging noise, but one of the guards slid his own weapon across the ground to land at Lucian's feet. Heart hammering, he tried to identify Rufus, but he did not see the captain's helm. Perhaps the priests had been selective in whom they'd chosen for this assignment.

"Well, Lord Lucian?" Camilla purred. "Are you willing to forsake your vows?"

His palm practically itched for that sword's hilt. Ajax's and Dog's mournful cries blended together in hideous harmony, and Lucian wanted nothing more than to make someone pay. These murderers, these cowards who had poisoned Erasmus. Lucian's scarred hands fisted.

Protect Ajax. Defend Dog. Avenge Erasmus.

But . . .

If Lucian lifted that sword, he'd throw himself back into the dirtiest game ever played. If he attacked, those cowards would *win*.

Instead, he slumped to his knees.

"Come on! Fight!" Ajax screamed. But Lucian placed his hands upon the ground, bowed his head.

"Please. Take me instead. Whatever Ajax is guilty of, I've done worse a thousand times over."

"How noble." Camilla sighed. "How like Erasmus." Lucian shut his eyes; her speaking the emperor's name was like a lash across his soul. "Unfortunately, you possess many of the same characteristic defects. Guards." Lucian did not look up as she gave the order. "Let's see if he really is as principled as he pretends. Run him through." He could hear the smile in her voice. "Let's check his instincts."

Stay. Do not move. It's all over, anyway. Lucian waited for the three circling men to launch their attack. This death was far too good for him. It was the only injustice here.

The men screamed.

Lucian's head jerked up as the soldiers exploded in clouds of red mist. Cursing, he wiped his eyes, spat the warm, coppery blood from his mouth. Three suits of armor, and three weapons, clanked to the ground. Steam rose from the remains.

Everyone—the priests, Lucian, Ajax, the soldiers—screamed as the ground rocked beneath them. Deep, wicked cracks stretched across the courtyard. Lucian's breath stuttered.

Emilia. No.

The ground stopped shaking, and he whipped around to see Emilia standing in front of the palace door, her hands held out before her in an almost protective gesture. Her eyes were dark in the pale orb of her face.

She collapsed to her knees and began rubbing her arms. Her teeth chattered. He could hear it from where he knelt, and he could hear her wretched sobs as well. Somehow, Lucian could sense the power smoldering inside of her. She'd used too much, for his sake.

"Stop!" she wept.

Lucian had not anticipated that kind of power. He had not truly known her.

As Emilia froze in mid-sob, trapped in stasis by the priests, Lucian rose.

"Let her go!" he yelled.

"I've had enough of your hand-wringing, Lord Lucian," Petros snarled. "Either stop us or be silent."

Lucian ran to Emilia and knelt by her side. She was a living statue, only the steady rise and fall of her chest proof she was still alive.

She had given everything for him. Didn't she know? Didn't she realize he was the most worthless creature alive? No, no, he hadn't known her, and she hadn't known him.

"I'm sorry," he whispered as the guards bound his hands behind his back and dragged him into the palace. Ajax followed, with two guards escorting him.

Dog continued wailing as they shut the palace doors, leaving the injured dragon alone in the dark.

62

Emilia

Emilia's screams remained locked in her throat as Petros brought out the chaotic's helmet. She tried calling on her chaos, prepared to smash everything around her to pulp if only she would not have to face the horror of that contraption. But the chaos was still within her, frozen by the priest's stasis. He was powerful, too powerful.

Petros approached with that helmet, the same type she'd seen on that girl years ago. The priest relaxed his magical hold on her enough to pry her lips apart and insert the mouthpiece. The lower half of the helmet was strapped around her neck and chin, the mouthpiece slipping down her tongue to pin it into place. After adjusting the straps, Petros fastened the top half of the helmet. His pinched face was the last thing she saw before the metallic darkness. There were no eyeholes in this helm. She could not see or speak.

Her harsh breathing echoed. As she lay there, she felt Petros affix two metal containers to her hands, binding them at the wrists. She couldn't move her fingers now. Lying on a bed, she heard the *clank* of chains as they bound her body to the cot.

Emilia could not move, could not see, could barely think with all the darkness around her. She could not touch.

If she didn't know what was around her, she could not destroy.

Footsteps filed out of her cell; yes, she was in prison. Emilia heard the distant echo of Petros's voice.

"Can you hear me?" he asked. She tried to move again. Impossible. "Good. I was concerned one of you might have been chaotic after that assault on the Volscia party. I will admit, I did not think it would be you. You were too much of a mouse." Emilia gurgled in her throat, and saliva flooded her mouth, making the tongue depressor painful. "The rest of the competitors will be brought here. None of you can be trusted. The Dragon picked a faulty crop this time around."

He patted her arm. Her stomach seized as he sat beside her on the cot.

"You wanted to take the throne as a chaotic, didn't you? You wanted to spread your poison throughout the empire?" His voice became a whisper. "That is heresy beyond even what I have committed."

Murderer! Liar! It didn't matter if Emilia was the same; she wanted to hurl those words at him. She screamed low in her throat.

"Don't think yourself the victim. Those soldiers you destroyed had families of their own. There's nothing to burn now. There will be no box of ashes for their loved ones. You did that, you evil, wretched thing."

Evil. Could an evil being turn things to beautiful crystal?

But . . . she *had* destroyed the Volscia ballroom. She *had* killed Huigh. She *had* murdered those three men with a mere twitch of her eye.

"I believe you know what we do to chaotics in this empire, but I wanted to assure you that your punishment shall be tenfold worse. We'll do the vivisection and the nails and the boiled lead." His hand trailed down her thigh and squeezed her knee-cap. Emilia tried, but of course she could not take herself out of his hateful grip. "But we're going to break both your legs before we begin, right here, and flay you from the tips of your toes to the shattered joints of your knees. We'll cut off your ears as well, and every one of your fingers before we finish with you. Why? Because it will give us pleasure and for no other reason. Only after all that agony—and after we have set fire to your hair and blistered your scalp—only then will we allow you to die."

Emilia felt as if she were standing at the precipice of an endless fall as the priest rose.

"Pray to the Dragon to protect your soul, if a demon like you knows how to pray." Petros left, slamming the cell door behind him. As Emilia lay in the blood-scented darkness, she whimpered.

Nothing. There was nothing to be done now.

She had exploded every scrap of bone, blood, and muscle inside three living bodies with a mere thought and the will to guide it. She'd grown so distracted by the shiny novelty of her gift that she'd ignored the destructive limits of her power. She'd done it to save Lucian, yes, but was that an excuse?

Petros was a murderer, but he was also right.

Evil had to be purged from this world.

63
Hyperia

Hyperia paced her cell, from the pitiful cot to the barred door and back again. She was a dragon in a cage. This insolence would not go unpunished, no matter whose throat she had to crush beneath her foot by the end of the night.

"What is going *on?*" she bellowed, kicking at the door. It rattled but did not budge.

She had been dragged from her bed by several of the imperial guard, not even given the opportunity to dress or find shoes before they hauled her through the palace and escorted her down a twisting flight of stairs. Her nightgown of pale golden silk was useless against the cold of a dungeon. Hyperia's feet were ice, her skin rippling with gooseflesh. But she would not give her jailers the satisfaction of watching her shiver.

The imperial prison lacked the ostentatiousness of the palace's other areas. No gold or pearl decorations down here. Instead, a long, dimly lit corridor of twelve metal cages, six on either side. Hyperia had been thrown into one, and the guards had left her alone to pound and scream.

Except that Hyperia was not alone down here.

To her right, Lucian paced as well, his anxiety matching hers, though the focus of his concern was different.

"Emilia!" He kept yelling the girl's name, hands gripping the bars as he peered into the cage to his right. While Hyperia couldn't see the Aurun girl, it concerned her that she hadn't heard anything out of her.

Across the hall from Hyperia was Ajax, and beside him sat Vespir.

"Why are we here?" Hyperia roared.

Vespir threw up her hands. "I don't know! They dragged me out of bed!"

Hyperia noticed that she and Vespir were both in nightdress, while Ajax and Lucian were fully clothed.

"What did you two do?" she growled.

Ajax merely sat with his back against his cell's bars and gazed into the distance. Hyperia knew in a keen, animal way that this was his fault. Whose else could it be?

"Do they know what we discovered?" Hyperia called to Lucian. Finally, he turned from yelling for Emilia and spoke to her.

"I think so." Lucian's voice trembled.

"Because of him?" Hyperia pointed at Ajax's lumpen figure. Lucian winced but nodded. That little *bastard*. Hyperia kicked at the lock, a high kick that rattled the cage door to its foundation. Her heel smarted. "You idiot! I wish we'd let that basilisk poison you."

"Don't yell at him!" Vespir slammed against her own door. "We don't know what happened yet."

"He tried to make a deal with the priests so he could become emperor. Didn't you?" Lucian asked, his voice hoarse.

Ajax nodded, his shoulders slumping lower.

"You *idiot*!" Vespir wailed.

While the servant girl shouted at Ajax, Hyperia sought Emilia once more. Lucian stepped back farther into his cell, lending an unobstructed view. The girl had been chained to a cot in the center of her cage. Hyperia gaped at . . . What was on her head? Why had they chained *her,* and not the rest? And why did that helmet appear so unsettlingly familiar?

"Lucian. What happened to Emilia?" Coldness grew in her stomach.

"It's my fault," he growled.

"That helmet . . ." Hyperia could not bring herself to say it, so Vespir did.

"A chaotic?" The servant girl shoved her face up against her bars to get a better look. "I saw an execution when I was a kid."

A pinched, sick feeling radiated outward through Hyperia's body. The explosion of chaos at her family home during the Game; the cracked ceiling, the screams; the dead lord, bleeding out at Hyperia's feet. Granted, she had killed that man herself, but only as a reaction to the attack. She just couldn't believe it. It had all been *Emilia*?

Chaos. Damnation. The embodiment of evil, with wild red hair and sorrowing eyes. That *bitch* had tricked her. Hyperia had even liked her better than the others. She went blind with fury.

"The Aurun will pay for this. They had to know," she growled. Then she paused. "Lucian. Why do you say this was your fault?" It couldn't be what she was thinking. "Did you know?"

"You're wrong about her! If I'd only picked up that sword, she wouldn't have had to protect me!"

Hyperia focused on what was key. "How did she protect you? What did she destroy?" She gripped the bars. "Did she kill anyone?"

Lucian buried his face in his hands. Yes. Yes, she'd killed. Monsters always sought blood.

"If I must die to prevent a creature like that from ever drawing another free breath, I'm glad," she snapped.

"That *creature* saved Ajax against the basilisk."

Good, finally that noble monk bullshit was falling away.

"And wreaked havoc on my family's lands. After we left the Game, do you think that the guests were simply allowed to leave? I'd be surprised if most weren't thrown in dungeons, awaiting trials to test for chaotic ability. She is like all true chaotics: clever, deceptive, and rotten to her core. She is evil."

"You of all people shouldn't give lectures on good and evil."

Footsteps approached. Hyperia stepped back as the captain of the guard opened her cell door. He wore no easy smile now and would not look in Lucian's direction.

"My lady, you must come with me," he said.

"Where?"

"Their Graces request your presence."

Was she first to die, then? If so, Hyperia would meet her fate with the calm of a true Etrusian. She walked out of her cell, the captain and two others at her back. While Lucian called out, desperate to know what was happening, Hyperia centered her soul.

Julia. My baby. I'll be there soon.

They marched her up several floors. She assumed they'd be taking her to the throne room, but instead they guided her toward the priests' bedchambers, situated on the other side of the palace from her own. Hyperia frowned. Why were they going *here*? The captain knocked and led Hyperia into a sitting room papered with golden silk. The furniture consisted of over-stuffed couches upholstered with orange-and-blue satin in fine Karthagon style. Camilla was perched upon a settee, a cup of coffee before her on the low polished table. The priestess waved Hyperia over.

"Sit, my lady." She gestured to a couch.

"Where am I to die?" Hyperia asked simply.

Camilla blinked. "Well. Not here. Have some coffee. Some cherry-and-walnut cake, perhaps?"

Hyperia did not appreciate games. A door off to the right opened, and Petros entered.

"You know, then?" Petros asked. He dismissed the captain and the guards with a nod. Soon, it was only the three of them. Hyperia had no weapon upon her, no way to defend herself. "What Ajax discovered?"

No need to dissemble. That was weakness.

"You killed Emperor Erasmus."

"Yes, because he had a chaotic spirit. Chaos is the great cancer upon civilization." Camilla sipped, her pinkie in the air. "Thankfully, you display no such affliction."

"So. You are *not* going to kill me?" Hyperia was puzzled.

"Perhaps not. That depends." Camilla replaced her cup. Petros stood behind her, his hands gripping the couch's back. "On your obedience."

"How so?" Did they wish her to become their servant? A spy?

"Become the empress," Petros said.

Hyperia blinked. "I don't understand. I won the Trial?"

Camilla looked back at Petros, and the priests exchanged glances.

"A winner has been selected." Camilla sighed. "You, alas, were not chosen."

"Ah." Then it was over. After a lifetime of having it drilled into her—*win, win, win*—this should have dragged her into the deepest chasm of despair. She felt oddly light. Perhaps she was numb to the pain, the adrenaline overpowering her senses like having a limb lopped off on the battlefield.

"But . . ." Petros stepped nearer. "The choice was unacceptable."

Hyperia frowned. "Who was chosen, then?" She hated to

question anything—she would not be like Emilia—but she couldn't help herself. "And *how* were they chosen?"

"It doesn't matter. You are *our* choice, my lady. Or should I say, Your Excellency?" Petros stroked a thin finger along his cheek. "Our bargain is simple. Keep our secret regarding Erasmus and be the orderly empress we all know you were born to be. In exchange, we shall crown you and kill the others. No one will need to know—"

"That Emilia is a chaotic?" she growled.

"Yes. She goes away. They all go away." Petros spread his hands. "All hail Hyperia Sarkona. Does it not have a fine sound?"

"But . . ." Hyperia struggled to wrap her tongue around the word. "It is a *lie*."

"Are you so ready to die for the truth?" Camilla asked.

Hyperia imagined the first rider, Aufidius, charging on dragonback against usurping nations. She pictured him carving out the heart of his friend, his enemy, Caius Martius. Weakness must be purged. She thought of Erasmus, scribbling away his mad heresies in a dingy room beneath the aerie. She conjured an image of the imperial city's walls crumbling with a massive tremor of the earth, the buildings falling under mountains of flame. Her own body, gored and lifeless, resting atop a heap of corpses.

Hyperia pictured Julia's laughing face as blood gushed from her neck.

"Yes," she said at last. "I will be your empress."

64

Ajax

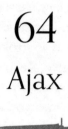

Ajax sat and thought about Dog. For a while now the others had been shouting at Ajax, but he barely heard. What did it matter?

Please, just tell me that someone went out to throw a blanket over him. Dog got so cold in the open air at night.

Dashing traitorous tears from his cheeks, Ajax stood and walked to the wall, wishing like hell he had a window. He wanted to see Dog one last time. Dog wouldn't be able to go back to the aerie now; he couldn't fly without sight. What if, to put him out of his misery, the guards had already taken their swords and . . .

No. Ajax shuddered with the thought. His soul would have died with Dog. That's what the bond between dragon and rider was, right?

Ajax rubbed the heels of his palms into his eyes, envisioned the infinity of stars blanketing the sky. Dog would never see the sky again. He'd never fly again. And if Ajax could just tell him . . . just tell him he shouldn't have come to protect Ajax's sorry ass. Dog never thought about himself; that was his biggest problem.

Guess I screwed us up. Ajax imagined saying that as he ghosted his knuckles across the dragon's snout, right between the nostrils. It was soft as velvet there. Dog would *hmph* in contentment and wrap his tail around Ajax's left leg. Dumb dragon.

Idiot dragon. The others are right. You're stupid! Useless! The words burned in Ajax's throat. He'd never felt hate like this, a cancer that knit his bones together, snaked through his innards like a parasite. Made him whole. Why Ajax? Why Dog? Why? *Why? What'm I supposed to do with a blind-ass dragon?* He could just picture Dog listening to the torrent of abuse as he faced Ajax calmly with blind eyes.

By the black depths, such feelings weren't worthy of an emperor. They weren't worthy of a shitty child.

Ajax was a feral, nasty thing, all bad angles and ugly teeth. Every day he looked into the mirror and anticipated that great man who was only a growth spurt and spray of stubble away.

But now he imagined hurling abuse at the only thing that—

That . . .

At twelve, Ajax had been embarrassed when his egg hatched to reveal a misshapen, thoroughly bizarre-looking dragon. He'd kept his eyes down as the runt trailed him through the dingy castle halls, squeaking and gawping and flapping its batlike wings. The Tiber bastards had teased him for it relentlessly. He'd finally tied the dragon up in a burlap sack and hung it from a tree branch, hoping something would come along and swallow the damn thing.

Dog had chewed his way out of the sack and waddled home, chirping and desperate to play.

And when Lysander had beaten Ajax's ass and left him crying in a corner, Dog had crawled over, plopped himself into Ajax's lap, and licked the boy's tears away with those flicking dragon kisses. Dragons couldn't abide salt water, but Dog had done it to make Ajax smile.

The only being in the castle that cared whether he laughed or cried.

Ajax had always grumbled that they were an uneven match, and he'd been right. He'd been right. Dog was worth two of him.

Misery swelled in his chest, lumped in his throat. Ajax fell to his knees, clasped his hands on either side of his head.

"I'm sorry," he whispered to a dragon that couldn't hear him. "I'm so sorry. I'm sorry," he whispered over and over.

"You should be," someone snapped.

Vespir watched him with volcanic rage. Lucian glowered from across the corridor.

Ajax could barely stand *feeling* anything, and he wouldn't let anyone see his pain. He stood and put his back to the wall, gritted his teeth.

"Just go away!" he howled, wrapping his arms around his body, closing himself like a fist.

"I'd love to, but I can't, because I'm *in prison!*" she shouted. "You just had to screw us over, didn't you?"

"At least *you* won a damn challenge!" He put his face near hers. Granted, Vespir loomed over him by a few inches, so it wasn't as threatening as he wanted. "You had a shot! I had to take what was mine!"

"The throne isn't *yours!*"

"It should be! I want it more than you!" No, he needed it. He needed to occupy a space only he could fill. He wasn't an extra, a by-blow; no, he was indispensable.

"You brat," Lucian growled. All this time, he'd kept pacing and watching Emilia—who looked terrifying, incidentally. The helmet gave her the appearance of some nightmare beetle. Ajax had never seen a chaotic chained before.

But first, back to Lucian and his insufferable smugness.

"And *you*. If you'd picked up the damn sword, your girl-friend wouldn't be like this right now!" The larger boy gripped the bars. Veins corded in his bull neck; he looked ready to tear the place apart. But of course he didn't. Lucian shuffled away, like a good boy. Ajax's lip curled. "Why don't you just admit it? You're shit at this peacekeeping thing!"

"Don't yell at him. This is *your fault*." Vespir kicked at him through the bars. "Why did you do it? You can't possibly be this stupid." She scoffed. "You should've thought about your dragon if nothing else. Who knows what they might do to—"

"*Shut up!*" he howled. Ajax began kicking and kicking at the cell door, imagined mashing the priests' faces to pulp. Through the clanging, he heard Lucian tell Vespir what'd happened. His fault. His fault his dragon would never see the stars again. His fault. His.

"Ajax. *Ajax*." Vespir sounded calmer now. He stopped kicking, wiped his arm across his eyes. Couldn't see through the stupid tears. "I'm sorry. They should burn to ash for doing that to Dog."

Trust Vespir to take a dragon's side, if nothing else. But he appreciated it.

"I'm . . . I'm sorry," Ajax muttered. He wiped his nose on his rough sleeve. "I know I screwed up. You just . . ." He couldn't think of what to say. What he felt was enormous, a gigantic monolith he had to describe while blind. "You two . . . You don't know what it's like to be born like me."

"To be born low?" Vespir drawled.

"To be born *bad*." Her silence egged him on. "Those images from the Truth doorway? I mean, before everything got weird. They were pictures from the past, maybe?"

Vespir and Lucian both grunted in understanding.

"I . . . I never met my mother." Ajax's thoughts were

scattered, beads from a broken necklace rolling across the ground. "She left right after I was born. And my father, Lord Tiber, well, he's a prick. A monster. He . . . Sometimes if he can't get a woman who wants him, he just . . ."

Vespir made a soft noise.

"I kept seeing it over and over. On the island, in the halls around here. It was driving me crazy. And he, my father, he must've done it to *her*, because why else would she leave me?" The heavy weight kept pressing on some tender, invisible nerve. "I just wanted to win, you know?" His chin quivered, and his voice broke. "Because then at least what she went through wasn't pointless. Then at least I'm not just some grimy bastard who's alive b-because of evil." The tears fell, and he didn't try to stop them. His entire body convulsed with his sobs. No one had wanted him. His father had been looking for pleasure, his mother not looking for anything at all. Ajax wanted to coil inside of himself like a snake and disappear. "But now I screwed up, and Dog's blind, and . . ." His voice broke. "I'm sorry. I screwed it all up. Please. Please. I'm sorry."

Ajax couldn't get any air. He crumpled in on himself, lay on his side shivering on the floor. Alone.

"Ajax." Lucian did not sound so angry now. Sniffling, Ajax looked up. The larger boy crouched by the door of his cell, a rough gentleness in his eyes. "I didn't know."

Vespir knelt alongside the wall nearest to him. She didn't look quite as forgiving as Lucian, but there was a sort of acceptance in her eyes. At least, Ajax hoped that's what he saw.

"I think I can help you," she said.

Ajax wanted to huddle away from the kindness in her voice.

"How? We're all in the same mess."

"I think I can help with Dog." That got him good. Ajax crawled over to her. The girl held up her hand. "I'm not here to judge you, but I'm also not here to make you better, Ajax." She didn't sound cruel, only matter-of-fact. "You're going to have to listen to me."

Sympathy with no bullshit was exactly what he needed.

"I will." He tucked his chin to his chest, too ashamed to meet her gaze.

"Come on." She reached through the bars. "First, your father's awful, but that doesn't mean you are. All right?" She squeezed his shoulder, the closest she got to gentle. "Next, Dog is *your* dragon." She said it like a prayer. "That kind of bond can't be bought, and it should never be severed. Right now he's lost in the darkness, but he might be able to see again. Not with his eyes, though." She placed her other hand on his forehead. "With yours."

"How?" he whispered.

She started talking about a Red, and how he could "lock in" with his dragon. The more she talked, the more it sounded like a made-up fantasy you convinced yourself was real when you were drunk, but he was not about to say that. Vespir talked about "letting your eyes go out of focus" and "taking down the wall between you and your dragon." When she'd finished, Ajax glanced at Lucian, who appeared blank.

"Uh. You ever tried this?" he asked.

"No," the Sabel boy said.

"I understand it sounds strange, but it does work. I've never formed the bond when I'm not with Karina, but maybe you could if you tried. Close your eyes. Imagine reaching out to Dog. Try to touch him."

"This sounds kind of impossible." Ajax was not the theoretical sort.

Vespir's mouth curled downward sharply. "Fine."

"Wait. I'm sorry." He reached for her when she pulled away.

Damn idiot, chasing her off when she was trying to help. Lucian watched them in silence. Emilia . . . Ajax wasn't sure she was even still awake. She hadn't made a noise since they got here. It was unnerving.

She wouldn't be like this if it weren't for me. He winced. *Is she really chaotic?*

He'd always thought of chaotics as so . . . frightening. It didn't fit with the Emilia he knew.

"Don't apologize. Just try it," Vespir said, snapping Ajax to attention. Her dark eyes were as serious as anything he'd ever seen. With a sigh, he shut his eyes and imagined . . . Dog? Dog flapping his wings? Dog panting, his forked tongue lolling out the side of his mouth? Every image Ajax ever conjured of his dragon had Dog doing something ridiculous. He couldn't help laughing. "Don't laugh at him." Vespir whacked his hand. Ouch. "You aren't his master. You belong to each other."

Not Dog's master? But Ajax was clearly the more intelligent partner.

And Dog was clearly the better. Ajax's stomach sank.

Ajax's other half. He'd always been annoyed to have such a dragon, one that loved to play and snuggle. Idly, he'd wished Aufidius had been his mount when he'd first seen the Hydra. Who wouldn't feel imperial with such a beast? But Dog was the love from which he'd shut himself off. Ajax thought of rubbing his knuckles against the dragon's snout. Curled up beside him in the aerie some nights, Dog's wing tucked about Ajax and holding him snug and warm against the dragon's gurgling fire belly. The first time he'd seen Dog take to the air on the end of the handler's lead, the dragon's joyous squawking and the flap of his wings.

Freedom. Joy. The two things Dog loved above all, except Ajax.

Ajax somehow could *see* Dog now, the faint outline of

him. The curve of his back, the tiny nibs of horns. A second and the image vanished, but Ajax reached out an invisible hand and touched the creature's snout. Dog's eyes were bisected, dried blood coagulating on his jowls like thick, viscous tears. *Sorry, boy. Sorry.*

And Ajax . . . *felt* his dragon. A ripple of something like love shivered down Ajax's outstretched invisible arm and through his body. He opened his eyes with a gasp.

"I think . . . I think I felt him."

"Is he all right?" Vespir sat cross-legged, didn't seem to find any of this odd.

"He hurts, but he's alive. He's scared." Ajax could have just guessed any of that, and it'd probably be true. But there was something in the way he'd seen Dog—the detail of it, not the basic image Ajax carried in his head. It was as if Dog had perked up as he heard Ajax's voice. Ajax's temples throbbed. "Vespir. Thanks." He hung his head. "I'm sorry."

"I know," she said. Not "it's okay" or "I forgive you."

They all sat in that quiet, waiting for the guards to come. They waited a long time, but there was nothing angry in their silence now.

If this was the end of the world, it was nice to have friends.

65

Emilia

Emilia floated in darkness, much like when she was a little girl and would go down to the seaside caves—her father had told her it was too dangerous, but she loved bobbing in the blackness, listening to the slosh of water coming through the narrow aperture.

In this void, she could hear the others' muffled voices. Nearest was Lucian, crying out her name, and then there was Ajax howling in agony. Finally, Vespir, her voice low and musical. Emilia was only just able to hear her words—the Red, dragons, connection—and they flowed over her, filling her mind with blissful images of dragons cavorting through the sky, riderless and free. Hopefully, she'd hang on to those happy dreams for comfort when they began slicing her body apart.

Emilia.

Was that her father? Lucian? The deep, masculine voice was one she seemed to know well, yet couldn't place. She tried to sit up but of course could not. Her limbs were heavy in this weightless void.

She lay in blackness and waited. Like the persistent beating of a drum, her name resounded again and again and again.

Emilia.

Emilia.

Emilia.

66

Hyperia

———————

As dawn lit the sky, Dragonspire's bells tolled in unison and crowds flooded the city streets. An emperor had been selected. Soon, dancing would begin in the great fountain square, and they would roast boars for this evening's citywide feasts. Children would buy pink and blue sugar dragons from market stalls, gambling dens would lay bets on which competitor had won, and the brothels would offer discounts. The city noise did not reach Hyperia from this high up, secure in her palace. All she could hear were the bells.

Hyperia reclined in a bath of buttermilk and rose oil as attendant women dressed in black and gold—her new retinue—buffed her nails and washed her feet, then laid out her ceremonial gown of imperial black, symbolic of a combination of all the House colors, belonging to all and to none of them. Acolytes had measured and swiftly designed outfits for all five competitors, in order to be prepared for any victory. The dress was of midnight-black satin, with a fitted bodice and skirts that molded themselves rather daringly to her hips and thighs. Sleeves and an outer skirt of fine black gossamer lent a ripple to her movement. A collar of golden dragon scales fastened around her chest and neck.

She rose from the bath, was dried with lush, cream-colored

towels. Her handwomen arranged her hair in a golden wave that cascaded to her shoulders. Dressed with ritual, she slid her feet into slippers of pure gold filigree. The golden sword she had won in the Hunt provided much needed weight at her side. She walked into the living room of her new imperial apartment. The priests awaited her on a couch, enjoying a snack of grapes. Petros stood, still chewing.

"A true empress," he said, smiling.

From there, the priests led her down the halls and into a richly appointed antechamber, one that opened through double doors onto an enormous terraced balcony overgrown with bougainvillea. Hyperia could only faintly hear the crowds, but she'd no doubt they lined the golden avenues below. They'd cheer when they saw her.

Glasses of sparkling wine waited on a table, alongside a pillow of black silk. On it rested the imperial crown, fashioned from gold to resemble a ring of dragon's teeth. In the center, a ruby of the deepest, bloodiest red glistened. The gem had been cut in five points. Five Houses. Five dragons. One ruler.

Soon they'd place this upon her head and take her out onto that terrace before the assembled masses. Then the gold Volscia banners would fly alongside the imperial black, and her glorious reign would commence.

"Leave us." Camilla dismissed the attendants, who shut the door behind them. The priestess lightly slid Hyperia's sword from its golden sheath. "Might we take this, Your Excellency? It is customary to appear unarmed for the viewing."

Hyperia watched as Camilla set the weapon on a sideboard, beside a tray of roasted figs and thinly sliced ham. Hyperia faced the open doors. The morning wind kissed her cheeks.

"The first Volscia ruler in nine generations, isn't it?" Petros clucked his tongue. "Your family will be proud."

"I have no family," Hyperia said serenely, gazing at the

bright day. "My mother and sister are dead, and my father will soon follow."

"Er, it was truly a blessing that the Dragon sent you to this Trial. If we had been forced to choose from amongst those other four—" Petros began, but Hyperia stopped him.

"The Great Dragon did not send me. He chose my sister, and for that I killed her." She faced the priests. Camilla, she noted, glanced at the sword. "We all understand what it is to murder someone."

"For the right reasons." Camilla beamed. "Your Excellency, you showed the true heart of a dragon when you slew your sister."

"Did I?" Hyperia traced a fingertip along the points of her crown. "When I first came to the Trial, I was certain I'd been tested and passed. I saw only my duty." She smirked. "Some may call me unimaginative. But I am not blind, you know."

"Of course." Petros sounded as though he were humoring her.

"And what the Truth showed me was unmistakable." She curled her lip. "Killing Julia . . . was the wrong choice."

"Erm. Excellency, it is forbidden to speak of what you've seen in the gateway."

Hyperia ignored Camilla.

"I've realized why. Why Julia was called and why I was denied my birthright. It was your fault." She glared at the priests. "When you killed Emperor Erasmus, you tipped the scales into chaos. Perhaps the Dragon responded by choosing a different crop of contenders from whom to select. We firstborn are trained our whole lives to be strong, ruthless, efficient, powerful, and proud. Perhaps the Dragon looked upon the others— the oddities, the soft, the broken—and decided to try His luck with one of them. For a while, I thought I alone was the true contender in a sea of misfits."

Hyperia's voice did not waver as two hot tears slipped down her cheeks.

"But I was the greatest freak of all. I killed my beloved sister, my baby. For nothing."

"For a throne," Camilla goaded.

"For a *lie*."

"Excellency, you've proven your wisdom beyond any doubt." Petros approached as he would a tiger's unlocked cage. "Yes, perhaps our actions resulted in some . . . unintended side effects. Perhaps we rocked the world out of balance, but *you* have righted it. You are ten times the emperor that Erasmus was. You are our *savior*. What does it matter if salvation is based on a lie?"

Hyperia wiped her cheeks, took a glass of wine, and toasted them.

"To the empire, then. Long may it flourish under my rule," she said, and drank. Petros beamed.

Hyperia smashed her glass against the table's edge, and with one lithe blow, she slashed Petros's throat open. The man upset a chair as he fell. Hyperia was upon him in an instant, the warmth of his blood decorating her cheek and chest as she stabbed him again and again through the eyes. The man's face became a slab of torn meat; his hands ceased fumbling at her shoulders, and his gurgles died.

Camilla screamed. Hyperia knew she had a mere second before she was frozen into stasis. With lightning reflexes, she grabbed the tray of drinks and flung it at the priestess. Camilla's attention went to the flying object, and those two seconds were all Hyperia needed to tackle the woman against the wall.

"Guards!" she bellowed, pinning Camilla with her knee while shoving the priestess's head back. Hyperia's other hand brandished the sharp, bloodied glass under Camilla's chin. The woman sobbed as guards rushed into the room, fanned around Hyperia with swords drawn. Camilla could do nothing now.

"Petros." The old woman wept for the dead man. These two had likely been inseparable since they were young. The best of friends, probably closer than most married couples. What a pity to lose the other part of yourself.

Hyperia knew that feeling too well.

"Yes. I will become what I was born and bred to be," she hissed in the woman's ear. "I *will* be empress, but lawfully crowned. Do not tell me who won the Trial; it does not matter. Until the others are dead by my hand, I am no legitimate ruler."

Hyperia had come too far, and done too much, to accept a lie now. If she had allowed this—allowed Petros to live, allowed Camilla freedom, allowed them to kill the other four on Hyperia's behalf—she would have been forever a puppet.

Duplicity. Pure chaos.

She'd inherited a magnificent tree squirming with worms. Rotten to the core.

It was obscene.

If Hyperia spared a drop of pity for the other four in those cells—even Emilia, hateful monster that she was—she locked those feelings away.

Julia. Your death will *have meaning. I swear to it.*

Hyperia choked Camilla, and the priestess's eyes rolled back into her head. Unconscious. Hyperia shoved her to the captain. Rufus gazed at his empress in shock.

"Excellency?" he said.

"Confine her to her chambers, and set guards to watch over her. Bind her from head to foot. Before I reveal myself to the crowds, the others must die." She straightened her shoulders. "I must be the one to do it."

If the others died at her hand, that horrific vision of a burning city could not come to pass.

Hyperia took up the crown then and settled it upon her head. A perfect fit. She sheathed her sword and gazed at herself in a floor-length mirror propped in the corner of the room. She was exquisite, a woman in black satin with golden armor and a golden sword and a crown of gold.

And a face and body spattered in blood. Hyperia did not bother to clean herself.

She had entered this Trial golden and bloody.

Best to finish as she began.

67
Emilia

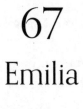

*E*milia.

That voice resounded in the negative spaces of her mind, and Emilia was falling into an endless void with only that voice to catch her. "Who are you?" she whispered, though she couldn't move her mouth.

Can you not guess?

She had stopped hearing the others a while ago. Now there was only she and this phantom visitor. Not her father. Not Alex. Not Lucian. Who, then?

In the blackness, a great orange eye opened, reptilian, with a narrowing black slit through the center. It beheld her soul; Emilia felt every lie she'd ever told, every wish she'd ever cast bubble up to the surface, and the harsh rays of some celestial light shined upon them. Even though she was bound to a bed, she wanted to drop to her knees.

Impossible.

"I'm hallucinating."

Perhaps.

"You can't be the Great Dragon." The last few words trembled in her mind.

I can be many things. That is your name for me, perhaps.

Emilia was half-afraid and half-hopeful that she'd simply gone mad.

"Then . . . then how can I speak to you now? Why never before in my life?"

Your soul is merged with your dragon's, and when I called your dragon to my Trial, she linked to me. You and I share a connection we could never have had otherwise.

"So you approve of this Emperor's Trial?" She couldn't help the heat in her words.

Not of what it has become. This Trial, this empire, has grown into a twisted version of what we once imagined. Even now, centuries after my physical death, I am ashamed of what I helped create. I would right these wrongs.

Emilia would have enjoyed a more in-depth philosophical and theological discussion right now, but she was about to brutally die. Her concerns had to be more practical.

"Can you take my chains away, then?"

Only you can save yourself, my lady. But I will help, if you allow it.

The draconic eye closed, and Emilia was swallowed up in an explosion of visions. She found herself gazing upon a vista of green rolling hills and cerulean skies. Through those skies, dragons cavorted in great number. Unsaddled. Riderless. Free. She watched as a pair descended to earth where a man on horseback awaited them. The dragons settled their wings, opened their mouths, and spoke to the man. They spoke, with glittering voices like a handful of coins.

The dragons were *speaking*. Emilia could barely believe it.

Fifteen hundred years ago, dragons were born into this world. With them came the dawn of order and chaos.

"Yes," Emilia said numbly. She knew that the great families of old had sifted through the remains of a long-cooled volcanic eruption, and in those ashes they had discovered jewel-bright eggs. She knew those eggs had hatched, and dragons had come into the world, but she never knew that those creatures could speak.

For centuries the ways of man and dragon were neighborly, but separate. Until Cassius Oretani, the chaos lord, rose up to bring the other Etrusian lands under his sway.

Yes, Emilia had known all of this. Before her, the scene dissolved as if wiped away, and a new image formed in its place.

Five people, two women and three men, stood before an enormous dragon. They were on a large marble veranda open to the summer air. One of the men, dressed in robes of blue—Antoninus Sabel, Lucian's greatest ancestor—strode forth to stand before the dragon.

This dragon—the Great Dragon—was a massive creature, over sixty feet in length. His scales were the color of burnished bronze, his eyes deep ochre, and his unfurled wings seemed to block out the sky itself.

Antoninus Sabel, soon to be the first Etrusian emperor, settled himself upon the Great Dragon's back. The other men and women, the rulers of the other four great Houses (and Emilia could see her ancestor, Marcella Aurun, among them) bowed in unison to Antoninus and the Dragon.

When Oretani grew to be too much of a threat, the voice whispered, *I told the other Houses to form as one army, led by one person. I chose Antoninus as my rider because he was the first to ask how he could help his people—he alone did not seek power. I have always thought the meek to have a keener understanding of human nature than most great men.*

The scene shifted, and Emilia watched Antoninus and the Dragon soar through the air to fight Cassius Oretani. Emilia caught a quick glimpse of the famed chaos lord, a young man with long black hair and a crimson mouth, riding a dragon of the purest white.

Before Emilia's eyes, Oretani took a sword to the stomach. He and his dragon spiraled downward.

The five families fought Oretani's people to a standstill. They trapped them in their territory to the west, frozen in stasis for all time by the orderly magosi. When the battle was done, all of us agreed that, for the good of the world, the power of chaos must be bound.

"If they bound chaos, how am I a chaotic?" Emilia could not let this pass without an answer.

Think of chaos as water poured into a cracked earthenware jar. The majority of it is contained, but there are leaks. It is a good thing, too, for all of us that your chaotic kind still exist . . . because of what happened next.

Emilia now watched the scene shift to Antoninus, the other lords and ladies, and a horde of orange-robed orderlies clustered around a table. They appeared to be arguing as, perched around the enormous pavilion, the Great Dragon and several other dragons watched, their tails twitching, their wings settling.

We dragons helped create the binding spell. We were foolish to assume that there would be no consequences to locking away half of all magical ability. And we paid the price. When the spell was done, and chaos bound away, so too were the tongues of all dragonkind.

Emilia watched as the Great Dragon and the others jerked as if shot through by lightning. They began to lash their tails, to bite at one another, to roar and flap into the sky in a disorganized mass. Antoninus and the others were startled and watched in seeming horror.

"Then why didn't they undo the spell?" Emilia asked. She felt as ill as if she were watching a murder.

Because if a meek man receives power without first developing a stout heart, he can become a natural tyrant.

Emilia was forced to watch Antoninus beckon the Great Dragon down as though the noble beast were a dog. When the

Dragon obeyed, he who'd been the savior of order and the lives of how many millions of people, the first emperor petted him like an animal. Antoninus smiled.

Emilia couldn't look anymore. Blackness rushed back over her, and she mentally sobbed in relief.

"So dragons are prisoners? Including Chara?" Emilia felt raw throughout her body—what little she could still feel, anyway. Chara, her best companion, the creature she'd tickled and kissed and whose scales she'd brushed . . . was that creature her slave? The thought nearly broke the tenuous thread of her sanity.

But you, and only you, Emilia of the Aurun, may set them free. Free them, and free yourself. Will you make that choice?

"What do I do?" Dimly, Emilia realized that she was no longer questioning the hows and the whys of this insane miracle. Perhaps Camilla, monstrous as she was, had been right about one thing: logic was the enemy of faith. Later, Emilia would find that thought disturbing, but right now she clung to that faith—her only hope.

A chaotic dragon rider must break the spell. Any chaotic may break a binding spell, but only one whose soul is connected with a dragon may break this one.

"I don't understand."

Think of the binding as a great invisible chain stretched across the entire world. To render a chain useless, you must only destroy a single link.

Emilia understood.

"If I can break the binding on my own dragon . . . ," she began.

Then the spell will shatter in every dragon's mind, and chaos will be unleashed once more.

At that, Emilia paused. She would give her life to save Chara, but . . . what she had done could never be forgiven.

"Isn't it better if chaos never comes back? What if the Oretani return?"

Chaos is as natural as order. One should not exist without the other.

No mention of Oretani.

"But I've only ever hurt people."

There is life in chaos as much as there is death. There is the potential for needed change. And . . . you may save lives.

The others. They would be put to death as well. Lucian. Vespir. Even Ajax. She could not . . . she could not allow it. So what if she'd been born bad? She had not chosen it, but she *could* choose how to shape her future. If she had one. If she chose one for herself.

And for Chara.

"What do I do?"

Reach out for your dragon. Feel the link in her mind, and break it.

Might as well tell her to dance the color mauve. But Emilia recalled what Vespir had told Ajax about locking in on some sort of Red. Emilia breathed and tried to do as the other girl had instructed. She cleared her mind and imagined her invisible hand reaching out through the iron bars and the stone walls. She pictured flying through the air, her spirit light as a sigh, and she imagined Chara rising up to meet her in this darkness.

Emilia could have sworn that her dragon actually appeared, milky white, ruby eyes shining with inner fire. Emilia reached out her invisible hand. She could *feel* the thin, silken sensation of dragon scales. This was Chara, her soul. Her beloved friend, condemned to a lifetime of servitude and silence.

No one should ever condemn a woman to stay quiet.

Shaking with the effort, Emilia imagined her hand passing into the dome of the dragon's skull. Emilia's breathing grew haggard; there was *something* resisting her, some pressure shoving against her hand. It tasted like iron on her tongue, this lock. This spell. Emilia gasped and cried out in pain.

Break it. Break it.

Emilia heeded the voice and pressed back harder. Her mind felt liable to snap with the pain. Perhaps . . . she changed her mind. It was not a lock, but a silken purse with the top sewn shut. Much easier to open. She began to pick at the thread binding that precious jewel. Her muscles, her mind, her will burned against this impossible spell. Too weak. She was too weak.

And then, her chaos prickled at the back of her neck and hummed at the tips of her fingers. With a deep breath, Emilia let the chaos slide down her arms, over her knuckles, kept it small as it approached the spell in her dragon's brain. Give the power too much freedom, and Emilia knew she'd crush Chara's skull from this distance.

Slowly, carefully, the chaos ate at those threads, and Emilia pictured the purse unravel and fall away. She felt something *pop*, something invisible that shocked her and shook her stomach and tickled her ribs. A white-hot explosion of *noise* like the howling wind cascaded over Emilia, rushing into her soul.

"Emilia!"

The voice that called her now was feminine and sweet, familiar as her own breath. The voice—her Chara, her dragon—called for Emilia again and again as chaos exploded over the world, rippling through flesh and bone and stone and steel. Emilia's back arched, and she gasped as the blood and flesh inside of her sparked with power.

Chara was free.

And so was Emilia.

68

Vespir

Vespir listened to the tolling bells and knew. One look at Lucian, seated on his cot with his head in his hand, was all the confirmation she needed.

"All hail the empress, Hyperia Sarkona?"

"I should have known," Lucian replied.

"Wonder if she was the real winner." Ajax, seated against the bars nearest Vespir, wiped his eyes. Clever boy.

"Someone should be down soon enough to kill us all." Lucian stared at the floor. "Traditionally, we go first. Then the dragons."

Yes. Karina would die howling for Vespir to save her. Hot, furious tears blurred her vision.

"Then we'll fight." She clenched her fists. "When they open the cell doors, we'll charge."

"Lucian? You up for a fight?" Ajax muttered.

The Sabel boy cursed, stood, and retook his customary position of looking at Emilia. He called the girl's name again before resting his forehead against the bars.

Ajax shrugged. "Guess that means no."

There would be a way. Vespir tried to think of places to kick a soldier: the groin, the instep. Could she break a nose if she had to? She'd never trained in fighting, but her arms were wiry from years of lifting hay and tack and wrestling hatchlings. Plus, she'd fought alongside her siblings in a thousand village skirmishes with other children. She knew how to bite an ear and pull hair with the best of them.

"We need a plan." Vespir licked her lips as she glanced at the closed iron door that led to the twisting staircase. Soon she'd hear the thud of boots. "Ajax, what do we do?"

"Pick a lock, if possible." He started jiggling his door, trying to snake his arm through the bars. "Maybe if—"

Vespir's ears exploded with a ringing scream. No, more than a scream. It sounded like the simultaneous shattering of thousands of panes of glass. Vespir slammed her shoulder against the bars, deafened by that thunderous crashing.

Tears streamed down her cheeks.

"What is happening?" she felt herself shout; she couldn't hear her own voice. Dimly, she saw that Ajax's mouth was open in a silent scream as well. Across from them, Lucian had taken a knee.

And then . . .

The shattering stopped. Through the ringing in her ears, Vespir made out a voice, one she had never heard before and yet knew so well.

"Vespir? Vespir!"

She gripped the sides of her head, but nothing would get that voice out. Not that she wanted it out. The more the strange, familiar woman called for her, the more Vespir thrilled.

"Who's there? Where are you?" she called.

"You hear it, too?" Ajax shook his head. "That man?"

"It's a woman, though."

"I hear a woman, too. Calling my name," Lucian rasped. He slapped his face a few times, as if to make sure he was really awake.

Vespir gripped the bars as she climbed to her feet. Then her hands slid down the iron as it became slippery. Freezing cold, to boot.

Vespir gasped as the bars of her cell transformed from iron to ice, the metal freezing in the span of heartbeats. Vespir backed up and watched the others' bars transform as well. Ajax leapt away with a shout, and Lucian cautiously pressed his palm against the bar. Then, decisive, he stepped back and kicked clear through the lock, the ice shattering into chunks. Vespir stared as he fashioned a door. Standing outside, he looked to Emilia's cage.

It alone remained ironbound. Cursing, he started pulling at the gate as Vespir, and then Ajax, followed his lead and kicked their way to freedom. Vespir stumbled out of her cage to stare at the now-dripping prison cell. How? Impossible.

"Vespir," the woman pleaded. Vespir clutched her head again. Maybe this was how they died. Perhaps the priests were already killing them by driving them mad. But no, she was free. That was no trick.

"Emilia!" Lucian continued to shake the bars.

"We need to get out of here, man." Ajax grabbed the Sabel boy's arm, but Lucian shook him off.

"You know what they'll do to her," he rasped. He tried yanking the very gate out of the wall.

The bars transformed, changing from iron to sand. Lucian tumbled to the floor. Blinking, he crawled back and watched alongside Vespir and Ajax as the chains that bound Emilia, the helmet on her head, all melted from steel into mounds of fine sand.

Emilia shook her head free as she sat up. Iridescent grains still clung to her purple velvet dress. She spat and rubbed her eyes. Cursing, Lucian stepped into the cell and helped her to her feet.

"Emilia? Did you . . . ?"

The Aurun girl ran fingers through her tangle of hair and grinned. Vespir had never seen such a radiant smile in her life.

"I'm. *Free.*" Emilia laughed.

Then she coughed up blood. It bubbled onto her lips, dripped down her chin. Ajax grunted in horror as Emilia turned around to take care of herself, Lucian gripping her shoulders.

"Are you all right?" he cried.

"Fine. Fine. I think it's too much power right now." She turned, having wiped the blood away. Her face appeared pale, though her eyes were fever-bright.

"What's going on?" Vespir croaked. Emilia told them in a soft, hurried voice what she had seen in her black prison. The Great Dragon, or at least she thought it *might* have been, and the secret history he'd shown her. The dragons' bondage, and chaos's binding. How Emilia had severed the chain and freed the dragons and chaos.

Freed the *dragons*?

"You mean the voice I hear in my head . . . Is that Karina?" Vespir's heart jackrabbited. Was it insane to be so violently excited while the world fell apart around them? Karina. She had to find her dragon.

If she could speak to her beautiful girl for five minutes . . .

"We need to get out of here." Lucian supported Emilia, her arm around his shoulders; she still appeared glassy-eyed, her body as weak as her power was strong. "If the four of us can get away, we can come up with a plan to expose the priests."

"I like the getting-away-from-here part." Ajax bolted for the stairs. Vespir and the others followed, taking the steps two at a time where they could. Soon. Soon. If the palace were in shambles because of the sudden chaos, maybe they could slip away to the aerie. Perhaps, even though she was spitting blood, Emilia could be useful if they ran into an enemy.

And above all, Vespir was as excited as a child at the

midwinter festival at the prospect of seeing Karina, hearing that velvety voice in a real conversation.

They ran up the winding stone steps and emerged into the palace corridors. No one was around. They took off, all four together. The main entrance hall was to their right, the door beyond. They broke into a run, rounded the corner.

They skidded to a sharp halt.

Forty feet ahead of them, Hyperia waited with a legion of imperial guards before the door. The Volscia girl wore a black gown, a collar of scales, and a crown of teeth. Blood decorated her front, much as when Vespir had first met her. Though *this* blood looked fresh.

The priests were nowhere to be seen.

Vespir turned to run, but another squadron of guards blocked her escape route. Swords drawn, they awaited Hyperia's signal.

"Shit," Lucian growled. He hugged Emilia tighter. "Hyperia. We just want to leave."

"To spread word of Camilla and Petros's treachery? No need. I've taken care of them myself," she replied coolly, unsheathing her sword. Vespir's legs felt rubbery.

"Then we're done. We all agreed not to kill one another," Lucian said.

"That was before I understood the terms of our agreement." Hyperia's eyes flashed. "I can't allow a chaotic to live. Besides, to make my ascension honorable, I must kill all of you by my own hand."

"Honorable?" Vespir choked.

Hyperia's chin tightened. "You're all a threat to my legitimacy. Especially *that*." She pointed at Emilia, who wobbled on her feet like a newborn foal. Lucian tried to snatch her back, but Emilia put him off.

"We've been lied to our entire lives," Emilia said. "There's so much we still don't know. Didn't you hear that noise, Hyperia? Don't you hear your own dragon's voice?"

Hyperia's calm mask slipped.

"That's Aufidius?"

"When they locked away chaos, the orderlies and Emperor Antoninus suppressed the dragons' ability to speak and think. Aufidius is free now. Can't you hear him?"

"I can. Do you know what he's saying?" Wild light kindled in her gaze. "A single word: *kill*."

Of course. Vespir shuddered.

"I won't listen to more of your heresies." Hyperia settled into fighting stance. Behind her, the imperial guard waited like a sea of black. "Come forward, and die."

69

Lucian

Lucian's instincts urged him to the attack. It would be so easy to disarm one of the soldiers and lunge for Hyperia. His eye twitched as he imagined lopping off her sword arm, blood gushing from the stump—

Just as he had done over and over, slicing soldiers through their bellies so that the rope of their intestines slopped onto the ground.

You swore to never lift a finger against another living creature. Do you only keep your vows when they're easy? he thought.

"Hyperia. Let us go." He would be calm.

"That is a *phenomenally* stupid request, considering everything I've just said." The empress strode to meet them. Emilia stepped forward, her hands raised. The thrill of seeing her in action again clashed with Lucian's horror at what might happen.

"It's not a request!" Emilia cried.

Though she growled, Hyperia did hesitate.

"Fight me on equal footing, you coward," the empress snapped.

"Fighting you with a sword wouldn't be equal, Your *Excellency*," Emilia returned. Her voice was low with confidence now; the stammering girl had melted away. Emilia flung her arms forward and the marble floor rolled and pitched like waves on the sea. The soldiers collapsed in a crash of armor, screaming as they were bandied about. Hyperia managed to keep her feet, but cried as the marble sea became more restless, rising in sharp peaks as if whipped up by a tempest. Hyperia was about to be bowled over when—

Blood.

Emilia coughed a spray of blood. Lucian saw it speckle the tile. She collapsed to her knees, fell forward onto her hands. She spat more dark, syrupy blood. No. No. He knelt and took her into his arms, stroked her wild hair. Her eyes, dark circles like bruises beneath them, sought his. A bubble of blood wavered on her lips as he cleaned her chin with his sleeve.

"It hurts," she moaned, and pressed her face into the crook of his arm. "Like something's stabbing me."

"Don't use it again. We don't know how much you can take."

"But if I don't . . ."

If Emilia did not fight, they were left with a useless Lucian, an inexperienced Vespir, and Ajax. The boy was quick enough with a dagger, but they faced Hyperia.

Lucian pressed his lips to the crown of her head. Emilia made a small noise at the kiss.

"Stay here," he whispered into her hair. "Take her, please." He gave her to Vespir and Ajax. Vespir cradled the girl against her body, and Ajax patted Emilia's arm. Wide-eyed, the Tiber boy balked as Lucian got to his feet.

"You're gonna . . . ?"

"No. Just talk," he said. Emilia gasped, her face as white as chalk. Dried blood flaked at the corner of her mouth. A relentless pressure built behind Lucian's eyes and in his throat; he would not let them have her. Or Vespir.

Well, he couldn't let Ajax die, either.

Lucian turned, held out his hands. "Hyperia. Emilia is *not* your enemy."

"She tried to kill my soldiers."

"She tried to stop you from killing *us*. She could have killed you instantly if she'd wanted."

"I've had enough of your failed attempts at diplomacy, Lucian. Either fight me, or prepare to die."

Desperation welled in his chest.

"Then kill me, but let the others go!"

"You severely overestimate your worth, don't you? A common trait of men," she spat. "Why would you satisfy me, when Emilia would live?" She bared her teeth. "A man who does not fight to defend his principles is no kind of man. You say you're atoning for your past, but you are *running from it!*" She grabbed a guard's sword and flung it to clatter on the floor by Lucian's feet. "There's nothing more loathsome than confusing weakness with goodness. Now, take up the sword!"

She was a monster.

She was . . .

Lucian thought again of that old man curled around his grandson, their charred corpses cooking in the winter air. He recalled hacking men to pieces—men who fought in homemade armor, carrying pitchforks from harvest, battling against Lucian with his silver armor, his longsword, his troops, and his dragon.

He had wanted to forget, but the path to redemption was not to hide from his skill. It was to use it well.

She was right.

He would never take up arms against an innocent again.

But Hyperia was no innocent.

Lucian picked up the soldier's blade.

"Thank you," Hyperia whispered.

When Lucian closed his hand around the grip, it felt like coming home after a long day. He swung it through the air a few times, listening to its song. Then, he crouched into a Masarian fighting stance, one best suited for lithe and leaping combat. His prior tussle with Hyperia proved she would not use blunt force. He would have to outwit her as much as outfight her.

With a roar, Hyperia charged.

Their swords clashed. The echo rang through the hall as they began their lethal dance. Up, down, up, up, lunge, parry, thrust—yes, it was a dance, and steel provided the music.

Lucian remembered every step. Hyperia's skirts whirled in a storm of satin. She nearly managed to get him through the side—she'd used her flowing sleeves as a distraction, drawing his attention with their flutter. Damn, she was good. As Lucian attacked, he realized she might be the first worthy opponent he had ever faced.

"Yes. Good, Lucian. Good!" Hyperia's fervor bordered ecstasy. He lunged, and his blade ripped through her skirt—damn, a few inches to the right and he'd have had her. He managed to duck just in time to avoid her sword as it whistled overhead. A few shorn strands of hair tickled his neck—he'd been inches from death.

Sweat dotted his temples as he deflected her. She had him on his knees now, attempting to weaken him until she could make her killing blow. When he swept his leg to knock her over, Hyperia vaulted into the air, landing perfectly on her feet. Lucian rolled backward and regained his footing. Both their chests heaved, their eyes bright.

"Enough of this," she growled. Hyperia feinted left, then came at him with a spinning thrust.

He'd seen it before: the technique she'd used on him after the Hunt.

If this had been his first time witnessing it, she'd have gutted him for sure.

Snarling, Lucian flung himself out of reach. As Hyperia sailed past, he elbowed her in the back. She fell to the floor, all the wind knocked out of her, but even that couldn't stop her. She wheeled on the ground, sword arcing in a strike from below. Lucian roared as he parried her thrust—and his blade bit flesh. His steel sliced a thin red line across the forearm.

Hyperia's sword clattered to the ground.

Lucian kicked it away. His boot forced her down, and down she stayed. Hyperia gasped as he laid his sword tip at the hollow of her throat.

"Yield."

"Kill me," she snarled. She even gripped the flat of the sword, ready to plunge it into her own throat. "It's the only way to stop me."

No begging. No crying. She was prepared to die as she'd lived, without weakness.

"No," he rasped. "I've defeated you. Honor demands you let us pass."

The eyes of the entire room fixed upon him as Hyperia struggled to her feet. She glared with simmering hate as she retrieved her sword and stepped backward into the throng of her guards.

"What're you doing?" Ajax shouted. "You won!"

Vespir shushed the boy as Lucian met Hyperia's eyes. Her jaw tightened. She could fight again, but Lucian would fight as hard, and he would win. He had the taste for it now and saw the realization in her eyes.

She wiped a hand down her face.

"Kill them all," she growled.

Lucian spun around. Emilia and the others began crawling

away from the horde of soldiers at their backs. So. Hyperia *had* weakness.

"Get behind me!" Lucian yelled to the others.

"Stop!" a voice shouted. Rufus stepped forward. The young man's dark eyes glowed, even beneath the oppressive shadow of his helmet. "We will not touch them."

Lucian knelt, cradling Emilia as he looked up in shock. Hyperia faced her captain.

"I command it!" she roared.

"You fought for your crown, and you were defeated. The guard is for Lord Lucian." Rufus met Lucian's gaze, and his old friend smirked. The captain held his blade at eye level. "We do not serve false emperors!"

As one, the imperial guard put up their swords as well.

"Lucian! Lucian!" they cried.

Lucian pressed Emilia over his hammering heart.

"Everyone, lie low," Ajax muttered, clinging to Vespir's arm. "I have the feeling she's about to get *mad*."

Hyperia turned in a slow circle, violence in her eyes, as she beheld the imperial guard standing against her. She could never get at them now, Lucian realized. He squeezed Emilia tighter, sighed when her own arm wrapped around him.

"You. *Bastards!*" Hyperia shoved herself through Rufus's ranks. The soldiers gave way as she sped for the door.

"Let her go!" Lucian called. The great doors opened, then boomed shut. "It's over."

"I can't believe it," Vespir said. "What do we do now?"

"Take a minute to breathe." Ajax slumped against Vespir's shoulder.

"Are you all right?" Lucian tipped Emilia's chin so that their eyes met. He had never seen such softness in her gaze.

Something moved within him at the sight.

"I need to rest. I feel like . . . broken glass inside, but—"

"Oh, *shit!*" Ajax leapt to his feet.

A semicircle of stained-glass window decorated the area above the grand entrance. A large dark shape blocked out the window's light, speeding closer and closer until—

Lucian hauled Emilia to her feet as Aufidius's golden head crashed through, raining shards of colored glass to the floor. The Hydra roared and spewed flame as Rufus and the soldiers by the door fell to their stomachs and crawled. One of them did not duck in time and was burned alive. His smoldering corpse lay amid slivers of blue and yellow glass. Aufidius roared again. Lucian felt his bones rattle as he and the others crawled to get out of the blast zone.

Thump. Thump. The doors began to splinter and bend. The Hydra was using its tail to break down the entrance. Once it was cleared, the bull would be able to shoulder his way through and go after the people within. Even if they ran, Aufidius could scorch this building from the inside out; the carnage would be extreme, and the palace itself could crumble. Lucian clenched his teeth. Why? Why had he been stupid enough to assume that would be all?

"I think," Ajax said, "letting her go was a mistake."

70

Vespir

What about the dragons?

Vespir kept hearing that plaintive voice in her head. *Karina!* Vespir thought, pressing a finger to her temple as if that'd help. *Are you all right?*

"Vespir!"

So far, that was all she could hear: her name, repeated.

If Aufidius and Hyperia dared to touch her girl, Vespir would kill both of them. Gritting her teeth, Vespir surged to her feet and watched from behind a marble pillar as the door splintered further. The Hydra used his talons to tear through the entrance. Guards sliced at the dragon with swords. Lucian led some more soldiers around the corner, wielding long spears. They threw the weapons, which sank into Aufidius's haunch. Roaring, the dragon retreated.

Vespir waited for the creature's head to reappear, but it didn't. Sunlight shone through the now-broken window. A full minute passed.

"Is it over?" Emilia gasped. She'd been propped up against the pillar and tried peering around to look.

"Wait here." Vespir raced through the soldiers and debris, her heart trammeling. She dared poke her head outside through the broken door and found that Hyperia and her dragon had really vanished. The path to the aerie was clear, and Vespir could still hear Karina's voice. She could even see Dog, shivering in the center of the courtyard. Aufidius had not hurt him.

"It's okay, boy!" she called.

Then she heard Aufidius's roar, distant but still bone-rattling. Great gouts of flame appeared as Aufidius sped through Dragonspire. The creature blasted buildings and swooped lower. Vespir froze, realizing the Hydra's game. He was going after the people in the streets.

They were defenseless. Vespir imagined children burning to ash as they sobbed for their parents, men and women screaming in agony. Her legs nearly gave out at the thought.

Her stomach dropped. Hyperia had gone absolutely mad. That, or . . . she was trying to draw them out.

There was no escape.

"She's burning the city!" Vespir shouted over her shoulder. Lucian's eyes widened in horror at her words. She watched him instantly gather the troops. Rather, they clustered around him naturally. As Lucian hurried to discuss a plan with his soldiers, Ajax came up beside Vespir, peering out the door. When he saw Dog, he deflated in relief but still did not run outside. The boy bit his lip and looked to the sky, probably waiting for Hyperia to descend on them at any moment. Vespir ran back to confer with Lucian.

"How fast can we coordinate with the city guard?" Lucian asked the captain. "We have to get as many people away from her as we can."

"Getting to street level will require a bit of time. Technically, the imperial guard is never supposed to leave the palace. Ten stories is a lot of stairs," the captain replied.

"Order the soldiers down, then come with me. My dragon can carry two long enough to get us to the main outpost. We can start evacuations from there."

"If Hyperia comes after us?" Rufus asked. Lucian paused. A Drake carrying two passengers could never hope to out-maneuver a bull Hydra.

"I can distract her," Vespir said, catching their attention. Hopefully, she sounded more confident than she felt.

"You might not be able to outrun her," Lucian said.

"You need to get the people to safety, and what she *really* wants is us, the competitors. She'll leave everyone alone if I show, even if I can't stay ahead forever . . ." Vespir took a shaky breath. "You'll have enough time."

"I can't ask you to do that," Lucian said, horrified.

"No. You can't. That's why I'm telling you."

Lucian squeezed her shoulder. "Then good luck."

While Rufus and Lucian gave their orders, Vespir rushed for the door, doubling back to drag Ajax along with her.

"You're going to help me," she said.

"What'm *I* supposed to do?"

"You're going to try reconnecting with Dog. When you do, come and support me against Hyperia." Vespir cursed as Ajax yanked away.

"I *can't*. Even if I connect with him, Dog is blind." His eyes tightened in pain. "I'm not getting him killed!"

Vespir grabbed his shoulders, all but shook the boy.

"If you climb aboard with no saddle or bridle and place your forehead against the back of his head, it'll help. Physical contact makes it work. I swear you can do this!" She gripped his hands. "Don't you want to give Dog the sky again?"

"Yes, but I don't want him shot down five minutes later."

"You won't. Karina and I can buy you time while we let Lucian and Emilia get the people to safety. Trust me." She stared into his eyes. "Will you trust me?"

"If you stop digging your nails into my skin."

Vespir dragged him outside by his wrist, plunging through

the shattered door. Ajax raced for Dog—his fear melted when he saw his dragon.

"Dog!" The dragon's fright changed in an instant. The beast trundled toward the sound of Ajax's voice, weaving a bit to find his way in darkness. Vespir watched the boy grip his dragon by the jowls and press his face to Dog's snout.

"Climb aboard. Quickly," she said. Ajax did as she asked, and Vespir stroked Dog's nose while she instructed his rider. "You have to let your mind go. It sounds odd, but you need to let yourself be equal to him. Two sides of one coin. Yes?"

Ajax shifted between the dragon's wings. He looked rather pale.

"What if I can't?"

"Then wait here."

"You'll die, Vespir." He said it with certainty. "Your dragon's too small."

"I won't die." She made a fist. "I'm the greatest rider in the damn empire."

She needed to believe it.

All of the dragons were out of their stalls, congregating in the center. She could not hear Chara's or Tyche's voices; she heard only their chitters and groans. But Karina lunged at Vespir, and the other dragons made way. Her dragon, with her brown riverbed scales, her flat, hornless head, her wide amber eyes, and her curved tail came up to Vespir, stretched out her long neck, and spoke.

"Vespir! My little Vespir!"

It was a voice of baking bread, of calm nights in front of the fire, of warm hands smoothing her hair, of home. Overwhelmed, Vespir pitched forward, only for Karina to break the fall. As Vespir clung to her dragon's neck, she heard that voice once more: *"I've got you now."*

Vespir couldn't see through her tears. She felt as though a warm, wonderful liquid had filled her.

"Karina," she whispered. "How?"

The dragon's eyes held an amused gleam. She cocked her head to the side, nosing Vespir's hair.

"It's like I've never seen you before," the dragon whispered, her voice—sedate and playful and young and old—reverberating in Vespir's mind. *"As though I've dreamed you for years."*

"I used to imagine talking to you, but Plotus told me it was worse than crazy to think that way. But . . . how? It's like you're in my mind."

"There's much I still don't understand, but we dragons have lived in bondage for generations. That much I know by instinct."

Then . . . Vespir had made Karina her servant. Her *slave.*

"You mustn't think that." Karina tutted, sniffling at her cheek. *"A dragon's bond with their rider is the most precious thing in this world. It is a choice. And it makes the joining of man and wife appear quaint."* Karina booped her nose against Vespir. *"A demonstration of my love, my little Vespir."*

Vespir decided to retire the word *boop.*

Her hands trembled as she stroked Karina's snout and the flat of her head. A scream of joy welled, blocking her breath. Karina . . . Karina was free.

"Can I hear the other dragons?" Vespir asked.

"I don't believe so. Once, perhaps, but . . . now it seems a dragon bonds with a rider, and a rider with a dragon." Karina extended her neck, looking over the top of Vespir's head. *"Though I'd be surprised if the others start off with as keen a bond as we share. After all, you and I have connected several times."*

"I need to stop Aufidius." Once she'd have simply jumped aboard, but now she needed permission. "Will you help me?"

"As if you needed to ask."

Vespir climbed onto Karina's back. She did not need to lock in now; the Red flashed before her eyes at once. With a few flaps, Karina brought them out of the aerie and launched into the sky. The wind whipped through Vespir's hair as they turned for the smoke in the distance, for Aufidius. And Hyperia.

Hopefully, the others would join them soon.

Vespir wondered what their dragons sounded like.

71

Ajax

"*Master Ajax!*" Dog said. "*For far too long the full extent of my mind and the complete expression of my feelings have been suppressed. For that, I apologize.*

"*But verily, who have we to blame but those putrid individuals that locked away the true spirit of dragonkind? The fiends believed they could chain us like mere chattel, but how we have been vindicated—how we now laugh and scorn their errant ways! Ah, to articulate the grandeur of my own experience, and to share it all with you, is a dream to which I did not even realize I clung. But forsooth, 'tis no longer a dream; now, reality.*

"*Master Ajax, though I am blind, my spirit merges with yours, and my heart is as your heart. Your presence steadies me, and if I did not cherish you before, I do so now, and shall devote myself unyieldingly to your safety, your security, your happiness. An oath of fealty cannot be too great—a promise of fidelity unwavering, of love unquestioning, of devotion unparalleled is yours as ever, my dear boy.*

"*Ah, so many words to speak!* Maladroit! Pineapple! Antidisestablishmentarianism! Fluffy! *Oh, and guess what? I love you! I love you! I love you! The best words of all! Huzzah! I love you!*"

Ajax gaped. "What the f—"

"*Fibula? Another excellent word! Tra la!*"

72

Hyperia

Hyperia would kill the others—or burn down the world trying.

Her heart synced with the beat of Aufidius's wings as they targeted the screaming people in the streets. These crowds dancing in celebration, these musicians playing timpani and blowing dove-pipes, these feasts spiced with tamarind and coriander, she would destroy them all. She was no empress. Those who did not rule by right must conquer.

The world would burn, and she would watch through her tears.

Julia. My baby. I'm sorry.

Her sister, dead for nothing. That chaotic bitch, Emilia, would live, and Hyperia . . .

She had betrayed her own heart. Beaten by Lucian, she had set the soldiers upon the other competitors to preserve her throne. Dishonorable. Weak. Cowardly.

She had killed her own beloved one for *nothing*.

Her mind splintered. She welcomed the collapse of all her senses.

"Kill." Aufidius's bass thrummed through her body. *"Kill. Kill."*

Her dragon repeated that one heavy word over and over. Hyperia wept, tears drying in the wind as soon as she shed them.

"Aufidius, help me," she whimpered. Her mind folded in on itself. Why couldn't she stroke his snout, let his wings shield her from the world? The Hydra roared, angry at her weakness. Hyperia clutched the horn of her saddle as her mount jerked quickly to the left, going sideways. Any more blubbering on her part, and she knew the dragon would buck her to the winds and let her plummet to her death.

"Kill! Kill! Kill!"

There was no escape from this. Hyperia bit back her pain.

The other four could not stay idle in their golden palace while Hyperia demolished the capital. Soon they would come.

I will burn this city to the ground. Thousands will die in the streets, and . . . and our five bodies will lie together among the ashes.

As dismay got its teeth in her, Hyperia tried to smile grimly. If that heinous image she'd seen in the gateway of Truth had been inevitable, at least it meant they would all soon be dead.

"Kill."

"Yes. Kill them all," Hyperia growled, eyes watering in the heat as her dragon spewed torrents of flame. The air stank with sulfur. They soared above pinkish-red terra-cotta rooftops that formed a winding labyrinth of shops and homes. The buildings ignited; smoke billowed into the air; the aroma of roasted flesh flooded her nostrils as men and women burned. Her dragon roared in ecstasy, and Hyperia's heart sang with him. She alternated between relishing the screams and wanting to throw herself into the inferno below. What was she? If she did not have her identity—empress, sister—she was nothing.

Let her be a butcher, then.

Through the smoke, Hyperia saw a small, darting shape fly beneath them. The creature, the dragon, spouted flame, rose on the winds, and tried snapping at Aufidius's tail.

Karina.

Vespir rode her minuscule beast, which shot above Aufidius,

expanding her little wings to block out the sun. Hyperia squinted, shielded her eyes with her hand.

"We're not done yet!" Vespir shouted, her tone cutting as any blade. Vespir's dragon made an upside-down loop before taking off at impossible speeds for the palace.

Yes. Hyperia would restore her honor by hunting down the finest dragon rider she had ever seen. Total annihilation could wait.

Nothing to fear. She had foreseen Vespir's death as well as her own.

"Go," she hissed. Aufidius winged his way over the rooftops of this wretched city. Soon enough, Karina grew from a tiny dot to a dragon. Hyperia would overtake these lesser creatures.

"*Kill,*" Aufidius snarled in her mind, blocking out the sound of screams. Yes. Kill.

Kill.

Kill.

"*KILL.*"

Hyperia's roar mingled with her dragon's as they attacked.

73

Vespir

Vespir wished she had seen more of Dragonspire before it was on fire. Karina tucked her wings and made a spectacular dive into the buildings' canyons. They soared past marble balustrades, past glimmering shop windows, and down cobblestone avenues lined with trees. The air shook as Aufidius roared behind them. Vespir dared a peek over her shoulder. The larger dragon couldn't follow Karina into the streets themselves, but his deadly breath more than made up for it.

"Pull up!" Vespir screamed when Aufidius spewed flame into the boulevard, roasting at least half a dozen people. Tears streaked her face as Karina rocketed into the sky. Hyperia was a murderer, yes, but Vespir hadn't truly believed her capable of killing like this.

"She's gone mad," Karina murmured. *"That dragon is a monster."*

"We need to draw them back to the palace. Can we make it?" Vespir wrapped her arms around Karina's neck and laid her cheek against the dragon's shoulder.

"In the open air, my speed may not be enough."

"I know." If they dodged through the city streets, they could avoid Aufidius, but it would involve more death. Vespir could not let that happen. "Please try."

"For you, anything."

They flew, Vespir struggling to stay calm as she heard Aufidius's roar. She screamed as flame shot overhead, nearly roasting the back of her neck.

"Vespir!"

"He didn't get me."

"But if he does . . ."

Fire couldn't hurt Karina, but Vespir was utterly human.

"Can you hook your heels under my legs?"

Vespir knew what Karina was suggesting and wished to the depths that she didn't.

It was the only way—Aufidius would not miss next time—and they were closing in on the palace . . .

But if Vespir let go . . .

She hooked her heels and flattened herself against Karina's back.

"Now!" Vespir screamed. Karina spun around, belly up to Aufidius, Vespir protected behind her back. All good, save for the fact that Vespir now dangled one hundred feet above the ground, the strength in her heels and arms all that prevented her from tumbling into oblivion.

"I will, I will, I will," she chanted, gritting her teeth as her legs began to tremble. Her thighs burned—she couldn't hold like this forever. As pain started shooting through her legs, the sky overhead lit with flame.

Vespir would burn to ash and join her brother Casca. They'd toss a little wooden box of her onto the family kitchen table.

One heel slipped, and Vespir screamed as it dangled in the air and began to pull the rest of her body after. Karina trilled in response, quickly soaring upward so that Vespir was seated once more. Wings flaring to fill with wind, the dragon rose above Aufidius. But Vespir felt her friend weakening—Karina was too small for a fight like this.

"Can we get around to the palace gardens?" Vespir called.

"We won't make it," Karina replied grimly. As the dragon spoke, Vespir realized that her left leg felt wet. Glancing down, she saw her pajama pant soaked in blood from ankle to calf. For one second she thought she'd been gored and hadn't felt it yet with all the adrenaline, but she noticed the curved gouge running along the top of Karina's leg, which bled freely. Vespir's mind seemed to shut down. Her girl had been injured. Badly.

"When I bit at his tail, he snagged me with his talons," Karina murmured. The dragon bobbed on the wind, sinking lower with every passing second, and Aufidius was nowhere near tired yet.

"The spire," Vespir gasped. The fifty-foot protrusion gleamed directly before them. "Latch on to it. Rest. We can launch off if we need."

Karina chirped and soared ahead. Aufidius rose behind them, his gold scales glowing like fire in the morning sun. Karina made it to the palace, and Vespir was tempted to have her swoop low and try to hobble inside, but Aufidius would be on them before they could make it to shelter. The spire was their last chance . . .

To do what?

Karina gripped the spire with her taloned feet. Her wings, each tipped with a claw at the top joint, took hold as well, leaving Vespir to dangle against her dragon's back. They were safe.

But not for long.

"Here they come," she murmured. Aufidius and his golden rider homed in on Vespir's location and hovered over them. Karina shifted and groaned, and Vespir touched the soft place between her dragon's shoulder blades for comfort. "If it gets too bad, I'll jump off," Vespir whispered.

"Where you go, I go."

Stubborn dragon. Vespir loved her for it. She fought against the urge to lower her head as Aufidius rose before them, his wings at their full forty-foot span. The Hydra's jaw unhinged, and fire gathered at his throat.

Shaking, Vespir stared at her death.

74
Ajax

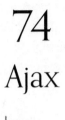

"Can you see yet?" Ajax had his forehead smashed up against the back of Dog's skull, his eyes squeezed shut tight as possible.

"Do not worry, dear master. I know you're doing your best, as always." Dog's tail thumped.

"It's not master. You're my partner, Dog. We're the same."

Mean it. Ajax had to *mean* it. The world was falling down around them, but the only thing he could do to fix it was to bond with this dragon. Let Dog see again. Depths below, the whole thing sounded so *stupid* . . .

"I believe in you," Dog said, his voice tender and small.

Logic had no place with dragons or with love. Ajax grunted and didn't shut his eyes so tight. He let his mind ease up, felt Dog's breathing match his own, and tried to reach out with invisible hands to touch the essence of his dragon as he had last night. Their souls linked, their minds merged, their beings formed as one. The Red flash that would unite them hovered just out of reach.

He could feel it. Ajax could feel it drawing closer and closer and—

Nothing. Just him sitting with his eyes shut. He cursed and

sat up. Ajax's head jerked at the deafening roar of a Hydra, and he watched as Aufidius swept into view. Gaping in horror, he spotted the tiny figures clinging to the spire. Vespir and Karina.

Aufidius had them in his sights. Ajax placed a gentle hand on the back of Dog's head.

"We're too late," he said.

75

Vespir

The fire built. Vespir wondered if she should tell Karina to drop and hope they managed not to splat on the roof below . . .

"Wait," Hyperia boomed. Aufidius growled but slowly shut his jaws. The eye-stinging heat of his flame disappeared as Hyperia unsheathed her sword.

What was this girl *doing*?

"Now. Set down, and fight me," Hyperia shouted, lifting that sword overhead so that the rising sun fired it. The girl really was incredible. Even now, she wanted her duel.

She gives orders, and servants obey.

Vespir thought of her mother and father, of Tavi, of all her brothers and sisters bowing to people like this for generations.

She thought of Casca's ashes on the dining room table.

She'd been born on her knees . . . but she didn't have to die there.

Time. This was all about buying time . . .

"No," she shouted back. She climbed to her feet, balancing on Karina's shoulders. Though she wobbled, Vespir remained steady. "If you want me, you have to come to me."

"You have no honor," Hyperia roared.

"No, *you* don't!" Vespir gripped the spire, her hand sweating. Vespir stared Hyperia straight in the eye. The blond girl's expression slackened. She might've expected this insolence from Ajax, but not the servant. Never a girl like Vespir. "You're broken. I'd rather see anyone else on the dragon throne. *I'd* be a better choice." The most surreal part was that she meant it. "I am never going to obey you ever, ever again, you *bitch*."

Hyperia reacted as if Vespir had physically slapped her. Aufidius opened his mouth, and fire collected at the back of his throat. Vespir slid down her dragon's back and hung on as Karina scrambled to get out of the way. This was madness. How were they supposed to survive? But Vespir thought again and again, hold on. *Hold on.* Was Karina speaking those words, or were they her own thoughts? The two seemed indistinguishable now.

Flame licked just below them. Vespir's eyes watered as they climbed higher. "Where are we going?" she shouted.

"Farther up."

Vespir clung as they neared the top, screaming as Aufidius swept up to meet them. He blocked out the sun, Hyperia looking over his shoulder with her face twisted in fury. Smoke poured from out the dragon's mouth, and embers fell to sizzle against Vespir's cheeks.

Vespir saw Hyperia mouth the word *fire.* Flame built in the dragon's gullet.

She could feel Karina's trembling. If they launched, they'd only be able to spiral to the ground now. The dragon's injury was too deep, her body too tired. Vespir hugged her friend tight around her neck, laid her cheek against those silken scales, and prepared.

"Gawp."

Dog, flying beautifully, emerged out of the smoke overhead

and let out a giant, warlike cry. Ajax, his blond hair undone and flowing in the wind, his face scarlet, screamed in triumph.

The pair slammed on top of Aufidius and Hyperia. The girl dropped her sword, which cut through the smoke and disappeared below. She fell forward, just managing to keep her seat. Aufidius belched smoke as the surprise attack propelled him down.

Karina released her claws, dropping fast as Aufidius was speared through the spire's tip. It tore into the center of the golden beast's body and out his shoulder. Blood rained onto Vespir's upturned face. It smelled awful, like shit and oil. Coughing, she wiped her eyes and listened to the Hydra's screams. The air moved rapidly next to her, blowing her hair into her face. Someone circled her as Karina struggled for purchase.

Ajax and Dog. The mad boy and his mad, wonderful dragon.

Karina and Vespir let go of the spire and spun down through the air, scrambling for a landing while Aufidius bellowed his defeat.

76

Ajax

The Red—whatever this was, this locked-in thing—felt like someone had their thumb pressed in the center of Ajax's brain, but he loved it. Wherever his eyes scanned, he felt Dog's scarred, sightless eyes move as well. This union tugged like a line hooked between their souls.

At some point, he would worry how much Dog could "see" when they weren't flying together. Specifically, like when Ajax was bathing or whenever he finally found himself taking things to the next level with a girl (someday, somehow, somewhere, something, with someone, please before he died or turned thirty). But that was for when they weren't in a damn life-or-death battle.

"You did it!" Vespir crowed, circling on Karina. The two dragons fondly chirped at each other. "What a beautiful boy!"

"Thank you!" Ajax yelled.

"I meant Dog!"

"Oh!"

They landed, Ajax grinning as he slid off Dog's back and went to Vespir.

"You . . . okay?" Ajax wheezed. Ash and blood smeared her cheeks, and she smelled like a smokehouse. He grunted when the girl threw her arms around him.

"Thanks." Vespir smiled. Then, "Though I wish you'd warned me you were going to do that."

"How about we start with 'Thank you, Ajax, oh uniquely handsome dragon master, for saving my damn life.'"

"Technically, Dog saved me."

"Then thank Dog."

"I will!" Vespir kissed the dragon square between his gouged eyes. Dog nudged Ajax's shoulder as Vespir returned to Karina.

"I like her. Her dragon is pleasant, as well. Quite lovely, in fact!"

Ajax couldn't get used to having that plummy voice in his head. "I can't believe I used to make you fetch sticks," he muttered, abashed. "You should've refused."

"Yes, but . . . I love you." Dog's tail thumped on the ground.

"Oh no." Vespir looked up as an unearthly scream pierced the sky.

Aufidius struggled to free himself, but his movements were slowing. His body continued to slide down the spire, now coated in oily black blood. The dragon's wings drooped. The long, perfect neck hung limp, the head swaying this way and that in the breeze. The screams came from Hyperia as she clung to her dragon's wing.

Even with everything Hyperia had done, Ajax had to turn his face away as Aufidius breathed his last.

With a scream that bit to the bone, Hyperia plummeted to earth.

Despite her injuries, Karina managed to flap off the ground, roll, and catch the girl in her talons. Ajax winced as the dragon bobbed in the air, her strain visible. But she managed it. Karina deposited Hyperia beside Ajax. He instinctively shied away, wanting to hide himself behind Dog, because Hyperia felt . . . wrong.

The Volscia girl sat there, her shoulders slumped, her hands dropped by her sides with her palms facing up. Her hoarse breathing was slow, her eyes open in a look of confused horror. Her expression reminded Ajax of someone desperately working to wake from a nightmare, but there'd be no waking from this.

Hyperia's very soul had been Cut.

The girl placed her hands on the sides of her neck, then her cheeks, as if she were trying to remind herself that she was real. Hyperia tilted her head back, gazed to the sky. She dug her fingers into her hair, and her face tightened with agony. Still, she did not scream. She suffered in horrendous silence.

Ajax wasn't the most sensitive guy in the world, but he started to cry. He put his hand on her back, just to let her know that someone was there.

If it happened to me, I don't think I could go on, he thought.

Hyperia finally slumped across Vespir's lap. Vespir stroked the girl's hair. He'd never seen such a sorry expression in his life.

Ajax had helped do this, which made him want to vomit. Dog nuzzled at Ajax's shoulder. *"It had to be done."*

"What happened?" Lucian stumbled toward them, Emilia by his side. He waved a hand to clear some of the smoke, allowing Emilia to lean on him as they shuffled along. Some of the imperial guard escorted him. Tyche waited behind her rider, tilting her head at quizzical angles.

"Aufidius is dead." Emilia didn't even have to glance at the spire. Her face crumpled. "I didn't expect it to be so . . ." With a pained grunt, Emilia lowered herself beside the blond girl. "I'm sorry," she murmured. "None of us wanted this."

Emilia's face and voice were apparently the incentive needed to restore some life to Hyperia. She pushed Emilia away.

"Don't touch me. Demon! I tried . . . I tried . . ." Hyperia finally began to weep. "I tried to stop it!"

"Stop it?" Emilia sounded baffled.

"Chaos." Hyperia rolled her eyes to the blue above. Her lip

quivered. "The priests . . . lied. I was not . . . the true victor. One of you . . . You were all selected . . . because of a flaw. Don't you see? I may be a freak, but you are all . . . abomination."

Hyperia clutched the sides of her head. Ajax draped an arm around Dog's neck for comfort. What in the depths was she talking about?

"I know . . . I seem cruel," she growled. "But everything I have ever done was for my empire. I've never wanted . . . *anything* . . . for myself." Her voice choked with tears. "All I wanted . . . was to live with honor. And *you*." Some of the old Hyperia smoldered behind her glassy expression. "Chaotics. Murderers. Hypocrites. Illiterates. Bastards. Thieves. Liars. Cowards." She gave one long, loud wail of agony. "*You're* what the Dragon really chose! This world is *garbage*."

"You need help," Vespir said quietly.

What did Ajax feel? Besides guilt, he just wanted this to end.

"Don't touch me," Hyperia snarled as Vespir tried to help her up. The Volscia girl staggered to her feet, swaying like a drunkard. Her golden crown had fallen off in the chaos. One of her diaphanous sleeves had ripped, leaving her arm bare. Hyperia's face was dirty. She looked worlds away from the pristine beauty he'd first met. Well, she'd worn blood on her face back then, too.

"I don't care what I have to do," Hyperia said. She sounded so calm, switching from one extreme to the other, that it freaked him out.

"Huh?" Ajax asked.

"*Master Ajax!*" Dog swept one of his bat wings around the boy. Ajax struggled.

"What the—"

There was a dense, meaty *tearing* sound, and the spire finally ripped clean through Aufidius's corpse. The enormous dragon fell to the earth, its wings fluttering uselessly. When it struck the ground, the body burst wide . . . and the fiery acid within its stomach cavity flooded the area in rippling blue flame.

Shit.

Ajax leapt onto Dog's back and held tight as they surged skyward. Vespir and Karina joined him, as did Lucian and Tyche, with Emilia perched on the saddle before the Sabel boy. The soldiers raced to shelter in the palace doorway. Ajax watched the acid fire scorch most of the landing area. Damn, what if Hyperia . . .

But she was gone. After the fire had burned itself out, they found no trace of her.

77

Lucian

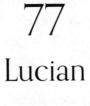

"How is the city?" Lucian asked Rufus as servants began to clear away the debris. "What kind of damage was done?"

"Most of the central fountain square was annihilated." Rufus shook his head. "The city was designed for riders, but no one ever thought there'd be a dragon attack here. There were no plans in place. Several buildings burned."

Lucian had sent Tyche to help manage the flames, as Emilia had Chara. Though she had to be careful, Tyche could carry containers and drop water onto a fire. So strange to have sent Tyche on a mission and not have to ride upon her to carry it out.

"Lucian. My love," she had whispered when they properly faced each other in the aftermath. She had prodded her snout against his chest, an action as familiar as anything he had known throughout their life together, but her silken voice had teased his mind. He had pressed his forehead against hers and let their thoughts intermingle. Thoughts of flying and thoughts of blood.

The images of those burned corpses in the north quivered with pain.

"I'm sorry, Tyche. Never again," he'd whispered.

She'd cooed, rested her jaw upon his shoulder, and forgiven him.

"There are other problems for you to deal with," Rufus said, reclaiming Lucian's attention. "The five families are waiting to greet their new emperor or empress. They are, needless to say, very confused." He cleared his throat. "Lady Aurun in particular has been . . . difficult."

Poor Emilia.

"Also, there's the priestess." Rufus raised an eyebrow. "What would you like us to do with her?"

"It's not what I'd like, Rufus. I'm not your emperor. In fact, we need Camilla to tell us exactly who needs to receive the imperial crown."

"If you say so." Rufus cleared his throat.

"What?"

"I didn't just declare the imperial guard against Lady Hyperia. I declared us for you. The imperial guard is the emperor's to command."

"I'm not the emperor."

"Not yet." Rufus grinned. "But all you need to do is place that crown on your head, Excellency."

"Don't call me that." Lucian didn't mean to snap. "What if Emilia were truly chosen? Or Vespir? I don't have a right if I wasn't picked."

"Lady Hyperia didn't have a right, either. Her move failed because we wouldn't back it. But we would back you, Lucian."

"Rufus. I want you to follow the true emperor."

"So do I." His friend's brilliant, dark eyes crackled. "And I know who he is."

When another guard summoned the four of them to go down to Camilla's jail cell, Lucian walked with a tight pain in his shoulders.

There were only a few iron-barred cages left in the imperial dungeon. Much of the jail floor was covered in water from the rapidly melting ice. Emilia blushed as she lifted her skirts to walk through the puddle.

They stood together, the four of them, and faced the priestess. Camilla hunched over on the cot, her steel-gray hair tangled. The soldiers had locked her arms behind her, and Rufus placed a hand upon his blade.

"If you attempt anything, my people have orders to run you through. Be careful, priestess," said Rufus.

"I suppose the days of 'Your Grace' are behind me," Camilla muttered." She lifted her head. To Lucian's surprise, her eyes were raw from crying. "Petros. What did you do with his body?" She sniffed. "You gave it to his dragon, yes? He must be eaten!"

"That can wait," Lucian said. "Frankly, I can't believe Hyperia left even one of you alive." It sounded cold, but after what this woman had put them through, he did not feel inclined to mercy. He never would have made a successful Sacred Brother.

"Petros and I may have miscalculated with the five of you—" Camilla began.

"You lied," Lucian growled.

"We . . ." Camilla sighed. "Yes," she whispered. "Because you discovered our secrets. None of you—not even Hyperia—were a good choice for the dragon throne. It would be only a matter of time until total pandemonium. Do you want civil war? Insurrection in the streets?"

"You say that we'd be the empire's downfall, but I don't think things are running well even now," Emilia replied.

"Of course you wouldn't," Camilla spat, hatred splintering her eyes. "Chaotic!"

"Don't be a fool." Emilia was more centered than Lucian had ever seen her. Her steely gaze wrestled with Camilla's own. "You know what I did down here," the girl said. "Chaos is unbound once again. I should thank you. If you hadn't backed me into such a corner, I might never have been desperate enough to try. Did you know the dragons were our prisoners? Our *slaves*?"

Camilla shuddered. "Don't use that word."

"It's the truth. Isn't that what order prizes above all else? Or do you think that truth is only necessary when it gets you what you want?" Emilia gripped the bars. Everyone noticed that they began to quiver, and everyone held their breath. "A voice in my head told me what to do. It called itself the Great Dragon. Isn't that who *you* claim to speak for?"

"That's heresy," Camilla said, choking. "He . . . He does not *speak* to anyone!"

"Then how do you claim to know what He wants? How does He let you know which competitor He picks for the throne?" Lucian asked.

The priestess gnawed at her lower lip.

"I . . . I can't tell you. It's a sacred mystery, taught only to those chosen as high priest or priestess. It's worth more than my life to tell."

Lucian snorted. "Convenient."

"How can you be certain it was Him?" Camilla asked Emilia. "You're being led astray by evil, girl, and you don't even know it!"

"If evil freed Chara and all the rest, then maybe evil is just what we need." Emilia did not shy away. She was fire and fury. Lucian became warm just looking at her.

And if he felt a bit nervous that some voice had told Emilia how to free chaos, he kept it to himself. Surely she knew what she was doing.

"Tell us who was chosen as emperor," Lucian said, hyper-aware of Rufus's eyes on his back. Even if someone else was chosen, Rufus might have been serious about accepting no one but Lucian. After all, he'd defied Hyperia; he might do it again. If that happened, Lucian would fight to stop it. But . . .

But on the throne, he could do so much. He knew now that he was no holy man cut out for good, quiet works. He must work to dismantle this horror show of an empire. He *must* have that power. What if . . .

"What if," Emilia said, "we *didn't* learn who won?"

"What?" Camilla blinked in horror.

"What?" Vespir said.

"What if *I* won?" Ajax frowned.

"What do you mean?" Lucian asked, and Emilia gazed up at him with those determined eyes.

"Whoever wins," she said, "will be a bad ruler."

"But I could be the best bad ruler we've got," Ajax muttered.

"We're all blind in certain areas. I know nothing of the world; Vespir knows nothing of politics; you, Lucian, know nothing of magic. But together?"

No. What she was thinking was too impossible . . . wasn't it?

"The four of us. That way, whoever *was* chosen does rule, but not alone. I have my knowledge and my magic. Lucian, you know the military and the politics of expansion. Vespir knows the people, and dragons, better than any of us." Emilia smiled at Lucian, at Vespir. "And Ajax . . ."

No one spoke.

"I'm crafty?" the boy offered.

"Yes, that. Anyway, power wouldn't rest in only one person's hand. The four of us would be able to reshape the world as *we* want it to be. The poet Valerius once said that gods dreamed of empires, but devils built them. We've been ruled by devils for so long. Let's be gods together."

Reshape the world. Rule nobly. Lucian had yearned for it. And to have the others with him—to have Emilia at his side, guiding him as he guided her—quickened his pulse.

He heard Rufus grumble, and Lucian understood why. Nothing like this had been tried, ever. This would be an empire still, but an empire with multiple leaders, leaders with multiple talents and weaknesses. Dangerous, yes, but perhaps the only true way forward.

"You're mad," Camilla whispered. "That's a child's dream of how things work! You can't do this! The five families will never approve."

"We don't care if they approve," Lucian snapped. The lords and ladies of the Etrusian Empire had built a system perfectly suited to them. There would be no true justice without a thorough dismantlement. "Use your authority to present us as the Dragon's selection." He had never felt so calm in his life. "Or"—Lucian narrowed his eyes—"we can reveal what you did before having you executed."

"You can't possibly ascend without my blessing." Camilla sounded wary, though.

"It would be more difficult, but it could be done. And either way, you'd be too dead to know how it all turned out." The threat flowed easily from his lips and sickened him.

Vespir winced. At least one of them felt the gravity of threats.

"Hey, one-fourth of a crown is better than none at all. Well, Camilla?" Ajax leaned against the bars. "Are we the Sarkoni now? Do we all have to wear black? How long does it take to get a few more thrones made?"

"Choose," Emilia said.

The priestess hesitated.

The next great turn of their lives rested on this woman's decision.

"I believe . . . we must all bow before our emperors." She got wearily to her knees. "All hail Emilia Sarkona and Lucian Sarkonus and Vespir Sarkona and Ajax Sarkonus."

"All hail." Lucian nodded at Rufus, giving the order. He

would still sit the throne. Apparently, that was enough for the captain.

"All hail," Rufus called. The guards dropped to their knees as one.

Vespir blushed madly as she watched the room genuflect. Ajax grinned.

Lucian felt Emilia settle close by his side, and his blood flowed like fire in his veins.

And if something inside him whispered *You don't know what you're doing*, he shoved it away.

Because Emilia was right, as usual. It was time for them all to be gods. And dragons.

78

Emilia

She would not buckle or bend.

The five families had gathered to pay homage to the new emperor or empress. Emilia ordered that they be taken to the terrace room, the antechamber before the grand balcony upon which the new emperor was to be presented.

The families were, unsurprisingly, stunned when the four victors entered in their outfits of imperial black. Unfortunately, the golden crown was still unaccounted for, but there would be time to craft new ones. The black satin and velvet made the point quite nicely, anyway.

Lord Sabel and his daughter both looked aghast; Lord Volscia simply sat down; Lord Tiber grunted in surprise; Lord and Lady Pentri appeared very quiet; and her own parents . . .

"I don't understand." Her father furrowed his brow. Alex, meanwhile, seemed delighted. Apparently, he'd forgiven her for those trade ports she'd gifted the Pentri.

If her brother was still on her side, she could do this.

The priestess, who had to be aware of how carefully the four victors and their imperial guard watched her, smiled as if trying to swallow curdled milk.

"The Great Dragon has made a rare selection," Camilla said. "After all, wasn't the emperor Antoninus the least amongst the five great lords and ladies? Didn't the Dragon select him to rule according to his meekness?"

"Does this have something to do with why our dragons can talk to us now?" Dido of the Sabel demanded. She didn't look too pleased. Emilia recalled Lucian's tales of campaign bloodshed. Perhaps Dido's dragon had had some choice words about that.

Camilla cleared her throat, but Emilia felt the priestess had spoken enough.

"Yes. The dragons lived as our slaves for many years," she said. "I simply freed them."

"You?" Emilia's mother sounded blunt with disbelief. Then her eyes widened as she imagined what Emilia—and only Emilia—could have done. "Oh."

"This is very simple." Emilia edged Camilla aside. "The Dragon's grown tired of how useless you've all been." In her heart, Emilia cringed to say that the four of them had been the Dragon's choice—it was a lie. But lies had been used to wreck the world for so long. Perhaps the world could only be healed by another falsehood. "It was time for a radical change. The lowest member of each family was selected. Together, we will work so that this world does not run further into the ground."

"What do *you* all know about statecraft?" Lord Pentri snapped.

"Not much." Emilia smiled. "At least, not the sort of statecraft of which you would approve."

"Is my House to be left out of this brave new world?" Lord Volscia inquired. He didn't look at her.

"Your elder daughter killed your younger. Julia would have stood here otherwise—I'm sure of it," Emilia said.

At that, the lord merely stood and walked out. No one watched him go.

"This is how it will be," Emilia continued. Her eyes tracked from one face to the next, memorizing the expressions she found there. If they looked pleased, or at least indifferent, she noticed; if hostility simmered under the surface, or their lips twitched, she remembered that, too. "It was suggested that we kill the dragons, and the eldest, of every House to prevent insurrection."

There were gasps. She could practically hear Camilla grimacing. It had, of course, been the priestess's cheerful suggestion.

"You wouldn't dare," Dido growled.

"We said no," Lucian replied. "The Cut has always been barbaric. From this day forward, it's done with."

Murmurs now. Confusion. *Some think we're weak for not Cutting,* Emilia realized. She was going to have to be very, very careful with everyone in this room.

"However, all of your dragons are safely perched in the aerie right now, and the imperial guard has thrown its support entirely behind us," she said. Of course, Emilia knew that the guard were partial to one person especially. Suppose someday Lucian decided to make a play for greater power, with Rufus and the rest backing him?

She let that thought slide. For now.

"If we gave the order, everyone here would be killed." Emilia remained stoic, even when the room cried out in horror. "Consider how merciful we are."

"We're supposed to bow to a *servant*?" Lord Pentri glared at Vespir. The girl's gaze bored into his.

"An empress who was a servant," Emilia replied evenly. "Yes. If you want to live."

The old bastard grumbled but turned away. From the corner of the room, Antonia stepped into view, wearing a gown of green silk, with seed pearls woven into her black hair. Emilia noticed that Vespir stood a little taller.

Antonia regarded them all with wondering eyes.

"How exactly will you govern this vast empire of yours? When a dragon is born with two or more heads, it dies in confusion," Lady Pentri snapped.

"Actually, there *have* been two-headed Hydra who lived very long lives," Vespir said. Yes. If anyone would know those particulars, she would.

"And we have other powers." Emilia turned out her palms, felt the chaos pump in her blood. She focused upon the chandelier overhead. The pendants of crystal morphed into delicate rosebuds, the flames to flapping monarch butterflies. All the Houses leapt to their feet in horror.

"Chaos?" Lord Tiber looked as if he had fallen into a nightmare. "Who did it? Kill them!" he bellowed.

"Chaos is free once more, and under my control," Emilia growled. This time, the reverberations through her body were not so bad. When blood dripped from her nose, she wiped it away before anyone else could see. "It's going to take its rightful place alongside order once again. Isn't that so, Your Grace?"

Camilla could barely bring herself to whisper yes, but it was a yes all the same. Now the families understood. Emilia had the power of chaos, the backing of the church, and the support of the imperial guard. Those who did not bow would die.

Emilia had studied these people her entire life. She knew that, Lord Sabel excluded, every one of them cared for their comforts more than trouble. If she could not bend their will to hers . . . death might be the only option.

She hoped it would not be.

"The choice is yours," Lucian said, surveying the room by her side.

The priestess kept silent.

Finally, the heads of the four Houses drew into a small circle. Their discussion was brief, and when Lord Aurun faced them again, Emilia could read the decision in his eyes before he spoke.

"All hail the emperors and empresses of Etrusia," he grumbled.

She made certain to look him directly in his eye as she gestured with a flick of her wrist. *On your knees.*

His lip curled, but her father obeyed.

Emilia's mother followed his example, as did the Pentri and the Tiber and the Sabel. Lysander openly wept with fear and possible confusion. Antonia was the only one who didn't bow right away. Instead, she crossed to stand directly before Vespir.

"Excellency," she said, lowering her lashes as she swept into a deep curtsy. But Vespir cupped the girl's chin.

"I don't ever want you to kneel," she whispered. Antonia stood, tears trembling in her eyes. Vespir whispered Antonia's name and kissed her. Antonia slipped into the other girl's arms with a sigh.

"All hail *us!*" Ajax crowed. "Time to let the empire see its new face." As the boy walked over to his so-called family, he flicked Lysander's ear. The older boy's face grew beet red, but he did nothing. "Hey. Thank me for that, Lysander."

"Thank you, Excellency," he snarled.

"I like the sound of that." Ajax flicked the other ear. "Do it again."

The four waited as Camilla took to the terrace, where a large copper cylinder meant to amplify her voice waited upon a stand. Emilia heard the priestess's voice ring out, loud enough to reach half a mile away:

"All hail the Dragon's wisdom. All hail truth's conquest over falsehood. Today, a great four-headed dragon has been born. All hail the Sarkoni: Emilia Sarkona, formerly of the Aurun; Lucian Sarkonus, formerly of the Sabel; Vespir Sarkona, formerly of the Pentri; and Ajax Sarkonus, formerly of the Tiber. All hail your new emperors. All hail the Sarkoni. All hail!"

Camilla bowed and gestured for them to take their place. Emilia walked to the terrace's edge, Lucian on her right, Vespir and Ajax to her left. The four peered over the balustrade at the veritable sea of people gazing back up at them. Even if corners of the city remained on fire, they had still come to see their emperors and perhaps to understand what on earth had happened.

The faces in the crowd were still. Emilia noted a ripple of turning heads, people asking one another what in the depths was going on.

"Uh-oh," Ajax grunted.

But then, hands extended up for them. The murmur of the crowd broke into a roar, and Emilia heard them shouting for the emperors. The Sarkoni. Hail to them.

She raised her hand and waved, and the crowd waved back. To be on display to this many pairs of eyes was exhausting, but she smiled.

"Do you think this will work?" Lucian murmured in her ear, while the families watched them warily from behind and the crowds rejoiced before them.

"Too late to turn back now," she replied. She flushed as his hand traced the small of her back.

"Then I'm lucky we're in this together," he said.

She had no ready response.

✳

Night had fallen by the time the families trundled off to their apartments throughout the capital. Inside the imperial home the other emperors reveled, along with Antonia. Emilia needed a moment to herself, however. She traced her path through the labyrinthine gardens, listening to the crickets and drinking in the perfumed air. When she arrived at Truth's doorway, she inspected the pair of stone doorjambs. The pitch-black void had returned; perhaps she might take another stroll inside.

No. Too much truth could be a dangerous thing.

She touched a sleeping rosebud and turned it to pure gold. Beautiful.

Emilia coughed, winced as blood splattered upon the burnished flower. It felt like a boot had kicked her in the stomach. More practice. That's all she needed.

The hairs on her neck rose as a twig snapped on the path behind her. "I don't love being followed, you know," she said.

"You never did," Lucian replied, picking an errant petal from his shoulder. "You yelled at me whenever I tracked you along the cliffs."

"Because you tried to push me in."

"Once, and only as a joke. I'd go in after you if you ever fell." He smiled.

Yes. He would.

"Are you all right?" Lucian asked.

"The chaos? It's in my control, at least. I've been thinking . . . The Drag—the *voice* told me that when they locked chaos away, it was like an earthenware jar with a few small cracks. I was one of those cracks. All of chaos was trying to get out through me. No wonder I had accidents. But now the power is evenly distributed. It's better."

Better, but in some ways more dangerous.

"Do you think the priests might have had a point about me?" she asked. Lucian frowned. "I exploded three human beings with no more than a thought. Perhaps no one should ever possess such power. Maybe it *is* wrong. Maybe the dragons losing their tongues *was* the right price to pay." She nibbled at her lip.

"Why are you talking about this now?" Lucian sounded baffled. "You're the dragons' savior, Emilia. You're a hero."

A hero. Boys like Lucian believed in such things. Emilia had read far too much to trust anything was so simple . . . but she didn't want to think about it tonight. She was tired of always thinking. And with Lucian beside her, the stars above and the garden fragrant around them, she felt so many things. Things she'd believed had been locked away, imprisoned inside her body.

"Can I ask you something?" Emilia murmured. His silence answered her. "Now that you're willing to fight again . . . have you made peace with what you did?"

"No." It was a soft answer. "I don't deserve peace. All I can do is work so that no one else ever makes my mistakes."

"Ah." Emilia frowned. "I'm sorry that I was weak with Hyperia. If I hadn't been, you would have kept your vows."

"No. I would have fought anyway. I had something to protect," he said.

"Oh." Her heart picked up pace. If only she'd been around people these last five years. If only she knew how to toss her hair or playfully grab his arm. If only they did not have an empire to govern and a balancing act to maintain between four people. If only . . . "We should go."

"Wait." He touched her hand as she began to walk away. "You said that you killed the first boy you ever kissed."

"What about it?" Emilia flinched.

He made her face him and brought her hand to his lips. The sensation of his kiss was too brief, but deliciously warm. Her body pulsed with chaotic sensation.

"Wh-why did you do that?" she breathed.

"A reminder that things can change," he said.

And that was that, for tonight. For now.

They wended the path back to the palace, the future fragile in their hands.

Elsewhere

The girl heard the fishermen whisper about her. She spent her days huddled in a corner of the boat, listening to the slosh of the waves and the uncertain murmurs of the sunburned men. She rubbed the place on her arm that had once boasted a pearl bracelet; she'd paid for her passage with it.

Sometimes the girl remembered her name. Other times she wanted to forget.

She gave them her pearl earrings in exchange for a rowboat. When they lowered her into the sea a healthy distance from her destination—they would go no nearer, not on their lives—the men called her a fool as she rowed away.

The girl's arms were always sore now, and her mind distant. Only half a heart beat in her body.

They took something precious from me. She could barely recall who "they" were, but she hated them.

Though she could forget her own name, she never abandoned her purpose.

So she rowed to shore, a sun-bleached expanse that grew impossibly large the nearer she came. Gulls cried overhead as if calling her back from the brink.

But she had her dagger and her purpose.

By the time she reached land, the sun was at its apex in the azure sky. Sweat soaked, she staggered onto the beach and gazed up a winding path to the top of a craggy promontory. The wind whispered along the shore. There was no sound of life here. Not a bird or beast, not a human voice. There was only the sea and the empty sky.

The girl climbed the path, walking because she could no longer fly.

She came to the top of the cliff, her sandaled feet white with limestone dust. Blading a hand over her eyes, she found the surrounding area filled with statues.

White chalky faces. Wildly gesticulating poses, backs warped and stretched, arms flung high into the air. Some poor bastard had been frozen standing on one foot. The dust whispered among these trapped souls.

Beings suspended in time. If she listened closely, the girl could hear the hum of magic.

The Chaos House. She stood among them, these prisoners of order's stasis.

Once, a red-haired girl had said that the blood of a noble heart could break such a spell.

Her right hand traced the gilded hilt of her dagger, the sole luxurious item she had kept. She had come to this land as a pilgrim in rough cloth and sandals. She had nothing. She was nothing.

The wind loosened a coil of her blond hair, dancing it behind her like the tail of a kite.

Her hands were numb as she grasped her dagger. Fear fluttered through her, but she had already suffered a much greater agony.

Even if the curse would not break, better not to go on like this.

And if it did break . . .

If it did, the weak would be culled, and the strong survive. Survive to fight a war, to put down chaos once again and uplift order. The empire needed to be tested, that was all. The empire, now ruled by that "four-headed dragon," the Sarkoni. The *abomination*.

If she must become the destroyer of all she held dear to save it, she would.

Her body trembled as she drew the blade.

When faced with weakness . . .

She closed her eyes and scarcely felt it when the knife entered. She only grunted when it angled underneath her ribs.

. . . cut out its heart.

The girl collapsed to the ground, her blood soaking into the earth.

As she faded, she realized that death was not as she'd imagined, a black depth that stole over her like the tide. It was hot white. The sun's blaze turned her closed eyelids red so that she could pick out the veins.

She barely heard it when *they* began to move around her. Barely heard the crunch of their footsteps. Her eyes fluttered open when someone stood over her, blocking out the sun. She gazed up into a shadowy face.

"Not dead *yet?*" the person whispered.

"No," she croaked. "Not . . . yet."

Hyperia of the Volscia gave a bloody smile.

Acknowledgments

Thank you to my editor, Chelsea Eberly. Getting to the end of this book very nearly killed both of us, but it was a journey I'd make a hundred times over. Ours is a fruitful creative partnership, one that's made me a much better writer and an all-around nicer person. A good two-for-one deal.

Thanks to my agent, Brooks Sherman. No one else has as good a heart or as sharp a mind. The pitch-black sense of humor is also top-notch. Thank you for strategies, for hard work, for integrity, and for letting me ramble on and acting like what I say makes sense. I owe you several.

Thank you to everyone at Janklow & Nesbit and Random House for all your incredible work. Thank you to Casey Moses for the amazing cover design, Ken Crossland, Shameiza Ally, and Barbara Bakowski. Thanks to Wendi Gu.

Traci Chee, Tara Sim, and Emily Skrutskie: The Avengers may have disbanded, but Thor + Tony + Cap + HULK will never die. Thank you for all the good and joy you add to my life. It's a whole lot. More than 3,000, even.

Alyssa Colman, for helping me fix this novel, for feeding me, and for friendship. Having you ten minutes away is one of the truest blessings in my life.

Alexa Donne, for laughter, free movies, good wine, and excellent conversation.

Gretchen Schreiber, beautiful friend, keeper of all books, and knower of everything BTS.

Erika Lewis, for being a rock, making me laugh, and teaching me how the hell a map works.

Brandie Coonis, my light and whimsy in dark places.

Alyssa Wong, whose mere existence brightens my day.

Jack Sullivan, for helping with fight scenes and generally knowing absolutely everything.

Josh Ropiequet, for making life far more interesting and introducing me to *Schitt's Creek*.

Amanda Santos, for all the best book discussions.

The Rosenblums: Mike, Alison, Jordan, and now Isabella. Love you.

The friends I wish I saw more of, because such is the life of an author: Alwyn Hamilton, Kelly Zekas, Emily Duncan, Christine Lynn Herman, Adam Sass, Paul Krueger, S. Jae Jones, Margaret Rogerson, Kerry Kletter, Brittany Cavallaro, Laura Sebastian, Kiersten White, Robby and Terra Forbes-Karol, Gwen Katz, Allison Senecal, Zev Valancy, Ronen Kohn, Parker Peevyhouse, Rosamund Hodge, Ian Randall, Grace Fong, Adriana Mather, Tobie Easton. We'll always have Twitter, or at least Instagram, which I shall never, ever update. Ever.

To my Clarion 13 loves, I miss you. I need more Rocketship Spatula in my life.

To Robert Crais, for talking me out of a tree when I was sure this book would suck, and for giving damn good advice.

My family, who are always there, and Bentley, the newest member: Thank you for everything.

Finally, to the booksellers, librarians, bloggers, and readers who make this job worth doing: Thank you for the gift of your attention. I'll keep striving to be worthy of it.

About the Author

JESSICA CLUESS is a graduate of both Northwestern University and the Clarion Writers Workshop. After college, she moved to Los Angeles, where she served coffee to the rich and famous while working on her first novel in the Kingdom on Fire series, *A Shadow Bright and Burning*. These days, she sits around thinking about dragons far too much, and enjoys it.

jessicacluess.com